Wole Soyinka

SEASON OF ANOMY

Wole Soyinka, the first African to receive the Nobel Prize in Literature, is a distinguished playwright, novelist, poet, and essayist of global stature. Born in Nigeria, Soyinka studied at University College in Ibadan, Nigeria, and University of Leeds, England. Soyinka's extensive body of work includes several poetry collections; more than twenty plays; five memoirs, including *Aké: The Years of Childhood* (1981); and three novels—*The Interpreters* (1965), *Season of Anomy* (1973), and *Chronicles from the Land of the Happiest People of Earth* (2021).

INTERNATIONAL

SEASON
OF
ANOMY

SEASON
OF
ANOMY

A NOVEL

Wole Soyinka

VINTAGE INTERNATIONAL
Vintage Books
A Division of Penguin Random House LLC
New York

CONTENTS

1 Seminal   I–II   1

2 Buds   III–V   33

3 Tentacles   VI–VIII   91

4 Harvest   IX–XIII   155

5 Spores   XIV–XV   295

1

SEMINAL

I

A quaint anomaly, had long governed and policed itself, was so
singly-knit that it obtained a tax assessment for the whole populace and paid it before the departure of the pith-helmeted assessor,
in cash, held all property in common, literally, to the last scrap of
thread on the clothing of each citizen—such an anachronism gave
much patronising amusement to the cosmopolitan sentiment of a
profit-hungry society. A definitive guffaw from the radical centres
of debate headed by Ilosa, dismissed Aiyéró as the prime example
of unscientific communalism, primitive and embarrassingly senti-
mental. To the governments that came and went it posed neither
threat nor liability. Thus it was that Aiyéró, unique beneficiary
of a three-quarter century of accidental isolation was permitted
to be itself. Until its rediscovery at the time of the census . . . the
tourists swamped Aiyéró, then the sociologists armed with erudite
irrelevances. Even the Corporation, intent on its ever-expanding

cocoa drive took note of a new market for cocoa-bix and cocoa-wix. Ofeyi, the promotions man took his team down to Aiyéró.

Why did they all always come back? Aiyéró's young generation Ofeyi meant, asking the question of Pa Ahime. What makes all your youth come back?

The Elders of Aiyéró, adopting the wisdom of its parent body Aiyétómò, sent Aiyéró's young men all over the world to experience other mores and values. Income from boat-building provided Aiyéró's main income but these young men also sent back a portion of their earnings to the communal fund. It was an act of faith by the commune to send the restless generation to work at whatever new industries were opened in the rest of the country, trusting that the new acquired skills would be brought back to aid the already self-sufficing community. And this was the unusual feature which intrigued the cocoa promotions man. They all returned. The neon cities could not lure them away. The umbilical cord, no matter how far it stretched, never did snap.

What brings them back, he again and again demanded of Ahime who played the role of Chief Minister to the Custodian of the Grain. What makes them different from the rest of their generation who succumb to other life styles and values? But the old man would only reply, that is like asking me why we came, why we are still here, why we live. The answer is, I do not know.

Ofeyi sent his campaign team back to Ilosa and remained to find out. Iriyise remained with him and, soon after, he began to wonder if his resolve to remain in Aiyéró had been entirely his or if it had to do with a sense of rediscovering the woman within that questioning environment. She took to Aiyéró as a new organism long in search of its true element. He began to wonder which provided him a cause for his long hours of unrest: Aiyéró, or simply this woman who seemed to change under his touch.

After the second week the Custodian sent for him. He was a

very old wizened man with eyes that seemed permanently hooded, until they burst out with a sun's after-rain intensity and clarity.

"Ahime has been telling me about you. We've had quite a number of people come to visit us, some have even stayed as long as you have. Tourists and government men—those don't stay long—the government man is usually the tax man, and he always finds his money waiting so there is no longer reason for him to stay. Money!" He spat the word out, paused as if he needed to regain his strength. "But you, why are you here? Ahime says you are not working for a degree. The ones who stay as long as that are usually trying to make a higher degree out of us so they can earn more money. They call themselves sociologists I think. Isn't that right Ahime? Or else a journalist who wants to take photographs to sell for money." He leant forward, his chin over his hands which rested on a stick. "What are you looking for? You sent back the rest of your cocoa band a long time ago. Why are you still here?"

Laughing, Ahime revealed that Ofeyi had asked why the young men of Aiyéró came back. The old man blinked. "Is that true?"

Ofeyi admitted that the phenomenon did make him curious.

"And you haven't found out yet?"

"No. To tell the truth I haven't even found out if that is the only reason I have stayed here so long."

The eyes shot open from behind the lids, regarded him for a long time. He spoke slowly. "Will you make me a promise?"

Dubious, Ofeyi said that he would try.

"Any time you find out, even if it is a long way from here, you must come back at once and tell me."

On the way back to the guest-house Ahime made a surprising revelation.

"Do you wish to know why the Founder wished to see you? He won't mind my telling you. Not that he has confided in me, but I know him well by now. I should."

"Yes. I should very much like to know."

"He is searching for the new Custodian of the Grain."

"Custodian of . . . you mean a sort of food commissar? Minister of Food Supply or something like that?"

Ahime smiled. "No. It is a title we don't use much, except among ourselves. We don't have much use for titles come to think of it but of course it is easier for duties to be defined by labels. No, the Custodian of the Grain is . . ." Then the old man broke into a roguish laugh. "Well why don't I leave you to add it to the list of things you wish to find out in Aiyéró?"

Two days later he did find out. Simply by putting the question directly to one of the natives of the place. Unable to believe the answer he went to a second, then a third and fourth. The riddle—it was not even worth calling it that as the question was answered simply and directly—confirmed in him a growing suspicion that there was a slightly insane element, if not about Aiyéró itself, then certainly about its elders. Casually, pretending that he had not yet discovered what office the Custodian entailed, he asked the old man if he had been serious about the matter. Ahime was too wily to be fooled.

"Oh you've found out already have you?"

He denied it hotly. The old man rubbed his chin. "Hm. Then tell me why the idea terrifies you. Why do you imagine I have gone clean out of my mind?"

"I know where I am going" Ofeyi retorted. "Clean out of here!"

"You have found out everything you wished?"

"More than enough." Seriously he added, "I cannot tell you how much I have valued your hospitality. But to even think of me as successor to . . ."

The old man placed his arm around his shoulders. "Aiyéró adopted you almost as soon as we set eyes on you." He nodded briskly. "Yes, it is true. It was an unusual encounter for us, you and your strange assortment of entertainers. It did not take us long to see that there was more to what you did than your slides and Mobile Cinema. All those tattered films which tried to teach the farmer what he had known for the past ten generations! But your casual—or maybe not so casual, certainly instructive side-shows at odd hours of the day . . . well, it was startling to find your message was the same as brought our community into being long before you were born."

"You have earned the right to your contentment," Ofeyi said. "But even the state of content can become malignant. Like indifference. Or complacency. Already you are near stagnant . . . please don't take offence."

"No, no. You know I value frankness," Ahime reassured him.

"Well, your children travel the wide world, achieve all sorts of experience in their own right and still return to the tiny pond to settle. It's admirable but . . . it encourages in-breeding. They seem untouched by where they have been, by the plight of the rest of mankind, even of our own people."

"We find no virtue in agression, son. Evangelism is a form of agression."

"I know. That is a contradiction which I have yet to resolve within myself. All the same . . . oh I don't know how to convey to you the smell of mould, stagnation which clings to places like this. It can prove paralysing in a crisis, and our generation appears to be born into one long crisis."

They trod the shoreline in silence. For a moment Ofeyi thought he caught a downcast look on the face of the old man, the first time he had found even the faintest suspicion of such a mood on any face in Aiyéró. Ahime stopped, stood before him and held his eyes. "Maybe the same thought has occurred to some among us. Have you thought of that? Why do you think the Founder began to think of a total stranger to succeed him as Custodian of the Grain? The meaning of grain is not merely food but, germination . . ."

Ofeyi waves his hands helplessly around. "Within this constriction?" He shook his head. "The waters of Aiyéró need to burst their banks. The grain must find new seminal grounds or it will atrophy and die."

"Then join the community" the old man challenged. "We have long recognized our need for new blood."

"No, no. You cannot guarantee what would come of that. You have your own people."

He parted from Aiyéró the following day. "You'll be back" Ahime shouted across the water. "I shall welcome you back on this same beach."

He could not resist the invitation to the funeral. Nor was that all, he went a full week early; there were still questions, possibilities in his mind. Aiyéró promised much, tantalized him with answers, potencies. It had to yield something to his search.

He gave himself to it, grateful for Ahime who took charge of Iriyise, infatuated beyond belief by the gin-and-tonic siren from the godless lights of the capital. Ahime schemed to draw him to Aiyéró through her, sent women of cunning kindness from his own household who grew so close to her that he saw little of her from day to day. He did not mind. When he looked for her he found her locked deep in talk with strange old women whom he did not wish to know. Then he woke one morning and found she was no longer by his side. Instead there was old Ahime fussing about his breakfast, the creases on his face one happy enigma. "Don't look for your woman" he said, "she is getting to know the heart-beat of this earth of ours which you take so much for granted."

Iriyise returned mid-morning in the midst of the old women. She came in a white-and-ochre wrapper, antimony round her eyes, a solid bangle of ivory on her neck—how did they get those heavy things onto a woman's neck! Ofeyi felt himself excluded by such transparent numinous excitement as flushed her face . . . how little I know of her, how very little after all. When they were at last alone she would only say, it filled me Ofé, it filled me completely where I had felt so empty. I know I am now complete. Who on earth, what on earth could have taught her to say that, whose only knowledge of fulfilment till now had been the aftermath of love!

Nor was that the end of her power to astonish. That same night as they lay in bed—he had been afraid that her new world might indeed exclude the ecstatic aspects of their bond—she turned to him and suddenly, irrelevantly, out of the deep inward absorption that came upon her after hours of love that betrayed no abatement in ardour, she simply said, "Don't hold up our people much longer Ofe. You belong to us before all others. *Us!*"

He did not grow to understand, merely marvelled all through the ten days of the Custodian's lying in state, the ten days of red chieftain caps, of flaunting cockatoo feathers, coral riches, ivory bangles, iron emblems, brass and silver, the smell of tanned leather, deep resonances of wooden gongs, the red froth of malt wine in fired-clay throats, a deep ferment of sweat, voices, clay and hide timbres, metallic percussions.

Camwood vistas and chalk. Walls in bark-gritty daubings of camwood, chalked doors and doorsteps, wide swathes of chalk below the camwood against beaten clayey earth. Rushes of red barley in the fences, chalk belts on massive tree trunks, posts, bamboo piers and the storehouses of the waterfront. The lagoon dissolved its daily tribute of camwood. And Pa Ahime's voice through it all patiently admonishing . . . why do you insist on calling our country Aiyéró? Say—Aiyéró. Ró! If you find the world bitter don't foist your despair on us. Aiye ti wa ró. It works, it is upright and balanced because we have made it so. Ofeyi mumbled his apologies, then grew querulous in turn . . . why do you make such fuss about a little tonal deflection? Ah, the old man wagged his head, it tells a lot you see. It isn't only that you change the meaning to what it isn't, to the opposite of what it is, but it tells a lot of your state of mind. You've been defeated by life and it shows in your tone.

"Is it time to tell me the secrets of Aiyéró?" he asked him finally.

"What do you wish to know exactly? Our story is a long one."

"Well, let's begin with why you broke away from Aiyétómò."

The old man sighed. He turned and looked away over the waters to the earliest working theocracy on the coast. Aiyéró made no effort to deny its parenthood but was reticent about the cutting of its umbilical cord.

"We do not believe" the old man began, "in the shackles of memory. We are here, we prosper and we know harmony. It suffices. It is the first principle we teach our children, they grow up despising dead knowledge whose nature is the nature of what is gone, dead, rotted. This is not to say that we keep things hidden. All our people know from where we came, and they know that we founded Aiyéró to seek truth, a better life, all the things which men run after. They also believe that we found it. That is why our children always come back."

"So do the children of Aiyétómò" Ofeyi pointed out.

The old man turned triumphantly on him. "There you are! What greater proof could you have of the wisdom of our ways. Because you see, they are also the ways of Aiyétómò. We seek no converts, we indulge in no futile recriminations. The way of Aiyétómò was—accept what we have made or go freely. There came a time when our founder, the first Custodian of the Grain felt he could no longer follow the path of the old prophets. He stood up in the meeting-house and gave voice to his new-found faith. He set off to found a new homeland, and those who believed him followed him. When our children grow up and ask questions all we tell them is—yes, Aiyétómò is our parent-home, but if you want to find out more than we've told you, get in your canoe and row yourself over. You will be welcomed."

"And are they?"

"Of course son, what do you think! Even total strangers are welcome there as here. The curious among our own people learn what they can, but they always return here!"

"Do they learn the truth?"

"Who knows? Does it really matter? All that counts is that they see a difference and they choose. A blind man can see it at a glance—they worship one god, we another."

"So that was the cause of the break."

"One of many. But we don't tell our children that. Why should we? It then becomes too large a thing in their lives. If they conclude for themselves that is the reason, so be it. There are other differences, matters of trade, matters of personal lives, children, teaching, ownership—oh the list is endless. But it was religion that caused a split in that first community. And it happened at the time of the slave trade. Yes, it was that simple. As best as she could Aiyétómò protected her people. But one day one of our young men had this thought. He told himself, we base our lives on the teachings of this white god yet the bearers of that faith kill, burn, maim, loot and enslave our people. It is time, he said, to return to the religion of our fathers."

The old man spoke with the pride of one who had witnessed the moment of triumph, the glitter in his eyes was not the borrowed flame of the historian. He went on to confirm Ofeyi's observation as he tapped himself on the chest and continued, "I am the last survivor of those who witnessed the scene at the meeting-house. I was a mere boy but I understood. I did not even speak to my parents before I followed the wild-eyed man and those who sprang to follow him. It was a strange revelation, to find that many had felt the same thing, but only he had dared rise in the meeting-place and testify."

"And he founded the religion of the Grain?"

The old man shrugged. "Why give it a name? We don't give it one. We don't even think of it as a religion, only as a way of life. Call it a philosophy if you like. Don't you yet understand the nature of our Founder? Fleeing from one self-contradictory deity he was not likely to stumble so easily into the pitfalls of another. No son, his concern was to found a way of life, a near-copy of what he grew up with in Aiyétómò, but without paying lip-service to dubious gods."

Ofeyi smiled. "What do you call all this then?" The sounds of drums were not far and from time to time they could see distant groups of dancers across the field, hear the thud of feet and the flash of bangles in the sun.

"We have observances" Ahime conceded. "We have our rituals. We are a farming and fishing community so we acknowledge our debts to earth and to the sea. And when a great man dies, a founder, we pay him homage. If we wish to take one full year burying him it is still less than his dues. For a people who own everything in common what we spend merely returns to us."

"As with earth?"

The old man stood still, stared thoughtfully at him. The look in his eyes could be pleasure or surprise. "Say that again" he said.

Ofeyi frowned, repeated the phrase.

"And where did you learn that?" the old man demanded.

"Is it something to be learnt?" Ofeyi demanded in turn. "You forget our first meeting. I came here with a message remember?"

"Ah yes of course. The land to those who till it. . . ."

"The sea to those who fish it. . . ."

The old man stroked his chin, smiling. "Yes . . . and I told our departed Founder. I said to him, here comes a man who brings us our own view of life. And he said simply, give him the run of the meeting-house . . . how strange. . . ."

"What is strange Pa?"

"When Aiyétómò, our parent community turned its back on the world, the founding Elder always said someone like you would turn up from the outer cesspit of the land, a stranger who would take our message to the world. But you came here instead, to us the offshoot."

Ofeyi laughed. "Yes, I came in search of converts. Aiyétómò, Aiyéró, they were here all the time while I brought models from the European world. . . ."

Ahime stopped him. "No. It was a most beneficial thing for us, your coming here all puffed with your sense of mission. It was good to know that our ways have always been the dream of mankind all through the ages and among people so far apart. Peoples as different in appearance as the cocoa-pod from a yam tuber. Eating and drinking differently, worshipping gods with no common ancestor, and yet . . ."

In the hours before dawn the song-leaders from the dead Custodian's household followed Ahime through the sleeping town, swift dark-brushing motions of maroon loin-cloths. All paths must be trodden in the pre-dawn hours, heads bent to the ground, acknowledging no one and seeing none. A low moan rose, thrilled in the slumbersome air, the earth gave answer in trembling accents, a lead voice prompted the sleep-washed dirge of earth and a sudden motion of feet would thud in velvety unison. The dark figures swayed backwards, leant into the yielding night membrane, uncoiled in a python lunge upwelling into a dark-toned monody.

Then they leapt forward again along the path, sending soft vibrations along the path.

Blood, oil, colanuts red and white in clay vessels at every crossroads, slain pigeons at every spot where a founder had fallen, sacrificed or finally rested, at every meaning left behind by the first progenitors. The departed were appeased, venerated, welcomed, touched and brought among the living. The new deceased was on his way.

Finally the hands of induction were swallowed by dawn. They gave way to a fleet of canoes which came over the water from the parent town Aiyétómò. Red ochred fences opened out in a flow of age-groups, joined the criss-currents of processions, paid homage at the house of death. The town was dressed in pride of exhibition.

Gun-bursts, tang of powder, angry dispersions of kites. The hunter groups filled their guns with wild metal, shot down branches and pulped the fibrous trunks, filled the air with rubble as they fired into wall-corners. A coconut disintegrated, driving white-fleshed shrapnels over rooftops. A pawpaw turned to red mash. The kites circled the hunters from a safe height, swooped down as they disappeared and snatched up the shreds of red-headed lizards.

Torches at night. Pungent trails on rings of flames, night forays by the tireless hunters, raconteurs of history chanting, stamping, mumming the gory course of divine lineages, a tapestry unravelled, masks in stirring possession by fireglow . . . all moving towards the climax of bright red sluices.

Ahime leant over to his adopted son and whispered, "At the time I told you of, there were no hunting clans in the parent community. Fish was the mainstay. And the question our Founder asked himself was this, How shall we defend ourselves if the slave-raiders come again? You asked what our religion is and I answered you truthfully, none. But among others we grant Ogun pride of place. You've seen our smithy at work. Look at those guns—men come from all over the country to seek the best from us."

At the least, Ofeyi thought, looking around him, it all restores the jaded psyche. On the huge four-poster bed the Custodian lay in state within an alcove of the outer wall, facing the iron and wattle roofs of Aiyéró. Submitting to a sensation of floating Ofeyi watched the body levitate towards the four golden ostrich eggs which crowned the bedposts. He took the place of the dead man, sinking deep in the feather-bed. Two electric fans blew flies from his face to the distant hum of Aiyéró's power station. There were crowds in the trees, scrambling for places to look their last on the face of the Custodian, they hung on fences, dangled from posts and tumbled through the hedges. Distant drums and voices, female, announced the approach of a new woman's guild. Why are the nostrils of a corpse stuffed with cotton wool? Ah yes, to keep the flies from climbing in. Laying eggs of putrefaction. Even a founder's face is not immune. The alcove choked in fumes of camphor.

The guilds approached, danced, retreated, leaving sinuous waves between the corpse and fourteen noble bulls penned before the alcove, one for each of the thirteen prior departed founding elders of the town. They were proud-horned, rich-humped, their brilliant ivory torsos rippled in the sun. Among them leapt the acrobats, in violent cartwheels, the female stilt-dancers bestrode them writhing suggestively above the humps, stooping low till their raffia skirts just covered the humps, only to twist away and leap over the herd looking back with mock-rebuke at the large watery eyes. The swirl of loincloths daubed ochre, chalk and indigo turned the pen fluid, as if the enclosure were one vast churn of milk. Until Ahime nodded quietly to the leaders, and the arena drained slowly of movements. The pillowed head of the Custodian had merged into shadows of the alcove, leaving the white shrouded form and the death-bed faithfully white to the eyes. The songs fell silent, the shouts retreated into subdued murmurs: a prelude of dedication before the climax of bright red sluices.

A thrill of anticipation communicated through his wrist. He turned to Iriyise whose fingers had sought his and found that her gaze was far away, her mind surrendered still to the Mysteries of that dawn of which this was the wider communion.

All eyes turned on Ahime. He rose, his yet supple fingers, dark and sensitive against a white wrapper which looped his shoulder. He moved among the arches of ivory in the pen, a fragile, near-feminine grace among the virile splendour of the bulls, raised his other hand in a moment's brief dedication while the gathering bowed their heads. He let the hush hang for a while, then he gave the command they all waited to hear:

"Plant the horns!"

To the rumble of renewed anticipation a group of young men rushed into the pen, picked up the trailing ropes, pulled, tugged and created space among the bulls. The old man raised his arm again as soon as the manoeuvre was completed, he was now the self-conscious performer, orchestrating details of the pageant, immaculate in white smock and wrapper, a silver glint from a neck-chain as he turned to survey the positioning of the bulls. The men, two to each bull, now kept their eyes on him. An occasional bellow came from the beasts themselves, who otherwise submitted to the drill with a mild questioning interest. When all appeared set to his satisfaction he brought down the arm and, one after the other, in no particular order but with earth-shaking thuds that brought a tremor to the feet of the furthest in the congregation the bulls were felled. It was a deft, near-invisible manoeuvre, a multiple exposure of swift complementary motions of one rope. Rear-feet and head, there was a moment to catch the surprise in the eyes of the bull, to watch the rope ripple along its length towards the target, a precise jerk of the massive head and suddenly the bull was down, both horns firmly anchored in earth and the adepts of this rope-trick instantly over the prostrate hulk, fastening the legs together with swift accomplishment.

A nod from the old man and they left the enclosure. He stood alone among the fourteen ivory throats tendered to the sky, taut lines of veins and tendons which curved and plunged into throbbing breast chambers. Distended eyes betrayed a now present fear which strangely was not given voice. Ahime was a reed of life in the white stillness of a memorial ground, a flicker of motion among marble tombstones. An intuitive priest, he knew better than to disturb the laden altar until his followers had drunk their fill of it, he let the ponderous mass for the dead emit vibrations of abundance, potency and renewal, binding the pulses in his own person, building a force for life within the circle of the pen until he judged the moment right for the magical release. They saw him feel softly within the folds of his cloth, watched his hand emerge with a slender knife, a mere flutist blade, so insubstantial did it appear against the pillared throats of the bulls.

Iriyise beside him, a distant stillness. Her ivory neckpiece had merged with hidden rapids in the bulls' convulsive throats. Caryatid and timeless, only the warmth of her fingers reassured him of her living flesh, a willing presence at the altar.

Ahime moved with feline balance, his hand poured back the drapes which fell away from his shoulder as he bent over the bull nearest the alcove. The cloth fell again so he caught it over the left arm and kept it there pressed against his waist. His knife-hand moved once, slashed deep and drew across the throat. The taut skin parted easily, opening to a layer of translucent membrane, yielding in turn to tendons and a commencement of red mists. Suddenly the white afternoon was showered in a crimson fountain, rising higher and higher, pumping ever upwards to a sun-scorched sky. Ahime stepped back quickly but not so far that the falling spray should not find him. His white vestments bloomed suddenly with small red petals and a long sigh rose, fell and filled the air with whispers of wind and the opening of buds. He moved swiftly now, the sighs of release were woven among the spreading mists, a thousand eyes followed the motions of the priest whose flutist blade was laid again and again to ivory pipes, tuned to invocations of renewal. Opening the vents of a rich elixir, he of the masseur's fingers stooped at each succeeding sluice-gate, a fountain-head covered in rime, his arms were supple streams in a knowing course through ridges bathed in a sun's downwash. He nudged the ridges' streams awake and they joined their tributaries to his fountain-head. A deep beneficence rested over the motions of his hands, opening red sluices for the land's replenishment.

The jets climbed strongly, the springs seemed interminable. But at last even those cavernous hearts had no more to give; a last spriglet of blood blossomed briefly, then the flood was dammed. A last gargle came through a blocked-up drain, a final shudder of love gave all to a passive earth. But the depleted hulks over which a miasma now lay retained for the congregation their power of emission. Ahime walked around on the inside of the pen, flushed and communicant. Anxious hands reached out to touch him and those hands touched other hands and faces, transmitting the essence of the sacrifice to the furthest in the gathering.

The entry of the butchers, armed with huge blades, axes and choppers, followed by women with huge bowls, trays and pots of water wrought instant transformation in the mood. But flutes, drums and voices breaking out from among the crowd continued to dispense the bulls' elixir even as the flesh was hacked, the guts squeezed and braided, and the enclosure turned pungent and heady in the mixture of blood and faeces. The heads, smeared in froth and blood, haunted by flies lay in a heap. Potsherds of blood, pocked by entrails slowly congealed in the afternoon whose shad-

ows had begun to lengthen. The women lit fires, undaunted, even
exhilarated by the prospect of a night-long wake. The first potloads
of malt brew approached on the heads of children. Bundles of fire-
wood accompanied the arrival of clay and iron cauldrons and cans
of oil. Dwindling into the dusk, voices called to the Custodian:

> *Watch O watch for us*
> *Who stay a while*
> *For we have soothed your path*
> *Who leave us now*

Pursuing him into the distant regions of his new abode, imbuing
him with all the sympathetic potency, the healing and reproduc-
tive promise of the earth-bull union which they had witnessed
they exhorted:

> *You dip your hand in the red clay bowl*
> *The gods eat from*
> *Lay your hand upon my earth*
> *Shower me with rain*
>
> *Lay your hand upon my roof*
> *Fill me with children*
> *Lay your hand upon my body*
> *Bless me with health . . .*

Ofeyi's mind had moved away with the retreating voices, away
from the immediate presence of the dead man, and the noise of
hacking and tearing in the enclosure. Suddenly the singing seemed
to be right before him, he looked up to see that some women had
broken away from the working group in the pen, had surrounded
Iriyise and were singing and dancing before him. When his eyes

acknowledged their coup they laughed, broke off and danced back into the pen, taking Iriyise with them.

That night he told her to pack for an early morning return. Her face fell with disappointment but he promised: "We are coming back. Right now we have work to do."

The old man sprinted out to meet him as he beached the Corporation motor-boat and helped out Iriyise. "I have been listening for the sound" he said. He glanced mischievously at Iriyise. "Did the woman lead you back?"

Ofeyi shook his head. "I have come with schemes" he announced. "Official schemes."

"I am content, even though I don't know what they are. There are some people who must approve their needs only in terms of the need of others."

"You are too deep for me Pa Ahime."

Ahime shook his head. "We are simple people in Aiyéró. Welcome to you both."

Even without the results of comparative tests—Ofeyi had returned to base with a pouch of Aiyéró's soil—the firm dank earth that commenced only a short distance from the coastline was visibly cocoa earth. The idea that came from his first encounter with the commune was only one of many that sought to retrieve his occupation from its shallow world of jingles and the greater debasement of exploitation by the Cartel. The pattern could be reversed, the trick of conversion applied equally to the Cartel's technical facilities not merely to effect restitution to many but to create a new generation for the future. A new plantation within the communal, labouring, sharing entity—seed through nursery to the mature plant and fructification—Ofeyi envisioned the parallel progress of the new idea, the birth of the new man from the same germ as the cocoa seed, the Aiyéró ideal disseminated with the same powerful propaganda machine of the Cartel throughout the land, taking hold of undirected youth and filling the vacuum of their transitional heritage with the virile shoot.

In Aiyéró's meeting-house where all new projects were discussed Ofeyi caught Ahime watching him curiously. His request was stated simply: a portion of forested land for his scheme— co-operation of the people of Aiyéró and their patience, especially when the intrusive cameras began to turn and threaten to violate their long-treasured insulation.

Ahime presided thoughtfully, taking no part. The people listened, discussed without arguing, asked questions, put forth ideas and listened again. Iriyise sat among the women, her presence provoked a flow of celluloid images; he translated them to the gathering, simply. The people of Aiyéró gave their assent, set aside acres of virgin land for the scheme.

Even the Corporation gave its approval.

The forest was cleared, sown. The founding ballads of Aiyéró were unearthed, a new body of work-songs grew from the grain of the vanguard idea. Iriyise abandoned the circuit of Ilosa's lights, the earth of Aiyéró held her deeper than any bed of eiderdown.

In wrapper and sash with the other women of Aiyéró, her bared limbs and shoulders among young shoots, Iriyise weaving fronds for the protection of the young nursery, bringing wine to the sweating men in their struggle against the virgin forests. Again and again Ofeyi allowed himself the pleasure of astonishment at her transformations, her unending capacity to learn. From merely singing praises of the "cocoa complexion" she had burgeoned in unforeseeable directions. Now she could even tell a blight on the young shoot apart from mere scorching by the sun. Her fingers spliced wounded saplings with the ease of a natural healer. Her presence, the women boasted, inspired the rains.

Then the ardent bloodhounds of the Cartel began to sniff out hidden roots. Unseen fingers combed his workshop, leaving a trail of ransacked papers and tapes. They turned over the shooting-script to experts, pored over each word and queried phrases. The work-songs stuck in their throats.

"Mr. Ofeyi, this is not quite the outline which we approved at the meeting of the board. The story of the cocoa plant from seed to ripening. . . ."

"And the life of the community. The parallel life of a child from seed—well, as near as we can get to that of course—to maturity."

"Even so Mr. Ofeyi . . . !"

The uncut and incomplete footage was re-run for the hundredth time, the sound-track played over and over again by the tenacious bulldogs of the Cartel. . . .

"Mr. Ofeyi, this Corporation thinks that perhaps you should take leave of absence. A study leave. We will arrange your itinerary to take in as many countries as possible where you will be able to see how they do these things, perhaps borrow a few ideas . . . America, Japan, Germany and so on. The Americans have the greatest advertising know-how in the world. They really understand the profession, that is why they are such a prosperous country. The Secretary will inform you of the arrangements. We want you to understand that the Corporation is quite happy—generally—with your work, we merely want to obtain the best possible from your talents. See the Accountant in the morning. He has instructions to er . . . ensure that your tour is as comfortable as possible. The Corporation likes to keep its employees as happy as the employees permit. You understand?"

Ofeyi understood. The Cartel still had hopes of his eventual salvation.

"What happens to the existing footage?"

"Oh, we'll keep it in our safe. It will be there when you return. There is no hurry after all. You can begin all over again on your return or shoot a new documentary altogether. The idea is most valuable, but there are other suitable lands and communities beside Aiyéró." He smiled. "Well, enjoy your trip Mr. Ofeyi."

II

Time expired, the prodigal returned.

At the root of his new sense of urgency was the airport encounter with the lone wolf whom he had mentally begun to refer to as "The Dentist." It drove him straight to Aiyéró the moment his plane touched home ground, almost as if he feared, not a weakening of resolve, but that a sinister potency of the Cartel might penetrate and forestall possibilities that yet existed only in his mind. The air of Ilosa where the plane landed appeared instantly filled by the corrupting agency of the Cartel and its many subservient alliances. Uncertain even now what strategies the new confrontation demanded, he trusted to that inspiration which he constantly derived from Aiyéró's calm sufficiency but wondered what the old man Ahime would make of that self-effacing priest of violence, the Dentist, whose single-mindedness had resuscitated his own wavering commitment. Ofeyi's sole doubt was whether such a force could ever be truly harnessed. The unexpectedness of their encounter was matched only by the other departure from the real programme of his study tour, a restorative idyll with the Asian enigma, Taiila. The airports of the world seemed to have turned hunting-grounds for alienated souls.

Ofeyi began to search for a blunted language which would best describe the Dentist to Ahime without hardening him in opposition to what he now considered a necessary alliance. A selective assassin? The term sounded meaningless, the point of assassination being that it is selective. An agency of retribution? A pre-emptive support? The last seemed closer to the Dentist's declared principles of scotching the snake before it had time to strike. Ofeyi's sceptical snort anticipated the old man's response to all such transparent efforts at making the Dentist's role any less stark, so he gave up the attempt. The Cartel had killers and used them; the Dentist would redress the balance, at least to some extent. As his motorboat neared Aiyéró, he began to rehearse the arguments in his mind.

But what he first asked Ahime, after the embrace and the welcome was, "What did he have in mind exactly, your late Founder, when he made me that improbable proposal?"

The old man fluttered his hands. "Why do you continue to call it improbable? Even a child can be Custodian of the Grain."

"Yes, but a child does not reek, as much as I must have done, of complete alienation from his way of life. I came to Aiyéró directly from wallowing in the filth and compromises of Ilosa."

"Then why are you here?" the old man asked him. "Why do you keep coming back?"

Ofeyi met the frank eyes of the old man and admitted simply, "I need something from Aiyéró."

Ahime waited.

"What would you say" Ofeyi began, moving to the point at last, "if I told you that I now respect the claims of violence?"

A flicker of surprise showed in Ahime's eyes but he merely shrugged and said, "The founding history of Aiyéró had its roots in violence."

"Even so," Ofeyi reassured him, "violence is not what I want from here. Just the same, the sowing of any idea these days can no longer take place without accepting the need to protect the young seedling, even by violent means."

"Go on" Ahime urged. "Tell me exactly what you want from us."

Ofeyi shook his head. "To begin with it is what I would like you to accept. Such as the need to form a common purpose with forces which are . . . well, let's just say—not exactly peaceful in their methods. Even if it contains the risk that such forces may run wild and endanger the meagre scaffolding. . . ."

Ahime stopped him. "All this has to do with your travels, am I right? New books you have read perhaps or new societies you have studied?"

"No. It is more to do with a new kind of person I encountered." And he proceeded to describe the encounter with the Dentist and the logic of the man. Ahime listened patiently then commented,

"You speak of sowing a new idea. But surely you have also heard that saying—sowing the wind and reaping the whirlwind?"

"The storm was sown by the Cartel, Pa Ahime. Unless we can turn the resulting whirlwind against them, we are lost."

Ahime thought it over in silence. He returned finally to the question that still troubled him most. "What will this mean for us in Aiyéró?"

"Nothing, if you mean from the Dentist's own activities. Aiyéró is my own province. I don't know what essence of leaves or bark you inject into your children from birth; I only know that it innoculates them against the poison of places like Ilosa, against temptations such as the Cartel can offer. I believe in Aiyéró."

Ahime betrayed a little glimmer of triumph. "Then why don't you simply stay here with us? What more do you seek?"

Ofeyi shook his head. "The healing essence which soothes one individual or some stray dog that happens to wander into Aiyéró is not enough for the bruises of others I know of. They require a very different form of healing."

"How do you know?" the old man retorted. "There are essences which no one sees, which may be slow in taking effect. Why do you think we pay such attention to ritual sacrifices?"

"That's just it!" Ofeyi snapped, "You have never broken off completely from your parent stock. You still indulge in these grandiose illusions. It's rather like those white monks who have stayed within their citadels of stone, shut off from the real world of evil, offering little candle-puffs of piety on behalf of the hideous hunger of the living world and even, presumptuously, of the hunger of the dead."

Laughing, Ahime admitted, "Well, that really describes us. We don't ignore the dead in Aiyéró."

"No you don't. You claim intercession from the dead and rotted same as those monks. Do you know how a friend described it? Matter of fact it was the Dentist, and he was referring to a girl I met about the same time as he. She wanted very much to become a nun. It was something of a tussle Pa Ahime, I have to tell you about it sometime. If I had been superstitious I would have thought that she was miraculously sent to save me from the path of damnation as represented by the Dentist. You know, good angel on one side, bad angel on the other."

"What became of her?"

Ofeyi laughed. "You don't fool me Pa. What you really mean to ask is, what became of Iriyise during that episode? We-e-ell, to tell you the truth, Iri was never in serious danger. I don't know how, but that woman has become indissoluble in my mind from the soil of Aiyéró. Taiila on the other hand is . . ."

Tired of waiting for him to find the right words Ahime reminded him that he had been on the point of repeating the Dentist's verdict on the girl.

"Oh it was nothing profound. Just a crack about her trying to run a two-way commuter service of requests and counter-requests between the living and the unknown. That is the business of monasteries. Seriously Pa, Aiyéró is rather like that. That function is not enough. It won't do for those whose needs I have encountered face to face, needs which I have seen men bleed and die for, from the lack of fulfilment."

"We have been called everything" Ahime commented drily, "including a pocket Utopia."

"You know what that means?"

"Oh yes. Our sons bring back all forms of literature. I have little to do with my time these days except read them. And I come to the conclusion over and over again that there is really nothing new on the surface of this earth." He gave his mischievous chuckle—"Or in the next. Men's minds have travelled across vast distances and embraced one another. Travelled vast periods too, both backwards and into the future and embraced one another. For good or evil. That knowledge teaches both humility and pride."

"You think that's what your people find out for themselves? Is that what brings them back here?"

"You still bother your head with that riddle?"

"Don't you ever ask them yourself?"

"Why should I?" Ahime demanded. "That is as much as to say I don't expect them back, which is hardly true is it?"

In the middle of the night Ofeyi started out of sleep, an inspired certainty rendered the prospect of sleep futile for the rest of the night. He scrambled into his trousers and rushed across the sleeping township to Ahime's compound. It was at least three in the night but, even without the light which still shone from a window in Ahime's house he would have knocked on the door and broken the old man's sleep.

Ahime opened the door himself. "Come in Ofe. You haven't slept I see."

Ofeyi began to apologize for the late visit but Ahime stopped him. "I was not asleep. At most I sleep four hours in the night. At my age, sleep becomes less and less essential." He laid aside the book he had been reading. "I like your Mao" he commented. "You can see I have been reading things to make sure I can meet you on your own grounds. He is unique this Chinese isn't he? A man of simple truths and a large experimental farm. For the first time I feel like undertaking a journey to meet a man I have only encountered on the pages of a book. After all, it is the time of life to travel . . ."

"Pa Ahime . . ." Ofeyi interrupted.

Ahime turned and looked into his face. "Oh, I see you did not come here to pass the night in idle discussion. All right, let's sit down and be comfortable."

Ofeyi sat in a chair opposite the old man. "I have come to make you an offer."

Ahime nodded slowly, his eyes alert.

"You have men all over the country," Ofeyi said. "In nearly all of the major towns. They are scattered all over, in every factory and industry. Lend them to me for two years. After that . . ."

Ahime raised his hand. "No, no conditions. Just tell me why you want them."

Ofeyi spread out his hands. It was this, or leave the entire initiative to other, more drastic, means. The goals were clear enough, the dream a new concept of labouring hands across artificial frontiers, the concrete, affective presence of Aiyéró throughout the land, undermining the Cartel's superstructure of robbery, indignities and murder, ending the new phase of slavery. His look indicated that he had expected this to be as obvious to the wise Ahime.

"I did not mean what you would make them do" the old man said. "I meant, why the men of Aiyéró?"

"Because they live by an idea, their lives are bound up by the one idea. I believe they cannot be corrupted, or swayed."

The old man nodded briefly. "They are yours."

Blinking, Ofeyi enquired, "They are mine? Just like that?"

"Oh I shall get our Treasurer to give you a list of where they can be found. That's how we know where they are at any time, by the addresses from which they last sent us their surplus earnings."

"But I can't just go to them and say . . ."

"That I sent you? Of course you can't. Because I don't send you. They are all free men who live, as you say, by a certain idea. If your own goals correspond to that idea, then all you have to do is go to them. I doubt if any of them has ever joined a political party even out of curiosity, they know all about them from close enough quarters. But if your idea fulfils their own constant readiness for service . . ."

Ofeyi stood up. "I promise I. . . ."

"No promises" the old man insisted. "Suppose you consent at this moment to be Custodian of the Grain, staying with us in Aiyéró, what's to prevent you doing what you want with these men, working at your own pace until you have persuaded the whole community to go along with you, freely using our resources in the promotion of your idea? Or even splintered the community and taken with you those who are swayed by your persuasive vision of the larger community to which we all belong. You see, it is in fact only a modest part of what we offered that you have demanded of me."

He accompanied Ofeyi to the door. "After all the battles of the world, one needs a resting-place. And often, in between the battles. Aiyéró was created for such needs or perhaps, let's simply say, it can fulfil such needs. Oh, I nearly overlooked this, when you have spoken to the men and they are yours, tell them that what they normally send to us in Aiyéró now belongs to the cause. They will know that we have consented to it. Well, that's all I can think of for now."

Outside, Ofeyi stood still for some moments, staring into the night. The spontaneity of Ahime's support overwhelmed him, taking on an even more deciding aspect than the earlier genesis of the strategy itself. He turned to the old man and asked, "Have you no doubts at all?"

"Doubts upon doubts, thicker than the night around us." His teeth gleamed in his face. "I quoted you the reply which our Founder made to me when I asked him, many years after Aiyéró had established itself firmly and stably, the same question as you asked me just now. Of course I have doubts!"

Ofeyi grinned. "Sleep well Pa Ahime."

"Sleep well, son."

He heard the door shut gently behind him.

2

BUDS

III

In the beginning, there was nectar and ambrosia
A golden pod contained them . . .

But the Chairman was no longer riled. He could afford to smile
his benediction on the orchestra . . . do carry on, carry on fools. It's
not who begins it but who ends it. And we will. We will.

Favoured of gods they made the cosmos rosier
The gods wiped the dribble from their beard
And snores of thunder soon were heard
For the elixir also bred divine amnesia

Ta-ra-ra-ra-.ta-.ta--ta---. The Chairman even supplied the coda in
his head. It was different at the beginning when he raged at the
perfidy. Now he could even afford to be amused. He ran his hand

over his chin as if to treat his fingers to the rich dribble of nectar before it vanished into mere imagination. Damned weeping Jeremiahs. Envy-ridden flea-bitten social dregs! As for Ofeyi—it was clear, he had learned nothing. The Corporation had wasted money on him. He had returned truly incorrigible.

> *The cocoa-pod became their sole desire*
> *Its food alone sustained them*
> *Thou golden honeycomb, they sang to a golden lyre*
> *Pure ambrosia-laden beans*
> *Womb of nectar—oh, joyous paeans*
> *Dear Muses, let this fount your songs inspire.*

If one didn't know, yes, most sophisticated, very very. Eminently suited to this gathering. Fortunately the guests don't understand . . . sounds straightforward enough, just like our local praise-singers, though come to think of it, never heard them wax so lyrical over the cocoa-pod. Palm wine yes, or pounded yam, but never cash-crops like the cocoa . . . yes, he knows his stuff all right. Knows how to bite the hand that feeds him too . . . oh, best smile on now. Betray nothing.

Zaccheus had finished his saxophone solo so he took the chance to slip down from the platform to pay his respects to the Chairman. He met the bandleader with expanded arms. "Allow me to complement you Zaccheus, your band sounds better and better every time I hear them."

"That's kind of you Mr. Chairman."

"And that song you're playing now. . . ."

"You like it sir?"

"Beautiful, beautiful. We must have it made into a record."

"I'm glad you do. We thought there wasn't a fitter place to launch it than at your party."

"But that is so kind of you Zaccheus, so very kind. Did you write it yourself?"

"No Sir! I put the sauce on it afterwards but you have to thank Ofeyi for the bone and marrow. We kind of share the meat so to speak. . . ."

The Chairman looked bewildered. "I'm afraid I don't. . . ."

Zaccheus laughed, apologetic. "Forgot you aren't quite in on the verbs sir. What I mean is Ofeyi does the main thing and I help in on the arrangements. Words and music all his sir and quite a dishy combination it is."

"Oh yes indeed, very dishy Zaccheus, very dishy. I couldn't agree with you more. By the way I hope your band is well looked after."

"Sure Mr. Chairman. We don't lack for juice."

"Good, good good. Just remember the house is yours. Feel at home."

"Thank you sir, we sure will. Gotta get back on the . . ."

"Of course of course. Don't let me delay you."

> *But though it gave the immortals a new complexion*
> *As though gold rust had stained them*
> *And celestial banquets flowed with the new concoction*
> *When they looked below and there was Man*
> *With glowing skin and cocoa tan*
> *They longed oh how they longed for a mortal infection.*

Stumped, the Chairman scratched his head. In spite of serious tutoring packed with samples by his I.Q.—the Intellectual Quota on the Directors' Board—until he grew confident in his own ability to spot the most subtly disguised insult or subversiveness in the campaign lyrics, a phrase or two did manage to stump him. But the code was broken—as he begged humbly to inform the

Cartel—and he had gradually become convinced that there was no word, no symbol, no picture, nothing whatever which had ever put up for the campaign—at prodigious expense from our profits gentlemen!—which did not contain a hidden dose of anarchy.

Just then he spied his I.Q. battling his way through the melee of wigs and medals and champagne glasses. Just the man! Perhaps he had listened to the last verse. But I.Q. did not even give him a chance to put his question. In his hand he held a flapping rectangle of paper and the Director sighed as he saw that it was another of *those* posters. The man came up panting:

"Have you seen this Sir? It was stuck right against the pillars of your driveway. One on each side."

The Chairman examined it, raced his mind to uncover the message before his analyst identified it for him. A picture of an opulent glutton with a mouth wide open to cram into it a mammoth-sized slice of the cocoa-pod. Beneath it the legend read: THE GOLDEN SLICE. With ill-disguised irritation he heard I.Q. explain, quite unnecessarily:

"After that loud-mouthed Jekú leader who boasted he would have his golden slice of the national cake."

"Yes yes I can tell that is the meaning. What I want to know is how it got stuck outside my gates. I have two of my own watchmen and both the police and the army are here in force. As you know we are expecting . . ."

"Oh yes I heard that. Is it true?"

"Yes indeed it is. How embarrassing if he had had this to welcome him to the party."

"Oh I don't think the reference would have struck him. Even so Mr. Chairman, they are getting very bold."

The big man crushed the poster between his hands and I.Q. hurried to take it from him and hand it to a steward then passing through with a tray of refreshments.

"It does not matter" the Chairman said at last. "We will take the necessary decisions and act on them."

He moved away to attend to the comfort of his guests, indifferent to the dripping of a new nectar and ambrosia verse . . .

> *The sweet-toothed ones alas lacked all moderation*
> *No man-made laws restrained them*
> *They milked the cocoa-tree in a mass operation*
> *They drained the nectar, peeled the gold*
> *The trees were bled prematurely old*
> *Nor green nor gold remained for the next generation*

Ta-ra-ra-ra. ta-. ta--ta---. I.Q. collared a brandy from a passing waiter and reflected what Ofeyi's facile explanations would consist of this time. Surely the reference was undeniable. He would hardly call it a cautionary tale against over-planting the land. . . .

Threading a practised route through gloves and guffaws the Chairman recited the table of ranks through his head: One pip make one captain, two pips make one major, three pips make . . . oh dear, got it all wrong . . . one pip, one lieutenant, two pips make one captain, three . . . when do the crowns begin and wasn't there supposed to be a bar somewhere? And where do the blasted sergeant-majors come in anyway! Mind you they can always be separated in appearance . . . ox-like and ready to salute at the slightest provocation . . . one crown make one . . . damn! Chief Biga! Pity spoilers like Chief Biga could never be kept out completely. How did such a creature acquire such power—actually one of the Cartel? The Muscle Quota no doubt. Was he Batoki's tool or was Batoki his fool? The one's deviousness complemented the other's crassness. Biga enjoyed his hatchetman reputation. Crude as a pig's bladder . . . one, two crowns—but are they crowns? At the most a Lieutenant-Colonel, just call him Colonel. . . .

"Ha-llooooo my dear Brigadier, how kind of you to come."

"No, it was a great honour for me to be invited."

"Not at all not at all. You people are so busy running the affairs of the state, piloting the awkward ship of the state, trying to get the country ship-shape oh dear I could go on forever. But that is because we know what you are doing and we are proud of your achievements."

"You flatter us Chairman. We are just simple soldiers, all the work is done by people just like you. You are the backbone of the country. . . ."

"Dar-ling!"

"Do excuse me Colonel I think my wife needs me over there. Now promise me you will not hesitate to ask for anything you need, anything at all. I insist that you enjoy yourself in my house Colonel."

"I promise."

The Madame had called him but she did not interrupt her chatter until she was out of breath and then she could not remember what detail of her lecture she had called him over to confirm. Or to remind her of. So he half-turned aside to survey the huge lounge with a half-smile on his face beamed on the sector which was politely dedicated to his wife's circle. The lounge was filling up fast. The Chairman spotted Spyhole the muck-raker just coming in through the swing-doors and grimaced. An irreverent journalist but useful. He knew just what terms Spyhole would use to describe the occasion—A Glittering Gathering. And God knows what else. And out of spite he would ignore the formal opening of his marble fountain and his speech, the climax of the entire proceedings. Some smarty-pants tiny reference as an afterthought, he'd probably lie that he left early but discovered later that the Chairman's new fountain was declared open by Brigadier So-so-so whereas everyone knew that holier-than-thou Spyhole never left a party until shaming light of day shone on the last empty bottle. Envy! In a way he pitied them. There he goes. . . .

Spyhole encountered Zaccheus in a comparatively bare spot on the floor, dead-heat in a race to stop a loaded waiter from disappearing among the crowd for stripping.

"Spyhole!"

"Zaccheus man how's it going?"

"B-Sharp dead-on."

"Any tips?"

"Deadwood."

"Nobody got slapped yet?"

"Too much gold fluff man. You won't see a wig pulled tonight."

"I thought not. Corruscated scene of starch."

"And Madames and madamns and damnacadamns off their normal beat. All on their best behaviour."

"Ah well. You've got the vantage point up there. If you see anything . . ."

"Sure I'll signal. So long Spy."

Spyhole looked around, strolled towards the verandah. Fresh breeze from the lagoon. Big slice of state-reclaimed land. Across the garden he saw what must be the boathouse. What did the man want with a motor-boat since he didn't trust himself to anything smaller than an ocean-liner. Certainly had nothing but contempt for remotely dangerous relaxations. A tarpaulin-covered mound rose in the middle of the garden, concealing the glories of the fountain whose fame had monopolized all thought and conversation country-wide for the past month. The Chairman did not believe in hiding his light under the bushel. Spyhole strode around the mound, was surprised to see how much of the ground it filled, then recalled that it was a fountain-fishpond combination. The garden itself, high-walled, sloped sharply down towards the la-

goon. It gave him the sensation, suddenly, of being trapped in
an eroded pyramid fallen on its side, apex already sunk in the
sand-marsh. Across the verandah, figures twisted in and out of
the general congealment trapped in vestments richer than the
wildest dreams of Tutankhamun—Skyros the Lebanese owned
three-quarters of this clientele, Skyros with his grand boutique
that gleamed full of smuggled gold . . . Christ, why should these
powdered mummies be resuscitated!

Iriyise entered, bitched to the eyes and bitchy as hell. Yes, she
muttered, turn all and stare! Men, dribble. Women, turn to stone;
I hate your guts and you envy mine. Shrink back into your padded
bras and putty brains, it's me—Celestial! And that goes for you
wart-lip Lady K, cross-eyed chairbag of the Ladies' Sunday Club.
Shall I tell you where the Sir spends his Wednesday evenings when
he claims to be at the Rotary Club? Not with Iridescent mind you,
not though he lay his knighthood at my feet. But he makes do
with the consolation prize I found him and he doesn't really mind.
Anything will do after you, you . . . !

"Relax," Ofeyi hissed in her ear.

"I feel bitchy."

"Relax I said."

"They are all in debt to Skyros anyway."

"What is it to do with you?"

"Why did we have to come?"

"You know damned well. It's part of your duties."

"I won't perform I warn you. If the Chairman himself comes
and begs me on his knees . . ."

"We'll cross that bridge when we get to it. Come on . . . oh,
here he comes. Behave yourself now."

"Welcome welcome welcome. The Brains and the Beauty of a
successful campaign. Now the party is really complete."

"Thank you sir. It looks like a very good party."

"With the Cocoa princess herself here it will be remembered

as the party of the year. Come over here and let me introduce you to the Brigadier. I'd better warn you Princess, most of the men here are hoping like mad for one of your famous Personal Appearances. . . ."

"I hope you haven't been building up their hopes, Chief" she hissed, wincing as Ofeyi dug his fingers in her arm. Mystified, she protested the moment the Chairman deserted them to trap a loaded tray. "But you don't want me to perform at his private party surely? Do you?"

Ofeyi murmured, "I'm not sure."

"You should have warned me then."

"I've told you, I don't know yet."

He sounded distracted, so Iriyise sank into her own mental rehearsals. There were no more surprises. Suddenly Ofeyi had stopped adding to the repertoire, stopped springing new ideas on her just before a scheduled "personal appearance," choreographing her till the last possible moment. It was only a question of getting in the studied mood, composing face and body for the moment of public exposure. Zaccheus had learnt to tour the troupe with all the props and costumes. The worry was never hers, she merely submitted soul and body to his fantasies. The mammoth pod split open lengthways, or across its girth, top half opening like a lid. Iriyise rose from a bed of simulated giant beans as from sleep, stretched her arms. The orchestra played and Zaccheus, dressed in tails, handed her a cup of cocoa, bent on one knee and she stepped out on his back. And the multitude of headgears, neither wig nor shrub—Ofeyi called them seasonals—they came in green, gold, brown, amber, cream and blends of other colours. On the better equipped stage, the pod might rise through the trap-door, Iriyise sealed within it.

A strange feeling on the recreation ground at Shage Dam, a "gala night" arranged by the workers on a holiday. Ofeyi had urged her by telephone to be nothing but superlative, for Shage was the Cross-river outpost of the new idea. The workers were mostly men of Aiyéró. All day they worked to fabricate a trap-door, converting leverage power from one of the numerous earth-moving equipment idling on the site. It worked. Then came the short-circuiting, so Iriyise lay within the giant shell in darkness, forever and forever as it seemed to her. No speck of light filtered through the airholes, no sensation except one of being buried alive. But peacefully, without panic. Tingling for the moment of light and life. Then the moment of rising through the soil, light coming at last through the air-holes, little dancing peppermints. The pod lifted slowly, guided by unseen forces and emerged prow first, splitting lengthwise along its ridges into thin orange wedges. Iriyise, already floated out on a layer of palm oil under her skin stepped onto an earth-covered stage and, into a thunderstorm of applause. Then came her dance of the young shoot and in that open space surrounded by virginal trees from which the arc-lamps had been strung, top-laden also with workers from the site and the Cross-river villagers of Shage, all seeking the best vantage spots— but Iriyise saw nothing of the thousand eyes, only the feel of night or her limbs and that prolonged sensation of climbing out of her skin into a rainstorm, sprouting leaves and fresh buds from neck and fingers, shaking her hair free of dead leaves and earth and absorbing light and air through every pore. Deaf to every cue that came from Zaccheus' reed she danced, the green scrolls in her wig flew outwards into the night and showered the watchers. Palm oil ran freely in her veins until, exhausted, she gathered herself for the final leap, amazed that she landed centre of the small platform that still held the thin canoes wedge radiating from the trap. They closed to a loud sigh from the engineer that was audible to the furthest reaches of the amphitheatre. Back within her shell, lathered, she felt, not in sweat but in rich black oil she waited again to be freed. . . .

She heard Ofeyi's voice at her ear. "What do we have tonight? Duality of the Iridescent Smile—glass splinters for the ladies, love barbs for the men?"

Her tone a silky menace she enquired, "Did I look as if I was smiling?"

"It was difficult to tell."

"Well I wasn't. And I will never forgive you for not being there when I did my dance at Shage."

"Ah yes. Zaccheus said you were never more marvellous."

Her frustration only seemed to increase. "You would miss it. You have never seen me at my best. That's why you think I'm only good for"—her lip curled in self-contempt—"Personal Appearances at the homes of fat Corporation swine!"

"Keep your voice down and . . ."

"Yes I know. Relax. I can't. I have never satisfied you, that's why you don't make anything new. Your cocoa-pod is falling to pieces. It already opens about twenty different ways and one of these days it will open all ways at once and then you will get rid of me at last. And good luck to your next Cocoa Tits!"

Ofeyi gave his attention to the men who had delayed the Chairman in his hunt for the drinks tray. One of them he recognized as the Commandant's right-hand man; publicly he served as a Trouble-shooter for the Cartel. Young, full of power and the glory like the rest of them, only far more so. He was intensely busy at the Chairman's ear. Was it true then, that the Commandant himself would cut the tape on the fishpond with his own gloved hands? Not bad, not bad, even it was only a regional commandant. Ofeyi slewed his eyes sharply back to Iriyise as he sensed, rightly, that Chairman and Trouble-shooter were about to glance in his direction yet again. For some reason he felt a great unease.

"You didn't listen to anything I said did you?" Iriyise accused him.

"I heard you. When will you learn to cope with company like this? You still let them upset you."

"I don't."

"They are nothing; I thought I had proved that to you a hundred times."

"Then why should you make me perform for them?"

"I haven't said I will. But it may be necessary, They shouldn't think no one knows what they are planning next!"

She frowned. "Ofeyi, what are you talking about?"

"Nothing, nothing." His manner became decisive. "Go and get ready. Tonight you will do the Pandora's Box. Go and tell Zaccheus." And he vanished into the crowd.

"This is not," beamed the proud host, "simply an occasion in the home of a private citizen. Oh no, I assure you ladies and gentlemen and Distinguished Personalities you would not be here to join me in the unveiling of this er . . . this . . . to be present at this wonderful occasion if it were simply so. Nor would such a busy man as the Brigadier himself be here to do us the honour of the unveiling. Yes, it is a symbolical event as you will see for yourself. This country owes its prosperity to the industry of one significant plant. It lies in its little farm, not making noise, just minding its business, not causing trouble, it is not he he he—an agitator shall I say?" He continued after his audience had duly rewarded him with approving laughter—"it is indeed the little lily of the farm but one that toileth in silence and feeds the multimillion mouths of the nation."

The applause broke, swelled, obediently faded away at the upraised palms of the Chairman. "When therefore I commissioned this little thing here, I said to the . . . er . . . the man who is to do the job, the artist I mean to say, I said to him, this thing is to commemorate our mutual gratitude to the cocoa plant, so whatever you design, make sure that the matter is naked to the eye as clearly as I am seeing you now. Well let me not speak too much. It is not me who has to be unveiled; my better half standing over there did that a very long time ago." He allowed the laughter to die down on its own, then stretched his arm towards the waiting Brigadier. "So let me call upon the Brigadier over there who has been so kind as to come and honour us by the unveiling of this fountain, this symbolical cocoa fountain which we all so fervently hope will never never dry from its eternal underground sources. Ladies and Gentlemen, Distinguished Guests—His Excellency the Regional Commandant—the Brigadier!"

Conducting his orchestra on cue, Zaccheus brought forth a flourish from brass and a roll from drums and swung into a martial tempo for the Brigadier's immaculate precision steps to the waiting silver scissors, held out by the Chairman's lady, ribbon-side of the fishpond and nestling on a blue velvety cushion. A dozen cameras flashed and did not stop again for another half-hour. The Brigadier bowed, took the scissors, took her hand and implanted a kiss upon it to thunderous applause and delight. He was a resplendent figure the Brigadier, groomed it seemed from a nineteenth-century Venetian court—appropriately, it had to be conceded, when the dust-sheet fell away and the glory of Italian marble was revealed to the benighted audience. Only the Chairman's running commentary jarred from time to time the viewers' contemplation of a Florentine moment in the heart of the festering continent.

White-coated servants gathered up the dust-sheets and pulled them slowly backwards. The fountain pool, itself a fish-pond was indeed scooped out in the shape of the cocoa-pod, floor and sides laid in tiny tiles of amber. From the centre of the pod rose a noble plinth, a marble arm from the enchanted lake, which for Excalibur upheld a blue marble platform upon which sat an armoured knight, equestrian. At the horse's feet writhed a monstrous dragon, scales of silver, tongue of bronze, fiery, fire-flashing eyes of onyx. It was transfixed by a ponderous silver spear and pounded by steel hooves of the noble steed.

"We all know the story of St. George and the dragon I think" the Chairman expounded as the applause rose and fell and the oh-ahs quietened. "Well, you may not guess that what I have done here is to put it to symbolical use. Which is why I specially hoped that one of our new rulers would be able to unveil the masterpiece in person. St. George seated on that horse there as you can see is representative of the new order which is battling the dragon which represents the forces of our greatest national enemy—corruption!"

"Hear hear, hear hear, hear hear . . ."

Spyhole, listening from the vantage point of the bandstand poised his journeying glass a few inches from his lips and turned slowly round to Zaccheus. Together they exploded in laughter, ducked behind a screen as a few pairs of eyes turned round in their direction.

St. George fixed his gaze beyond the scene, intent upon a mission which did not involve the present company. A head-casque covered his head in tradition but the eyes and a nose-bridge were permitted to vulgar gaze. Hannibal, Alexander or even Boadicea, it did not seem to matter, he sat symbolical upon his leaden steed, oblivious to the important gathering that had come to honour his full-sprung birth. To yet another burst of demented drum roll and trumpet rampant a servant turned a hidden tap, the Chairman shouted out a frantic "Stand back a little ladies and gentle-men" and the water leapt out through a dozen gashes in the beast and through its serpent-tongued mouth, heavily fluoridated—the Director explained that dragon's blood is blue but this was lost in the vociferous approval that greeted the display. There was little left of applauding energy when the final wonder was perceived.

As the rush of water mounted to a level required of the hidden mechanism in the plinth, St. George, horse, dragon and platform began to spin, slowly and clock-wise on the plinth. The hardiest victims of *déjà vu* were won over and joined in the applause.

"Ladies and Gentlemen, Distinguished visitors"—he bowed and bowed to unending cheers—"Ladies and Gentlemen, the bar is still open, more dancing to our famous Zaccheus and his Cocoa Beans orchestra. And . . . please attention please, attention Ladies and Gentlemen . . . I think we are even fortunate enough to be able to promise, later, a Personal Appearance of none other than our Cocoa Princess, in one of her famous presentations, the title of which I'm afraid is being kept secret till the actual moment."

Pandora's Box, its denouement subverted to the private ends of sky, clouds, sunset and air-currents in the stratosphere, left its creator Ofeyi with a sense of superfluity, the watchers with a hint of cosmic threat. After the initial cautionary villains, so familiar to the farming audiences, had emerged from the black-painted pod—the same long-suffering, multi-purposed pod—after them came the unexpected. Four familiar faces, puppet-form, suspended also from balloons, faces whose identities none, not even of those present, dared claim to recognize—Ofeyi had counted on this— faces whose names were whispered with dread even in the hardiest sanctuaries of the underworld. These, the real powers of the Cartel unfurled with linked arms as the balloons flew higher and the strings were unravelled. In the uneven movements of the balloon barrage they appeared to do a slow macabre dance of the magic circle, heads slowly turning side to side in contemplation of a prostrate world. With the extra buoyancy of the larger balloons they soon overtook the lesser hazards, the drippy scaly microbious shapes that hovered lazily over the garden while Zaccheus at his clowning best leant, panting, on the lid he had hastily shut. But his moon-horror face was no longer acting as he saw the four bogey-men. Until they emerged after the weeds, the viruses, the swollen shoot and other plagues of the cocoa farmer he had not suspected their presence in the box.

The applause was mild, uncertain. It hovered between a refusal to recognize the four linked figures—the "terrible quads" according to the christening of their own genteel circles—and realization that failure to applaud the technical display was admission of their recognition. The guests mostly began to wonder if they would ever attend another garden party. If one was not safe from such dilemmas in the very home of one of the top servants of the Cartel . . . !

Iriyise waited in the lower half, waiting for Zaccheus to cue her for the commencement of her tiny-voiced plea "Let me out, let me out." But Zaccheus was paralysed by the fear of what other outrage lay within Ofeyi's conclusion to this divergence from the norm. Iriyise crouched among the props of aerosol, seeds for supplementary crops, fertilizers and rolled up banners suspended on balloons. She heard the scattered applause die an unnatural death, a hush descend upon the garden. The music which had been kept at skeleton strength by a few pieces in the orchestra faded also. Second Trumpet dropped to a lower octave and Voice-Guitar could barely mumble tune and lyric. Finally they gave up the struggle. Iriyise sensed an unhealthy stillness, turned cold in the womb of the pod.

But the chill that had begun to set on the garden had not been caused by the appearance of the bogey-men alone. Perhaps it was the presence of armed men in the garden that prompted it—the Commandant had come with a bodyguard of nearly forty and they mingled among the guests with fingers on sub-machine gun triggers, as much at ease as the waiters who, regulated simply by clear-cut duties and apparel, are the true urbane beneficiaries of all ostentatious events. And so the armed men, natural dealers in death and thus the most superstitious were first to notice and to be affected by a phenomenon that had commenced in the sky some time before, but had remained unnoticed until the ascent of the sinister Cartel quadruplet. Whispering among one another, they soon communicated their unease and the cause. Other eyes which had followed the marionettes found themselves face to face with a spectacle which began by astounding, then, as memories were awakened, ended with a cold apprehensiveness. There was no one present who did not remember the morning when the country had woken to the knowledge that their destiny had been taken in charge by the once-invisible men of the gun. It had darkened abruptly that day and many swore that the morning mist over the lagoon had dripped distinct black globules on the leaves. The hardiest rationalists had conceded that the short, fierce rain was out of season. And the pall that accompanied it, indefinable as fog, eclipse or mottled mist had been dark enough to force them to switch on full headlamps as they drove to work over the bridge that hung, barely visible over the lagoon.

Standing around the cocoa fountain, their hardihood strained by alcohol that had seeped through and softened the protective carapace of scepticism, they like the other more portent-happy spectators no longer brooded on the latest outrage of the Pod. Their minds had shifted now to wondering if the sunset that now confronted them in some way bore a related warning to that non-rise of the sun that ushered in the barrel power of the unnerving guests in their midst. The tropics spawned some startling sunsets, but never one like this. Within the closure of the toppled pyramid each man and woman began to feel trapped, alone with doughy lumps of cirrus clouds, set vulnerably against an open hovering furnace. Oblivious of cricks commencing in their necks, their skins absorbed a fear communicated from neighbour to neighbour, unable to tear away from the mesmeric host of foetus shapes moulded and ejected from a kiln on the horizon, wafted by currents they could not feel within the pyramid. The shapes moved towards the dome centre of the sky, in a steady, unbroken formation. Briefly it looked like a recumbent flock of sheep, again like rows of dressed fowl through a display window. It even took on the brief suggestion of even rows of cocoa pods but, again and definitely the sky dislodged its pastoral teases, settled finally and lavishly for a blood-lit evocation of biblical horrors, flickering around a star that led and moved and guided the shapes over a mangy den—plagues and visitations, the Massacre of the Innocents.

The Cartel marionettes had long sailed beyond vision, nodding to the last into a sunset apotheosis. The sunset-rinsed host settled directly over the garden. Details glowed, translucent networks of tender veins and arteries, the soft unearthly faces were curled inward to the navel, massive foreheads tinged, like the softer underbellies and folded limbs, in a flickering purple hue.

Half the visible sky was now covered. And, to heighten the growth of an oppressiveness individually directed at the watchers, when the foremost row had all but reached dome zenith, hearing an ever-present sough of dark wings in their arm-pit squelch of apprehension, sensing the line almost flush with a line of division in the fear-distended lobes of their brains, the wind dropped suddenly and the host hung motionless. Now it was only the sun whose motion they could feel sinking deeper and lower, leaving its emphatic pace to be reflected in the somnolent eidola above their heads, their eyes glued to the responses of these shapes, to their vascular modulations, a pulsing of violent and purple intensities, uniform as if they all drew heartblood from a common source. Their far-side of the sun was the spinal curvature, again of a uniformity contrasted in sluggish grey and a smear of blue. The pulsing, the greatest source of disconcertion grew clearer though weaker, a late twilight hour on a neon-infested metropolis, a comfortless view from that sunken, closing alley.

Zaccheus had recovered from the shock of the Cartel appearance and was impervious to the goings-on in the sky. Recalled to the tradition of his profession from the moment of the final disappearance of the Cartel quartet he roused his men, took the microphone himself and began to sing . . .

In the beginning, there was nectar and ambrosia
A little pod contained them
Favoured of gods, they made the cosmos rosier . . .

Accustomed as she was to violent and spontaneous changes in the programme it did not make much sense to Iriyise, trapped still in the beneficent sector of the Pod. She began to scratch gently, then, finding no response, changed to outright bangs. And the rehearsed tinniness which the role demanded was completely forgotten as she began to scream:

"Let me out, let me out you drunken bastards!"

IV

⸻

The meeting was called to order.

The Trouble-shooter tried his first joke of the day: "If only it were as easy to call our Co-ordinator to order, ha ha?" No one laughed. Deeper even than the cause that had inflicted him upon the corporation was his presence resented. The decision of the Cartel to send their own man to sort out a mere wayward employee implied a total loss of confidence. (The thought of danger did not occur to any member—who could threaten the Cartel!) In spite of the outrage of the previous week, in his own house, it was inconceivable. And then, for the Chairman at least, there was the personal aspect. A firm believer in personal diplomacy, proof of "having the ear of—you know who I mean . . . ," he had sent his little handwritten squeak of protest through an intermediary to the Cartel. . . . "I humbly beg to remind you that this is a matter of concern to me as Head of the Corp. responsible for the day-to-day admn. of etc.

etc." Only to have it returned by the same courier with a contemptuous footnote which called him the head of that "headless corpse
which should be interred as quickly as decently practicable etc.
etc." Something in the manner of the Trouble-shooter suggested
just the kind of time-serving, power-drunk opportunist functionaire etc. etc. who would send out such a witless piece of effrontery.
And that garrulous face—how else could the impertinent footnote
"delivered by hand" have become the source of sly winks and guffaws in the night-clubs and casinos whenever the members of the
Corp. appeared with their mistresses.

It was small consolation that the joke quickly backfired. The
name stuck. The Cocoa Corporations, regional fronts for a thousand conspiracies of the Cartel became known as the Headless
Corpse. Figures of terror became, overnight, objects of sniggers.
The Cartel however remained no laughing matter. The Chairman
refused to be fooled by the inane grin which failed to mask the
arrogance of their Trouble-shooter.

Pompous too, the Chairman decided. Performing for relegated
clods whose authority he had usurped, armed with the power of
assignment from the Cartel. He shuffled papers round quite needlessly and spoke like chapters from a book. "I have made bold to
make a spare copy of each of these reports. And the sales graphs.
It is only right that the Co-ordinator should have a copy of everything as the indictments are read. We don't want him to complain
that he was not dealt with according to strict canons of juridical
procedure and natural justice."

The Chairman shut his eyes and crossed his hands over his
paunch. The Secretary complemented this gesture of long-
suffering by raising an eyebrow and slackening his own mouth.
He had been worsted in the preliminary skirmishes—the Trouble-
shooter had come into the boardroom on his own to view the
arrangements and insisted on the Chairman's personal chair for

himself, and right at the centre of the mahogany table—"where I can look this dangerous character in the eye." The Secretary had stammered that this was the Chairman's private chair. And place. Only to encounter the cool stare of the functionaire. "I am not here as an observer but to conduct a serious enquiry."

He was now relaying more or less the same sentiments to the assembled board. "If you would be kind enough to er—give your-selves some kind of observer status today gentlemen while I try to adopt my own methods in this rather crucial enquiry. . . ."

The Chairman detached a hand laden with heavy rings from the cross of martyrdom on his paunch and indicated his indifference in a casual wave. "Do carry on as you think fit." Keeping his eyes rudely shut the while.

"I shall do so" the young man promised. He glanced again all round the table, guessed accurately that they spent most of their infrequent sessions between snores and the crunch of colanuts and dismissed them from his mind. A hundred and one recommenda-tions on the future of the Chairman roved through his mind and gave him some solace. He turned to the Secretary:

"Send in the Co-ordinator."

The Secretary remained loyal, turned first to his Chairman. The worthy man's eyes were not as firmly closed as he would have the Trouble-shooter believe. Restraining his cheeks from showing his pleasure he nodded with gravity.

"Yes I think we are ready. Send in Mr. Ofeyi."

After which, the Trouble-shooter took charge.

Ofeyi entered the room as the Secretary held the door open for him. He paused to place an envelope in the hands of the man, caus-ing him to look back to his Chairman as if to enquire what this trifling diversion might mean. But the Chairman had resumed his pose, and this time his eyes were truly shut. He had seen far much more of Ofeyi than he wished for the rest of his life. The Secretary shut the door, glanced at the envelope to ensure that it was marked neither Official nor Urgent and returned to his place at the end of the table.

The Trouble-shooter beamed on the man he had come to try, pointed to the chair on the other side of the table. "Do be seated Mr. Ofeyi."

He waited for the chair to stop creaking. "You will not know me of course. I have been loaned to this case from the Head Office. I am here with the full knowledge and approval of the military government and will report back to the Cabinet office after my investigations are completed. The Commandant of the region is personally interested in this case. He considers it his duty to step in when a crisis threatens more than the immediate parties of that crisis. And, I regret to have to inform you, it does so in this case. The country's economic health is affected. Your activities Mr. Ofeyi, have begun to cause both the Corporation and the Government very great concern."

He now cut off the beaming welcome abruptly and selected a xeroxed graph, passed it on to Ofeyi.

Ofeyi examined the graph. He had begun to wonder if he had not made a mistake in changing his own plans of non-participation in the get-together. But the transformation of the Commandant's personal representative—Ofeyi had recognized him at once—into the Cartel's Trouble-shooter had intrigued him. After thrusting his letter of resignation into the hands of the Secretary he had succumbed to a curiosity about the real status of the Trouble-shooter. Now he wondered if he had not willingly walked into a trap. He fiddled with the graph and waited.

The Trouble-shooter continued. "The graph represents, you might say, one of the credit sheets in your balance book"—he grinned and looked around the table—"if I may borrow a metaphor with which everyone here would be very familiar. It shows the sharp decline in promotion expenditure since you took over the cocoa campaign for the Corporation. I understand that you cut down on many redundant posts and even undertook the writing of copy yourself, without extra remuneration. Naturally, what with throwing so many people out of the enjoyment of virtual sinecures, you were bound to make some enemies. Human nature, we all understand it. This is why we were disposed to discount for so long those sinister reports which began to come in on your activities. . . ."

Ofeyi broke his silence. "If I may make a suggestion, just to cut short the proceedings . . ."

"One moment Mr. Ofeyi. I am conducting this enquiry and I understand all about procedure and I can assure you also that I have no interest in prolonging the session one second longer than absolutely necessary."

Seated next to the speaker, the Chairman grudgingly admitted that this handling of Ofeyi, whom he regarded as the most devious employee he had ever encountered, was masterly. The Cartel-Cabinet representative continued:

"I have brought out these details merely to assure you that we do possess a full record of your campaign activities throughout the country, some of them very very dubious indeed. And I think it my duty to let you know why we have ignored most of these reports up till now. The results were positive and what we wanted was positive results. The country became cocoa-conscious, thanks to your drive. We no longer had to rely on foreign markets to dictate their own price to us. We have now built up a remarkable internal market for the first time in our cocoa-growing history." He paused, fished out a few more graphs and passed them to Ofeyi. "You may like to look at those also Mr. Ofeyi. In them you will find confirmation of everything I have just said."

Ofeyi waved them away, handed back the first graph also. "It's not necessary. We all know the entire history of Cocoa-bix and Cocoa-wix."

The Trouble-shooter shook his head. "I wonder Mr. Ofeyi whether you really do. I wonder whether you know the real extent of the multi-million industry which has developed from the hundred and one cocoa products in the country and the other hundred which are being developed even at this very moment."

"I do. I even know where all the profits go. What we don't know is where the workers disappear to, the so-called agitators."

An expletive, hastily swallowed and turned into a racking cough by the Chairman was followed by the long silence. The Trouble-shooter leant back in his chair and tapped the side of his nose with a pencil in a gesture which he had copied and developed for moments when he needed to rethink his tactics. In a quarter of a minute he had made up his mind and, smiling thinly demanded:

"Perhaps Mr. Ofeyi, this enquiry will prove even short enough to satisfy you. So let me ask you one question straightaway. Are you also—to use your own expression—an agitator?"

"No."

"No. Of course not. Nobody ever admits that they are trouble-makers. Let me put it another way then. Are you a communist? Or a Marxist? Or do you just call yourself a socialist?"

"I have read Marx . . ."

The Trouble-shooter snapped, "So have I Mr. Ofeyi so don't let us beat around the bush."

They stared at each other in silence for some moments. "If you must know, I disapprove of foisting cocoa-flavoured sawdust on the . . ."

The Chairman broke his self-imposed restraint, exploded; "What was that, young man? Who is foisting what sawdust on who?"

"Cocoa-wix and cocoa-bix. Not to mention cocoadine which

does not fulfil a single one of the hundred benefits it is supposed to confer on human health."

The Trouble-shooter turned down a corner of his lip in his best derisive manner. "I know that you are supposed to be a genius in promotion ideas Mr. Ofeyi. I've heard some of your songs myself, very catchy tunes indeed. I was not however aware that your talents extended to dietetics or pharmacy."

"No they don't" Ofeyi admitted. "But surely you must realize that I have taken the trouble to consult experts on the subject. They conducted the tests and their reports uniformly say . . ."

The Cartel spokesman banged his fist on the table. "And I must remind you that we also have our analysts, chosen and approved by the Government ministry. And we choose to accept their report rather than that of some disgruntled backroom chemist whose qualifications were probably obtained in Moscow!"

There was another pause, then Ofeyi commented, "You keep saying 'we' I notice. May I ask why? I thought this matter only involved a private concern—the Cocoa Corporation. Aren't you here simply as a government—er—moderator in an industrial dispute between employee and employer? Or are there other matters you wish to bring up?"

At the end of the longest silence yet, the Trouble-shooter began to replace his papers in the files. He did not look at Ofeyi again but turned to the Secretary at the end of the table.

"The enquiry is over. The Co-ordinator may leave now."

Ofeyi stood up, pointed in the direction of the Secretary's pile of papers and said, "The Secretary has my resignation." Then he turned to go, but not towards the door which the Secretary held open as wide as his mouth. He stared at Ofeyi who was headed in the opposite direction, waved his hand in protest but got no further than a prolonged stammer.

Suddenly the placidity of the room was broken as the Secretary rushed back to the table to fetch the letter while the Chairman sat up in his chair, spluttering with more astonishment than indignation at Ofeyi's retreating back. The Trouble-shooter misunderstood the cause of his distress and wondered why such a fuss should be made over a gesture that was predictable and typical of such stereotypes as Ofeyi. But the Director finally found his tongue.

"You can't go in there my friend. Use the main door over there."

Ofeyi already had his hand on the door leading into the boardroom. "If you have no objection I'll use this exit today."

"Stop!" The new order came from the Trouble-shooter. Ofeyi ignored this also and vanished.

And now it was the turn of the Cartel Inquisitor to betray signs of dementia. He leapt from his chair and dashed round the table, ran through the main door and out. They heard his studded boots clattering down the stairs, his voice, thundering across the empty hall below:

"Captain! Captain!"

The rest of the table, already moderately alert by the unusual shape of the meeting sprang up in alarm and demanded to know what was going on and was there going to be shooting?

An officer accompanied by a private with a submachine gun burst into the room and demanded, "Which of you is the Secretary?"

Eight pairs of hands pointed instantly to the cowering man. The soldier swung the gun round at him while the officer shouted, "Show me the back door!"

The Secretary rasped out a yessir and shot through the door which Ofeyi had used. They heard him repeating "yessir, yessir, yessir" all through the lengthy boardroom and out through the other door. Comprehending at last, the Chairman recovered his poise, reflected how thorough the Cartel continued to be and took consolation from the fact. The Trouble-shooter raced in, shot out again through the boardroom after the two soldiers. The Chairman assumed a new, contented pose, sighed:

"They'll get him yet."

A poster stared him in the face: WAKE UP WITH THE COCOA COMPLEXION. He felt sick at his handiwork. Worst of all was Iriyise's figure on it emerging three-quarter nude from the wraps of sleep. His fingers automatically searched in his pockets for those strips of paper which he had taken to carrying about for pasting over the last four words, leaving a truncated message for an interpretation of subversive suggestiveness. The voice of the Personnel Director mocked him from earlier confrontations:

"I knew we had chosen the right man for the job and you can ask anyone on this table and he will tell you the same. We wanted fine fine film in technicolor telling the people what a fine fine crop this cocoa is. Fine fine women dancing to fine fine music. Fine fine happy family round the table in every fine fine home. Already you have made cocoa the sine qua whatever you call it in every family. Even my wife wakes me up every morning nowadays with a steaming cup in her hand and she sings: Wake up with the Cocoa Complexion and go and make us some money ha ha. . . ."

Grumbling to Ahime over what he felt was a prostitution of his talents, he could only rouse the man to a shrug. "Food is sacred" he would say. "Cocoa is food."

"Is cocoa-wix food?" Ofeyi demanded in turn. "A craving is being created for this and other cocoa-flavoured sawdust. What the farmer earns the Cartel takes back in return for sawdust!"

Glancing back at the poster again he thought how Iriyise was like the food he ate and, in some measure, grown. The only brightness in a long progression of compromises. He headed for her apartment. Not that the Corporation spies would not think of looking there but Iriyise occupied a cell in a deep hive which had a practised history of the Early Warning System. The utmost exertion that he might be forced to make, if a persistent party did find its way there, would be a short walk through gloomy corridors and urine-drained courtyards to another comb until that danger was past. And Iriyise was Queen Bee of the hive. Within it he remained immune, protected by a maze of signals and burrows created by the worker ants.

A nauseating leer rose before him. It belonged again to the fat figure of the Personnel Director: "Ah yes we do know that you have been combining business with pleasure, but do we blame you for it Mr. Ofeyi? Do we accuse you of nepotism? No we don't. Because the result is what matters to hard-headed businessmen like us. Results Mr. Ofeyi, results! Who in his right mind would deny that in your whole country-wide search you could never have come up with a better choice of a Cocoa Princess? The public acknowledge it everywhere so who cares what private relations go on between you and the greatest asset of the Corporation. The point is, we don't then accuse you of nepotism do we? I mean to say Mr. Ofeyi, when I think of the things you have been accusing us of! Accusing fine fine people like the honourable members of the Board of Directors seated around this table . . . !"

Gaining the outer precincts of the hive within which Iriyise lived, his steps became a little jauntier. He began to hum one of the songs which even the ardent hounds of the Cartel had failed to sniff out in time and, afterwards, could not eliminate. It acquired instant conquest as much by its brisk, aggressive rhythm as by its memorable tune. He jigged across the gutter from side to side, trying to boost his apprehensive spirits by the cheerful melody. In his head Zaccheus and his Cocoa Beans orchestra roared into accompaniment.

Who's the friend of the cocoa farmer?
Insecticide!
What is the fate of parasites?
Fumigate!
Swollen shoot's like a swollen belly
Eats you dry and gives you hell-y
Fouls the earth and makes it smelly
Burn them out!

"Why swollen shoot Mr. Ofeyi? We eradicated the swollen shoot ages ago. There is no more swollen shoot on the entire west coast, none whatever. The World Health Organization itself declared this coast swollen shoot free, so why panic the poor farmer unnecessarily?"

A mere metaphor, Ofeyi reassured the Board. Swollen shoot is now common currency for any kind of parasite which plagues the farmer.

"Really Mr. Ofeyi?"

What's the might of the cocoa farmer?
Matchet and hoe!
What's the cure for weeds and nettles?
Uproot entire!
Root out the climbers and rotten creepers
They don't-sow-nothing but ardent reapers
Till harvest time they're heavy sleepers
Root them out!

"And this other verse Mr. Ofeyi? There are suggestions that . . ."

He came through a passage between two high fencing walls so narrow that an encounter with an oncomer could only be negoti-

ated sideways. The short passage opened into an exposed courtyard, the only area of potential danger in the hive. Ofeyi paused,
scanned the washing-line. The pair of brassieres that hung next
to a bamboo support was a familiar black-laced one. He counted
the clips that held it in place: three. Ofeyi stepped boldly into the
yard, whistling the same tune, loudly.

V

On *the* day, the Final Day of that public airing of flesh, recon-
ditioned wrinkles, artificial spots, deodorated pores, lightening
creams and obituary scalps—thus Zaccheus christened wigs—on
that day of breastful optimism, the favourite was missing. No
ordinary favourite but, the only justification—so wrote Spyhole—
the first and only justification he had ever accepted for the most
degrading exhibition on earth. Yet even Spyhole, after years of
lacerating contempt poured from his yellow columns on such
"travesties of black womanhood," even Spyhole had caught the
fever. And this began from the early eliminations, and into the
semi-finals.

"I still insist" he shrieked, "why must we ape this white charade!" But his voice was thinner than usual. Now it grew shrill
with a genuine alarm that came from knowledge of the seamy
world which it was his vocation to burrow through, to feast with

the maggots and acquire a carapace as the dung beetle, demanding, "Where is Celestial?"

No warning. No reason. The "Celestial Certainty" had vanished. A show for which he had, deeply, nothing but contempt had turned foul and sinister.

He mourned her in his columns, bordered his page in thin black lines and pronounced the beauty contest dead. He rose to heights of his lyric journalese wailing, Where is that Iridescent face that lit us through the abyss of universal ugliness? Beneath the sweet-sad face of the missing queen he placed the caption—A Celestial Certainty!

Garage touts, tycoons, secretive civil servants, diplomats and shopkeepers mouthed the single question—Where is Iridescent? Doormen, newsvendors, thugs, market women, street pedlars, colonels, smugglers, catechists, highway robbers and students shook their heads and said there was dirty business about. They all turned to Spyhole. He had created her so to speak because he had first drawn attention to her and he was the avowed misogynist. His columns, witty and sensational, banal but sensational, predictable but sensational first and last wrote the sentences that founded the myth. I despise women, he wrote, it is my duty to despise women for what they are, but I finally met a woman that wasn't a woman. When she vanished he swore to his readers that he would get to the bottom of her mystery though he had failed to get to her fascinating bottom. At the next bar which he entered to slake his journalistic thirst he was set upon and roughed up by three students. Celestial was not a subject for lewd cracks.

And then, just as suddenly, Iriyise reappeared. No explanation offered, no betrayal of knowledge of any fuss that surrounded her disappearence. Where were you Iriyise, but she would only reply, I'm back. She accepted her habitual homage, continued to hush hotel foyers with her appearance and drove diplomats to indiscretions.

"But where *were* you Iriyise?"

Once in a while she unleashed the caged tigress in her at some trivial or imagined provocation, engaging the riot squad and fire brigade in a night-long siege which ended only when, on the stairway or on the lavatory bowl or even in bed she fell suddenly, immortally asleep. It was the Brigade who named her Firebrand. And the name was taken up and absorbed into the lyric repertoire of her legend.

"Where *were* you?"

She raised herself on an elbow and looked down on Ofeyi. She had not expected his insistence. "You are a funny one. All you men . . . ! After all this time . . ."

"Where *were* you? And I am not men."

"But you want to know don't you? You all do."

"Tell me where you were."

"The sun came up and I vanished like the dew."

"I acknowledge that you are a good pupil, but answer my question."

"I was living up to my name."

"Forget the dew on the feet, answer my question!"

"And dew turning back, fading away . . ."

Ofeyi sighed. "I confess I have sometimes allowed myself to get carried away by your exceedingly euphonious name but . . ."

She shook her head suddenly in his face and he felt warm drops of moisture. "And that is a few dewdrops of malaria to keep you quiet." The effort exhausted her and she sank back again.

"You are wet all over. Is this the same Firebrand from which flying sparks ignite dead flesh?"

"I think I am ill" she conceded.

Ofeyi nested her head in his armpit and coiled her sweat-lathered body into his, her knees tucked into his groin. Something made her shiver and Ofeyi sensed it was beyond her malaria chill. Even so it took some moments for him to make sense of her next words:

"They wanted to kill me Ofe."

When it finally sank in he asked: "Who wanted to kill you?"

"Chief Biga."

"That gambler? He's the hatchet-man of the Cartel. What did you have to do with him?"

"Nothing. He threatened to burn my face with acid. I told him I preferred to be killed."

"But why? Stop talking in bits and pieces. What had he to do with . . . ?" He struck himself on the forehead. "Of course. Betting!"

He wrapped his arms round her and encased her completely. He felt the shiver die down and her body relax. "What happened exactly?"

"I found out later it was because he had lost thousands at the Casino. The finals of the Beauty contest were on just then and everyone seemed to think I was certain to win it. I suppose that was how the idea came into his head. I was in the hotel and some-one came and called me. Some Big Shot wanted to see me he said. So I went. There was Chief Biga in this posh suite surrounded by four or five of his thugs. You know what he said?"

"Go on."

"He held out one hand and said, 'Here it is. Two hundred cash.' Then he opened the other hand and said, 'Here it is, scarred face for life.' There was a tiny bottle in that hand. He smiled that fat smile of his and said, 'I want you to disappear for a while Celestial. My Pontiac is outside to take you to a private motel I own in Cross-river. On the house,' he said, 'everything was paid for a month. Drinks and food.' Of course I knew what it was all about, I had only to remember what a reckless gambler he was."

"Why are you trembling? It's all over."

"I'm afraid Ofeyi. Tell me not to go on this trip."

"Iriyise . . . !"

"Tell me not to go. I don't want to disappear ever again."

"Then DON'T GO!"

"I had never been so alone. They kept guards at my door day and night. There must have been millions at stake. I never went out. Saw nobody. And I had only just met you. It felt like dying."

"All right. When the band arrives I'll let them come in and see you. With this temperature no one in his right senses would expect you to leave your bed. Any layman can see you've got pneumonia and pleurisy and I don't know what else."

"What is pleurisy?"

"Who cares? All I know is that you are too ill to travel."

He barely caught her whisper. "No, just too frightened." But he felt her shiver again and could not mistake a fear which lay deeper than past recollections. He was helpless before it. Beyond a desperate longing, which seized him suddenly, to rock and croon to her like an infant he had no knowledge how he could combat the darkness that her fears had conjured up. It lay between them, murky and threatening. Reassurances choked in his throat, a protective love proved futile and reduced him to a fellow-sufferer. This fear, now so tangible that he could touch it all around him was made even more persuasive because Iriyise was not given to such forebodings, capricious though her other moods might be. Her eyes, larger and luminous from the effects of the fever stared straight, it seemed to him, into the heart of an event whose definition however eluded her. Ofeyi now felt her fingers bite into his arm though her voice had turned drowsy:

"Don't go to sleep Ofe."

"I won't," he promised.

Where their skins touched he felt a soapy lather of sweat. She grew smaller, curling herself tightly into his body. He felt she would sleep now, her fears would pass and she would return to her elusive, unpredictable self.

The room, down in a kind of semi-basement on a level lower than the distant street, was insulated from the traffic roar. The street itself was several houses and a junkyard away. Iriyise's cell was buried deep in the vast honeycomb creating in its muffled recesses the morning hour which Ofeyi called the White-Collar Silence. It began just after the workers had departed for office and the housewives had not begun to stir themselves for the shopping spree, the hair-dresser rounds and the jewellery hunts. An earlier silence, one he loved even more was the Petty-Traders' Pause. First came furtive noises, the rustle of baskets and wares gathered and sorted. A little change went into tins, a kettle simmered, some pap bubbled on the hearth, a breakfast was eaten in silence. Drugged motions, even in the eating of breakfast. The splash of water at the morning wash was muted. All sounds sifted through as though in awareness of the larger army of sleepers in household or large compound who needed and deserved their extra hour of oblivion. The quiet opening and closing of doors. Shadows stealing forth with scrolls of mats, trestle shapes on which they would sit by their stalls. In the streets terraced pyramids made from packing cases were unveiled where they had stood all night and all year; from their impossibly vast recesses the wares emerged for display on the wooden terraces of the stands.

Those roadside queens of the petty trade, ethereal in the morning light before the earthy transformation for their confrontation with bargaining humanity! They move like wraiths through alleyways. Even burdened with the day's merchandise they are creatures of another world, their plump forms made even more shapeless by wads of wrappers and a money-belt securely round the waist. They leave the home with a softness extracted even from the key turning in the lock, from the two halves of a window married into place with a sleight of hand, a mere shush in the growing twilight; a final tug at the multitudinous folds and sash then footsteps fading into distance to minister to the needs of strangers . . . and a live, palpitating silence that follows their departure, a hive falling back into a last recoil before it joins the common frenzy in glare of daylight.

Morning after morning Ofeyi savoured it all, wondering which of these phases of morning had formulated Iriyise's childhood. He tried to picture her in a context of sounds that would accompany the resuscitation of a white collar executive household. A chorus of Smith's alarms, zee-ee-eths of curtain rods, the rusty creak of levers on glass louvres, running bathwater, electric buzz of razors, Madame's high-pitched querulous morning voice and the clink of silver on china? And the garage, then the car doors opening and slamming perhaps? It did not seem to matter. Iriyise could be raised in a foundling home and there would only be differences of detail in her, not of essential nature.

With the tinny coda of a bicycle bell the White Collar Silence finally descended on the morning, a deep contented sigh, a winnowing of synthetic impurities. Brief though it would be it was a period of exorcism. Sounds reached him only through walls and distance, through the dens of iniquitous ecstasy in which Iriyise's neighbourhood was honeycombed, sifted through her black glossy mop of hair and gentle breathing which told him that Iriyise had finally fallen asleep. If she could have another hour of such peaceful sleep before they arrived or he could stop them before they broke into the house . . . but there wasn't much chance of that. Alone of all the cars that came into that area only the long American amphibian risked its fenders and paint on the ninety-degree turn through narrow wall corners into the courtyard. The driver would bring it right up to the window and toot his damned horn. Two notes, A Natural and B Sharp, swore Zaccheus.

If the notes sounded flat he judged that the battery was running down.

Ofeyi decided to slip out from under her and prepare to dash for the courtyard at the sound of the amphibian.

She stirred, called his name. He lay still, hoping she was only half-awake. She was, but then her arm moved from its angled rest on his chest upwards, her hand dug in between his neck and the pillow, imprisoning it more securely. She began to breathe in the even pace of a deeper sleep and he woke an hour later to see her face above his, propped on an elbow.

"You fell asleep."

"The spirit was willing but the silence was deep."

"What got into you suddenly? Why ask me that question after all this time?"

He shrugged. "I don't know. Oh yes I do. A song came into my head." He hummed a brief tune. "Oh where were you Iri-yi-se . . . where-o-where-o were you? Yes, I think I'll ask Zaccheus to work some more on it."

"Is that all of it? Sounds rather lean to me."

"Don't try to be clever. When it's completed you'll hear it. Not a moment before."

She prodded him in the chest again and again. "You are the one trying to be clever. I know why your mind went back. I am going on this tour, you are not coming and you are afraid I'll end up with a big businessman up there."

"They don't like argumentative women up there."

"We'll see. Now tell me who you have arranged to bed down with the moment my back is turned."

"Your very best friends, naturally."

"Don't joke about it. Who have you got in mind and don't think I don't know."

He shrugged, composed himself and waited to hear the latest

divisive effort of her so-called friends. When it came it was bull's-
eye and he winced. "You think I haven't heard of Miss Career
Diplomat?" She cut short his protests. "I suppose she understands
you better than I can. Is it true she has a degree in something
administration?"

Marvelling at the detached curiosity of her tone, he nodded yes
before he could stop himself. She leapt on him then in fury, a fist-
ful of his hair in either hand and Ofeyi felt his scalp about to be
lifted clean off. "So there is someone! You knew who I meant right
away!" He seized her wrists and tried to calm her down. "Your
fever Iri, stop it!"

"You are going to her. You would even bring her here, I know
you."

"Use your brain now. I can't come with you because I've
resigned. I am no longer on the campaign staff! But I must first
take a warning to the old man in Aiyéró. He must get the word
round to our people."

"It's a lie, I know you. You cooked it up."

"For the hundredth time—I must dash to Aiyéró!"

He pressed her backwards onto the bed by the wrists and
pressed her down with his weight. Even as his body touched her
he felt her vibrant skin, expectant.

"Look at your skin Iri, you are burning."

"It doesn't matter."

Malaria, fever and sweat he took her. Their mingled sweat
soaked the sheets and she clawed as he sank into her. Then she lay
quiet. Her mood continued strange. He had expected she would
say: "that should keep you till I get back but of course you are just
a woman wrapper." Or boast that her smell on him would kill off
any woman who touched him in her absence. She did not even
make him declare that no woman "of your sort" ever filled him so
completely. Instead she pushed him off, then half-lay on him. Her

hair strayed and tickled his nostrils. When she spoke it was with a calm, distant consciousness of what she actually uttered.

"I don't want to die yet."

Startled, he could only gape and try, futilely again, to traverse the distances in her wake.

"I don't want to die yet." And then she appeared to come back to him, teasing but earnest. "Even though you've ruined me. I've never leant on a man the way I lean on you. No one." There was a moment's silence, then she turned at a sound outside. "I think they are here."

The huge ship slurched round the sharp corners of the building, taking off its customary grains of cement and losing in turn a square inch or two of its own paint. A lush note rent the early morning silence on the paved courtyard. Before the car came to a complete stop a waddly figure stepped out in unbuttoned jacket and staggered slightly. The car braked prematurely and Zaccheus was half knocked against the door. He looked reproachfully at the driver who merely shrugged and said,

"Boss, you'll kill yourself one of these days."

"Blame the car then. It feels the same moving as standing still." He was already yards away, excitement over his cherubic face.

Iriyise let down a corner of the curtain, then pulled it up sharply. Another figure, a lean brief-case of a man with a satanic beard had also stepped out of the car. He wore a Tyrolean hat with a pink feather. Iri had rolled off at the sound of the outer door opening and pulled a sheet over them. Ofe glanced at the door.

"Did we lock it?"

Zaccheus burst into the room and Iriyise shouted at him, "Lock the door after you."

"What's the matter?"

"Lock it—quick!" To Ofeyi she said, "The fool's brought Aristo."

But the salesman already stood in the doorway, grinning benignly into the room, his arms outspread to accept the tribute of welcome. "Iridescent, where is she?"

Iriyise reached an arm behind the bed and her fingers closed on a shoe. Zaccheus gestured helplessly. "I thought the man was waiting in the car. Look, Aristo . . ."

A mauve shoe flew through the air, barely missing the Tyrolean hat. Aristo ducked out of sight and Zaccheus slammed the door. A tornado now erupted from the bed, fought its way into a dressing-gown snapping at Zaccheus, I'll have it out with you later, ignored his protests and flung objects around until she found a weapon. Ofeyi calmly wound the discarded sheet around himself. Before Iriyise quite left the room they heard Aristo's voice outside the door protesting, "But why throw shoes at me Celestial?" Zaccheus clutched his head and shouted, "You bloody fool, you mean you are still waiting?"

Then the door flew open and the first blow of the heavy coat-hanger took the surprised Aristo flush in the mouth. "You think you can burst into my bedroom uninvited?"

"Lady . . ."

And then, suddenly wiser he turned and fled down the passage, Iriyise in pursuit.

Ofeyi shook his head. "That girl is going to collapse on you on this tour."

Zaccheus had opened his instrument case and begun to piece his saxophone together. "Who? Firebrand?"

"She's ill."

"She's tough."

A loud plea from the hunted man outside made them look out the window. Iriyise had him trapped between the car and the wall but could not reach him with the hanger.

"That chick ill? Aristo doesn't think so."

"What is he doing here? Are you taking him on tour with you?"

"We ain't taking him nowhere. But he's coming. He's got his limoswim parked by. How come he can get hold of a Corporation plush anytime he likes, that's what gets me. Why all the perks and quits?" He exclaimed suddenly, "Hey, Firebrand ain't horsing you know. If that stone had got him . . ."

"He asked for it."

"Christ! We nearly lost the Prince of Sales just then. He had better just get out of it."

"Iri doesn't like men who carry tales. She doesn't mind it from women so much."

"What tale has he been carrying?"

"About me. Nothing serious, just mischief."

"Not to the Corpse was it?"

"Yep. He's just a fool."

"He is dirt!" Zaccheus exploded. "Haven't we got enough trouble with those Corporation fatsies without he stirring up more crap. He's Dirt!"

"He's just a fool. He thinks if I get the sack he'll get a chance to sell her to his big friends. That's how his mind works. He's just a silly man."

"Yeah? Your funeral man. Got any cocoaine?"

"In the cupboard. Pour me one too."

Clicking his mouth in rhythm Zaccheus reached up in the wardrobe. "Pour me one-two, one-two, one-two; pour me one-a-two . . ." He took out the bottle and fished out two glasses from the junk on Iriyise's dressing-table. Voices drifted in from the courtyard where the rest of the band had poured out of the car to plead for Aristo's life. Zaccheus flung open the curtain and told them to "leave the lady be. Maybe she's got good reason for what she's doing." Turning back into the room Zaccheus pulled out the cork and took a long sniff. "Man, it's ripe."

"Straight from the source."

They clinked glasses and drank. Suddenly Zaccheus swore. "It was him wasn't it? Before he knew what cocoaine actually was, went and told the fatsies we were sniffing dope. Man, I would have drowned his head in a butt of the stuff if the lads had let me."

Ofeyi smiled at that. The thought of mild Zaccheus holding a man's head down in a butt of cocoa wine . . .

"Ho, you don't believe me eh? Ask the boys. I was that good and mad I could homicide the bastard." He suddenly examined the bottle closely. "Hey, you and Celestial are slow. But I suppose you have riper things to do with your time."

"What's that supposed to mean?"

"Isn't this the same bottle we brought back from Aiyéró?"

"Same one."

"You've hardly touched it. Man, I'll never forget that party. That was some education. If anyone had told me all that condensed milk in the cocoa-pod could throw such humane-killer punch. . . . Say, how's it coming on? Government going to legitimize the stuff?"

"Not a chance."

"Not even with all the songs of praise the chemist boys are singing on the stuff?"

"Zack, you forget who owns the shares in all those foreign sounding distilleries. Not to talk of the imported foreign liquor trade."

"Yeah. That's a mess. But what the hell, it makes the stuff more exclusive to the congosentries . . . hey? What you laughing at?"

"Where did you pick up that word?"

"In the report. It said, the congosentries can distinguish between the cocoa wine from one kind of soil and from another."

"Cognoscenti."

"Oh. And what's that?"

"Them that knows."

"What? Oh. Fancy me thinking it was some forest guards in the Congo or some such stuff. How come they make up words like that. Trying to frighten the poor farmer who's going to read it that's why."

"Pour me one more."

"Sure. Pour me one-more, one-more, one-more." He flipped the curtain aside. "Yeah baby. Kill the damned runt."

Aristo made a desperate gamble, flung open a rear door and plunged through the interior of the chariot, cracking his shins on the scattered instruments. He snatched open the door on the other side, tumbled almost at the feet of Iriyise who was too surprised to stamp on him more than once before he gathered himself and lunged for the sole exit out of the courtyard. A rain of missiles and curses pursued him.

Zaccheus wiped his mouth, and ran the scales up and down his saxophone. "I'll just blow that last song for you so you'll have an idea how it's grown."

Before he could complete the first bar Iriyise flung the door open. "The rat got away. And you Zaccheus, why did you bring it here? Bursting into my room like he's the landlord or something."

"Baby, blame me. But we're late baby. When is your bath?"

"What about the rest of the boys. I only saw three in the car."

"Getting breakfast. We'll pick them up on the roadside."

"Oh-oh, so now you want me to come along and play *Bolekaja*, picking up your early morning drunkards along the road. . . ."

"Baby baby baby . . ."

"I am not your baby. Go and pick them up and come back for me."

"Baby they know you. They know if they get here at noon you will still be in bed. So they insisted I drop them round the corner where they can booze until you choose to get ready. Nothing will shift them until they see you. Baby, it's like it isn't quite dawn for them. They don't believe the sun is out until they see Celestial . . ."

"Don't sweet-talk me. . . ."

"Why not baby. You know it's Aristo that's got you so damned awkward. Why shouldn't I sweet-talk you out of it. What's Zacky running the damned bunch of genius for if . . . hey, and that's something else. Dig this . . ." He blew a rapid phrase on the saxophone. "You know what that is?"

Her curiosity was aroused. "I haven't heard that one."

"Course you haven't. Listen to some more. And you ain't heard the words even so you don't know nothing yet."

"Who wrote it?"

"I ain't telling. Seems to be about somebody's mother. He's flying man, flying. Handed me the song yesterday and I've been trying out a few arrangements. Maybe the band will let you hear it tonight maybe not."

"Why should I care?" Flinging herself back on the bed.

"You would if you knew who wrote it." Hardly stopping he began to intone,

> *Never again Mother-of-Dawn*
> *Never o never again*
> *Don't ever leave the light again*
> *The dwarfs are spitting on the sun . . .*

"Yeah Ofeyi, that's the line I want to tell you about. There's trouble with that. You'll have to give us different words or . . ."

"So it's him."

Zaccheus hit himself on the mouth and moaned, "Oh Papa Zacky!"

Iriyise turned idly on her side. "It's a change anyway, judging from that little bit. Though one can never guess what he's hidden inside it until they come for him."

"Hey, you don't think . . ." Zaccheus stopped dead, turned reproachful eyes on Ofeyi.

"Don't you know him yet?" Iriyise threw at him, irritated.

Zaccheus shook his head. "No, it's straightforward. You're getting jittery Firebrand. I've read all the lines, you don't get lyrics more straightforward than that."

"You are simple. Ever known a straightforward number from him?"

"Ofeyi . . ."

"Oh shut up the pair of you. And you, get out and take that shower."

"I'm dead."

"I'll count up to three. One . . . Two . . ."

"Oh damn you—*man!*"

She gathered her towel and sponge and flung out of the room. Opened the door and thrust her face at him. "They'll get you yet, and don't say I didn't warn you."

Zaccheus poured another drink of cocoaine and gulped it. "Hey man, friend, comrade . . ."

"Shut up Zacchy. There is nothing wrong with the song."

"If you are sure . . ."

"I said it's straight. Now let's hear the whole thing."

Zaccheus looked relieved and abashed, began to adjust his mouthpiece. "It isn't that we wouldn't have done it anyway. But not up yonder, no siree, not up yonder. Man, they are not nice people those Cross-river Fatsies, they are not nice people at all. Here at least your friends will know what happened to you before things go too far."

"Are you going to play the damned thing?"

"Coming boss coming. Man, you and Celestial are real touchy this morning."

He blew softly, lingering over each phrase and caressing the notes. At the end he took the instrument slowly from his mouth, let it hang from his neck and rocked his head from side to side.

"I don't know why I let Celestial give me that scare. There is no thorn in it man, not with a melody like that. Just ambrosia man, nectar and ambrosia like you name it in that other number."

Ofeyi laughed. "You want me to change the words round."

"What? Oh no. That's mere words and spikes—not that the tune isn't sweet and seductive and all that. But this . . . ! Hey man, why don't you just stay with us. I mean instead of being also *against* them, just be with us. Leave them alone to go to hell where they're heading anyway."

Shaking his head regretfully Ofeyi told him, "It is not that simple Zack. There is no such easy division."

"You can keep it simple if you want to. B Sharp is B Sharp. Call it C if you like but when Zack says B Sharp that's what it is. And if you want you can keep things clear and simple like I do. Man, you're just too fond of sniping. You and Spyhole, you're twin brothers. Snipers. You got telescoping lenses stuck in your eyes all day long."

"We all share the same air Zaccheus. When they breathe in it, they foul it no matter the distance."

"To hell with you man. Let's get down to business." He broke off suddenly and dashed outside, returned a moment later with Iriyise in tow. "I want you to hear this right. Celestial, you sing it best as you can."

"What about my bath?"

"Later baby, later. Right now we've got a problem."

"What other problem now?"

"No, wait till you hear it." He fussed around the sheets and came up with a page. "Line's gone, can't find it. Aha, got him. I'll blow you the line and you sing to it—Never in the fettered dark. Got it? Never in the fettered dark." She repeated the words. "Good, here goes."

She sang the words, he playing along with her.

"Once more Celestial, just one more time."

When they had finished he folded his hands and looked at Ofeyi.

Ofeyi stared back, then gave an idiot grin. "Don't get it maestro."

"What do you mean, don't get it? I'm asking you what it sounded like. How did the words hit you?"

"Look man, say what you've got against it?"

"Got against it? Who said I've got anything against it? Did I say I got anything against it. Celestial . . ."

"All right" Ofeyi sighed. "Why do you like to beat around the bush? Too literary?"

"No no, who said it was too literary. I don't say anything about that. But who is going to sing it? Fettered dark! Man, that mouth ain't built yet that can sing that and make me believe it. I mean man, is it opera . . . ?"

Ofeyi leant over and took the bottle, poured him a drink. "Zack, I'll change it. I'll think of something else."

"Before we leave? I want to launch it on this tour. Man, it will knock them."

"This very minute. If you can manage to shut up."

"It's a deal."

"Whew! If you'd only stop beating around the bush. You and your elephantine notions of tact."

"Who is talking now?" Zaccheus protested to the world in general.

"You men want breakfast?" Iriyise asked. "Because I'm taking that bath right now and I won't go in the kitchen afterwards."

"Who wants breakfast? Me, I've been up since I left the club, teasing out that damned tune and the words. Why not? I don't mind. I know a work of love when I hear one and if music be the food of love, I've breakfasted."

"Two eggs or three? Or shall I send the driver for some *akara* from the next street?"

"Coffee dear lady, just coffee to go with some ninepence *akara*. If you happen to be frying eggs for yourself I'll keep you company to the tune of two. Otherwise no breakfast ma'am." He helped her into her slippers and opened the door for her. "Baby, until you said it I just didn't know how hungry I was." He shut the door when she had left and rested against it, wiping imaginary sweat off his brow.

"Man, you never knows whether that lady is on your side or not. Did you hear her? She offered to make breakfast."

"But she always makes breakfast."

"Yeah, sure, sure enough. But not after a scene like that. Not after a blowup with a rat like Aristo. She's changed I tell you man. Changed. Ask around if you don't believe me. Until you packed her off into the bathroom I didn't dare believe we'd set off before tomorrow. You're modest man, you're real humble if you think that was nothing."

"Do you want this verse changed or don't you?"

Zaccheus tiptoed to a chair, pressing both lips together with his fingers. He poured out the last drops of the wine and sank into a corner, hoisting his short plump legs onto the leather pouff. Raising the glass against the light from the window he began to hum:

> *Hail, Golden mammary*
> *Healer of memory*
> *Make me a child again*
> *Suckled on sweet cocoaine*

He went into a delighted chuckle, "I don't care what they say man. You have the genius. I say—did those Gboròlu cats deliver the goods?"

"It's under the bed. I'm taking some with me to Aiyéró."

Zaccheus sat up sharply. "What!"

"Shut up and sit down. I have bad news for them so I must sweeten it with something."

Zaccheus moaned. "Oh God, oh God. Ofe, promise me there'll be something left when we get over there. Promise you won't let those savage adopted ancestors of yours get the damned lot down their throats."

"There'll be something left."

"One look Ofe. Just one peep."

Ofeyi shrugged. "But if you let it out it's here before you leave town you know what will happen."

"Don't I know it" and he whipped up the bedspread. "Oh God Ofe, oh God oh God oh God. I can't think all these demijohns are loaded with the stuff."

"Smell it if you don't believe it."

"Ofe man, this will really turn a corpse over. Not even the schnapps-weaned ancients down that village can demolish all of it in one week. We could call there on our way back and give a show."

"That's what I keep telling you. Now shut up or you'll leave one verse short."

"Sorry sorry I forgot. You can't blame me for getting carried away." He shot back into his seat and did not move again until Ofeyi threw a scrap of paper at him.

"Man that's quick . . . hey, do you see what I see?"

The window was sill-level with the floor of the courtyard. Aristo's face showed suddenly, crouch-form through a gap in the curtains, arms free swinging, orang-utan. He scratched softly on the bars. Zaccheus shook his head in disbelief. "Do you see him? Hey what's the matter with you Aristo? Can't you use the door instead of playing monkey at the window?"

"She's locked the door."

"So?"

"Let me talk to Ofeyi maybe he can simmer her down. I have to come with you on the trip so I've got to straighten myself out with her can't you see?"

"Who says?"

"Let me talk to Ofeyi."

"Get lost Aristo." He pulled the curtains shut and picked up his saxophone. "Read the new version when I get to the spot man." Aristo rapped on the bars again and Zaccheus pulled back the curtain. "Look man, you've got business with Iriyise, so you come in and you settle your business with her. Don't interrupt this conference once more or I'll shove this tube down your throat."

"Will you open the door for me?"

"Goddamn you man aren't you the one who boasts how tough you are? I thought you liked irate lovers for breakfast."

"Woman is different. I don't backchat an angry dame. Not if she is called Iriyise."

"Look Mr. Loose-mouth, I got business. Either you shut your big mouth now or you point your yellow feather backwards and beat Jesse Owens. Or knock on the door and try your sales talk with her. You're the big sales shot aren't you? We'll see how you get on with the one person who can muck up your record on this trip."

Ofeyi laughed. "Now you've got him really worried."

"Hell has no fury says the Good Book. Celestial will snarl all his lines on this tour I know that. He's going to come back with a blank order book. Eleven of us cramped in that beat-down Chevrolet, the damned Corporation wouldn't even lend us a van though we promised we'd foot petrol and repairs. But he gets a damned big Mercedes all to his little self. You know Ofe, I ask the runt if he could give a lift to a couple of the boys, just to ease us out you know. You know what he tells me?" He switched to a ludicrous falsetto. "We-ell, it's this way Zack, say it happens I get to pick up a chick on the way. An extra body in the car would cramp my style see? Two is company, three is a crowd eh? Yah, that's what he tells me."

"Forget it. Want to try out that line?"

"Sure sure, don't know why I let myself get het up about a punk like him."

The door opened to the sound of sizzling and Iriyise entered with a loaded pan in one hand and a tray in the other. Zaccheus rushed to her aid, made space on the table by knocking his instrument case to the floor and cursing the emptied bottle.

"Try not to spill the coffee" Iriyise warned.

Ofeyi glanced up at her and marvelled again at her changes of mood. She caught his eyes, smiled and went out to the bathroom. Gone, wiped out in entirety were all traces of the morning's apprehensions, the clairvoyant intensity that went into her fevered utterances. As for the hatred in her eyes when she chased Aristo out of the house—and he knew that in those moments it was real; threats to Ofeyi she felt as menaces to her own life—even that hate was gone. Aristo could walk into the house now and would be met by a cold contempt—that of course she would retain. She would not once open her mouth to him on the trip or acknowledge his existence. And she did possess this gift, she could speak through the most strident, most assertive being without efforts or seeming contrivance. He smiled inside of him, plunged into the eggs.

Breakfast was long finished, Zaccheus was purring satisfaction through his saxophone when the door opened, noiselessly. Iriyise passed through the music and ordered him to turn around while she changed. Zaccheus without a break in the notes chuckled and changed his position, Ofeyi folded his hands behind his head, marvelling at the apparition of a goddess bathed in a purple curtain-filtered light. It seemed to him that the room was mysteriously still, that the moment was frozen and replete. On Iriyise's head the shower protection, white crimped rubber became a bowl of husked milky grains, a tumulus of icing. Her eyes no longer acknowledged their presence, they had turned inwards, into her rites of transformation. She slipped a bronzed limb behind a mahogany-and-glass panel of the wardrobe, there were quiet, supple movements as she selected robes and jewels, then her face emerged to test the choice against her skin, expressionless. She moved behind a folding screen but her presence still filled the room and held it tranquil. The mound of grain floated briefly in air, was replaced by a sheen of hair, black silken corn tassels through which she ran her ivory comb. She teased the fringes, pressed them into place and shook them out again. Emerging at last, sheathed in a spadix mould of home weave, she stood between the mirrors of the wardrobe doors and receded into infinity with myriad duplications.

"Well?" She had turned to the two men, her arms hanging down and the palms turned outwards to them, joining them in a casual intimacy.

Conjurer, incantatory words floated through Ofeyi's lips. He got up from the bed at last, wrapping the bedsheet around him and walked towards her. Zaccheus, the mouthpiece merely wetted by his lips fought for definition of the sight that now confronted him: Iriyise, still, except for her eyes which followed Ofeyi's motions, and Ofeyi in the loose white wrap, sanctified by love-stains, prowling her on cat's feet, priest and vestal in mutual adoration. And why not, thought Ofeyi? Vision is eternally of man's own creating. The woman's acceptance, her collaboration in man's vision of life results time and time again in just such periodic embodiments of earth and ideal. It was not a question of beauty, or of perfection. It was simply that however briefly, with that transience that was a seal of truth on its own nature, Iriyise would reveal within her person a harrowing vision of the unattainable.

Zaccheus wetted his lips, conceding to the general air his ultimate accolade, "Madammadonna . . . madammadonna . . ."

"He's right" Ofeyi said, his eyes unwavering from the presence.

3

TENTACLES

VI

"The child who swears his mother will not sleep, he must also pass a sleepless night." Thus Batoki, tunesmith of proverbs. He summed up the resolution of the Cartel and turned over to sleep. Stung, crazed by months of insomnia, the Cartel had at last identified its tormentors and organized a return harassment.

The move was anticipated, the counter-measures had been worked out in advance. Ahime waited only for such a warning to send couriers off to the new outposts of Aiyéró. The men would expect evictions from their homes, punitive taxations, loss of jobs, even arbitrary detentions and trumped-up charges. The strategy was simple. The men would leave areas which had become too hot for further functioning, change places with others. The Aiyéró presence would be maintained. Ofeyi tied up his boat and climbed inland.

Inwardly he took pleasure from the knowledge that Aiyéró,

once the comic Utopia, had become a moral thorn in the complacent skin of the national body. While it remained quietly in the
backwaters, a quaint tourist diversion, nothing ruffled the composure of the Cartel or their allies in the successive power shifts.
That aspect was perhaps unfortunate, that the movement had been
traced directly to Aiyéró, to any particular region of the country.
Anonymity would have served more effectively. Still, they could
not hope to keep the identity of the cadres secret forever, in fact it
was a marvel that the genesis of the movement remained hidden
for so long. The Cartel had long tentacles to begin with and, now
that it had identified itself with the new power from the barrel its
Intelligence had become redoubled. The new alliance had been
made manifest. There was the unmistakable boldness in the air.

He had come as far as the pen of the sacrificial bulls when he
saw the figure of Ahime approaching him, the old man's eyes fastened on his and strained with anxiety.

"What's the matter? Have you heard?"

The old man nodded.

"Well, it's happened much later than we expected."

The old man scanned his face. "I don't think you know."

His voice was slow. His tone raised the scale of reverses far
higher than Ofeyi had any cause to expect. Apprehensive now he
asked, "What is it I do not know?"

"You haven't heard the radio?"

Ofeyi shook his head. "I've been on the lagoon all day."

"Come with me."

In the meeting-house the old man stopped and made Ofeyi sit
down. Then he broke the news of the magnitude of the disaster.
Ofeyi's face froze slowly, stunned.

"There is one glimmer of light" the old man consoled him.
"Yesterday, even before any news came from the radio, a man came
from Shage. They had received warning from their co-workers

at the dam, from the Cross-river people themselves. They held a meeting, all of them, and decided to stop work until the troubles subsided. That was the advice given to them by the native Cross-river workers. There at least we did not fail."

"It seems a pitiable fraction" Ofeyi muttered, "if that is all."

"It may not be" Ahime said. "But even if it is, the community at Shage was the most important. Or don't you believe your own words any more?"

Ofeyi tried to rouse himself, conceding that Shage was central to the less obvious penetration of Aiyéró through the land. Old villages had been uprooted, inundated and replanted making the concrete achievement visible, the marriage of the physical and the ideal. Even as the dam grew and the hydroelectric promise moved towards fulfilment, the men of Aiyéró sowed their seeds in the soil of the new communal entity. Shage was even placed strategically, an almost symbolic settlement on the Cross-river border itself. If the bond had been strong enough there at least, to make the Cross-river workers save the aliens in their midst. . . .

"I would like to talk to the man."

"He is waiting in my house."

Then he burst out with the other fear that had tugged at him since Ahime revealed the ruthless, indiscriminate sweep of the Cartel's campaign of re-assertion: Iriyise who had just left for Cross-river, and Zaccheus with his band . . .

It seemed an endless dusk before Ahime led him into the court-yard of the meeting-house and through a cluttered grove. The caryatid ringed grove was a surprise to him. The path at the end of it sheered off abruptly, a cluster of deciduous creepers parted to reveal a break in the walls. A quick warning from the old man saved Ofeyi from slithering down the sudden moss-covered slope into a spread of water hemmed in on all sides by seemingly impen-etrable mangrove. A canoe with both paddles and outboard motor, long and sleek, nosed the shore-line, yet so still and archine was the bough-vaulted pool that it appeared no more than a fallen pod from an extinct species of the silk-cotton tree, the pool itself a subterranean lake whose surface had lain unbroken by man or fish for a long millennium.

The silence enveloped them, unyielding. Ofeyi's eyes, gradually allied to the emerald gloom discerned at last an outlet from the pool; he wondered if this led to the sea itself or simply into yet another bowered escape from time. Neither leaf nor straggle of vine seemed out of place; a dense-textured drape hung round the pool, sealing them within the dark preserve of spirits, placid and protective.

Ofeyi wrestled free of the spell. "Why have you brought me here?"

"To recover yourself, and think wisely. If you need to, use the boat. It is not wise for you to be seen in the Corporation boat any more. Leave it here, we'll know what to do with it."

"You think I shall go back to Ilosa then?"

"It is more likely you will want to fly to Cross-river, but bear in mind what I have said. I shall send the man from Shage to talk with you. No one will come here to disturb you."

"You are so swift to plumb a man's needs" Ofeyi remarked, gratefully.

"Is it such a mystery? You need a peaceful place to think. Join me in the meeting-house when you are done."

"Don't send the man just yet. Let me have a few moments by myself."

Ahime looked a little dubious, then shrugged. Ofeyi heard his soft footsteps brushing the moss along the path.

Failure. Was this the smell, the colour, the phantasma of failure?

The shadows closed around him. Ofeyi felt grateful over again for Ahime's tact, predictable though it was. Felt privileged to have been left alone in what he guessed must have been the private sanctuary of the late Custodian. It seemed a well of restoration, used perhaps in those moments of "doubts upon doubts" which Ahime had revealed that other night.

And then, inexplicably, rose the conviction that this had served as sanctuary also for others in the not so distant past. The noise of slavers' raids broke through the silence and a feel of massed anxious flesh wafted through time and assailed his pores. He sensed the waiting, watchful eyes of Aiyéró's fugitives through mangrove twists and archways, merged with the Cross-river whiff of violence, rape and death.

Iriyise, Zaccheus, blissfully unaware, driving straight into a holocaust that had already commenced. . . .

Skirting the edge he sleep-walked to where the canoe lay, pushed the sheath of pitch and corkwood onto the pool and sat on its cross-bench. It drifted, its prow towards the faint outlet he had observed. He felt borne on a vintage fluid and potency of the past, as if invisible denizens of that space had laid their hands on him. What answers shall I make you then, you restless questioners rising from dank silt-beds? How change your whitened bones into something rich and strange? The lines had haunted him from his first glimpse of the pristine moment—full fathom five his father lies . . . of his bones are coral made . . . those are pearls. . . .

The pool stank of history. Slaves, gold, oil. The old wars. Sightless skulls, blood, sweat and bones, agony that lay on seabed, silenced cries forever mingled with black silt. Ever-present energies from the past, staring sockets that demanded that living eyes see, learn through their terror, through rings of past hollowness, empty visions, skeletal fingers webbed in mud, imprints of experience signalling renewed demands . . . this spent energy, this spent error, this violent, untimely cycle of waste renewed a demand for transformation. What would his paddles turn up from that rank

bed of history if he dug deep enough—what, beyond the inter-
twining of matter and deeds! It defied a break in awareness, the
oil trade flowed into a smell of death, disruption and desolation,
flowed in turn into tankers for the new oil. Ofeyi fed this symbio-
sis with faces of prospecting teams he had chanced upon . . . the
Italian covered in flea bites of every shape and hue, and the beefy
engineer, scarred and mangrove tendoned, breaking into the quiet
of the creeks on apocalyptic footsteps. Bulbous chromium tanks
sprouted from the warts on the Italian's face, the prominent veins
of the other dived under his earthy flesh, surfacing and re-diving
like sea-serpents, curving up for a surface run of pipe-lines and
diving into earth again. Restless eyes flitting in a treasure-hunt of
fluids through burial-grounds of the unknown, knuckles snapping
to the rhythm of drills and detonators sending shockwaves through
placid arteries of clay and stone . . . rotted leaves and wood, peat,
shale; yet the long latent metamorphosis would erupt. Looking
up at the rich black fountains, at the protean flow that answered a
thousand demands he wondered what answer he must make to the
puzzled dead searching in the living for the transformation of their
rotted deeds, thoughts, values, tears, bile, decadent and putrescent
memories, searching for a parallel transformation to that of rotted
earth-flesh reborn into life-giving oil. From the archine strength
and failures, what interchange effected? Within the fluid, rancid
energies, what new state of being abstracted, answering a million
demands?

Embarrass me no more with your accusations, he murmured.
Ask your questions of the Cartel who will drain the oil as they
have the milk of the cocoa.

Enervation snared him in a dark sheath on a surface that closed
up its scar. Paddling in somnolence, a little of the water seeped
through the floorboards as he manoeuvred the prow away from a
widening slit in thick forest wrap. The quiet bred a greater dis-
quiet, the news from Cross-river re-surfaced in serpentine coils,

asphyxiating, ringed him with a paralysing knowledge of futility in thought or motion. Both seemed fated to tend towards the starting point. The refutation of change brought moments of despair. Behind the canoe, even the lake conspired to breed spores of this paralysis, closing up the scar of passage, blotting out the challenge of the voyager, substituting a statement of immutability even for this simple rite of passage. Ofeyi muttered, Camouflage! The regenerative powers were only jealously contained within the pool, hidden but attainable, awaiting only the rightful challenger. It awaited only the precise trigger to arouse it to its function within convulsive, rock-blasting, honing tides.

Ofeyi grimaced in self-mockery, blotting out the ghostly illusions of hope. This pond denied even its undertows, presenting a clean slate of perpetual calm. The rower confessed to envy.

The outboard motor sat like a huge malevolent toad on the stern of the canoe, another challenger to the innate rhythm of the place, obscene and gross in its hidden power. It created resentment in Ofeyi, forced him instinctively to side on this point with the paddle's subtler propulsion, its near sacramental union with psychic nuances of time and place. Ahime was himself like that paddle, creating motion within himself and within his environment without a hint of stress, without disrupting the pristine balances. He had held him back from the first instinctive headlong rush. What will you change? If the men of Aiyéró are dead, what can you do? If they are in danger, how can you help them? I love Iriyise like a daughter but her fate was never in my hands. Nor in yours.

Yet someone, a group with desperation enough had plotted her fate and the fate of others. And he . . . no, this was one danger to which, in spite of the horrors that raced through his mind, he would not expose himself. No regrets. No remorse. No will-sapping self-recrimination. Unless . . .

The Dentist! Unless the Dentist had been right after all. The

Dentist with his unassailable logic of extraction before infection. Extract the carious tooth quickly, before it infects the others. And the Dentist had accepted his, Ofeyi's leadership, placed the final responsibility on him. What alternative to his could have prevented the insidious process of mass infection, exposed daily by proximity, hunger and need, human weakness and deprivation, exposed to temptation by the passage of sweetmeats, cunning, corrupt confections. What choice precisely did I make, he demanded of the brackish pond. His paddle clove the water, the ripples strove against with self-protective need for stagnation to swallow up the markings.

The magic mirrors, the sub-aqueous crystals of time-fragmenting cycles persisted. Iriyise surfaced through ripples in the heavily sedimented goblet of wine and he stopped the idle motions of his finger. From merely stirring he began to revolve his glass in the light, marvelling at the illusionary wonders of a coarse, full-bodied glass of wine.

He stared in the full-length mirror that doubled the depth and length of the muted cave of passage. A bloodless orchestration of dead melodies and acoustic magic blotted out the roar of angry jets that rose and landed just without. Swathed in some animal fur, expensive, she entered on flat sandals. And her eyes were as sleepy, ocean-bedded as ever. He questioned his interest. A need for encounters far different from confrontations that lay four thousand miles away. He transformed the stranger to no less than Iriyise, in spite of the much lighter cocoa skin in the dim tranquilizing light. Her pace was a shade less leisured than he remembered, but this seemed natural enough on the thick carpeting. He insisted that the texture of flesh was the same; if he touched it it would radiate the warm thrill of velvet in the dark. He eyed quadrupled reflections of a tone of golden syrup in the cave of mirrors. A shawl slid off one shoulder, a slender arm gathered it, replaced it round her neck.

Iriyise he murmured, what are you doing here in this staging pool of Europe?

The transit lounge turned familiar earth, for this sorceress was known to him. Homesickness? He indulged the warm delusion. He was alone with her, the secret word had been spoken and he was led, a lone night guest into a virgin's lair. Given that he had created her, her face, her own vulnerable shoulders pronounced her virginal.

No matter, the spell remained intact. Not even the nervous rasp in his throat could break it as he signalled the waistcoated barman for another raw glass of wine. The lamp of nostalgia and escape soon came crashing down, its myriad reflectors splintered and embedded in his flesh. The doors swung open and a stranger intruded, flesh and blood. Ofeyi winced. He was black too. Ten to one he would speak to him.

The man seemed copper-coloured and his hair was covered in what could be dust. Before long Ofeyi saw him glance indifferently into the mirror. Eyeing the virgin? The stranger's presence renewed his longing for familiar earth. A soft near inaudible swish, yet his ears caught the sound of his first distraction, the shawl sighing to the ground. He rose, retrieved it and received the startled thanks of two large, impossibly luminous eyes. Indian? All practised openings failed him at the crucial hour and he stammered back to his seat.

So be it then. The voyager consigned himself to guardians of hospitality of the road. Lead me where you will, so be it some handmaid of dawn be found waiting at the end.

He twirled the glass stem between his fingers. The male intruder watched him from beneath deceptive eyelids. Raging now from boredom, indecision, Ofeyi railed at those who had forced the journey on him. Why should I roam these barren, condescending shores to learn—? What had they called it? A-ah, promotion methods! He slammed his glass back on the table muttering,

"I'm returning home!" It splintered in his hands. The stranger looked up, the virgin also. The starch corruscated waiter arrived with dishcloth and chiding glare. He ordered another glass of wine.

With Iriyise unbound, unearthed, salvaged, transformed and fresh created, a grand design for the Cocoa campaign had crystalized in the flash of their first encounter, leapt from his hot brain entire. Goddess, Princess, Chrysalis of the Cocoa Grain, around her burgeoned a thousand schemes and devices, a panoply of adulation and Svengalian transformations, ending her immaturity and self-prostitution. And then, at the very commencement, banished to a six-month Study Tour! He swallowed his wine in self-pity, turned again to linger over the part-bared shoulder of the virgin at the bar. Strange, she could be Iriyise, even her skin was right. Just then, the hidden loudspeakers began to speak.

But it was the girl's reaction to the cancellation of her flight which sent his heartbeat quickening once again. She turned towards the source of the announcement in disbelief, her mouth drooped in distress and she appeared close to tears. Gathering her shawl and overnight bag she made for the door. Ofeyi scrambled to his feet and followed her.

Only to have the stranger step in his path. "Excuse me, are you from . . . ?"

"What?" Embarrassed at the involuntary irritation in his voice he turned to face the interloper. "What is it?"

"I hope you don't mind . . . I heard what you shouted just now, when you broke your glass."

"Yes?" (Insensitive, interfering ass!)

Oblivious to his impatience the stranger continued, unruffled. "Can I buy you a drink? I guessed you were a compatriot and when I heard you exclaim a moment ago."

"Where are you from?"

He did not wait for an answer however. Stung by a sudden conviction that he was delaying too long he rattled at his countryman "One moment, I'll be back!," sped through the doors and slowed down only when he found her at the airline desk.

For the first time he remarked her extra-long mannequin legs, the only part of her that appeared to have developed to full maturity. He watched them wade delicately creating ripples in the pool that lapped his mind, stirring up visions of Iriyise.

She looked up as he stood beside her. "Oh, were you also on the cancelled flight?" He lied affirmation, nodding in triumph.

The stranger was sitting patiently when he returned. Elation drowned his feeling of guilt at his abrupt departure.

By way of apology he offered, "Let me buy the drinks."

The stranger smiled in turn. "I am sorry but I didn't realize . . . I hope I haven't . . . ?"

Ofeyi reassured him, then asked, "And how long have you been away from home?"

"Six years plus. I was a student of dentistry." He hesitated, stopped, then asked in turn, "And you?"

"A mere three months, but already sick of it."

"How come?"

"I miss everything." Then he surprised himself again by blurting out, "The so-called study tour was forced on me. I despise myself for not resisting it to the last."

The stranger waited, not bothering to disguise his expectation. Ofeyi shrugged. "You want to hear all about it? It's the same old story. Nothing is secret any more about the plight in which we've found ourselves."

He said nothing while Ofeyi sketched for him the affair of the Cocoa Campaign, culminating in the suspended shooting of the Aiyéró film. Only then, smiling with a slight superior condescension did the Dentist comment:

"Rich black earth or rich blackguards—you can only shoot one." Then he elaborated as Ofeyi caught the disturbing note and looked up. "Working alone that is. Now if you had a different kind of technician assisting you, you could shoot both, working together. Working together" he repeated, then stood up.

"You will remain here for a while? In this country I mean."

"I can break my itinerary, go anywhere" Ofeyi admitted bitterly.

"Try and remain here, if only for a few days. After all, the advertising business is quite flourishing here too." He flicked his head towards the door. "And your oriental friend?"

Ofeyi grinned. "A fascinating woman. I was trying to get her to see the cancellation of her flight as an act of God. She seemed to think so already—but not on my account!" he added ruefully.

"I can offer you my apartment" he said. "Why don't you stay for a few days at least. We have much to talk about."

"All right. Thanks."

A shimmer of vapour from gasfires at evening. Toast and reverie morning and evening. A frail figure of paradox, young and solemn who tried to draw the world within her inward peace—"I want the world in here, within me, but first, I must submit my conscience to the universe."

"Listen Iri . . ."

"Don't!" Her young eyes grew hard and angry for the first time since they met.

"What's the matter?" He was really taken aback.

"Not any more. At first I was not sure, now I know it is the name of some woman you know."

He fell silent. "Yes" she continued, "I knew I was right." She broke into the more familiar smile. "Now that you have admitted it I am no longer angry. But don't use the name any more."

The moment passed, the outer world was re-interred, in its place only the two large eyes which filled the sitting-room, luminous votives moving on invisible radials to the centre of the universe. Taiila turned and looked at him. He understood her language by now and knew that she was inviting him to join her. He shook his head and said, "I have told you not to wait for me."

She sighed. "We pass and re-pass each other but you will not step off your circling path. You are trapped on your violent circumference Ofeyi. Why won't you rest?"

"Mire and mud, for some these are the paths to beauty and peace. We may meet at several intersections, you and I, the mystery virgin of a transit lounge. . . ."

She came forward and took his hand. "But you still don't believe it was fated. You think it is all an accident, my brother a doctor in your country, our plane cancelled on my way to visit him, and just you and I in that lounge. You still don't believe it was all destined. Can't you see I am meant to save you?"

Ofeyi tried to infuse his voice with all the sincerity he felt. "Believe me I envy you your glimpses of redemption. I really do. Only you must believe also in my own commitments. Leave me to track my own spoors on the laterals, Taiila. Moreover," he added, "if we were destined to meet so was my meeting with the Dentist."

Church bells, fresh snow timbred, air that became clean music, the black steeple and chimney skyline in a crisp winter air. Savagely crunching beneath his feet the cotton deadening of commitments, he accompanied her to her observation post to view the line of nuns walking endlessly towards the sound of vespers, seeking the infinite in mists, trudging along her vision of radials gathered into the heart of an impenetrable stillness.

Blackbirds pocked a world of snow, plunging into white horizons of her infinite silence.

"Let's walk" he suggested. "My shoes soak up the snow standing on this one spot."

"Is that the only reason?"

"Why? What other reason could there be?"

"You resent my watching the nuns."

"You are silly" he chided. "I want to stretch my legs, perfectly simple."

"And I want to stretch my soul. I want to stretch my soul to embrace the infinite."

"Listen sister . . ."

"Don't call me Sister." She turned away, walking briskly. Her lips were drawn in disappointment. "I did not expect you would try to mock me."

At first he did not understand. Then light broke and he tried to explain. "I didn't mean sister like Reverend Sister. Just sister, the way I would say brother."

Her smile drew against the bleak landscape. "I know. I like to see you contrite."

"And I'd like to spank your impudent bottom."

They walked back slowly to the house. "You should be a doctor" she announced, with the frowning solemnity of one who has given deep thought to a problem. "You are a beautiful person you know. Inside of you I see so much beauty."

Ofeyi thanked her, caustic-toned.

"Oh you are quite beautiful outside too" she went on calmly. "But that is not important. The true doctors are the real healers, and healers radiate beauty. That is what heals you know. The beauty they radiate from their own persons."

They were back in the flat. He warmed his hands against the gas fire. When he turned she was standing directly behind him, watching him sadly. He raised her paradoxical face, a mixture of adolescence and experience and tapped her chin with a finger.

"You are very wise, of that I am sure. And beautiful inside and out. And if you are both things, why this fascination with a nun's life. Have you really thought it out?"

"A nun too is a form of healer, and healing is beauty. . . ."

"And healing takes many forms. There is the way fire heals. And the way wind heals by tearing down and blowing dirt into void. Even if one is blinded by too sudden and too much light, it reveals inner truth. I also seek beauty, but that kind which has been tested and stressed. Only such beauty lasts. Be a nun if you insist, but stop preaching at me."

"I don't trust men of violence!"

"You should not eavesdrop on private discussions."

"I could not help overhearing . . ."

"Then you must forget what you heard." He took her hands in his and spoke more gently. "In any case you heard an argument, nothing more. You should know from what little you heard that I also do not believe in violence. But I see it, I recognize it. I must confront it."

She turned away from him and sat on the window-sill. Ofeyi felt his being sink inwards in a sigh closed to the pain on her fragile face. Through half-shut eyes he addressed the ceiling. "These encounters destroy a man bit by bit, they dam up passages of clarity, the essential. Do you understand? My feelings are incoherent. I meet you, grow towards you, I think of the mystery of even encountering you. I am aware also of the growth of self-deception, because you stand for only one part of my longing. . . ."

"The peaceful part?"

"Yes. The stillness."

Her face was suffused with sudden radiance. Ofeyi stared at her in surprise. "I know I shall be able to help you attain that. Some day. I know that everything is linked. You must believe that. And I am striving to obtain a glimpse of the entire network. I know I will arrive at a state of detached consciousness where I shall stand aside and comprehend it all in one instant. Even if it lasts only one moment, it will be enough for me. And for you. Yes, for you. That is what makes me happy."

"For one so young, you seem to strain for a glimpse of the doorway to death."

She stretched her long neck through the window, straining to see the receding procession of nuns. It made him think of a swan framed against thin icing on a lake at twilight. "There could not be any beauty to equal theirs" she murmured. "To spend a whole life in self-preparation for that moment of perception of the infinite. To perceive, understand and be at peace. Ofeyi tell me, can you think of a more complete moment of harmony? Is life not unbearable without belief in such a moment?"

Her breath stopped as a knock sounded on the door. They glanced at each other. She spoke wistfully, "Your host knocks with such gentleness, but it is the knock of a violent man. Even if I had not met him or ever heard him . . ." She hurried away towards the bedroom, shut the door firmly behind her.

"Come in" Ofeyi called out.

The youth from the airport encounter entered, carrying a small suitcase. Small and compact though it was it hit the floor with the dead resonance of heavy metal as he set it down. "It is all in here" he announced. "When do you plan to leave?"

"Tomorrow if there is a flight."

The visitor's eyebrows lifted in surprise, his head turned a fraction towards the bedroom door through which Taiila had disappeared, his eyes asked the question.

Ofeyi shook his head, his grin though slightly soured in regret reassured the man. Glancing towards the door just to make sure it was not ajar Ofeyi said, "Surely you did not think there was a serious dilemma?"

"I wasn't sure."

"It is strange" Ofeyi said, "but she herself thinks in terms of little else but destiny. Everything—destiny! Our encounter at that airport lounge. Your happening along at the same moment. She weaves all the strands in a private accommodating mesh and outside of that . . . nothing exists. I am not sure mind you . . . if you hadn't happened along." He shrugged. "I was at that stage of self-pity, negativity and I don't know what else. Maybe you've been through it also, the stage at which one asks, what is the bloody use?"

He gestured towards the arm-chair. "Whisky? Oh, I forget . . ."

"No, it's all right. I am . . . no longer on duty."

Ofeyi glanced at the suitcase. "Yes . . . to quote a title from the world of fiction—mission accompli?"

The youth smiled apologetically. "I'm afraid I am not familiar with the world of fiction. In fact, I rather despise it."

Vainly attempting to keep the scorn from his voice Ofeyi retorted, "Aren't you overdoing the Lenin bit?"

"No, no . . ."

"You see everything as a threat. No drink while you are engaged on—even on long distance business. As for women, art, music . . ."

The youth held up his hand. "It is only a habit of discipline I have acquired with time. As for Lenin, no, he merely distrusted those aspects of the arts which he found will-sapping. A natural precaution." He grinned disarmingly. "Why are we quarrelling anyway? What you have told me about your work, your music for instance, how could I be against that? It was sufficient threat to the Cartel of organized robbery and murder to send you packing on this leisure trip. As for women, well, I am looking forward to meeting the famous Iriyise. . . ."

"We'll drink to her." Ofeyi poured out the whisky. "And to that

suitcase. One is as essential as the other—depending," he spoke
with slow emphasis, "on mental attitudes."

They drank. A thoughtful silence fell on both. The youth paced
up and down, suddenly restless. He burst out suddenly, "You have
thought what to do if they search it?"

Ofeyi spread out his hands. "But I honestly do not *know* what
it contains."

"I am sorry to have to ask you to do it, but I have been too long
away. No contacts at home, nothing! And—I dare not be anything
but clean on arrival!"

"Listen, let us assume the worst. My position is clear. A chance
acquaintance asked me to take the suitcase back for him, even paid
the excess charge on it. That is my story and you don't have to
bother your head about any slip-ups."

The youth's eyes remained bitter, swearing through narrowed
lips. "Bastards! They are all so stupid, so shortsighted. To pass
dossiers on us to our worst enemies at home."

Ofeyi was somewhat surprised at the passion of his resentment.
The pattern was wearisomely familiar. A violent change of government, the new leaders courted recognition from neighbouring
power, offered dowry in the form of wanted fugitives from that
area of repression. Sometimes trussed and wrapped like mail-bags.
And dossiers complete with aliases, photos, activities and lists of
connections. Dirty deals, the old bargaining in human flesh, a slave
market among the middlemen of the black continent, perpetuat-
ing their historic role in a lucrative betrayal of their own skin
and flesh. It boiled down to this, neither more nor less, sustaining
the putrid form of power with a market in flesh, an internal slave
route lined in shameless sophistries.

"At least you got out in time" Ofeyi consoled him.

"Stripped bare! Of comrades, contacts, equipment. Almost of
ideology. Christ! The lip-service those stooge leaders pay to lib-

eration movements! Why the betrayal, tell me that! Why, if we were such a threat didn't they simply let us go on to Mozambique. That was where we were training for, Mozambique or Bissau." He calmed down slowly, sipped his drink with increasing thoughtfulness. "Well, perhaps they did me a favour. I can put that training to some use on home territory. It has taken a long while to accept that cliché, but charity does begin at home."

"You have not forgotten our agreement?"

"No. I shall wait. I have kept up with the situation and . . . you have briefed me some more. But I'll give myself time to study it all over on the spot. I like to see, to get to know faces. Even those who . . ." He stopped short, drained his glass at a gulp.

Ofeyi regarded him with his former unease. "We should not work in different directions. . . ."

He met his gaze frankly. "I cannot guarantee that."

"Time!" Ofeyi stressed. "Time to educate on a truly comprehensive scale. Nothing can be achieved by isolated acts, we have to organize."

It drew a mere grunt of partial agreement. "Of course. But one cannot ignore the real incorrigible enemies who are impervious to education. The kind that hunted us down as soon as they came to power, the fat bourgeoisie who immediately began to suck up to them and lick their boots in public! What do you think I have done all these years of roaming around? What else was there to do except watch the pattern multiply itself and prove endemic throughout the continent! Bloated, ignorant armies hanging on to power until they drop like rotten fruit! A conspiracy of power-besotted exploiters across national boundaries, bargaining with outsiders against *us*! Lip-service to revolutionary movements to drown the cries of internal repression. Tell me friend, what are they selling? All this haggling and under-the-counter deals, what is the commodity? Us!"

Increasingly disturbed, swirling his drink round and round his glass, wondering how much of the personal emotion would go into settlement of the score of betrayal. The youth appeared to read his thoughts: "Don't worry about me," he said. "I speak like this only from frustration at my long inaction." The boyish grin returned. "And the effect of the whisky. That is why I never drink on duty. At the point of action the machine takes over. The decisions are made in advance because I must avoid the luxury of doubts. Don't worry about me," he repeated.

Dream-like in its drift round and round the pool the craft came again close to the outlet. Archways of overhanging boughs framed the narrow passage, a change in the motion of the paddle steered his craft at last into the passage and his face was flicked by sappy leaves. He made no effort to duck them. Fear death by . . . no, it was not a watery death he feared, only a death from error. And not his, but the death of others brought upon by faint decisions. And if those decisions were his, then it was worse than his own death, being the death of an idea, a stretching out of the passage towards his own eventual demise no matter by what name it went. A favourite title might be loss of faith.

To Ahime he had explained this, saying "No, I have no wish to die yet."

The old man shook his head at what he deemed delirious talk.

"To go into that place is to court death. Wait for the frenzy to die down. You can help no one. If it is given for the men of Aiyéró to be the sacrifice . . . it was a good cause."

Not sacrifice, he had thought bitterly, only more scapegoats to lay a false trail of blood away from the altar of the unholy god, Mammon. No, not sacrifice. Ahime, priest of the acrificial knife, he of all people should know better than to desecrate that word.

So Ahime led him to the pool. "Whatever bones lie beneath the water, the spirits that left from them must be beneficent ones, of that I am certain. Just sitting on the shore I drift off sometimes for an entire day. At the end I feel restored, rejuvenated. No matter what trials drove me there to seek its peace, they are resolved, as if an oracle had whispered in my ear."

The only voice that came was the call of Iriyise. And it was no whisper but a loud cry of anguish. And trapped voices of the men of Aiyéró who had gone out at his call, vanguard of the new idea. . . .

The channel opened abruptly into a wide expanse of water. He took his bearings from landmarks in the receding town, stood up in the craft and secured the engine over the stern. Seizing the cord firmly between fingers of his clenched fist he pulled. The engine roared into life.

He kept his eyes on the prow-riven sea, refused to acknowledge the lithe old man who had leapt out from the meeting-house at the sound and raced to the shore, only to be confronted by the receding churn of water. But before it vanished round the next curve of shore-line Ofeyi raised his arm in greeting, his gaze fixed steadily ahead.

VII

The soil of Irelu rose and spiralled in rust, the man who approached wore it on his head, a quiet freak with copper-coloured hair. There was even a patina of rust to his face, a thin layer of dust on fired-clay firmness. At that distance the cicatrice, three horizontal lines on each cheek seemed the handiwork of a light touch tatooist; normal skin growth had encroached on it until all that was left was the bare impression. Ofeyi watched him rise from the small circle of men in the inner-room of the beer parlour, noted his relaxed confidence as he approached his table and occupied the vacant chair. Ofeyi put aside the newspaper he had brought with him but the man took it from him, looked briefly at the date then turned it over to display a picture of the murdered judge.

"I did that" he said.

There was no boast contained in his tone, neither pride nor remorse, there was neither regret nor satisfaction. It was a plain statement of fact, made even more ordinary by his tone. Ofeyi found himself a little surprised by his own self-possession; it was after all the first time he had sat face to face with a self-confessed assassin. "The police haven't given a very good Wanted description of you."

"No" he admitted. "They haven't the faintest idea who they are looking for."

The man hardly belonged to the pattern of bestialities which had lately sprouted among a people whose character he, among others, had taken so much for granted. One grew immune to shocks, easily. Yet he had a feeling that he was looking at a completely new casting from the foundry of Olukori. Flawed? Or merely stressed to the demands of the time? There was a time when he should have pursued the answer to that. Now it was too late.

The hair held him fascinated. "How do you get around that?" He pointed at it. "It's turned more coppery since you got back. Is that from being back in the sun? It rather singles you out."

"Oh one wears a tight-fitting cap. Or dye it if absolutely necessary. I have only had to resort to that measure once."

It occurred to him then that his unusual hair might even be an asset. Very few policemen, unless they had actually seen it would think of including a copper head of hair in the Wanted descriptions. There was prolonged silence between them, broken by Ofeyi's embittered sigh. "You have not kept your bargain," he said.

The man looked puzzled. Ofeyi continued, "Oh, when it became clear that there was actually a lone wolf who handled things—that way, I could no longer pretend to myself that I did not know who it was."

"I hope you also remember that I am not a mercenary."

"No. I persuade myself you are still on the side of the angels."

He smiled at that. "If you mean the ones with the flaming sword, yes."

"Sitting in lone judgement over lesser mortals?"

"The times make it necessary."

Ofeyi read in his eyes calm acceptance of his role. A fatalistic complement to the popular insurrection in which feeling and rationality were bound together. Youthful as he looked, a lonely concentration of the will to action within his own person rendered him grave and aged. The picture of the dead judge lay between them and he gave it a long thoughtful study.

"That operation took three months to prepare. Three months is a long time in the urgency of our situation."

Operation! Usually the word came from the more hardened thugs, the crude strong-armed gangs who roamed the cities creating mayhem in strongholds of opposition. But he made it sound far more diagnostic, an inevitable course for a patient who had gone beyond the stage of simple medications. Nothing would serve now but the operating table, a clean, drastic surgery. Even the venerable vendors of compromise, miscalled peace, had come to recognize the failure of their surrogates. One after another they withdrew into silence, admitting the impotence of their solutions.

Even the churches, the mosques, the far more ancient shrines had ceased to call for the favourite panacea for a week of fasting and prayers, bored with the increasing futility of their pious voices.

Operation. Twenty miles from Irelu a woman was dragged from her bed, sliced open at the belly. She was not even dead when they left her guts spilling in a messy afterbirth between her thighs. A tax assessor, she had beggared many ruthlessly in slavish obedience to the Cartel. In those remote unchampioned villages, a man's failure to produce a valid tax receipt at the required instant meant seizure of his cocoa farms. Permanently. Then came the turning of the worm. The assailants stuffed her mouth with a roll of the court orders she had served on them and set the grotesque cigar alight.

The antelope's hoof, symbol of the Cartel manipulated party, Jekú, inspired the idea for amputations of their agents in Aro-oke. They were hunted down one after the other, a foot was hacked off at the ankle and stuffed into their mouths. The insurgents then carved a crude crutch from the nearest tree and sent their victim hobbling on his way—keep that message in your mouth they said, and deliver it to Chief Batoki.

A family of twenty, three generations in all wiped out in a noon of vengeance. An agent on the run from mob rage had fired wildly into his pursuers felling two, fled and barricaded himself in his own house. He was still scrabbling for more cartridges when they came upon him, a huge wave borne solely on pain and rage. Up the stairs fled all the inmates of the house, seeking imagined safety. The mob set the stairs alight, shot and cut down every being in the house who leapt or tried to creep into the safety of the bushes even on broken legs. A nursing sister, niece of the agent drove into the blood-crazed arms of the mob as she returned from work. Recognized, the yet unsated avengers raised her, she flew from arm to arm, was swung back and forth and into the flames. They howled and raged until the fires died down, running in blood circulations. They waited until the flames crouched lower and then razed the shell, tore brick from brick with peeled and scalded palms, tore off the iron sheets and bore them far from the scene. They wanted nothing left behind of that ill-famed mansion, nothing but the charred earth, the bones and blacked rectangles of mortar, nothing but the scorched imprint of the awakened beast of revolt.

Operation, the elastic word. It covered the seven-year-old son of a Returning Officer, subverted by the Cartel, a child left carelessly behind in his father's car outside his office while he took a secret footpath to the home of Chief Batoki to receive his ten pieces of gold. He came back to the burnt shell of his motorcar, the charred remains of his son in it and an impassive crowd gathered at a distance observing him. In his hand was the tell-tale envelope filled with soured five-pound notes. The crowd left him untouched.

It began with the slaughter of innocents by the Cartel's paramilitary troops, intimidating volleys loosed on markets and schools, slaying at random and spattering schoolroom walls with brains hot from learning. It turned into the fate of such licensed killers who ventured foolhardily into seemingly soft villages, found them deserted, demolished the huts and fired the crops then returned to their vehicle and drove back to report success. Only, in a mysterious fashion their skins had begun to burn beneath their uniform and, when they leaned forward in their seats a searing pain tore through their backs; they could not budge. No one could rid them of those uniforms, the cloth took off strips of their skin in the attempt. They died in great agony, nor could the government analysts identify what manner of lethal paste had been smeared on those seats while they were out destroying the crops.

The self-confessed assassin was saying, "There is a pattern even to the most senseless killing. All that we must do is take control of that violence and direct it with a constructive economy. Our people kill but they have this sense of selectiveness. They pick the key men, but they also kill from mere association. An agent is marked down for death. An informer is butchered. We cannot stop it even if we want no part of such righteous vengeance. But we must also set up a pattern of killing, the more difficult one. Select the real kingpins and eliminate them. It is simple, you have to hit the snake on the head to render it harmless."

Abruptly Ofeyi asked, "What do they call you here? I know you have all sorts of names with the police."

"The Dentist" he admitted, with a wry smile.

"And afterwards," Ofeyi demanded. "What do you envisage?"

"Envisage?" His tone rose in protest. "Why do you want me to envisage anything? Is that my field? I thought it was yours."

"Surely, when you—eliminate, you have in mind something to follow, something to replace what you eliminate. Otherwise your action is negative and futile."

The Dentist sighed. "Why do you people, you intellectuals or whatever you call yourselves impose on us burdens to which we lay no claim. I am trained in the art of killing. I utilize this acquisition on behalf of my society. In what art are you trained? I have watched your cocoa campaigns, I have followed your troupe about and I concluded that your mission is indeed to educate. Right? You stir up a dangerous awareness in our people—the mass is your self-imposed constituency—isn't that right? Self-imposed mission. But we have spoken of this before, you know where I stand in the struggle. I cannot shoot issues or mount physical guard over them. I take a simple view, but it happens to be the result of my experiences. You know what they are. I agreed for us to meet because I have a most important question to ask you. An opinion if you like. But not to answer questions which are outside my field. Don't ask me what I envisage. Beyond the elimination of men I know to be destructively evil, I envisage nothing. What happens after is up to people like you."

"All right. What did you want from me?"

The man stood up. "First I want to take you on a tour." He smiled. "A local one this time. I am trying to bring you in, not chase you out. The sights will be familiar to you but I think that few of you have really gathered what is about to happen soon. I want to introduce my constituency the only way I can. I have satisfied myself about your activities by the way, so it only remains for you to accept the fact that we are still allies."

"What activities do you know of?"

"You have been planting men from Aiyéró all over the country. That was a deep scheme, really far-sighted but it does not interest me. I know all about that piece of anachronism." He shrugged. "In my opinion you are all woolly-minded idealists but we can work together to destroy the Jekú. My contribution will be to lower your handicap."

He looked more like an executive civil servant than a killer, with a loyal squad of thugs at his command. They rose from the inner room as he stood up but a glance from him returned them to their seats. Only the very observant would have noted the co-ordinated motions of the men, and it sent a thrill of optimism up Ofeyi's spine. The Dentist seemed outside of it by his appearance, but the half-dozen men who had risen and sunk back into their beer so unobtrusively were a recognizable part of the increasing stream-lining of assassinations which in turn appalled and uplifted him. But the accusing fact remained however, that it was the lesser agents who perished. The masters remained inaccessible, heavily protected, flitting from hide-out to fortified rat-holes, playing a waiting game and callously buying time with a hundred lives and mutilations.

"I shall take you through this town, and a few others. Then we shall make a tour of Curfew City. Is that all right?"

"How shall we do that?" Ofeyi demanded. "How does one break the curfew?"

"Don't worry about that. First, my base. It's my home town."

"I didn't know that."

"Where else could I move so freely? If anyone gave me away here . . . no, no one could think of it!"

Such confidence seemed fatal. Ofeyi felt some surprise and showed it. The Dentist had suggested a far sharper awareness of human nature. However he continued, "My father was some kind of politician—in those days of kingship you understand? When kingship really meant something. Well, his history is not easily forgotten. We don't breed traitors here any more."

And beyond that he would say no more.

The city was baked bright clay from its laterite soil. It was startling to come upon a mammoth breadfruit tree full-leaved and in fruit in the midst of so much red dust and the general drought of Harmattan. The Dentist led him through a cutting which broke briefly onto a motor-road, untarred. They crossed it onto a foot-path and were closed in by drying ears of elephant grass.

"The Harmattan" the Dentist commented, "is the right season for insurrections. Fires burn faster, the winds fly drier, a people's anger spirals swifter in the dust of those miniature devil-winds building up into the cyclone that must sweep off their oppressors. I like the Harmattan."

"So do I" Ofeyi conceded. "But only because it brings me a feeling of euphoria, why I don't know. The flux of dust and light I suppose, when it isn't actually in your eyes, the dust that is, I get stings and prickles all over my skin. My body becomes pounds lighter."

"That is because you lose moisture. Look, here is one part which never quite feels the dry season. If you knew how much blood-shed that piece of land caused some fifty years ago. Can you sense change in the air?"

Abruptly the warm brittleness of Irelu had changed into humid air. Ofeyi sniffed greedily, glancing ahead to detect the possible presence of a stream.

"This area is so fertile, two villages fought constantly for it. Kejàse claimed that that road behind us marked the boundaries of the two settlements; Irelu said no, the boundary was further ahead, right up a fair length of the main stream which waters the valley. Such a stupid and unnecessary quarrel. There was enough water and land for every mouth in both villages."

"How was it finally resolved?"

The Dentist smiled. "By an act of God; at least so it was interpreted. One thing our people are good at is the formula that leaves no side of a quarrel in prolonged resentment. Today—worse luck for them—those who occupy such hallowed positions—well, wouldn't you call it that?—signs, omens, oracles, or the written law—their interpreters are a device society creates to safeguard justice which alone holds society together. Do you agree? So when those who are entrusted with that task betray it and sell their voice to corrupt forces . . ."

"Like the judge?"

The Dentist paused. "Of course. But I wasn't thinking of him in particular. Do you think I was trying to justify to you why he had to be eliminated."

"Weren't you?"

He shook his head. "I told you I am taking you on a tour of inspection. The past is still here with us, our history is preserved in these blooded streams. Tell me, when in those days a king betrayed the collective trust of his people what happened to him? Was it not usual to summon him, present him with a calabash of poison and invite him to retire to his chamber?"

"I'd like to see you inviting Batoki to take a pinch of cyanide."

"No. That is why it is necessary to force it down their throats. By whatever means we can find." His face twitched a little in distaste. "But they make their exit so undignified."

The judge in his terror, before the final payment was made . . . ducking down below the bench as a car backfired outside his court. The regulation issue of revolver had provided only a shred of comfort. It lay constantly in a half-open drawer below his desk but such was his fear that in those moments of imagined menace when his hands sought it, his fingers could hardly close on the butt. He ordered even his own state prosecutors searched. His thrice weekly tennis was first to go, then the Sunday worship. Then he gave up his Rotary Club dinners but not even this ultimate sacrifice was the one that he was called upon to make. In those early days, at the commencement of his sanctification of crimes from the bench, even of murder, obeying a call on the telephone or a whisper from the leader of Jekú he had earned the inevitable name of Daddy Cowboy—a gun had fallen from his pocket at a public function and the guests roared with laughter at his clumsy effort to retrieve it and return it into his pocket. Months passed, Daddy Cowboy was no longer seen at state functions, at charity fetes, he delegated his inspection of the guard of honour to others at the opening of Assizes, his greatest tool for destroying the enemies of Jekú and enriching their agents by unprecedented levels in awarding costs. . . .

"It was simple in the end, but it took three months of waiting, watching. And now the others are even more cautious."

They came to a curve in the stream. Across it lay a tree which served for a bridge. The Dentist stopped. "This was the act of God. At some point in their stupid battles there was a storm and this tree fell across the stream. A priest from Kejàse contacted his counterpart from Irelu and asked him if his kernels had divined the same meaning from the event. Naturally it had. The elders on both sides met and agreed that heaven willed it that the tree should bridge both villages in amity. End of war. Now they share everything in common. After three generations of polygamous birth increase there are still acres of uncultivated land." He kicked a stone into the stream. "The stupidity of human greed!"

He led across the bridge into Kejàse, pointing out the shells of the police station and the provincial courts. They were gutted by fire and stood stark against the fertile surrounds of the village itself. The pattern was all too familiar. These villages were not peopled by the same breed as occupied the commercial cities.

For those, even the bark of a guard dog was a depressing sound, since they were never asleep, never ignorant of the intrusion of night marauders in their midst. Their only prayer as their eyes shut tighter was that the raiders would complete their mission quickly and peacefully, clean the house of their possessions but leave them in peace. When the steps grew menacingly close, they snored loudly, abjectly. And even when, growing ever bolder, the robbers left huge gashes on their flesh as a memento of their visit they would pretend that they had slipped on broken glass. The land-worker was beyond such surrender. Even when his lips were compelled by a superior force to stay shut his wide-open eyes spoke clearly, saying, I take note of this event. Bound to earth in a visceral bond he could not conceive of existence compounded by self-betrayal. The act of arrogant, alien mouths gorging the product of his sweat, consigning him to rinds in punitive taxation, dispossessing him of land at a neutral stroke of the pen or a pronouncement of suborned judges could result only in one form of response. It built up slowly, flared into those sporadic flames as had begun to gut symbolic presences of the oppressing force. It had begun to mass together in a concerted sweep.

And the Cartel woke to the increasing rumble at its door.

The Dentist scuffed ashes in the burnt-out shell of the tax office and faced Ofeyi. "What did you think it would lead to, the doctrines you began to disseminate through the men of Aiyéró?"

"Recovery of whatever has been seized from society by a handful, re-moulding society itself. . . ."

"But not through violence?"

"What is the point of that question? I've never excluded that likelihood."

"Those who stand most to lose have woken up to your activities. What do you think they would do?"

"What they are doing now, uproot it where they can, destroy

the men whom they held responsible for the spread of the virus of thought."

"And how will they do it?"

Wondering where this sudden plunge into cross-examination was leading Ofeyi conceded a number of the counter-measures of the Cartel. The Dentist nodded thoughtfully, pointed to the rubble of official buildings.

"Will this stop them? Is that what you think?"

Feeling it was time for a change of roles Ofeyi asked in turn, "What do you think is the answer then? Your selective assassinations?"

The Dentist held his eyes for some moments. "I don't deny that neither my method nor yours will serve by itself. You have always taken your methods for granted, you can't envisage any means beyond converting inertia to a mass momentum. But the other side know that what they do is abnormal, it is against nature. And so they are compelled to act together, as an abnormal but organic growth. From the very start. There is one way to break such a growth apart and that is to pluck off its head. Pluck it right off. They make their own rules brother. We must make ours."

"But the end result of that?"

"You will insist on means and ends won't you? All right, we'll make a few more trips. The picture is not all bleak, I admit that. But while you busied yourself on the seminal rounds of the distant ideal, your friends have been ringing your fields in steel. In fact brother, the stranglehold is very nearly complete."

VIII

"Is that the dog?"

The clerk had not even bothered to turn at the cushioned clang of the carved, metal-studded doors but continued to rummage among piles of paper on a long table. The *dongari* advanced with his charge as far as the first pair of pillars, pushing him forward at every step.

The clerk turned slightly, demanded again, "Is that the dog Salau that no longer knows his mother?"

The *dongari* pushed his prisoner to the floor and the man cringed, his head between his arms to ward off expected blows. No sound came from him although spasms commenced around his jaws and his head bobbed up and down. On the raised floor at the opposite end of the hall, a seeming end of the world away from where the clerk had spoken, sat a turbanned figure at the sight of whom the prisoner had promptly lowered his eyes. Impassive and expressionless, permanent slits of boredom and disdain served for a pair of eyes. His figure filled a huge ornate chair. Without the velvet-covered footstool however, his feet would have stopped a good way short of the ground. A mildly hawk-like nose protruded also from a face that was otherwise smooth, flat, without lines or wrinkles.

Sprawled at his feet were a number of shapes in poses of seeming inattention. A young boy raised languid eyes from the comic-strip paperback which had engrossed him until then, looked up at the turbanned figure, then across the vast expanse to the creature who still cringed against the *dongari*'s feet. The boy fluttered his long lashes, giggled and sent his voice lisping down the hall:

"Is the dog mute then?"

He looked back at the turbanned presence and smiled, was rewarded by a faint indulgent smile from the immobile Buddha form. The *dongari* took his cue from the interruption, put his bare foot to the prisoner's rear and catapulted him forward:

"Crawl dog! The Zaki wants you."

Pausing from time to time only to present the salutation fist of homage in the direction of the dais the man called Salau hastily began his journey to the throne in a strange combination of movements: sometimes he dragged on heels and buttocks, then sprinted a quick yard at a crouch, hands hung low to the ground so that his fingertips retained a light contact with the marble floor, he slid a few more yards on one leg and half-buttock, his palm flat against the ground, then crawled whining on all fours . . . his movements were punctuated by a quick wringing of his hands, a trembling fist of homage and a quick gargle in the throat as he bobbed his head and saluted:

"Ranka dede, ranka dede."

He was halfway up the hall before Zaki Amuri stirred faintly, made a gesture, almost imperceptible except to the early spokesman, the clerical figure in a western suit. The clerk at the table stepped to the edge of the marble dais and shouted, "That's enough!"

The prisoner jerked to a halt, bobbed his head a few times and continued to mutter "Ranka dede." The boy with the long lashes giggled and threw his head back, reached vaguely into a bowl beside him, took out a sweetmeat at which he nibbled daintily. The other retinue on the floor gave the culprit brief glances from beneath hooded eyes and took no further interest in the event. Except perhaps one who appeared to keep his eyes steadfastly averted from the terrified man in the middle of the hall, unnecessarily, as the prisoner was beyond recognizing anyone in his condition. The man in the turban gave yet another faint nod of the head and the clerk turned interrogator.

"The Zaki wishes to know if you are the man who has sold your birthright for a mess of pottage."

The prisoner wrung his hands and turned from side to side. "Ranka dede . . . I did not know . . . I swear I was misled. . . ."

The clerk laughed. "Misled. Are you a goat with a halter round your neck? Misled! Perhaps we should put one round it now so we can know for sure whether we are dealing with a goat or a responsible head of a family."

"Ranka dede, ranka dede . . ."

"Strangers come to you, complete strangers from way across the river. Not even men of the faith but *kafiri!* They make you promises, bribe you and you agree to foment trouble among your own kith and kin. You proceed to sow disaffection against the subjects of the Zaki!"

"No no your highness, I swear by Allah I am no trouble-maker."

The clerk's smile turned grim. "Well what are you then? That is what the Zaki would like to know. What are you? Go on, tell us."

Salau muttered silent prayers, raised his eyes to the arched ceiling in vain. He swallowed hard, then plunged into explanations he wished he had had time to rehearse.

"What could I do your Highness? The land was truly ruined. I am only an ignorant man and there was no one to advise me what to do. The land was barren through and through. Nothing grew, farming was impossible. And it wasn't as if I had a job to turn to, like my brother-in-law Abdul and one or two others. But for the mercy of Allah my little ones would have perished of hunger. Once or twice I even stood beside the gates of the mining company to beg from the whiteman—after all it was their doing that brought ruin upon the land. But the gateman chased me away. Imagine, he said I was dirtying up the whiteman's gate. When I came back again he called the police and they put me in gaol for a week. So what could I do your highness when these men came? The land was costing more to till than it yielded. I ask for the Zaki's forgiveness on an ignorant man."

"So when these blaspheming strangers came you thought Allah had smiled on you? They were visitors sent from heaven to make your fortune?"

"Forgive me your Highness. Abdul my brother-in-law misled me. He said the men were out to help poor people like us."

The clerk snorted. "To help people like you! Because where they come from they have no beggars of their own who need help? And your village head, I suppose he was sick or dying?"

Salau looked bewildered, rolled his eyes round the room in vain search for elucidation. He was startled back to attention when the clerk shouted: "Answer me! It's me speaking to you, not the wall."

"Your Highness will forgive me" the man pleaded. "I don't understand."

"I asked if you had no village head from whom you could take advice? Or is it everyday that strangers come to you and offer to make you money from useless land? Especially when you were already paid by those who borrowed the land!"

The man continued to wring his hands. "Ranka dede, ranka dede. I am a very foolish man, I can only ask you to forgive . . ."

"Not satisfied with your foolishness you even became the agent of these men. You went round to other villages stirring them up, deceiving them with promises of fortune from the sky."

The man leapt at a straw in the deluge of indictments. "No no, if your Highness will permit me to explain that, I was not their agent. . . ."

The clerk folded his arms, pursed his lips together and waited.

"I was no more than a guide, your Highness. They wanted someone to show them the area around the Mining Trust. What happened between them and other people, I swear by Allah, I know nothing of that. If you ask Abdul your Highness, perhaps he can tell. But I swear I did no more than act as guide."

"And just what do you know of this Abdul? This man who is to blame for everything?"

"My brother-in-law your Highness. He works at the Mining Trust as watchman. Your Highness, if you will permit me to explain something. . . ."

"The Zaki wants all the explanation you care to give."

The man swallowed several times, uttered a swift, silent prayer. "Your Highness, as you know, the white men have been digging on those lands for a long time. They pay us something but, what does it all come to your Highness? Nothing much. When they have finished with the land it is useless. Nothing but rocks. The rain washes the best soil away once they have been at it. Apart from a small patch here and there. A goat turns up his nose at the grass that grows there. Please your Highness don't think it is as if we were complaining. Ever since the village head called us together and told us they have the Zaki's permission we have let them dig wherever they like. But you see your Highness, when they are done, the land is well and truly finished. A man like Abdul was able to get work with the whitemen as a watchman, but the rest of us . . ."

The clerk turned sharply at a bored gesture from the Zaki, leant downwards and put his ear to his lips. The accused man prolonged his drone of woe until an impatient bark from the clerk cut him off in mid-word. The boy with the long lashes broke into a prolonged giggle, threw a half-bitten sweetmeat across the floor to the culprit and resumed his comics.

The clerk nodded in response to the inaudible movements of the Zaki's turbanned lips. "Of course your Highness, he has not told the whole truth." He spun round at the man again and screamed, "Did these men not tell you that the Zaki had let you be cheated by the Mining Trust?"

Salau shook his head in vigorous denial but the clerk shut him up. "You and Abdul, that was the story you spread round the villages. You wanted them to rebel against the Zaki! Don't lie dog! You wanted to set Cross-river on fire with the aid of those men."

The accused spread out his hands in weariness and mumbled pious denials.

"Speak up!"

"Your Highness, they said many things. But Allah is my witness if I said anything to others against the Zaki. I ask you, who am I to raise my voice against his Highness? Sure, they said the white people had ruined the land without paying us enough and Abdul said it was only right that we should get some of the profit taken away by the white man. The white man is not my brother your Highness. I saw nothing wrong in trying to take more money out of him."

"Can you read?"

The man blinked, taken aback by the change of tack. "Can I read your Highness? No, I . . ."

"This paper you signed, you and other discontented dogs, do you know what it really says?"

"Your Highness, Abdul read it to me. All it says is that I agree that they take up my case with the Mining Trust. They called it a letter of authority."

"Is that all?"

"But your Highness, what else could there be? Abdul read it to me. I even asked how much it would cost me. Abdul is my brother-in-law. He said it would cost nothing."

"And what would you say you illiterate fool, if I told you now that that paper you signed has given your land away to these men who say they have come to help you."

"*She-ge!*" The oath came out before he could stop himself. He bowed abjectly, touched the ground with his forehead and begged forgiveness. He launched into a wail of self-pity and demanded of the heavens what sins he had committed to be so put upon. Then he remembered Abdul and stopped, round-eyed.

"But Abdul! My own brother-in-law! Your Highness must forgive me but is it really possible that my own brother-in-law would do that to me?"

The clerk gave him a look of withering pity. "When last did you see your brother-in-law?" he asked.

The man scratched his head. "I must say I have not seen him now for a month. Which is strange. He always comes to my house at least once a week."

The clerk exchanged looks with the Zaki. For the first time, a tremor of a smile hovered around the lips of the turbanned presence. On the face of the accused, a look of consternation now replaced the earlier bafflement. Then rage. He shut his eyes and silently called down the wrath of Allah on the perfidy of a kinsman, even one of the mere marriage tie, who could do this to him. The clerk observed him carefully, exchanged another look with the Zaki who nodded slightly.

The clerk's voice now changed to one of fatherly rebuke. "Now you see what you have done by placing your affairs in the hands of strangers from the South. Your father is here. You knew that if you had any trouble all you had to do was come to him. If you felt that the whitemen had cheated you, the man to turn to for redress is the man who gave them his blessing in the first place. Is that not right?"

"Your Highness is right. I have been foolish."

"You and the others, your land now belongs to aliens who pretended to be your brothers. At least the whiteman only borrowed it. He paid you and returned it to you. And part of the profit he makes he pays into the Treasury. That is how we build you roads and hospitals and schools. But you let too much greed lead you to agitate against the Zaki, your own father who has done so much for you, the only one who knows how to handle these whitemen you grumble so much about. You sign a piece of paper which you can't read and suddenly you find yourself landless."

The bereaved man catapulted himself suddenly flat on his face, arms spread out. "Forgive a miserable, ignorant dog your Highness. I am only a child who got misled. Forgive us your Highness and help us get our land back from those accursed unbelievers."

The clerk looked down on him without surprise. He turned away, leaving the prostrate man with his face in symbolic dust while he informed the Zaki of developments that had taken place over the business. The Mining Trust had sacked all employees suspected of involvement in that and other agitations. This meant all non-natives of Cross-river. Abdul was safely in one of the airless dungeons of the local administration. He would be freed only when he had been tortured into admitting that he had misled and cheated others of their land. And maybe not even then. He was too far gone with the madness to be trusted. Once on the loose he might expose the forgery and resume his agitations. The plump man nodded. For the first time he spoke with some degree of audibility.

"I want a clean sweep of Cross-river."

"They have spread wide your Highness. Trouble has already begun in the cotton mills up in Darama. The man we sent to investigate believes it is the same men. All the strongholds of the Cartel your Highness, even the cement works at Suro . . ."

The big man gestured impatiently. "They must be swept out to the last man."

The clerk complained. "It is no longer possible to tell who are the men from Aiyéró. They are not newcomers. Many have been in Cross-river for years. It is only now they have begun to show themselves in their true colours."

"The natives of Cross-river know one another. Those whom they do not know . . ." The Zaki closed his eyes in boredom, and the subject.

The clerk bowed backwards, returned to the spread-eagled occupant of the central expanse of the audience chamber.

"Get up" he snapped.

The man dragged himself together wearily, resumed his former position, squatting on his haunches.

"You have no redress in law, you know that. An agreement is an agreement. There is nothing in this world so powerful as a piece of paper to which a man has put his fingerprint, in front of witnesses. Nothing can wash the fingerprint away. You have signed away the land of your fathers to robbers from across the river."

The man murmured, "Let our father help us if he can your Highness. There is nothing more I can say."

"How many able-bodied men are there in your village?"

After thoughtful frowning the man said there might be over a hundred. The clerk nodded, "Good. Get them together. Tell them what has happened. Let them all go round and take note where all the strangers live. Take note of where they work, where they go to eat and drink. Do you understand that?"

"We will do as you say your Highness."

"Do that, but no more. Do nothing more than what you are told."

"I understand your Highness."

"There is more than one way of obtaining justice. The Zaki has decided to forgive your past foolishness. But there is to be no more nonsense. Keep your mouths shut and your eyes open. Get yourselves ready. Wait until the Zaki gives you the word. Until then, do nothing on your own."

The man touched the floor with his forehead. "I know now the Zaki has forgiven his wayward son. *Ranka dede.*"

The big man stood up. Immediately all the recumbent retinue leapt onto their haunches and gave the homage of the fist. Excepting the boy with the long lashes who rose lazily to his feet, picked up the bowl of sweetmeats and minced onto the platform. Placing his hand on the boy's head Zaki Amuri swept out of the room.

The retinue rose one after the other, wandered through the chamber aimlessly. Two squatted back onto the floor and began to gamble with a well-worn pack of cards. Mostly they meandered outside, intending to pick up gossip, their noses already full of the scent of action and relief from boredom.

A lone figure, the one who had averted his eyes from the persecuted man slunk through the courtyard of Amuri's palace. Half-brother to the incarcerated Abdul, his was the first vague warning to reach the settlement at Shage. But even he was too late.

———

They had watched as the hundreds of combat-ready soldiers, paramilitary waggon-loads and armoured cars invested the city. The darting eyes of plain-clothes security men betrayed them, their lethal bulging pockets conspicuous as they sought to mix among the crowds. Mentally, mindful of their training, perhaps they succeeded. Physically there was no crowd for them to mix with. The people stayed at home, shops and offices were shuttered in this first daylight curfew in the nation's living memory. So the fearful secret eyes of order mingled among the shadows of store frontages, merged into trees and packing-cases, merged conspicuously with the silent air and waited. And it was their fear most of all, and the hungry prowl of those impersonal armoured cars and alien cartridge belts from Cross-river in the deserted city which conveyed a plain summons to death on the dusty streets, one that none of the hidden watchers could misconstrue.

Ofeyi felt its essence as the protrusion through a slanted ridge of a toxic tuber. A man stubbed his toe on it and maybe dies; death as sowed by these false farmers, the power-men, was planned to burgeon under the soil. The offensive outcrop was only a wilful, incidental wart, a mere tip of the iceberg that might warn or kill. The real death that the people were called upon to die was the death from under, the long creeping paralysis of flesh and spirit that seized upon them as the poison tuber might spread through bowels of earth. Those noisy individual deaths were merely incidents. The real extermination went on below.

Before the first train came to a complete stop there commenced an unholy racket of boots and rifles and metal-studded rucksacks as the men leapt, jumped, crawled between the waggons as if by pre-arranged signal. The sliding doors of the freight waggons gravelled open on burnt-out castors and ungreased tracks and the soldiers who were still half-asleep at the last level-crossing dashed through openings into the rusted goods-shed of the old abandoned station. The manoeuvre was all over in a few minutes and the train once again picked up speed, rolled onwards into the modern station where the reporters waited, officially invited to witness the baselessness of rumours of the daily haul of Cross-river soldiers into the rebellious city.

"Walk through gentlemen, examine the length and breadth of the waggons and see for yourselves. Perhaps you think they are hiding in these cotton-bales? Or among the groundnut sacks? Or maybe hanging on the underside of the waggons? Gentlemen, I think your informants have been watching too many American films. This is not the Wild West you know!"

In the darkness and rust of the deserted station, barely five miles away, the reinforcements awaited dusk and assembled their weapons. Metallic clacks issuing from the still and smokeless yard only deepened the desolation of the railway yard. The sun's reflection on glazed rails seemed strident; long after the last hiss of steam from the departed train flakes of rusted iron separated and fell off the sides of the rails. Ofeyi kept his mind on the motion of such peelings, felt the exercise dissolve tension raised by the morning's sinister incursion.

"Why come ye upon our peaceful people with such fuss and noisome fright and with devilish instruments of war. . . ."

But his companion would not even permit himself a smile. "Because we invited them. You have seen dogs lay on their backs and beg to be tickled. When a people do that, they are begging to be kicked."

"It is creepier than that shrine of curses at Gborolu."

The man merely shook his head. "This is far more effective. Curses fly in the air, same as bullets, but impotent."

Curfew Town—the name was bound to stick, ousting its real name Gborolu—had been wrung dry of all propaganda juice squirted through the Corpse's organs night and day. City of the

New Era, Future Cosmopolis, its spotless ultra-modernity was a symbol of the progressive and unblemished character of the men of Jekú. It was the planned city, it proved that Jekú had a plan. An old, crumbling village, primitive, clannish and locked in decadent rituals of vengeance had been transformed into a clinical exhibition city of factories, colleges and civic contentment. Against all unrest Curfew Town was assertively immune. No tendentious propaganda could penetrate its geometric bungalows and high-walled state of welfare being.

When ledgers were questioned which could not be explained even in terms of the ever accommodating roads and projects that defied penetration, Curfew Town absorbed the missing millions into its benevolent purity and experimental essence. Look at the prototype of the future city. Prototypes are invariably costly. We must experiment. The experiment is not yet ended but the natives of Gborolu are proof and witnesses of the new quality of life and justification of the cost of providing this. Here is a report of the Secretary and Auditor to the Board of Planning, himself a native of Gborolu and a luminary among the citizenry. . . .

"I shall show you a little-known sector" Ofeyi's companion had promised, "something a little different from the supermarkets, the real Gborolu that no man of Jekú dare penetrate."

It was already night when they came upon an undulating settlement of bee-hive clusters, parked the car and began to walk. Almost at once the heady smell struck them, and it required no further sniffing to establish its nature—strong, fermenting liquor. Successive rulers, beginning with the white invaders had striven in vain to suppress an industry that won fame, it was claimed, from the quality of the water from the wells. Next to the tell-tale clumps of camouflaged distilleries, the wells were the most ubiquitous. Hardly a depression could be found in which a well had not been dug; it was a saying also that what Gborolu did not kill

with liquor it cured with its waters. In the dark damp of fermenta-
tion sheds the old women of Gborolu also nursed strange fungoid
growths to which many, even from the far metropolis, turned for
alleged miracles of pharmacy when all else had failed.

They found their way to that ancient heart of Gborolu along
tracks which wound round low hills in serpentine coils, leading
unerringly to the wraiths of incantation which rose into the night,
vibrant and raw-nerved. It was a plaint of anguish and anger, and
yet demand and prayer also, uttered mostly with a determined
impatience. They were overtaken from time to time by broken
defiles of lamp-bearing figures; in the still air the incense of oil
rose and hung heavily, clogging the distant trill to which late-
comers were hastening preceded by the earthy smell of palm oil.
The Dentist led him onto a hillock; once on higher ground they
could observe the entire scene of a thousand flickering lights coil-
ing in and out of dark clumps and moving in the direction of
the chorus of incantation until at last they joined a vast basin of
lights from where the chanting had commenced. From the valley
bottom they rose higher and higher up the sides until Gborolu
became a subaqueous cave to whose sides clung thousands of tiny
limpets, luminous with soft dull metallic fires. From the centre of
it, propelled by an urgency of pain and bitterness came the chant
which became more recognizable as it was swelled by voices of the
new arrivals—a chant of curses and excommunication. Pausing
hardly for breath it rose and fell, shaped and toned as though by
those convoluting tracks through which they had come, modu-
lated around the rhythms of the hills, a blend of Gborolu's herbs
and unguents floating on oil exhalations from the burning lamps
of hate.

The names were audible to the listeners, and the intensity of
uttered maledictions . . . "water is enough for a load, may it weigh
you down but never slake your thirst . . . may you be remem-

bered as we remember carrion . . . the tree of hate you planted
has touched the sky of pride—it must fall on you when you shelter beneath it . . . the death of a viper brings joy to the farmer's
household—may you bring joy to the heart of Gborolu. . . ."

And the names, punctuating the curses, over and over again . . .
the Cartel quads, the Jekú leaders . . .

If a collective intensity could alter the course of history, or a
pooling of psychic strength alter the path of nature . . . it was
no less easy to accept than that organ peals and the sift of light
through stained-glass windows should operate on the lateness of
rains, averting drought and the threat of smallpox. A basin of oil-
lamps and crouching shadows actually sought to disturb the peace
of mind and material ease of the four-headed beast that trampled
their dignity with iron hooves? Yet it seemed credible, at least
significant. For these were the inhabitants of the new dwellings
of concrete and glass, among them were the upholders of the new
bourgeois conceit, yet they had turned backwards and inwards in
desperation to this old eternal community of feeling which made
every spot a shrine, a temple, a pool of agony or ecstasy, which a
community of feeling, sought to transcend limitations of tramped
self and transform it, in union with others, into a weapon for aid or
destruction of distant forces. Their need—Ofeyi was none too sure
of their faith—but their need was undeniably pervasive; it reached
him, disturbed him profoundly and seemed to alter the balance
of merely sensed forces in the night air. A collision between the
cry of Gborolu, and the nightly talisman of the Cartel, whose live
burial of a cow in the dead of every night sought to preserve their
potency and guarantee a lasting ascendancy over a people that had
lately begun to rumble and shift under their feet. . . .

But in addition, the Cartel possessed the bullets. Cowed by
superstition they might sow a live cow in their backyards but,
they raised a crop of armed serpents when the need arose.

At night the soldiers poured into the city. Silently. Obedient to the death infection of the beleagured town even more than their own need for silent movements. One understood now that more than one side played the game of Gborolu. The means of this curse was however tangible, the end was the embalming of an entire people even as they breathed, deadening their nerve centres, willing the vital organs to malfunction, ending all coordination among the physical and thought processes. The peace of the town would thereupon be presented to the world—a wax composure, a dead composition of serenity.

"Whoever first invites the other to death" said the Dentist, "literally has his cake and eats it. For the recipient to pretend non-recognition of the invitation is to accept his own demise. To accept it is to meet the first man on his own terms. To misinterpret it is to deny one's intelligence, in which case we lose our sense of wholeness after, which is a form of death. In exchange for the surrender we receive a permit to remain alive, but it is really a certificate of death."

It had gone beyond the mere imposition of a curfew. The many faces which peeped through chinks in the windows to witness the filtering of alien bodies through the city's alleyways were stunned; they admitted reluctantly that they witnessed a brutal extermination of their own selves. Alien forms had come upon their will to life with an ultimatum which left them unprepared. They knew in advance that an alien intrusion was not merely an abuse of sectional boundaries but far more painfully an irritant in the eye. Open or shut the eye remains bloodshot, the resultant flow of suppurated rheum unending until the irritant is removed.

"I still insist" the Dentist commented, "self-defence is not simply waiting until a lunatic attacks you with a hatchet. When you have watched his attack on a man up the road, you don't wait any longer. But you see, you rationalists have given birth to a monster child by pretending that the lunatic can be reasoned with. That is why our people die. Because you paced in silence at the incubation of a monstrosity, preoccupied with a study of the phenomenon. Tell me, if you took a mouthful of food and you felt an acid burn your mouth, do you roll it round and round on your tongue thoughtfully or violently spit it out?"

He drove the Fire Brigade car casually in and out of barricades without drawing more than casual, perfunctory looks from the patrols. Sometimes he even received a salute. They watched the grime and coal-dust coated soldiers multiply every moment. The few private cars on the road were stopped and checked. These were the doctors and the few "essential services" men who had been issued passes, the only relief from a festoon of khaki, steel helmets and bayonets. Ofeyi found his discomfort increasing with every sidelong glance that the Dentist gave him, a glance of subtle mockery and impatience.

He groaned, "God, how I long for peace. Peace, just peace, anything for peace, that much abused, much dirtied word peace. Just peace." He paused. "Yes, that is the problem. A *just* peace."

"You are calling on a rapacious beast. One with the most ravenous but selective appetite. The more it is fed with the wrongful diet, the more determined it is to wait for the genuine sacrificial meat. It is best to feed it properly from the first. Everything else is buying time with innocent victims."

Feeling himself challenged, Ofeyi began to speak urgently. "Listen, hesitation is one thing . . ."

"It is everything" interrupted the Dentist. "It means consolidation by the opposition."

"We are discussing means. I don't want to foul up the remnants of my humanity as others do by different means. Through surrender or compromise for instance. To accept any depredations on one's total personality is to cripple oneself in more ways than one." Ofeyi looked sidelong at his companion and grinned. "After a while, even the act of making love to a woman seems to take place under sufferance. I mean, the same senses are involved. And so pleasure, even ecstasy is tainted by the coarsening of the senses through compromises. So it is hardly worth it, not even the orgasmic moment of compensation for the torments of survival. The situation, social or political situation overwhelms, fouls and corrodes even the most intimate sensations. In such a situation one is only half a man, no matter how superhuman his woman swears he is. The sentient, sensitive totality of the man recognizes that he is only a mangled part of his human potential."

The Dentist drove through cordons of intrusive bayonets and levelled sub-machine guns. Once when it appeared that a senior, intelligent looking officer intended to take a closer look at the credentials of the occupants of the car he jumped out and took the battle to him. "Are you the commanding officer? I haven't been able to get anyone on the phone but I want to know whether or not you intend to provide any special guard for the petrol storage tanks at the Ministry of Transport. It is a fire hazard and a natural target for saboteurs . . ."

Ofeyi watched, admiring his nerve. Except for details of scruple, he found himself increasingly accepting the fact that they were kindred spirits. A rage engulfed him at his imprisonment within the dilemma, an exaggeration of the mere part against the whole. There was something a little unnatural in this process of resolving the ethics of assassination, preparing oneself to accept or reject the cold-blooded necessity with a minimum of feeling. Demanding in return only the residual sensation of a freed conscience, exhilarated, a dreamless sleep, the knowledge that one has taken decision on behalf of the guiltless inmates of overcrowded prisons, of innocents disembowelled on the point of stakes, shot in the silence of their homes, pauperized and degraded by a totalitarian maul, brained by leprous accretions that even devoured their own fingers in the reckless pace of gluttony.

If it were possible—yes, that was the grim temptation—if it were possible to ignore even the unformed, irrational whisper, the purely psychic intuition, to succumb to the peace of amnesia, expunge all knowledge and define freedom as the freedom not to listen; to read only the official newspapers, to avoid conversations, refuse to open letters whose origins could not be immediately identified and thus evade the cry of distant suppliants, to shut off the strident radio and exist only in the sterilized distillation of the experiences of others, to cling only to the moments of insulating sensuality . . .

He heard the car door slam, the Dentist's voice next to his ear demanding, "What were the ravages playing on your face? You didn't imagine we were in any difficulties did you?"

He denied any lack of confidence in his guide's resourcefulness. "No, I was merely thinking."

"You have an unbelievably expressive face! But we must get out of town immediately and change this car. I have another waiting just on the outskirts. A change of clothes and we can drive back in and resume our tour of inspection."

Ofeyi nodded agreement. As they drove towards the town borders he said, almost to himself, "Do you know, his children call me Uncle."

"The most notorious murderers and mass-murderers have been noted for their love of children," was the Dentist's dry comment.

"I know my people—they are cowards!"

Batoki confronted the raised eyebrows of his guests with a confident stare and repeated, "I tell you they are cowards. When you have killed a couple of them and put away some tens behind bars, the rest will behave themselves and toe the line. If they don't, add a zero to the numbers. Kill a couple of tens of them and put some hundreds behind bars. If that doesn't break them kill a few thousands and take no more prisoners. And let them know it. If that fails I give you permission to call me a bastard."

Over a champagne dinner for his associates of the Cartel, Chief Batoki gave vent to his contempt for his own people. But his real audience was Zaki Amuri the all-powerful tyrant of Cross-river. It confirmed his own loyalty to a sodality that transcended mere regionalism. The only party that truly transcends local boundaries, Batoki chuckled as he entreated his guests to his daughter's crabmeat delicacies—"is the party that runs the mint."

"And the guns."

All three in mufti turned to the speaker, the Commandant-in-Chief who represented the fourth arm of the Cartel. His late predecessor had occupied the same seat the year before. No one drank a toast to his memory. Perhaps this omission, even of a libation to the departed prop of the Cartel occurred to him at that moment as he handed his glass to a waiter to be re-filled. The glass was already full, his confusion increased. He scraped his boots nervously on the marble floor and gulped his drink, spilling some over his ribbons. Belatedly he felt that he had made a mistake coming in uniform. Somehow he had hoped that this would impress his own power on the group; instead it simply marked him as an outsider, a tool, a mere representative symbol. Probably dispensable.

Lamely he added, "The alliance of the purse and the gun is of course . . . I mean . . . the hope of er . . . I mean, national stability."

"That reminds me" Batoki said, "I mean to change your speechwriter. He is not reliable."

"I am quite happy with his . . ." The C-in-C's voice trailed away.

Not far away, rehearsals for the big parade continued. The quarterly meeting of the Cartel would be incomplete without full-dress airing of the props of power. It was both demonstration and warning. A flexing of muscles to bring waverers back to heel. Moreover—so claimed Chief Batoki—I look in the eyes of every man on parade and, where I sense disloyalty I speak to that man. When their officer hears me ask how fares that man's family and whether he would not prefer to be near them, he knows I never want to see that man within ten miles of us.

Publicly, the pomp, the ceremony continued to fill the hollow reed with seeming substance. The trappings of authority cloaked a universal abomination and Batoki became the secondary cause for a people's unanimity, expended though it was on hatred and loathing. Even to such a mockery of their strength were they reduced. Nerved to a pitch of destructiveness they hurled the granite boulders anyway, hurled them at targets far beyond their reach. The missiles fell short, fell often on themselves. The head they sought to stick on a public pike clowned through the passages and sounds of death, himself inaccessible.

Protected by an army of minions, Zaki Amuri remained equally immune in Cross-river.

Chief Biga paraded boldly where he pleased, surrounded by motorcades of his private army.

The Commandant-in-Chief carried out orders, made speeches as they were drafted by the civilian trio; but the genius of their language was Batoki himself.

And Batoki sowed a forest of bayonets in the sun, laughed through the curses of the people and mocked their tears of frustration. He was endowed with the patience of a lizard and he bridged time with mounds of the dead and mutilated.

In those fields which surrounded a bristling network of aerials and teleprinter waves the desperate gecko was decked in the

colours of authority. Amidst quasi-military manoeuvres, the provincial police bands polished their pieces while the shock-squads
polished their batons and boots while the drill-major in his baggy
shorts shrilled his orders at the ever increasing corps of recruits—
"Wait the corner, wait the corner before you sharp wheel!"—
himself the very antithesis of precision.

On that rehearsal trip Ofeyi had fastened on the discordance of
the drill major, his old parchment face a slip in bureaucratic post-
ings, more comic mascot than drill-major. It recreated an idyllic
image of slumber and fallen corrugated sheets, browsing goats in
thoroughfares and the solitary patrol of the village head in an ex-
serviceman's cast-offs. Remote from the present reality.

"I know my people" Batoki continued to insist, "I tell you they
are cowards. God must be on our side or he would never have
made them such cowards." This time, to his wife and daughter.

The brass band played Viennese waltzes. An officer in gleaming
turnout crossed himself repeatedly sword in hand, marched up
and down, inspected the lines with a stand-in for Chief Batoki.
The drill major with his bunch of recruits looked over to where
the professionals drilled and pointed the example to his wards.
"Look over there and see what you have to do." He sighed, bit
into a colanut and muttered, "Ah, in the time of D.O.s and those
white governors in their white uniforms and gold buttons, beautiful medals all the way across the breast. Now those were men
worth all this energy, not like these present fools . . ." He turned
sharply on his giggling row of recruits and they quickly dried up.

"Unfortunately" the Dentist muttered, "I've lost my telescopic
sight—smashed in an accident. A parade of this kind would have
been ideal. So I have to get closer you see. More risk. I can't afford
an error in decision because I cannot repeat the same trick twice.
So I have to know whose elimination will most weaken the Cartel.
We must be effective."

The guns of the rehearsing guard of honour—all from Cross-river, Batoki would not take a chance with his own people—their guns looked deceptively like toys. Varnish on the stocks appeared too shiny and the straps from which the guns were suspended over their shoulders looked like the retrieving thongs for cork missiles. That, and the games excitement on the faces of watching recruits made it all a Saturday afternoon village parade. Ofeyi pictured the ancient sitting on his verandah, firing cork missiles at stubborn goats.

"Czech made" the Dentist commented, handing Ofeyi his bin-oculars. "Fires twelve rounds. Pounds lighter than the average air-gun believe it or not."

Ofeyi put the lenses to his eyes and wondered how from the midst of this treachery that elusive justice could ever be retrieved. Tangled in a mesh of aerials, among high-tension hammocks and scrambled pulses and electronic codes, dragged along undiscrimi-nating air-tracks onto beetle-nosed troop carriers, to cordons of cartridge-belts and enslaved to one colossal usurpation of a thou-sand minds. One had to presume that they had minds, these drill-ing automatons. Something is bought at a salary, something is surrendered, something is swapped for the legal glow of dealing death. Whatever this was, it had been taken in hand, caught in the warp of one megalomaniac mind. To release these minds, it was difficult to escape the thought that the shortest and justest course was—to use the Dentist's phrasing—elimination!

The wires seemed to emit nothing but aeons of destruction. He felt his skin crackle under their bombardment. Among a wel-ter of images one that constantly monopolised evocation was the mystery of a woman dead of machine-gun bullets, whose hand still tightly clutched an infant's legs. The infant's head was a pulp of brain and bone. Did madness enter her with that same bul-let which first passed through the child that was feeding at her breast? The breast hung free and her milk had mingled in blood to paint a testament of damnation on earth, beside spilled peppers, an upturned stool and a bowl of pap. Even the soldiers had been afraid to touch her where she lay. A tourist, a total stranger had recorded the scene long after the departure of the death-dealers.

It seemed a sacrilege, with memories such as this, to admit to death-wish as contained in a refusal to accept the burden of decision when that decision could—if the Dentist was right—end all repetition of such images as this. The truth was too bare for self-deceit, the call for urgent action too strident for any evasion. The Dentist appeared to have set his course on the only possible sanity, leaving the rest slaves to rationalist or emotive fantasies.

"If we could line them all up, publicly, against that white-washed wall and shoot them, then we should. But we cannot. We lack the means. But we can take them out one by one, hitting them from safety. You must know that each successful elimination makes the next doubly difficult. My role survives on borrowed time; that time must serve the most effective purpose. That is where you come in, you have known them longer, so you must tell me who goes first." He gave one of his rare smiles. "I sometimes think it should be the member from Cross-river. Isn't he supposed to be the real power? If we eliminate him, Batoki would die of a heart attack, so that would be two with one bullet. Is that a merely fantastic idea?"

Ofeyi shook his head. "Batoki may appear obsequiously dependent on him but he is much tougher than that."

Demakin nodded slowly. "Yes, at other times I think that too."

There remained the miasma of unreality through which Ofeyi tried to cut by brutal phrasing. Shaking his head he said, "You do realize what you are asking me don't you? Who do I first assassinate?"

"Yes. You've seen their preparations, evidence of a costly

rehearsal for the real blitz. If there is a better way to stop them, tell me and I'll carry it out. Otherwise just answer the question—which of them must I first pursue and—kill?" He returned the binoculars to its case. "I have to plan. I do not forgive myself mistakes."

"You know almost as much as I do about them," Ofeyi grumbled.

"Almost, but not quite as much. If I choose and make a mistake, the responsibility is yours."

Batoki, acknowledged clown of the team, but also the subtlest strategist: did that make him the lynch-pin of the vicious ring? It was he who first thought of recruiting whites from South Africa into the Secret Police: "if their methods weren't good their minority wouldn't still be in control." Kilgard with his hunched back, rheumy eyes and scalpel thin smile became the forerunner of a trickle of experts on the many refinements of interrogation. And Kilgard was also fond of black children, stopped his car to chuck them under the chin, watched them roll and fight in the dust for his scattered pennies. He had no children of his own, sighed and told Batoki he envied him his beautiful family—in between reports and secret orders, at all hours night and day. Until he was so much one of the family that they also called him Uncle.

A habit of age deference, a virtue adapted from tradition, Ofeyi ruefully reflected, which their undiscriminating nature had also applied to him. Excepting Biye the eldest they all called him Uncle. She had quickly become the lady. As soon as she felt old enough she began to call him by name, her thin voice rising to a crescendo of shrillness in frustration at his failure to take her advice, echoing her father's words.

The enemy, to him, was not faceless, not without flesh and

blood. Ties. Even pleasant recollections of past association. Batoki especially he knew, had supped often at his family board, even flirted inconclusively with his precocious daughter, Biye. And Batoki had tried to use this link to tear him from his course. He heard the father's calculating comments in her salvationist intensity.

"Why do you mix with these gutter boys, these riffraffs. They are rotten with envy, their lives are built around nothing. Why do you pretend that you do not have a background as decent as ours for instance? You have nothing in common with them!"

"Listen to me Biye . . ."

"No I won't listen. You waste yourself on these dregs of society. They want to turn the country upside down because they have nothing in themselves. They want to drag everyone down to their own level. Can you imagine it, only the other day one of them, these so-called communists said to my father . . ."

His hand had sought hers and he tried to interrupt. "That is the trouble. You listen too much to your father."

"And you try to pretend you have none. You pretend you sprang from nowhere, you have turned your back on your own background. They are merely using you Ofe, you know nothing of how insecure and insignificant their existence would be without people like you!"

A loud, mocking whistle. "Whew! All these big words. . . ."

"Be serious Ofe. Look, my father likes you. He doesn't really understand you but he likes you. That is why he made the Corporation send you on that study tour, to give you time to cool down. They were beginning to round up troublemakers. Look, ask anything, any post you want. You know it's yours for the asking. My father really respects you. He respects your family. He wants to help you. So why do you abuse your intelligence by keeping company with these born losers?"

Depressed by her impregnable insulation, the crust of which had coarsened by daily proximity to such a man as her father, he could only offer her the simplest advice to take back to the man. "Tell him to leave the country, and quickly. Tell him to stop using you, to stop abusing your beautiful generous nature. You give with such admirable ease, so selflessly. But it is also thoughtless giving and this will only lead you to despair. He will eat you up. He is like those ancient witches of ours who must eat up their young to rejuvenate themselves. Don't let him eat you up!"

He felt the sting on his face, then the shock and wonder on hers as she realized that she had actually slapped "Uncle" Ofeyi. At that moment, he felt protectively drawn to her by her very fragility. In spite of the fawning and flattering which went with her status as favourite daughter of one of the "terrible quads," in spite of winters and summers in villas on millionaire beaches from Capri to Miami where she ran sands and fortunes through her fingers, in spite of pampering by a hundred commercial relations, the world-wide extended families of the Cocoa Cartel, the state balls and state parades and hostessing on nights of diplomatic assemblage on her father's lawns, her vulnerable self and lack of brains stuck scarecrow bones through affluent pretensions. She never could, despite her undoubted vitality, endure the punishment of pace. Often before the night was over, she barely managed to animate a face of crinkled negligee abandoned on a winter line, frozen in fragile folds. The shock of her impulsive action drained the last drop of self-assurance from her face leaving only a shell of tiredness and a suspicion that Ofeyi might be right, that she never truly permitted herself to think. It led to her breaking down completely, tearfully begging his advice.

"Take a holiday," he counselled. "Forget what is happening here. Divorce yourself from the enjoyment you have begun to take from being Batoki's daughter. Go and study something and leave your father to stew in his own juice if he will not take the advice I gave you earlier. Go to one of those summer resorts your father has bought himself with our people's money."

Too late he realized that he had again aroused her fierce loyalty. There was perhaps something admirable in such pride but Ofeyi shook his head in pity, knowing that she would only destroy herself in the process. And now to quicken that process, as he must, by nominating the father for prior choice in the round of elimination? And if another? Domestic scenes filled with other Biyes, Habibas, Chinyeres rising before his eyes.

And the other image also, in violent protest, the faceless mother whose fingers even in death rigor still clutched the legs of an infant with a pulped head. . . .

Biye's face was flashing past him, hissing, "I thought you could be saved but you belong in the gutter, you and the rest of the social failures who call themselves radicals."

Staring at her vacated chair he could only regret that they were not even her own thoughts, much less words. The crime of Batoki and his vulgar noisy circle became even more heinous, acquiring dimension in its deliberate corruption of susceptible minds, creating mindless captive loyalties from dependants by blood or by inducements. This intimate corruption of their power loomed larger in the scale of menace than the catalogue of brazen thievery and daylight massacres.

4

HARVEST

IX

Ofeyi turned the car into the lesser used road, feeling a need to gather and store within himself all the calm and peace that such routes could offer. Soon there would be none of the serenity on the face of nature, no moisture in the soil, no leaves on the wind.

They came to the grove of rain-trees, the famous stretch planted by a now forgotten missionary eccentric. It led from the small town of Omola and spread for miles in an arcade of interwoven branches high above the road. The sun filtered through in yellow shafts, weightless insubstantial bamboos, organ-pipes which yielded to contact on the car, ran lightly over the panels, ran through the windscreen and played on their faces. Birdsong came down those gilded pipes, played among the restful shadows.

Sensations, mere sensations. He felt as always dissatisfied, cheated. These golden wafers were so cruelly beguiling, he stretched his hand through the window and they danced all over his arm in elfin abandon. Within that glade they were cut off from the world, wrapped in a mist of sun motes in a forest of song. Ofeyi sank deep into the enchantment, consoling himself by thinking, I store it up for later needs.

He glanced at Zaccheus. He looked bound also underneath the spell. When the last pair of trees had diminished to a garden shrub in the mirror Ofeyi spoke at last. "Places like that seem to possess reserves of healing powers." And this idea of healing possessed him again in his legacy of an older experience. "I knew a man" he began, "some sort of madman, I suppose. His obsession was numbers. Weights and measures, distances, money. And he would rattle off these figures at a speed that gave you no time to catch on. You never knew what the figures actually meant for him or what he did with them—addition or subtraction, multiplication or what. He was a school-teacher before he went mad. Maybe he taught mathematics. He came round to the compound where we lived, once a week, sat down in the front room and proceeded to assess each household millions and millions of pounds. It had to be paid on the spot. After a long sermon of numbers he would accept a settlement of sixpence or threepence and enter it most meticulously in a ragged notebook, tear off a receipt and read out the balance owed to the last zero on the million pounds and the last fraction of the pence.

"Well, one day came the big surprise. A little girl in our compound was suffering from stomach cramps. There she was writhing on the pavement with no one able to help her. She was a playmate, my own age, so you can imagine what I suffered watching her agony. Then our madman arrived. At first he did nothing, just stood there watching. Then his eyes lightened up, he smiled—it was an awe-inspiring, beatific smile, he smiled as if everything had become clear to him. It was the smile of enlightenment. And he walked over to a grass verge, plucked up a tuft of grass, returned and bent over the girl, held the grass to her navel and began his familiar incantation of figures. Only there was a difference. He wasn't reading his usual electricity bills and water rates or any such familiar pattern. The style was still the same effortless recital, the skin off the surface of some deep cultic fount of figures but it was, in some indefinable way, somewhat different from what we were accustomed to hearing. Two minutes later perhaps, maybe less, the girl's thrashing stopped, she grew quiet and in another minute she was fast asleep.

"He sat beside her on that pavement while she slept fifteen, maybe thirty minutes. Maybe an hour. Time has rather different dimensions in one's childhood. The girl woke, saw him, screamed and ran away just as she used to. Some of the children were really afraid of him. But he only smiled, got up, dusted his trousers and said he must be away. Then he remained on his feet for a long stretch of time. He looked slowly up and began to stare at the stars while I waited to invite him to the house. I liked him and wasn't afraid of him, I believed in fact that he was my very special property. So I invited him into the house. But he said, oh no, not tonight, and began to move off. I ran after him and asked how he did it. Was it magic, I wanted to know. He smiled and said no, anyone can do it. I said, even I? Can I do it? He stopped, took my hands in his and looked at them for a long time. We both stood completely still under the starlight, he calm and still and filled with a remote self-assurance, I with my heart pounding fit to burst. And he gave that sweet-sad smile again and said, Oh yes, you especially. Now run back home.

"That was the last I ever saw of him, I or anyone else. He simply never came back. Now first tell me what you make of it and I'll tell you my own theories . . . Zaccheus!"

Zaccheus snored on.

Morosely Ofeyi remembered that bad news exhausted the

bearer much faster than good. If anything good tidings was a shot of adrenalin; on Zaccheus it would even act as a compound jab of hormones and the purest essence of caffeine. A lucky fact that, it had forced him to centre his feelings on that never before encountered image of the band-leader, sorry and bedraggled, an orphaned chicken, the lone survivor of a flood-swept brood. One look at him, and Ofeyi had braced himself.

Drawn by memories from her dark intuitions, he had returned to the same room on his return from Aiyéró and lain on the bed, feeling his apprehensive thoughts change course towards an affirmation of loss. And when it came he found himself strangely prepared, even welcoming. He watched it enter her room on Zaccheus' hesitant feet; the pressure on the doorknob and the silent opening door seemed part of the response to that cumulative apprehension that lay within. The sunlight pencilled thinly along the floor, widened to a yellow frame for that intuition to materialize. Zaccheus turned his back on the room, his big sheepish hands fumbled to re-lock the door, he stood on one leg and wished to turn back in flight, every phrase rehearsed a hundred times on the long journey back clean vanished from his mind. When he turned round again the jacket seemed to sag down his shoulders of its own impatient will, shabbily portentous. The door was not well shut; as it swung open again Ofeyi raised his hand to shield his eyes from the widening glare so Zaccheus took his cue from that, glancing briefly at the jar of cocoaine on a chair by the bedside.

"Hangover?"

"No. Come in and shut the door."

Again Zaccheus took so long that Ofeyi had time to watch him grope for words. So he sank back into bed and tried to return his mind to the mood of self-preparation that had assailed him since he woke up after the long journey back from Ahime's tale of catastrophe in Cross-river. His eyes had opened to the red ether of her room and he came out of sleep muttering, the world is dead and I am sole survivor . . . nothing left but shadows, nothing but shadows. . . .

Zaccheus, as a first confirmation was literally a shadow of himself. Ofeyi felt a little stronger and smiled. The musician turned on his padded, considerate feet and lifted a chair out from under the table without disturbing a dust mote. He was a large apologetic figure of pathos, moving about the febrile dark like a fat powdery moth. And then he flapped his wings down his side suddenly and bellowed,

"That was hell man, hell!"

Ofeyi spun out the moments, pushed the jar a little way on the chair and Zaccheus had to lean over sharply to save it from tipping over. He grasped it gratefully and gulped, cradled the jar on his knee against a heaving paunch. Egbo fastened his gaze on the film of amber in the glass, waiting. He watched Zaccheus take his time, glad now that he had chosen to wait there, in the room which was so uncompromisingly hers. Strangely he felt protected, even tightly sheathed against the impact of disaster. It was a sheath of her own colours, scents, sounds and textures. At first it had all but choked and constricted him, then it merely settled over him, lightly and evenly. Awaiting what he knew Zaccheus had come to say he consoled himself that if he had to be sucked into the vortex of loss it should be from within this sheath, he would measure out the desolation cup by cup and dilute it in her yet fluid essence, drown himself in it. In the region of his stomach he felt the beginning of anxious contraction and recognized in it the need to adjust to a yawning emptiness.

Since Zaccheus appeared to have finally lost his voice he asked, "Where is she?"

Then the words rushed out. "We didn't know a thing until it hit us. We didn't know the town was already soaking in blood and we just went on playing. Then they hit us. Not just the mob. It wasn't the mob that did for us, it was the soldiers themselves. The club is some way off the main road and that's why we didn't know a thing. We were right in the middle of a number when they broke in. From nowhere and everywhere. They just burst in man and the bullets began to fly. I had never been that close to those things man, I just didn't know what was going on. It was every man for himself. I'm telling you the straight thing man, call me what you like. I didn't remember nobody. Nobody, not even Celestial. I didn't remember God to pray to. Man, I just ran. The noise! You didn't see a thing with that noise going, don't let anyone tell you noise doesn't affect the eye."

"So you don't know what happened to her."

There was a long silence from Zaccheus, finally he looked straight at him. "Ofe, I do."

He swallowed, shifted about in the chair and swore. "Listen, when I got out of that hall—I don't really recall how, but I found myself running on the driveway—I found myself heading for a group of those bastards and they were heading straight for me. I plunged right into the bushes on the side and—don't ask me why, maybe I just thought it was the safest place, but I just began to shin up a tree. Maybe it was the right thing to do but they didn't pay much attention to me, just let loose a couple of hundred shots at the tree and moved on. Maybe they didn't see how I could survive that blast. I don't see how I did, come to think of it 'cause thick branches were falling in shreds all around me. They must have thought I was part of the crashing wood or something. Anyway I was still there, much higher up when the whole group ran back. They had Iri with them and she was scratching and cursing and kicking like you know how she can. They threw her into the Land Rover still screaming the town awake. Well I'm not a brave man Ofe, just the band is my whole life but, well I don't know how, but I couldn't let Celestial down. I shinned down that tree fast and ran to where B-Sharp was parked and drove after them. They were too busy sitting down on Celestial to keep her down to pay any attention to the big car following them."

Zaccheus swallowed nervously, got up and slammed the open wardrobe door against the wall. "Calm down" Ofeyi said. "Just tell me what happened; you already did more than most men would have done so stop kicking yourself."

"Well it petered out man, that's where it all petered out. I saw her carried into a house. Big house with high barbed wires and a large gate. I hung around for the rest of the day from a long distance. It was guarded by those wild men. Later I found that it belonged to some business man from down here. Some officer had taken it over for his quarters."

"The owner, do you know what happened to him?"

"Guess man. They split his family open before his eyes then dragged him live through the streets tied him to their Land Rover. I saw the rest of him where they tossed him. Two days and he still wasn't dead Ofeyi. His eyelids move, but that's all. The flies on him were more alive."

"You could find your way back to the house?"

"Sure Ofe but . . . wait a minute man, what are you thinking of?"

Ofeyi gestured to writing materials on the table. "Draw me a map how to get there."

Zaccheus stared at him for a long time. "You're crazy man."

"I said, draw me a map!"

"Nothing doing man."

"Zaccheus!"

The band-leader squared his shoulders stubbornly. "I'm not helping you to commit suicide so get it out of your head. What do you think man, just what do you think? I've lost my band. One-third died in the first rain of bullets, a third are dying or crippled in hospitals and the rest are scattered by now over the corners of the earth. I found our driver in the bush, not far from where the car was parked with all his stomach gone. Just what are you going to do with a map you tell me that."

Ofeyi stood up and began to put on his clothes. "It shouldn't be too difficult to find such a house anyway."

Zaccheus flopped down on the chair and rocked to and fro. "God help me, I thought you had more sense. I thought you had more sense man or I would have scattered myself all over the globe like the rest of my band sooner than come to you. I didn't have to, shit man I didn't owe you no bad news. I've been giving you eyewitness man, not something I picked up in the market. I've seen women's bodies lying there with the breasts cut off and children with their brains smashed on walls. What do you think I'm telling you man? Why do you want to go and get yourself killed? You think they don't know you there? You think they are not waiting for you?"

Ofeyi stood behind him, kneading his shoulders to calm him down. The plump figure blubbered like a child, Ofeyi gently forced his head forward as he worked the tensed muscles of his neck. The tears ran down unchecked, soaking his trousers at the thighs. "Damn you man, damn you to hell! Why can't you just let it break your heart like any decent man and go away and get it over with. I know what they are and I'm telling you even if she isn't dead by now . . ."

Ofeyi clamped a hand over his mouth. "Don't say any more Zack. I am trying hard to shut off my mind. Either help me or shut up." He released the imprisoned mouth slowly, turned back to fasten his shirt.

Zaccheus sighed. "I am not trying to be gloomy. But while I was there Ofe, a fly couldn't step out of doors to feed on the bodies without risking a bayonet or bullet in the guts."

"How did you get back?" Ofeyi asked him.

"By train, how else? B-Sharp is stuck out there, I don't want to see it ever again, no sir, not with the ghosts of all those boys hanging loose among the seats. Second Trumpet. Bass Guitar. You go out in the streets with a plate number which says you came from down this side of the river and man, you go right over the other side of that much wider river. After the first day of foolishness I just parked it some steps off the main road and forgot all about it. I didn't want B-Sharp for my hearse when it came to the point, although if anyone had asked me before I would have said, Sure, bury me in B-Sharp, I don't need no coffin." Minutes later he added, "It would be cheaper than a coffin anyway."

"You couldn't dig a hole big enough to contain it," Ofeyi countered.

"Who said anything about digging a hole? Have you seen some of those ravines up that way? They would swallow a liner, no trouble!"

Ofeyi gave him a little more time to collect himself. "Are you going to draw me that map?" he again demanded, making it obvious that he had asked for it for the last time.

Zaccheus shook his head with equal defiance. "Forget it man. I know she was something special to you. She was with me too, with all the boys, with anyone who had eyes on the skin. I know it was like falling for the way dawn breaks after an all-night stand. You think your marrow is all dried up and then the blood comes rushing up again when you see Celestial. What I'm trying to tell you Ofe is, this dawn won't ever break again. . . ."

"Will you draw the map?"

Zaccheus shook his head. "What I had in mind when I came down on the train was, Ofe's got to have connections, even among the khaki thugs. You can get hold of one of them and make him handle it. It's the only way man. . . ."

Ofeyi sat on the bed and faced him. "That also Zaccheus, that too. But you must know I can't stay here, not for one moment. Just draw me the map and I'll ask no more of you."

Zaccheus accepted what he had feared all along. Ofeyi would prove ultimately unreasonable, and he could not let him go on his own. He shrugged his shoulders, said, "Okay, let's go." Ofeyi hesitated a fraction, then nodded, planning to dislodge him just before they left town. Zaccheus guessed his intentions from the speed of his acquiescence, refused to quit the motorcar when Ofeyi began his round of pretexts.

Ofeyi thought hard while Zaccheus slept. It could have been just another raid. A private club, especially if frequented mostly by aliens in Cross-river would be a natural target for spoliation, yet his mind returned again and again to Aristo and his thoughtless, perverted antics. Once Ofeyi had asked him for his business card. Pleased and unsuspecting the salesman whipped one out of a breastpocket with practised flourish. Ofeyi knew what was on it; under the salesman's real name was printed, in gold cursive, his own self-imposed title: Aristocrat of Salesmen. Ofeyi took out a pen and scratched off Salesmen, substituting it with Ponces. Aristo knew what he meant when Ofeyi returned the card to him. Unabashed he laughed and boasted Iriyise would be riding in some big man's Buick before the year was out. "What do you want with her man, what does she mean to you? Nothing. Dames like her need to make it while the going is good. Don't mess up her chances, she's not your type." Then he changed tactics, placed a confidential arm around Ofeyi's shoulders and tried to pull him aside. "I'll make a deal with you. You go on taking your slice off the dame and I'll see that Sugar Daddy doesn't suspect a thing."

Ofeyi had done nothing to him. If he flattened him he would have picked himself up, dusted his Tyrolean hat and "mentioned" the incident to his client. . . . That's what we suffer Chief, that's what we get out of bringing two people together who need each other. You need her, she needs you. But does that dog in the manger know it? No. And when you try to tell him he bites . . . Something would change hands then, a token "danger allowance" in the line of duty. Aristo would weigh it casually, absent-mindedly, shove it in his coat-pocket with a—Yah, maybe I can use it to bribe one of the bandboys to take my messages. Saves me getting tangled up with that gorilla again. Ofeyi reflected often on the extended menace of the Aristos of his generation. A refusal in them to accept the mysterious nature of values, a sense of being personally threatened by a hint of such values which they had never entered and could not. They needed to deny the possibility, destroy it by levelling the threat with whatever was most recognizably corrupt. Their potential menace was unlimited because they failed to recognize the context of their actions beyond immediate benefit, benefit that was not even always tangibly material. No, there was only the pleasure of being associated with an act of desecration in order to buttress their own unreasoned denial with spurious grandeur. So Ofeyi responded by offering him Iriyise for himself—you take her, yes, why don't you pursue her for yourself? That makes more sense to me. Or don't you want her? And for once he saw Aristo lose his nerve, stare at him as he would a madman and take to his heels.

When Zaccheus woke up he asked him who had arranged their itinerary.

"Aristo of course. It's his new sales beat. We were there to do the usual for his sales drive. You know the routine."

"Yes of course. But was he there that night?"

Zaccheus thought hard, his eyes grew larger. "Hey, what are you thinking man? You surely don't think . . ."

"Aristo is a fool. He never knows quite what he gets himself into."

"No no I've told you. You've got it all cock-eyed there. It was a general no-favourite no-exception craze. He couldn't have brought those swine on us."

"Aristo is a thoughtless opportunist."

Zaccheus shook his head in firm rejection. "No man, not this time. You are way way off. When we get there you'll see what I mean. Not a ghost in the streets Ofe. Just the flies and the vultures and the bully-boys raking every movement with their bullets. Aristo couldn't move fast enough to exploit that situation."

"Maybe you're right. But they did come for her. They didn't just come to raid an enemy hang-out and maybe capture a beautiful slave. They came for her and were ready to kill the lot of you even without your standing in the way. They did not want any witnesses. Look Zack, they *knew* she was there. Whoever organized it knew where to find her."

"Sure they knew. Didn't we have posters all over the place?"

"Aristo had been trying to sell her to that gross Cross-river quad of the Cartel. I know he took the news of my last session with the Corpse to him—in person. By air. The trouble-shooter entrusted him with the report."

Zaccheus looked at him as if he now suspected his reason. "So you think Amuri set up the whole thing, shot up the town and extended it all over Cross-river just for one dame? Look man, I know Celestial does funny things to men. . . ."

"Iri was just a personal bonus. So was what was done to your band. They were after the men of Aiyéró everywhere. But they have to disguise it by unleashing death on a far wider scale."

The moth caress of Iriyise's scented room had not stopped the dreams of Anubis, the jackal-headed one, once he had absorbed the scope of the Cross-river event. He had fallen asleep thinking, this is the fifth face of the Apocalypse, the eighth plague that the

Judaic sorcerer had omitted to include—the plague of rabid dogs. Cramped half-asleep between the bed and wall he watched the thousands and thousands of the slavering bare-fanged creatures emerge out of the corner of the floor and rush him. He turned and fled but his feet were trapped beneath a boulder. Struggling in vain to free himself he hit on the only salvation and bared his teeth, pronged and flaring just like the swarm whose spear-point snouts were aimed in unison at his throat. Miraculously he found that his teeth were no longer human, that his jowls dribbled the dirty-ash, crimson-blotched spittle of a recent bestial banquet. His neck grew warm at the back as hairs rose on them in defiance and, most wonderful of all, the sound that came from his throat was a perfected howl, fiercer than their prey-scenting wail. Kicking his leg furiously he woke and found it wedged between the bedpost and the wall.

Was this the truth of man-wrought plagues, and was it the secret of their confidence, those men who unleashed such terror on the innocent? Was it the certainty that once the pack began to hunt, after the first selective base of a night of Long Knives the instruments achieved a transformation in their own nature and even innocents donned a mask of the jackal to ensure safety from the hunting pack? In turn becoming one with the nature of bestial transformations of the human mind. How else explain the thorough, undiscriminating measure of the mob infection, the unholy glee on the faces of women, even children. He knew what games they played with victims whom their men had left half-dead, could see clearly those who even filled the role of beaters for the hunt, flushing out half-crazed fugitives from their hiding-place. And even participating in the day-long games of mutilation.

"Do you think it is over?" he asked Zaccheus.

Zaccheus shrugged. "Last I heard the forces of law and order had taken charge. But they said that the very first day."

Thirty miles north of his question Ofeyi flung himself suddenly sideways away from the window against Zaccheus, taking the car to the other side of the road, one arm instinct-flung against the hurtling blur from nowhere. The car side-swiped a shea-butter tree and was partly hurled back onto the road, one set of wheels churning the sides of a runnel in a prolonged fight for control. Rear bumper and undercarriage finally brought the car to a stop after scraping a ten-yard furrow in the road shoulder facing the direction from which they had come. They leapt out in panic, half expecting the car to burst into flames. The springs still danced madly as Ofeyi took a step towards the object that had caused it all, a brown matted bundle that now lay motionless in the middle of the road.

Zaccheus joined him and they stared at the bundle. "Is it a monkey?"

"Looks like it."

It was quite some distance back. The engine was still ticking and neither of them had thought to turn it off. Ofeyi said, strangely, "We'll drive slowly towards it."

"Why, do you think it will bite. It's dead." And began to walk towards the body when Ofeyi pulled him back.

"Wait. That monkey is wearing clothes."

Zaccheus blinked repeatedly, shook his head. "You are seeing things man." And he moved again towards it.

"Stop Zack! Get in the car! We'll drive towards it." Laughing, Zaccheus refused to budge. "There has been no circus in these parts to the best of my knowledge, but come on let's go see."

Between his teeth Ofeyi muttered, "I hope the car isn't crippled." Zaccheus waddled round the vehicle to inspect the wheels, returned to announce that they were free of the mudguards.

Ofeyi shushed him, eyes still riveted on the object. Then he pointed to the side of the road where the object lay. A man had emerged from the bush, followed by another. Ofeyi said, "If we've hit one of them then there is no stopping. In these parts there is no word for accident, they simply deliver summary judgement. A life for a life."

Zaccheus bellowed out a loud laugh. "I told you it was a monkey. Look at them, they are hunters."

The men carried bows and arrows, daggers strapped to their upper arms. Two more emerged from the bush and soon they totalled eight. As they emerged they stood still, doing nothing, merely staring at their quarry on the road. Zaccheus sighed, "Ah well, to think I had always fancied a monkey skin. But they look too many for us."

Ofeyi asked, "So why are they standing there, just looking. Have you ever known hunters do that?"

"What are you talking about?"

"The normal hunter would rush the wounded animal at once or send one or two more arrows into it just to make sure. He wouldn't simply stand and stare at it."

The tableau held some moments longer. The two travellers had become part of it, immobilized by the strangeness of the sight, expectant also, wondering what was the meaning of the hunters' silent attitude. Ofeyi wondered if their car had been observed by the hunting group.

The monkey's skin took clearer definition as the sun broke through the trees briefly and shed a bright patch on the road. It began to look like a much lacerated skin, browned with grime and matted with burrs and twigs. At that moment also the hunters moved. They bent over the kill and one of them prodded it with the end of a bow, moved its head from side to side. From the distance where the travellers watched, it took on the appearance of a head-shrinker's handiwork.

"I could only see with the corner of my eye, and it happened too suddenly, but there was something about the way that creature flung itself at the car. . . ."

That, and the mystification of hunters who emerged from the forest not as avid pursuers but rather with the leisurely, relaxed motions of herdsmen who confidently followed the spoor of stray cattle, certain that the wanderer would be found within the stretch of pasture, unworried by the passage of time. And now, examining the casual cloak flung over their shoulder and the nomadic sandals, even the standard dagger strapped to their arms, Ofeyi became confident that they were herdsmen. They looked sweatless, as if they had participated in the chase in the certainty that they could not be outdistanced, that the victim was destined by its nature to remain within the circle of recapture. Ofeyi's mind reverted to that leap yet again, recovering details of the landscape of the road bank little before the leap. And now he was certain of large hunted eyes, waiting, certain also of a distinct flap of rags albeit mud-caked and burr-ridden and a head that, for all its skull-tightness was decidedly human.

A scene of stalking had surely preceded this. It took animation from the disintegrating tableau on the deserted road: the mea-sured pace of beaters on their own grounds in pursuit of a quarry that went round in circles. They would herd him patiently, beat the sparse growth on the perimeter of successive lairs towards the waiting line of hunters, primed for the despatch. The group had listened to his self-deluding cunning, his furtive breaks and exhausted crawl on all fours among the stunted camouflage of this scrubland. Feeding on roots, leaves, worms, retching as he ran, convulsing from unaccustomed juices and poisonous barks . . . how many days had they pursued this game? It grew clearer every minute, the passage of this fugitive who had sought safety in an isolated village, untouched (so he hoped) by the madness that had broken in the cities but in truth alerted for the prospect of such diversions where the cities had left off. From one arid death then, to this other, in a forest which cushioned its betrayal with springy earth, decaying wood and leaves that deadened the hunters' footsteps.

Finding the road at last, listening to the roar of cars and leaping madly towards that sound of safety and encountering only the real line of his killers, had he in desperation flung himself in the path of a far more humane death? For the moment continued to clarify, ceased to be a mere impression. A forceful trajectory danced before Ofeyi's eyes, emaciated claws that fought to clutch, even in that fractional moment. . . .

A movement from the stunned creature, a stirring in the matted rags, a twig, a tubercular arm scrabbled on the tar . . . again all was still. Only for an instant. The eyes of the watching group were suddenly alerted to the evidence that life still existed in him. Again the claw moved on as if it sought to smooth down the protruding pebbles. His elbow sought a feeble leverage on the ground and the head, a matted trap of seeds, berries, insect life, pollen and earth rose a little way from the ground. And only then was there animation in the eyes of his hunters who had waited, since their emergence it seemed, just for this moment. As if this flicker of life was a sign, a sanction and a command that must be fulfilled before it again petered out they swept him up, bore him onto the grass verge and held him by his wasted limbs to earth. The varnished skull of one—he seemed to be the oldest among them—rose above the others and his mouth moved, shedding what seemed to be a brief devotional fragment on the scene. Then someone unsheathed a dagger, placed it in his hand. It rose, glinted briefly in the sun and the old man stooped and drew it across the throat of the prostrate figure.

His hand moved again, this time down the body, the knife-tip drew a swift, practised circle on the crotch and his other hand held up the victim's genitals. He passed it to one of the many eager hands which also uselessly held open a jaw that had opened wide to thrust out pain. Into that mouth they stuffed his penis with the testicles. Then they all stepped back and looked on the transformation they had wrought.

Their faces betrayed neither thought nor feeling.

The blood had spouted briefly, there seemed to be little blood in him. As the mouth was held open to receive its obscene fodder it dried out, a weakened gurgle and red froth accompanied a final spasm of the limbs. His eyes stared unblinking at the sun. The men had vanished as silently into the forest as they emerged. Numbed by the scene and locked on the lifeless principal of the nightmare spectacle, neither Ofeyi nor Zaccheus had seen them go. They stood riveted to the enlarged emptiness in the stare of the dead man, incapable of motion or will. Zaccheus was the first to grow coherent, now that he had fought and controlled the bilge that rose to his throat.

"Pity he didn't die when he hit the car."

"Yes. Maybe he was trying for just that death."

"Look Ofe, these people, they never even cared to watch out in case a car came along. We were here, they never even looked our way."

"They saw us though."

"You think so?" His voice betrayed alarm. "I never saw one of them look this way."

"They saw us, that's why they waited such a long time, to see what we would do. They never stopped taking note of our presence."

Zaccheus felt cold eyes on him which he had earlier viewed as dispassionate, indifferent to his existence. Now with no other distraction, the eye-ridden bushes were turned on him and his exposed presence on that road. He began to turn nervously round when Ofeyi placed a hand on him and spoke softly.

"Don't move too suddenly Zack. I am going to start fiddling with the nearside of the car. Get in as if you were going to check something. Make it casual Zack and don't speak at all. Move!"

Zack obeyed him. He was no sooner seated in the car than Ofeyi leapt in beside him, shaking free of the paralysis which slaughter and mutilation had laid on him. A rustle in the undergrowth to the immediate rear of the car had clarified the unease in the roots of his scalp and he realized at once why the butchers had vanished so silently into the bushes. Thoughtless, or simply forgetful of the car's mechanical potency, one of the stalkers leapt in front of the car just as Ofeyi released the clutch. Zaccheus shut his eyes but Ofeyi watched the form sail over the bonnet and crash into the roadside shrubs. When Zaccheus opened his eyes again, forced against one side of the vehicle's unexpected centrifugal exertion, he found that Ofeyi instead of heading straight in the direction the car had been facing was doing a U-turn on the road so as to head back in their real direction. He began to voice his protests when he found that they were once again in the midst of the herdsmen who had poured in from the bush to help their wounded comrade. They scattered as the car roared upon them, its torn mudguard scraping the gravelly tar surface with the paralysing din of an infernal engine. The last moments, before they turned and fled, Zaccheus perceived with an air of wonder, the transformation of their impassive faces to one of disbelief, then fright and open terror. The approach of the vengeful wraith had made them human after all, responsive to fear, responsive to a superior force which held in its impersonal space a thousand possibilities that ranged from quick extinction to a lingering agony.

What he had not bargained for was the frenzy that seemed to have mounted Ofeyi in the head. He rounded the next bend in the road, stopped, swept through another U-turn that nearly landed the wheels in a rut and crept slowly back round the corner leaning out of the window to see as much as he could before the car revealed itself beyond the line of his vision.

"Steady on Ofe, what's the matter with you?" What he read on his face was a fanatic resolve to drive through again and again whenever the killers found the nerve to attempt the removal of their comrade. Zaccheus crossed himself, snapped out of his passivity and screamed at him, "Suppose the car stalls, have you thought of that. Suppose the car stalls just when we are right among them—snap out of it man! Stop taking chances and get us out of here!"

The sense Zaccheus made penetrated his cold, homicidal hate, restored him to a measure of normality as he turned the car round again after letting his head hang over the steering for what was, to Zaccheus, an interminably long time. But he was not so far restored to humanity that his eyes failed to scan the surrounding bushes as he drove slowly, hoping that some overweening folly would prompt some others of the killer group to challenge the passage of his chariot of wrath.

Zaccheus remained thoughtful. "Are you sure you ought to be going into this thing? It isn't going to be healthy for us if you intend to ram every single murder crowd that we happen on in the city."

"I'm sorry." He stepped on the throttle and tore out of the neighbourhood. Zaccheus pointed at the speedometer to slow him down.

He began to drive with more harmonic concentration, bringing his mind into flow with the functioning of the engine, washing his rage, then his over-responsive skin through air-stream, fumigating his psyche through the invisible exhaust. The captive body of wind within the car framed its own world among capricious elements, and that went also for the metal that defined it, a capsule in alien winds obedient to the touch of his fingers. Calmness returned, and with it a sense of exultation.

They drove through catland, the high grass expanse interspersed with shrub shaded waterholes, pocked by anthills, thorn trees, baobab and the locust bean trees. Beyond the vultures and a few hidden hyenas, nothing moved in these grasslands but the cats, and he came gradually to feel the existence of one, even of the advertizing variety right beneath his bonnet. It was a soothing sensation. Nothing filtered through into the saloon but the purring contentment of the sleek-furred creature coiled among the maze of wires, cylinders, bolts and knots. It defied the outer furnace of a sun that burnt fiercer as they moved ever northwards, passed a feral tingle into his fingertips which became sensitive to road surface, wind-drag, to sun haze and the shadow flash of passing vultures. His bare toes on the pedals traced the course of fuel atoms from the source of combustion, felt the easy rhythms of pistons in their cylinders. Leaves blew in his hair, the catwind sniffed his tyre spoors, he experienced again the oiling of his viscera as when he watched the mechanic slurp the dark viscostatic fluid—patronized by all the major firms sir, all those who have to depend on efficient transport—relaxing fully, he admitted that when the car spun seemingly on only two wheels he distinctly sensed the heavy colloid hold the vehicle in a maternal ease.

"I am all right now" he said to Zaccheus.

"B-Sharp, dead-on!" Zaccheus said. "I felt it the way you been handling this baby."

Through circuits of radiated calm and into the narrow rain-belt of Shage. The landscape turned deciduous. Heavy lianas tangled treetops close to the sky, braided by the leaps of monkey clans through dense, seemingly impenetrable ceilings in the forest. The silence had long died that accompanied them on the last hundred miles; suddenly the air was filled with the caterwauling crashes in this misplaced kingdom of Rana. Only Tarzan was missing, the ultimate primate of colonial fantasies, seated astride a trumpet advance and the flap-ears of pachydermous faithfulness. But nothing broke through the dense branches, nothing but the shrill escort of the long-tailed tumblers of Rana's court; they pursued them on their skyways of lianas into the rain belt, furious twilight demons shrieking execrations to the last. Ofeyi braved the unwanted escort as long as he could, then turned to Zaccheus who still remained in a semi-torpor from reaction to the last visitation:

"I don't know much about monkey lore. Are these mini-Tarzans pursuing us supposed to be lucky?"

"I'd like to take a pot-shot at the blasted chatterers" Zaccheus replied. "Just look at those vile bottoms. And who the hell are they baring their stinking gums at anyway? I once went to play at an army camp and I stumbled into their shower-room where the recruits were being de-loused. I tell you if these blasted monkeys knew how closely they resembled those bald-headed bare-arsed shit-scared recruits they wouldn't be so noisy."

TO DAMN: read the asymmetric lettering.

The board was nailed to a tree, an arrow by the same amateur effort pointed like a barbed monkey tail along a deep furrowed road, two deep tracks and a middle weed-covered hump.

Ofeyi braked, reversed and re-read the sign. "Must mean Dam. I thought we were close to the Shage project."

"Do we want to see it?" Zaccheus' voice was justifiably querulous.

"It may clean my mouth completely of that last encounter."

"I doubt any work is being done at the moment."

"No. But the works will be there. I only want to see something our men from Aiyéró have helped build in Cross-river, something to reassure me that all that is happening now cannot add up to zero."

The monkeys seeing a sudden erratic motion of the car cancelled their escort service, wheeled about and vanished into the forest, dispensing bare-gummed maledictions to the last.

The high-wheel base of earth-removers had created the hump; it threatened to suspend the car and leave the wheels dangling. Ofeyi took a set of wheels onto the hump and the other rode on the shoulder. The forest closed about them, ominously still and silent. Zaccheus voiced his fears.

"Listen man, suppose there are some of these wild villagers about?"

"We are not recognizably from the scapegoat town" Ofeyi assured him.

"But how will they know that?"

"The cicatrice on your face. Why else do you think I reconciled myself to your coming with me. Those horror scars have become our protective talisman. We can move at will."

Zaccheus thought over this for a long while. "Look, I agree it all sounds okay to you. Only as I keep telling you . . ."

"Don't worry. I don't take foolish risks. Before you made your way back I had already worked it out. If you hadn't showed up I was going to come anyway, taking a driver with huge tribal marks."

Zaccheus resigned himself to Fate. "All I know is the scapeclan has expanded to cover just about everyone who doesn't speak their language. Don't tell me in this wild outpost . . ."

"It is not a wild outpost Zaccheus. This is the one place the animals could not touch because the union was strong. They had a meeting here and they decided to suspend work at the first sign of victimization."

Zaccheus' face grew rounder with suspicion. "What are you keeping from me man? How come you know so much?"

"I don't know all that much Zack. Only that we did manage some work before the bloated Corpse exploded. New projects like the Shage Dam meant that we could start with newly created working communities. New affinities, working-class kinships as opposed to the tribal. We killed the atavistic instinct once and for all in new ventures like Shage." He saw Zaccheus' bewildered gaze, and he knew he was about to resume the old suspicions. "You helped too."

Zaccheus exploded. "Leave me out of it. I knew nothing of it and I don't want to know."

"Well you did suspect. And more than once. But you helped. Remember when Iriyise danced here? Look at it, here in this forest isolation a new tribe, the working tribe was created, far from the poisonous tentacles of those fogies of clannishness tribal power. Do you see how it was possible to create new entities here which not even the divisive greed of the cities could penetrate?"

Zaccheus shuddered and wound up the windows. "Just the same, I can't help feeling spooked. I'm not into this thing so I can only tell you I don't like the scene. Let's go back before it gets dark or we get trapped."

Ofeyi looked at him and conceded at last the legitimacy of his fears. "All right, we won't stop. I shall only drive round the site and I'll leave the engine running. All I need is a little reassurance that we did not totally fail. Before we get into Kuntua and I lose my faith to the rampant travesties."

Half a mile before they came on the site Zaccheus said, "I know now why it feels so spooky. There isn't a living soul within miles."

"That's what I keep telling you. The site is abandoned."

"Then why are the monkeys so damned free of the place? They

wouldn't have spread so far along the main road if the tractors and things stopped only recently."

Ofeyi explained it patiently. "Listen Zaccheus. They stopped work here days before the troubles began. The Cross-river locals among the workers had been brought into the Cartel plans and they reported it to the Aiyéró leaders. One of our converts was actually in the Zaki's retinue. But at the time they all thought it was simply an attempt to break their solidarity. The men of Aiyéró decided to stop work so as to anticipate the Cartel's move. When the locals brought further warnings they made the entire works close down. They all held a meeting and decided to go home. That was two weeks at least before the Cartel turned their jackals loose. Of course the site is deserted!"

They broke into clear ground, nearly plunging through the banks of a vast artificial lake as the road curved sharply along its banks. Above it hovered a low evening mist, pierced by the arm of a single crane. A dangling rope of corded steel with a massive hook at the end seemed to fish in the white, suspended veil.

"It's a dead place Ofe. Where is all that fog come from?"

"Must be something to do with the closed lake and the steamy forest surrounding it."

"Haven't seen anything like it since some impresario took my old band for a Christmas—New Year tour of the Scottish Wilds. Do you know the Fifth of Fourth or some funny name like that? They were building a bridge there at the time. That crane reminds me of it. The bridge stopped in the middle of the whole wide fifth or whichever they said it was and there was this crane hanging over the rough end of the bridge dangling into nowhere. You know the place?"

Ofeyi nodded. "That's a coincidence. I often stood at the top of a hill overlooking the river. That was when the Corpse packed me off on that tour. Ran into a girl, the one I told you about. We motored around a bit and visited the place. Firth of Forth, if you are interested in the real name."

"Well at least there were cars roaring back and forth on the nearby roads and lots of kilts and bagpipes. I don't hear nothing but silence here so why don't we just head out and find people of our own kind."

"I always thought" Ofeyi commented, "what a pity if the bridge was ever completed. It was perfect as it was, dangling in nowhere. Those painters and musicians who left some works unfinished, I suspect they did it deliberately."

"My grandfather would rush you to the medicine-man if he heard that kin' talk from you."

"It's quite true, believe me."

He broke off abruptly, hesitant as he opened the door. His eyes turned towards an incongruous pockmark on the surface of the lake. Stepping out, the stench was first to hit him, a wet slap of putrefaction in the face. Suspicious now he climbed up on a sand-bank and stared.

From that height the even mist was shredded, he now perceived, in a hundred places, opening patches of the lake to light, to a display of floating bodies so still that they seemed anchored. There was the marvel, although the bodies were swelled and the faces decomposed there hung about the scene a feeling of great repose. Perhaps the shroud of miasma dulled all sense of horror, or the abnormal stillness of giant machinery made it all a dream, a waxwork display of shapes, inflated rubber forms on rafts in motionless water, perhaps it all seemed part of the churned up earth, part of the clay and humus matrix from which steel hands would later mould new living forms.

I am lying to myself again he said, seeking barren consolation.

But it seemed vital now, indeed it seemed everything, to know, definitively, if the Cross-river voices that had assured him of their safety had been nothing more than a hoax, if the same voices had lured the victims back to work to await destruction. Unless of course they had been slaughtered in the safety of the new village and brought back, in a gesture of cynicism and contempt, to the lasting monument they had sought to build. Desperately he hoped that the Cross-river comrades were themselves part of the grotesquerie on the lake surface. Great though that loss would be, it was less than the total erasure of the essence of the idea. There was however no way of finding out.

The crane with its low hook seemed poised to fish out the recumbent figures. Ofeyi followed the line of cord to the derrick limb, to its pivot on the roof of a control cabin, down down to its mud-poulticed caterpillar wheels. Concrete mixer cauldrons with their dirt-caked smoke stack . . . he stopped. It was becoming a habit, running lines in his head to stop the negative flow of implications from stark reality.

Ranged in clearings among the trees—and he recalled with a sense of unreality that Iriyise had danced for the workers in one of these clearings, that the villagers had hung from the trees and applauded in this wilderness—the machinery lay deadly still, their raucous revolutions silenced by mud and rust. Brown claws, dead weights, slack iron jaws of monsters, caterpillar treads had churned and bucked through slag and swamp, angry rhinoceroses charging at prides of the forest, bringing them crashing down one after the other. Always they left the earth a little more naked, a little more exposed than before. The hope was that something took their place, and he meant something beyond the concrete structures. The silence erupted in his ears with the sounds of those iron mastodons in motion, and the army of rubber boots trampling earth into submission, the clangs of picks and shovels, blackskin, whiteskin, red and sweatskin, of levers, bolts and strains, a luscious mudbath for the flesh and metal bestiary to tear up earth and throw it back in stronger, fructifying forms. Underneath his feet sank the inchoate gurgle of electric power. . . .

But all around his immediate presence there was silence. Rust lay on the idle tools, mud had usurped the marked-out line of sluices beneath the artificial lake.

It all remained unfinished, and not sublime. Again, not for the first time in his knowledge the wrong sluices had been opened. It seemed that few enough hands sought the sluice gates of light and life, of truly making grow, turning moist and live. He turned away from this new offering to rejection and hate and descended the earthbank. He wondered now if he had in any case been standing on a hasty burial mound; the miasma which hung over the lake now seemed to seep from a source of hidden putrefaction.

Zaccheus held the car door open. Only then was he aware that he had also left the car and stood beside him on the mound. They drove off wordlessly.

Through his clothes he felt a contagion, as if the fumes had seeped through and had begun to spread a filmy hand over his skin. That, and the silenced sluices lifted his rage suddenly beyond the immediate, confronting the old man of Aiyéró with a rage that dared him to prove that his microcosm held the secret of a living harmony, that when his fingers reached to let moist sluices free onto the land, they overrode fortuitous idiocies of the new land spawns, the bureaucrats, the marionettes of power, soldiers and politicians, the technocrats and currency expounders. Again and again he pitted the mangled wrecks, the buried foetuses of still-forged entities, mothered and fostered in the humanistic will, pitted even their desecration in time against such self-sufficiencies as esoteric hinterlands . . . the sum was a slight memento, a tracing before his eyes which read: Iriyise danced here.

———

The trees began to dwindle fast, the leaves grew scrawny, the sky scorched to hot winds, locust bean trees sprouted occasionally among ant-hills which now rose to heights of scrubland trees. Drought pursued them in clouds of dust, twitched the stunted branches like predators' tails.

From a charred, barkless height, a kite rose from its watch-tower and circled the sky, gaining the rarer regions on invisible windstreams. Zaccheus had taken the wheel, Ofeyi leant back and tried to borrow eyes off the kite, scan the distant city for the object of quest. Foiled he turned his gaze on the gorges whose precarious sides sheered into the netherworld, a network of canyons and ridges writhed into a sunset-gory horizon, giant troughs whose linear base seemed pocked by tumours of dislodged boulders. Ofeyi found that he had begun to fill these chasms with people, the Anubis-headed multitudes of his dreams. They poured into the abyss from all sides, swarmed over the rim and raced downwards towards a promised feast, a coalescence of that feast whose sated aftermath he had just witnessed at the dam. Slavering on the bait-trail of the putrescent tumour they rushed dragging their young brood with impatience, abandoning them in headlong plunge towards the scent of an inhuman banquet. Drowsed by the hum of the engine a sensation close to what he had experienced in Iriyise's room came over him, that of being alone in the world. Only this time, he saw where the rest of mankind had rushed, and now his was the only consciousness observing the dark pulsating chasms of tearing, grasping, clawing, gorging humanity. He stood on the humped ridges, the proud-horned bearers of the healing elixir whose bronzed torsos reclined above the laden troughs. And there in his hand, Ahime's scalpel of light. The bulls did not await his command, his barely breathed, "Plant the horns." They turned their throats to the sunset and awaited the moment of sympathetic bleeding. With barely a gesture he moved from bull to bull, the fountains leapt up and rushed down the chasms of unbeing, rushed towards the banqueting ravines and inundated them from end to end.

He looked upwards at the shifting cloud-humps in the sky as yet undarkened by a hint of rain and muttered—When again?

X

Were these payments for the days of evasion? The price for his own private pity seemed inordinate. Unjustifiable even if proven.

A round concrete tower encased the fire-escape. Tiny air-vents which offered no handhold whatever, it would take more than mere miracle to score a direct hit with a grappling-hook before the scrape of iron attracted attention from a numerous household . . . the details and prospects flashed through the Dentist's mind as he surveyed the sprawling mansion bathed in powerful arc-lamps. Only the stair shaft was in partial darkness, monolithic and impregnable.

He pointed in that direction. "I could plant a heavy charge through the lowest of those vents but then it might simply destroy the building without so much as touching my man."

"He sleeps on the fourth floor" Ofeyi murmured.

"What wing?"

"That side. Next to the stair shaft."

The Dentist sighed. "What do they want with such excessive structures. Look at it! It is bigger than that Hilton mess in Gosara. How many live in it?"

"Just he and his family. Plus a few hangers-on."

"And bodyguards?"

"Of course."

Chief Batoki, Western arm of the Cartel Axis relaxed only when he was on the fourth floor of the house. Below him were three layers of safety, each guarded by beefy thugs armed to the teeth, though camouflaged in the normal uniform of house-servants. Above him was a half-open terrace patrolled by guards loaned by the Commandant, swinging itchy sub-machine guns. It would be a suicide-bent assassin who tried to break into his country fortress.

"This man has deserved death a hundred times over."

"What makes you so certain of what you are doing?" Ofeyi demanded. "What makes you so sure of what you have just said?"

The Dentist turned from their hiding-spot and put away his field-glasses. The inspection was over for him. An idea occurred to Ofeyi—why not bring about a confrontation?

"Wait. Why don't we simply go in? Perhaps you ought to meet him first."

The Dentist turned querying eyes on him but Ofeyi nodded. "Yes, why not? I'll take you in."

"You know them that well?"

"We are . . . not exactly friends now. But I was very close to the family once. I am always welcome there."

"All right."

"But don't take . . ."

"What do you take me for? Of course not."

They retrieved the car and Ofeyi took the wheel saying, "It is easier if I drive. The gatekeeper knows me."

He swung the car back onto the main road and brought it to the outer iron gates. Before they reached the sentinel box he could see the gateman already speaking into a telephone.

"I shall simply ask for the daughter" Ofeyi said. "We can wait in her private reception room while she arranges for us to meet the father."

"What will you say you want him for?"

"I won't need a reason. Until the whole thing goes up in flames and every man's position is boldly lit they will continue to hope for conversions. A visit like this would only mean I am coming to my senses. The whole family will rush out to welcome the prodigal son. By the way who are you?"

"I don't understand."

"I mean, who do I introduce you as?"

"Oh. Well, I'd better use the name on my passport. Call me Demakin. Isola Demakin. And say I have just come back from studies in the States."

"Have you studied in the States?"

The Dentist gave a faint smile. "I have studied everywhere."

They were met by Biye in the anteroom to the second-floor lounge. She looked at Ofeyi for a long time, keeping his hand in hers, then shook her head sadly.

"So you never did take my advice."

"No. And you haven't taken mine either."

"True. But who is in trouble now? Is it me or you?"

Jolted, Ofeyi asked, "Trouble? What trouble?"

She put her arm through his and began to lead him to her apartment. "Ofeyi, all these childish pranks you've been playing, do you think they are not known? It makes my father very sad. He had hoped you would think things over on your study leave."

He waited. Given time she would grow still more voluble,

reveal every detail of whatever reports had been blown towards this ear of the Cartel. She rattled on, "I don't know what you hope to gain by it except to get yourself hurt. If you knew how much time my father has spent defending you! He insists you are merely misled by keeping bad company. The others wanted to get quite drastic with you. Anyway, I'm glad you've come. You know he'll do anything to get you out of the mess. You could go on another tour."

She guided them onto a purple settee then recalled that Ofeyi's companion had not been introduced. Ofeyi pointed out that she had not given him a chance to open his mouth, introduced the Dentist. She laughed, pressed a bell and a white-jacketed steward arrived, disappeared again at a wordless order.

"You will both drink champagne won't you. Ofeyi hasn't been to see us for over a year so it calls for celebration. What does your friend do?"

"Nothing yet" the Dentist replied. "I've just returned to the country. I was studying in the States."

"What was your study?"

"Dentistry" he answered recklessly. But it struck no chord in Biye. Not a flicker in her eyes connected his profession with the notorious legend of the Dentist.

"Well, if you are looking for a post my father will be glad to do all he can since you are Ofeyi's friend. But I hope you don't think like him."

The Dentist smiled. "No. I'm afraid our politics differ somewhat."

She could not contain her delight. "Oh that is good, very good. I am glad to hear it. Perhaps you can exercise some influence on him. He is rapidly turning communist."

"Oh I wouldn't say that," the Dentist replied.

"Or anarchist. I think that is even more accurate."

Ofeyi asked, "Is that what your father now calls me?"

She flared up at once. "You never stop thinking of me as a child do you? You seem to think I have no opinions of my own. You are an anarchist, everyone says so."

Ofeyi held up his hand. "All right, all right. I haven't come here to quarrel with you."

"Yes, you have come because you are in trouble. It's at least a year since . . ."

"I came to see the family. I was passing by and suddenly felt like seeing you."

The champagne arrived in a silver bucket. She busied herself laying out the glasses while she challenged him to tell the truth. "You came because you are in trouble. For once you have managed to swallow your pride."

Then the steward coughed discreetly, hanging by the door. Biye turned and he beckoned politely to her. She followed him just outside the door and the two men heard the steward conversing with her in a low urgent tone. Her thin face bore a set angry determination when she returned to them.

"Ofeyi, I'm sorry but you have to excuse me. Daddy needs me. You know the house, so make yourself at home. I'll try not to be too long."

"Anything wrong?"

"Oh it's . . ." Her voice rose to a vehement shout. "It's Mummy again. She just won't learn that I also have my rights in this house. Wait here for me." She turned sharply and went out. A moment later she was back. "Ofe, can you come with me?"

Surprised, Ofe rose and met her by the door. "Come on, you are almost a member of the family anyway. Perhaps you can talk some sense into her."

Shying back Ofe began to protest but she had snatched his hand anyway and was dragging him away.

The harridan voice of a middle-aged woman reached them before they arrived at the heavy leather-upholstered double door at the end of the corridor. Biye was about to march straight in but she checked herself at the last moment. Pulling one half of the door slightly open, she peeped into the room and began to listen. Moments later she appeared still content with merely eavesdropping and Ofeyi began to squirm with embarrassment.

He whispered, "Don't you think I ought to go back?" But Biye shushed him clinging to his hand as to a safety-belt. With her other hand she pushed the door open an inch wider.

Batoki, shrunk to half his size appeared to shrink further into a deep arm-chair in a huge living-room festooned in gold framed photos of dead family forebearers, smiling reception scenes and parades. An enormous figure of a woman loomed over him, her lips vibrating in an incessant sizzle over the unfortunate chief.

"So? What is suddenly wrong with your tongue? Has Chief Biga cut it off at last? He's supposed to be your creature in the Cabal but it seems to me you are more like his boot-cleaner. So why don't you answer me? He's cut off your tongue has he? Because you can't bully him you think you can come into this house and take it out on me do you? You can't play god with your colleagues so you come back to the house to play god, is that it?"

The voice of the man whose form was wholly swallowed in the arm-chair uttered protests as though through a reed, "Control yourself Mama Biye, control yourself please. The whole household can hear you."

"The whole world will hear me before I take any more insults from you so answer my question and let us be done with it. Or don't you speak the language any longer? From what they say about you that's about the only thing your enemies fear from you, so use it now if your tongue is still loose in your head. Joke your way out of the question if you like but answer it. Am I taking the parade with you or are you going with that slut?"

The man pleaded. "You were there when I promised she could ride in the open car with us. You said nothing at the time. . . ."

"And why don't you take the whole family with you then? Am I supposed to be your wife or not? Why don't you go hunting round the obscure branches of the Batoki family and let them loose in their rags and lice to take the salute?"

"Abusing my family isn't going to help us solve this problem" he pointed out.

"Oho! Does it really hurt when your family is mentioned? And what have you done except heap humiliations on my own by using me worse than messengers in your office? What is that but belittling my family?"

"Mama Biye, is this not a disgraceful scene in the home of a man in my position. You say I use you badly, isn't it really the way you use yourself? I mean, if you must talk like a market woman. . . ."

Chief Batoki was seldom wrong. The insult had the effect he had expected, mild and plaintive though he had made his voice. Batoki's voice at its most lacerating always became a woodwind instrument, sensitively controlled. With sorrowing, downcast and furtive eyes, more sinned against than sinning, he let fall his sly insults, a light return to the foul-mouthed barrage with which he was perpetually flooded by wife, business or political enemies. While his wife heaved with rage and gathered her vocal powers for the next assault he let drop the next rebuke, coated in equal mildness.

"You know, sometimes you make me wonder. You really do. I mean there are times when you behave like an Ojuorolari. Really, if these toys mean so much to you that you cannot share them with your daughter. . . ."

Ofeyi made another effort to release his hand, longing for the peace and champagne in the sitting room. She clung harder to him, whispering fiercely, "Now you can see for yourself. You see the kind of life my own mother creates for me? Always wants to reduce me to nothing."

"Then why don't you get out!" he demanded. "Get out and leave them to their squabbles. This game is too dirty for you."

"It is my home, not hers."

Ofeyi sighed. "Biye, she is his wife. You are just the daughter."

She turned on him. "Ask Daddy. He needs me more than her. She knows I am far more use to him with all his contacts. All she does is disgrace him with her vulgar manners."

The lady of the house seemed to react most violently from just such imputations, the barb of which still smarted from the last similar pronouncement by Batoki. She plunged with relish into the task of demolishing the trapped politician, proceeded to level his pedigree to the dust.

"You Omiteru, *you*! You dare suggest I am Ojuorolari, one of those who never before tasted splendour? You! You dare group me with those upstarts who never in their lives rubbed shoulders with greatness?" She drew back a little, her eyes raked his cushion-engulfed body up and down and reduced him to the status of such slaves as, in those days when nobility was what it should be, would be slaughtered to accompany her father on his final ascent to a resting-place among the heavenly rafters. She burst into a prolonged artificial laughter which bordered on hysteria, broke it off suddenly to scream:

"Have you forgotten that you are what you are today solely by the grace of what I am? Because I will show you Omiteru. I will remind you, you and your nameless family, I will have to remind you from what dungheap your family used to scrabble for left-overs before I brought my name and wealth to raise you into something at which dogs no longer turn their nose!"

"Look here Mama Biye . . ." Batoki turned on his voice of cajolery but it only acted as raw pepper in the wound, as he knew it would.

"I don't mother bastards" she screamed. "So don't ever call me Mother-of-Biye ever again. Got rot my womb if that is what brought out that bitch." She spat viciously on the carpet. "Perhaps you should have named her Biyi. *Mo bi yi na*—worse luck for my womb!"

"Leave the child out of it. If it is anyone's fault, it is mine. The poor girl is not responsible for my blunder."

She missed the ambiguous wording, screamed "Poor girl!" and turned her eyes in a final appeal to heaven. "Do you hear him? Poor girl! How many broken homes has that"—she made a feeble attempt to catch the squeak in his voice—"poor girl to her credit? It's a wonder she has not even taken to procuring as a profession. She does it on the side-line for all your Corporation friends doesn't she?"

Scornfully now Batoki replied, "So we are now touting all the cheap gossip, are we?"

"Gossip! Doesn't she bring her disease-ridden friends for you to sleep with? Of course what else can one expect? There isn't a single streak of honest dealing in the family of the Batokis, there never was. She has inherited your blood, no doubt about that! I thought I could close my eyes to the number of houses you bought outside to lodge your mistresses but I never thought my own daughter would bring those free-for-alls for my husband to sleep with, under my roof."

"Keep your voice down if you must retail these stupid gossips. . . ."

"It is hardly your fault of course" she continued, raking him downwards again with contemptuous eyes. "It is the fault of those who took pity on the bare neck of the vulture and lent him a shawl. They weren't to know he would forget a time when the cold winds froze the blood before it could even reach his head."

That was a fatal game to play with Batoki. His rejoinder followed swiftly. "You should know all about wind and feathers. The turkey with a permanent itch opens her tail-feathers to the first wind that blows into a yard."

Mrs. Batoki stood still, open-mouthed for a long moment. Then she gave ground on that particular front, gathered her handbag and shawl. She had the ultimate weapon, a reminder that she was totally unselfconscious, uncaring for the demands of dignity in a public showdown.

"I shall be in that Cadillac when it calls here for you. Bring your procurer if you like and the whole clan of the Batokis. We shall find out then if the descendant of Adegunlewa, a princess in my own right was born to wipe the dung off the feet of the Batokis."

She turned off and, at that moment, before he could restrain her, Biye flung the door open and burst into the lounge. In his instinctive effort to restrain her he was catapulted into the room. Once exposed there was no retreat. Accepting the situation he stepped boldly forward and bade them a good-evening, only to find that his presence was completely ignored in the confrontation that followed swiftly on the flashpoint of Biye's entry. The mother's face underwent violent contortions.

"Get out! How dare you enter when I am talking to your father?"

She ignored her, went straight to the father. "Dad, I hope you haven't allowed her to bully you into changing your mind."

"Did you hear me tell you to get out?"

"I am talking to Dad," Biye retorted, regaining some calm.

"And I said get out you slut. Get out of this room before I fling you out myself."

Batoki settled down to enjoy his release from the strain of his own torment. No one could accuse him now of having set one against the other, a practice in which he believed implicitly, even in the domestic politics of his own home. When two dogs are fighting, he would advise, run off with the bone. If there is no bone anyway set them fighting so you can take a rest while they use up their strength. Biye was more than a match for the mother, and in a way she was continuing his fight where he had left off. He shut his ears to their slanging match, and drifted on to other problems. He had heard it all before, he was confident that he would come out of it with the advantage of having exhausted the troublesome woman without expending any more energy. Sad though he was when Biye's marriage broke up—Biye's happiness, he persuaded himself, was the sole purpose of his existence—yet he had experienced a measure of joy at the thought that he would now see her more often. But within months his wife had begun to resent his increasing reliance on Biye. In commercial and even government circles she became known as Batoki's deputy. That had galled the mother, a thought which brought a smile of pleasure to his wily face. The girl was an undoubted asset, the woman an embarrassing vulgarity. Through his reverie her voice now filtered in vicious demolition of Biye's pretensions. Batoki sighed. He knew how it would end and he wished they would hurry it up. Biye would be worn down by the sheer stamina of that formidable woman. That would be the moment for him to intervene, scoring an easy victory over the much weakened victor of that duel.

"You keep forgetting this is my home, not yours" Madame Batoki reminded her daughter for the eleventh time. "Neither you nor your father nor your entire family on that side can drive me out of it. You had a home and you lost it, you lost your husband and you are fast losing all chances of finding another."

Was it perhaps the right moment for him to interfere? "Oh come now" Batoki murmured half-heartedly. "That is not a kind thing to say."

"Then tell her to behave herself. Do I have to put up with all her nonsense until some poor fool takes pity on her. This house is big enough but she makes it a point of duty to get in my throat. I won't have it. Nobody does that to me in my own house. I am no one's slave here. I wasn't brought to this house in settlement of any debt and I am not a bastard. I didn't come here to pay off my people's mortgage, and I didn't step up in the world when I put my foot on your doorstep. You took me from the home of kings. My birth title is Omofayiwa, Omofolasere, Mosunmoloye, and if you don't know yet whose daughter I am go and ask whose mother is known as Asiwaju Ibode. . . ."

Batoki sat up in alarm, aware for the first time that he had delayed too late. She was mounting rapidly towards that pitch of hysteria with which he was only too painfully familiar. In that state, anything could happen. Even he was no longer safe from her physical violence. Acting with urgency now he tried to calm her down but she rode over his efforts, her voice rising with every word.

"I am no twopenny commoner whose chieftaincy was created by the civil service gazette. Am I now an object to be trampled under by you and your daughter, by this shameless harlot whom you call a blessing? You had better let her know whom has the voice in this house because I am warning you that I Mofolayelu, daughter of Asiwaju Ibode will not . . ."

Biye's voice cut through sharply. "And you I suppose are the Asiwaju Ibadi? You taunt me with losing my home but is it surprising? What else could one expect when the mother precedes the daughter to her marital bed? You should call yourself Asiwaju Ibadi—you've more than earned the honour!"

Ofeyi, tip-toeing his way out, stopped dead. The room seemed to have suffered a similar seizure. Biye, her eyes blazing betrayed a little hesitant motion, as if afraid that she had gone too far. Then Batoki gave a long sigh, sank back into his chair feeling, not for the first time, that his cup of humiliation had run over. Then the frieze was cracked open, a bellow of animal rage tore through the room as with the shout "Liar!" the mother flung herself on Biye who went down heavily under the unexpected attack.

Ofeyi remained indecisive, looking to Chief Batoki to move to the rescue. The little man moved at last, but his wife had already gathered herself for the next blow. She lashed out with her foot, Biye rushed her hands upwards to protect her face and felt her mother's shin across her knuckles. The demented woman now attempted to dig her heel in the girl's stomach but now Batoki had gripped her by the waist and was dragging her back. A final kick as she struggled in his grip took Biye in the ribs and Ofeyi saw her grimace in real pain. He rushed forward just as the mother fell back into the chair, smothering Batoki beneath a bulk he had underestimated. He gasped as though winded but Ofeyi had already scooped up the girl and was racing outside with her. The mother's abusive shouts followed them until they were out of hearing.

Back in her living-room he snatched the napkin from the neck of the champagne bottle, dipped it in the ice-bucket and tried to soothe her bruises. But she seemed far more concerned with reiterating the truth of the scandal.

"It's true Ofeyi, she knows she can't deny it. Dayisi never knew whether he was married to me or her."

Ofeyi threatened, "I'll leave if you bring that up again."

A matronly servant, one of the many who had begun to hang close when the quarrel rose in volume now entered, her face full of the tearful concern of the faithful poor relation. Relieved, Ofeyi handed over all further ministrations to her and only then did he realize that the room had been empty on their return. The Dentist was nowhere to be found.

He compelled himself to wait a while longer, hoping perhaps that he had merely gone to the lavatory but sensing intuitively that this was not the truth. For the same reason he could not enquire directly about the man with whom he had been seen entering the house. Not that his absence would be remarked if he was compelled to leave without him, but to actually make enquiries would be to draw attention to him—if anything were to occur afterwards. If? Coldly he asked himself what decisions the Dentist could have taken in his absence, experiencing a deep resentment that he had initiated what after all could now only be regarded as a reconnoitering entry into the house. Resentment came from knowing within himself that his intentions had been different. It had been a largely deceitful intent, a form of special plea which came from feeling that only a mercenary assassin would pursue the death of a man whom he had encountered in the most mundane domestic context. After that the victim ceased to be a faceless cipher, a factor in a social equation which must be subtracted for a working formula. The Dentist, he persuaded himself, in spite of the cold rust that seemed to fill his bones in place of marrow, the Dentist was no professional killer.

But where was he and what was he doing now? Most urgently, how was he, Ofeyi, to view his own position if anything took place?

Finally he found his prolonged wait no longer bearable and left the house. He drove out through the gates and, at the end of the long driveway he turned the corner into the public road and a figure stepped out from behind a clump of bushes. He recognized him at once and pulled over, pushing the door open.

The Dentist's tone was mocking. "And what did you think when you found I had vanished?"

Ofeyi countered by asking what he had been doing.

"I wanted to see if I could leave the house undetected. If I could then I could return the same way."

"Well?"

The Dentist shook his head ruefully. "No. I was challenged almost at once. I said I was taking a stroll while you were busy with the family. Then I walked towards the stair-shaft and tried to get out that way. Another armed gorilla sprang up from nowhere. I was already so suspiciously close to the fence that I had to undo my zip and take a pee."

"How did you leave?"

"Through the front gates. Thought I might as well spend the time doing some more viewing from the other side of the fence."

Ofeyi continued the drive in silence. The Dentist asked, "And how is the Batoki family?"

"Pitiable, as always."

"What?"

"I wish you had witnessed that shabby family scene . . . no, don't waste your time on Batoki. He is not worth killing."

The Dentist's face hardened and he turned a faintly supercilious glance on Ofeyi. "Shall I put that another way for you? What about this: the family is suffering already, don't bring any more misery upon them. Or: their opulence and self-indulgence has brought them no happiness, so let them extort and mutilate those who resist to their heart's content. Or this one: in spite of the thousand deaths that can be laid at his door, Batoki is a man of deep family attachments. . . ."

"All right, that's enough. You know nothing of my relationship with that family."

The Dentist narrowed his eyes in suspicion. "Oh, I see. Was

that why you took me into the house? To see Batoki en famille? And pity him?"

Ofeyi remained silent, staring straight ahead. The Dentist gave a sigh of one who had been through the dead arguments before and was weary of them. He shut his eyes and flung his head over the backrest. The rest of the drive was taken in silence.

XI

They now began to encounter the fugitive transports in droves.
Blank stares, emptied of all self-awareness filled these grossly
overloaded trucks which swayed past in twenty contrary motions
along different axes of the body. Miraculously the mass remained
together. And there were the private cars also, looking as battered
as their occupants. These people had a common characteristic: a
stare of resigned preparation for just that final unexpected blow.

"We are getting close to the river I think" Zaccheus said. "Near
Labbe Bridge."

At the bridge Ofeyi pulled the car off the road, wiped his sweat-
grimy hands and announced that he would take a swim. It looked
safe enough. On the other side they could see the patrols. They
stopped each fugitive truck perfunctorily, waved them on again.
They looked bored, contemptuous. From time to time one would
stroll around a detained vehicle, point nonchalantly at an article

that had attracted his greed. A television set perhaps, sometimes a brand-new sewing machine. The driver knew what it meant. He did not even bother to ask the owner. He quickly unloaded it, turned it over. Partly to observe this activity of the soldiers directly Ofeyi walked further up the river, resolved to swim to the other side.

But there was also the need to pause at the formal doorway to the territory of hell. It was a purely formal doorway; the terror had spilled over to outlying villages below the bridge as they had only too grimly discovered on the way. And the plague had been welcomed into the bloodstream of some who shared neither land nor cause with the Cross-river clans, but who, anxious not to be outdone in the predator game, preyed upon the victims as they passed. But Labbe Bridge marked the boundary of organized carnage. A few days before, the bridge itself had been a death-trap for many. The executioners had waited at such obvious points of escape and picked their victims at will.

Thinking of this Ofeyi walked further upriver, making for a tributary whose white sandbanks stood out sharply in his mind from a journey some years before. Coming upon it sooner than he thought he inspected it carefully, sniffed the air and peered into the bushes. It was possible that even this part of the river had shared in the haulage of putrefaction. Still, after this bridge it was even more certain that no stream remained unpolluted, no pool existed in which a man could throw a stone without bursting a bloated skin of decay. Not even the wells, for in their mindlessness the hordes of the Cartel had not refrained from soiling the needs of the living for pure sources. It took no energy to kill or maim, it took much to bury the dead. The wells and inland waters proved receptive, insatiable. When the streets were piled high and the vultures proved too tardy scavengers, glutted beyond their air-borne dreams in this mostly barren landscape, then the trucks moved in, gathered up the gruesome debris and tipped them even into reservoirs.

A train bearing refugees to safety had stopped over a bridge, emptied one waggon full of corpses into the gorge below. When the bolts were first removed the bodies simply fell out, tumbled towards the thin ribbon of water far below the narrow bridge. Then the sanitation men in their brown uniforms, handkerchiefs tied to their lower faces began to haul out the others one by one, prodding through the metal gaps to push into the void those which were caught between the girders of the bridge. Faces of survivors crowded the windows on that side, set faces followed the motions of this parody of acrobats through space and sunshine, the distant thuds of bodies bouncing from crag to crag of the bottomless gully. A child corpse flew right over the steel arch and plummeted down like a plump wild duck. The distant, barely recognizable splashes grew even more beggarly as the bodies dammed the trickle. Then the waggon door was raised, the bolts rammed into place and the train moved on . . . Zaccheus, fleeing back on that train had withdrawn his head after the first cascade of bodies, contenting himself with observing the changes that were rung in the faces of the hardier watchers. He felt that with most, with the few who stuck it till the end there was an element of compulsion, a resolve to brand the scene on their minds forever, ready for disinterment whenever the time should come. . . .

Scanning the surface of the tributary and around the confluence Ofeyi saw no evidence of such desecration. The sandbanks gleamed spotlessly. Not even the usual patches of drying cassava roots could be seen—the settlements around were mostly alien and they were now deserted. The words of Ahime came into his mind . . . the earth is our feeding grounds, the rivers our watering places; if we are contemptuous of them we will look to them in real need some day and find we are rejected. Food is sacred. . . .

He shrugged off his clothes and walked through the last yard of tall grass, splashed through a narrow fish-trap and flushed out a flock of egrets. They lifted slowly on astonished wings. Involuntarily he snatched at the nearest over his head, not really thinking he could succeed, the egret pulled away easily and, beneath their concerted wing-beat, invisible strings fastened on his outstretched finger-tips and passed beneath his armpits, lifting his nervous flesh above the water, canopied beneath a hundred white wings towards the ever beckoning peaceful, strifeless, cleansing migratory grounds.

They dipped him gently back in a placid lake, the water lipped him round the chest. He went beneath the cool waters, surfaced, floated towards the confluence and saw the egrets alight on the other side. When they rose again he shut his eyes and indulged in a renewed metamorphosis, merged into their ruminant habitat, a prime patient cattle for their clean elegant gleaning. Lazily he watched them alight on his hide, flicked his tail in contentment as they picked him clean of blood-infesting ticks. The water shut his ears to all cacophony, his nostrils to pollution, transmitting only the rhythms of cropping and quiet germination. An easeful, decay, ingestion, germination and renewal. Egrets feeding on his own skin, fearless.

The sun gleamed orange through his eyelids. The reeds passed him upstream from the banks, reeds in the fingers of an eccentric healer, whispering incantations over a child in agony . . . a curious breed those healers. Witch-cauldroned from the womb or stressed to a tensile purity by experience, by a slow painful self-crucifying search through life, even to the lethal charge which whitens their hair overnight but fails to kill them. Hands that stretch forth and scatter healing vibrancies as lesser men in their so-called triumphal progress scatter pieces of gold. If they are not found at will then events must bring them forth, the terrible individual needs.

Those secretive fingers with the sensitivity of grass, cattle and egrets, of ultimate repose—what chance do they have truthfully, against the tumoured belly of humanity with its periodic seepage of pus and bile into the living streams of earth? Ahime? Healer in magic insulation against such pervasive evil?

He shook his head in denial and to clear it of water, turned at the midstream sandbank which his head had just struck and began to swim back upstream. The water was clear and he could see clearly down to river-bed. No, the multitudinous dead did not seem to have passed or rested this way. The crystalline sands pebbled and broken-shelled seemed to restore a little element of hope, of increasing justification. Stepping out onto the bank his eyes encountered yet another lorry from Cross-river, it looked as if a slum home had been uprooted to its last floor-board and tied onto a bare truck. The residue of disruption. A rolled up blanket peeked out from a discoloured mattress—it hung down the side of the truck like a buffer against surprise. A dangling chamber-pot, a bicycle that had lost a wheel, then the baskets balanced on the pile and the familiar debris of faces stuck among the pieces. The bridge dipped into an abyss of denial.

In the early hours of Sunday they reached Kuntua. Day of rest. The town seemed bathed in the peace of an unspoken truce. A concatenation of church bells drifted over the city roofs, reinforcing a visible peace. They drove in silence, seeking the aliens' quarter.

Ten minutes later and they would have been part of the victims of the ghetto. The early quiet had bred a seductive sense of security. From a porter in the railway station they learnt that the predatory gangs no longer roved in bold daylight, their activities were confined to sneak murders at night, the unexplained fires and incidental looting. They headed the car in the direction he had given, missed a crucial turning twice and drove up an adjacent hill to survey the entire alien quarters. Straining to pick out the pattern of road ribbons far below in the ghetto a few unusual scurrying motions struck first Zaccheus, then Ofeyi. From their vantage height each building stood out clearly. So did the streets, albeit narrower from that height. A few pedestrians moved normally among the houses.

It seemed at first a normal Sunday morning in the strangers' district, inhabited mostly by "pagans" and Christians, all aliens to Cross-river. The quiet was accentuated rather than broken by the whinny notes of a pedal organ and the sluggish Sunday-breakfast replete voices of the congregation. They picked out the church building easily, dominated as always by an enormous cross.

"Praising God for surviving" Zaccheus surmised. "And praying for protection for the future."

Ofeyi added, "Perhaps a few imprecations for their assailants, it wouldn't surprise me. Not all these denominations hold with the forgiveness doctrine."

Frowning now, Ofeyi observed the commencement of jarring motions in the streets. From odd shadows, corners and even from behind a few hardly noticeable trees figures began to emerge. They moved like ghosts, swift and co-ordinated, silent and clothed in the familiar dusty travesty of white robes. It was evident that they were no Sunday worshippers.

More sinister however were the opposite (or complementary) movements which had also commenced. A handful of policemen who had been posted around the ghetto began to move outside the ghetto walls. In a few moments not one of them remained. The movements of the flitting dirty-white wraiths now became a rush. There was no longer effort to conceal the weaponry of matchets, bows, arrows and daggers. And a number of cans whose purpose the watchers could not yet define. A short while later, these apparitions had surrounded the churchyard. As if by prearrangement, a detachment of them rushed the church itself.

The action unravelled with chilling clarity. It had a definable beginning, a middle and an end. It began almost as a game, with the weaving and dodging among the houses and passages, expanded into a co-ordinated sweep as the hide-and-seek was jettisoned and the mob rushed into the churchyard, made instantly for doors and windows and began to slam them shut. The pious hymning changed abruptly to screams and even this new change was snuffed out, replaced by blows of hammer on nails brought from the clothing of the unbidden worshippers. Each move seemed choreographed, even to the last detail. Planks were raised, laid across the slammed windows, held in position by others, and hammered in by pre-selected groups. So efficiently was the manoeuvre carried out, so quickly was it over that it struck the watcher that could not be the first exercise of this nature by the group. One moment, all twenty, thirty windows and doors of the church were wide open, a minute later the church was tight sealed on the worshippers.

"The police!" Ofeyi muttered urgently. "Get in the car Zaccheus, get them here fast."

Zaccheus shook his head dubiously but Ofeyi pushed him behind the wheel. "You saw them leave," Zaccheus continued to insist. "It will only be a waste of time. And it's Sunday—you know what they are!"

"Don't go to the local stations. Go to the National Police. Drive directly to their headquarters and demand to see the highest officer. Hurry man!"

Nothing that they had heard so far indicated any connivance on the part of the National Police. The local constabulary had their dirty blue uniforms dyed in blood as deep as the red sash that they wound round their ungainly knickers. The soldiers did not bear thinking about. Hopefully, he waited. He thought of the Dentist at this moment with his rifle and telescopic lens and longed for his precise solutions. If even one or two were picked up from this distance, the rest would abandon the attack and flee.

A window was violently smashed from within, its sound carried crisply up the hill and ended the distanced wishfulness. He looked down to see a pew protruding from one window. Used as a battering ram, it had smashed a jagged hole through the planks but without forcing the window itself open. The end of the pew served only to block the hole it had made. Nothing could pass through. Not that it mattered in the least, for any would-be escapee would have been cut down with ease. To ensure that such a meaning was made plain to the trapped worshippers the nearest assailant loosed an arrow at the aperture. It embedded itself in the wood, at least half its length penetrating through to the church interior. Only then did Ofeyi observe that ladders had been put up, reaching to the roof, in those brief moments he had spent talking to Zaccheus.

Each act progressed from the last with bewildering precision. Distance turned it into a deadly mural, activated by nothing more sinister than an illusionist trick. A relay worked with smooth efficiency, passing the mysterious cans up to three or four men on the roof. They sprayed the contents all over the roof, found cracks and poured the liquid into the captive space beneath the roof. A different group performed a like ritual around the windows, splashing fluid on all wooden surfaces of the church. A third directed motion came from another group which piled wood and rubble of all descriptions against the two main doors into the church. Ofeyi knew for certain in what fluid the building had been soaked.

The deadly libation was soon over, the priests withdrew, waited for the trio on the roof to descend. They poured the last few drops from their cans onto the ladders and left them there. Ofeyi did not see the actual lighting of the fire, only the sudden inferno that leapt up where the church had been, and the ring of watchers around it stepping further back as the heat raged fiercer and black smoke began to obscure their vision.

The screams appeared to come from a long long way below earth. Loud crackles as if of sudden downpour on overheated metal sheets accompanied, then drowned them. Fumes from the petrol set up an unearthly haze high above the roof. Two kites were conjured up from an empty sky and hovered above the human kiln. Ludicrously the folk-tale to explain this homing of kites on fires passed through Ofeyi's mind.

An iron sheet burst its moorings, flapped grotesquely in the flames. As if this had been perceived by the trapped people and was accepted for a signal, some half-dozen windows flew open, smashed through as before by wielded pews. A general assault on other windows and doors began and the sound of battering-rams now mingled with the general roar of the flames.

It was a moment the attackers had awaited. As the first man leapt out an arrow flew towards the flames, transfixed him briefly. The figure staggered, recovered balance and fled towards imagined safety. More followed him, and so did the steady procession of arrows, thudding into their targets and wringing execrations from their lips. The last man turned, pulling at the shaft embedded in his throat and, crazed by the pain tried to clamber back into the inferno. Another arrow struck him in the spine and he shuddered, fell over the sill and hung there as flames licked his clothes and soon engulfed him completely.

After this all was still for a while within the church. The unbroken windows remained intact except for flames that had begun to gut them. Ofeyi wondered if the remaining worshippers had knelt down to await death or were praying for deliverance.

And then, simultaneously, both doors crashed open. An instant later the remaining windows were also forced and a mass breakout began. A giant led the way through the larger door wielding a large chair as shield and weapon. All the men followed through both doors and fanned out in a circle. None got far. Too great a distance separated them from the besiegers and they were cut down to a man by the seemingly inexhaustible swarm of iron barbs. The archers were unhurried. They picked their victim as he rushed forward, often falling at their feet as the last of the shafts found a vital part. The paved surround of the church ran with blood spurting one gory fountain after another.

Mutilations followed death, sometimes preceded actual death.

The women came out in a body, slowly, holding their children by the hand. They stood outside, a few yards from the burning temple. They waited. Conspicuous as a shield, a plea or an accusation for the rest was a frail creature nearly overbalanced by the heavy pregnancy that stuck out of her and seemed ready to weigh her to the ground. Ofeyi held his breath, unable to tear his eyes from the confrontation. Until that moment when her head jerked suddenly downwards to stare in surprise at the unnatural blossom that her womb had sprouted. Ofeyi sank to the ground, his back turned to the screams that rose from the paved altar of the Sunday sacrifice. He knitted his hands across the back of his neck, pressed it down between his knees and tried to blot out voices that damned his futility.

It seemed hours before he heard the sound of sirens. Moments later Zaccheus came for him and he let himself be driven past the scene. Uniformed men stood about the churchyard in a daze—the attackers had long vanished. The church smouldered peacefully amidst hushed voices and whispered orders. Innured to such wholesale slaughter, there was yet one spot on which they all resolutely turned their back, a spot covered by one frail body. Ofeyi too turned sharply away from the wet oval cavity where her womb had been. . . .

The desk-sergeant's face did not pretend to interest, much less concern. "You have reason to believe . . . you have reason to believe . . . my friend, we need more than that to take action."

Ofeyi damped his rising temper. "Someone actually saw her carried in forcibly."

His expression did not change nor did he stop the entries he had been making in a large register when they arrived. Ofeyi was not even sure that he had looked up once since they entered the station. "Someone actually saw her . . . you have reason to believe . . . we all have reason to believe . . . someone actually saw her. Where is that someone?"

He had cautioned Zaccheus against revealing himself as witness to the abduction. "He could not come with us. He fled to Ilosa and I can't blame him for not wanting to return here."

"I see sir. So there is no material witness here whose word we can rely on to take action."

"I am here" Ofeyi pointed out.

"I know you are here." The man conceded it drily and carried on with his scribbling. Ofeyi wondered what his next approach should be. The ceiling fan whirled noisily but the maddening scratch of the nib completely overwhelmed it.

Ofeyi renewed the assault. "I know the house."

"I heard you before" the sergeant replied.

"He described it to me and even drew me a map. I can take you there."

"I am not deaf sir."

Zaccheus hemmed, took Ofeyi aside and rubbed the fingers of one hand together in a standard gesture. "Do you think that might help?"

Ofeyi understood, nodded and dug into his pocket. Taking

out five pounds he queried Zaccheus. He suggested he double it. With the ten pounds folded in his hand he returned to the desk, raised a corner of the register and slipped the wad of notes under it.

The sergeant stopped writing, sighed as if in boredom and pushed aside the huge volume. He took out a smaller note-book from under his desk, then, with an impatient grunt as if searching for his pen, he contrived to lift the former register from his side and cast a swift glance at the thickness and colour of the notes which lay under its far edge. His expression suggested neither satisfaction nor the opposite. Without looking up he picked up the pen where it had lain all the time and poised it over the smaller book.

"What is your name?"

Ofeyi supplied it.

"And the details of your complaint?"

Half-way through a repeat of his narrative, he paused, thought hard for some moments. "Are you making a Missing Persons Inquiry or are you laying charges of kidnapping or what exactly?"

Ofeyi replied, "It's up to you to put it under what heading you like. All I want is help to look for this woman. If you came with me we could go there now. . . ."

He interrupted and said, "I will list it as Missing Persons Inquiry."

He ended his report with a flourish, looked up at them for the first time, but not even directly in the face, simply over Ofeyi's shoulder and vaguely above Zaccheus' head.

"It is a pity that the material witness is not here."

Ofeyi began to protest. . . .

"It is a pity" the man said stolidly. "You are sure he cannot be contacted."

Ofeyi offered to contact him by telephone if more information was required. "Isn't all that is important the fact that we know the house and that I could . . . ?"

"It is a pity" the sergeant resumed, "that we do not know who the witness is. There are many people missing in this town."

Ofeyi grappled vainly with the sequence of the man's pronouncements and began to wonder if this meant he was called upon to increase the bribe. Already the act, his first ever had bred nausea in him. He took the sudden irrelevant decision to snatch back the bribe which was still partially hidden by the register, if the sergeant's cupidity was still unsatisfied. The next question took him by surprise.

Flourishing his pen again the man said, "Name and address of witness please."

Ofeyi stared stupidly. "Name and address? He is over five hundred miles away. What use is that information to you?"

"We can contact him. I can use our police transmitter to ask our men there to contact him and acquire the relevant information . . ."

"I have all the relevant information here." Ofeyi's voice had risen to a scream. "*All* the information. I know the house, I know the date, the hour of abduction. I have the number of the army truck that took her to the house."

"Ah. So it was an army truck."

"Yes" Zaccheus confirmed. "A Land Rover."

The sergeant shifted his gaze to a spot one foot over Zaccheus' forehead. "A Land Rover belonging to the Army?"

"You know that already" Ofeyi snapped.

"And the people who carried out this abduction, they were, according to these notes I have taken, army personnel?"

Zaccheus intervened. "Officer, you have all this information already. We are only asking for assistance. If you can't help just direct us to whoever can."

"The people who carried out this abduction," he repeated, "they were, according to you, army personnel?"

"Let's go Zaccheus."

Zaccheus restrained him, took his place at the desk and said, "Yes sergeant, they were army personnel."

The sergeant put down his pen and spoke with disdain. "Can you inform me why you have not gone to report to the army instead of coming to the police?"

"Sergeant, you know the situation in this town better than we. Tell us to which army officer we should report the matter. Which barracks do we go to find such a man?"

"You should have reported the matter to the army" the man insisted.

Zaccheus turned away but the man continued. "You come here, make an accusation of kidnapping and abduction concerning the house which is now owned by a local respected citizen and you expect me to go and barge in there and start to search on the word of a witness who has not made material appearance to testify. . . ."

Ofeyi already at the door suddenly remembered. He moved towards the register at the same moment as the sergeant raised its edge. The spot was empty. Zaccheus held out his hand with the notes in it and announced, "I've got it boss."

They went out of the station ignoring the sergeant's bark to Halt there!

In the car Zaccheus said, "I knew it was a wild goat chase. They all have some of the blood on their hands."

Soberly Ofeyi cautioned, "We had better watch our step from now on."

"Yeah? You're just telling me that are you? The only sensible thing is watch our step out of this town, the faster the better."

"He wanted to know who the eye-witness was. He had no

intention of helping, but he wanted the name and where he could be reached."

Zaccheus shook his head in despair. "As the man said, the house of a highly respected person. In Cross-river highly respected persons are very high and very mighty . . . Ofe!"

"What is it?"

Zaccheus was quivering with suppressed excitement, a mixture of fear and discovery. "Ofe, listen. You missed what the man said. You missed something very important. That desk-sergeant said— which is now owned by . . . Do you get it? A house which is now owned by . . . ! But I told you who formerly owned it. A big businessman, one of our own people. And I told you what happened to him."

"What are you getting at?"

"But it was the soldiers who killed him and his family. And that sergeant wasn't referring to an officer, no matter how high he is, as a highly respected citizen. They do the dirty work, nothing more. They don't call them respected citizens. So when they went bumping off that family, they did it because the respected citizen wanted the mansion for himself. And if they took Iriyise there so soon after. . . . Ofeyi, do you get what I am saying?"

Ofeyi stared stonily ahead.

"Only one man is big enough to use the army that way. There is only one stomach large enough to gobble up everything belonging to the aliens in Cross-river. Zaki Amuri!"

"I know. There will be something for all the faithful. But only after he has had his pickings."

Zaccheus wrung his hands in distress. "Ofeyi, give it up."

Ofeyi shook his head to clear it. "We may. Perhaps we are not ready for him. But first we must make sure."

———

They were made to wait outside the gates of the Air Force Base for over half an hour, then marched into an office with two sub-machine guns at their back. In the hair-raising drive of the last one hundred yards, uniformed figures with levelled sten-guns had stepped out from behind trees into the road, forcing them to screech to a halt, then ordered them to proceed at a crawl along the last one hundred yards. Finally made to get out of the car, submit to a methodical search, walk the last few yards to the gate where two other armed figures escorted them, their backs itchy to the presence of the unwavering guns pointed at the base of their spines. The wait just outside the gate had lasted only twenty minutes but it seemed to have taken the entire day.

"They are actually gentlemen here" Ofeyi consoled Zaccheus. "We couldn't even have got this far in any of the army barracks. But the Air Force try to be gentlemen."

"I don't like gentlemen who carry guns."

"We should be all right here."

A call came through to the gates at last and they were escorted in.

In the office into which they were led a strange face confronted them, waved them politely to a chair.

"My name is Lieutenant Sayi."

Ofeyi began to explain what he thought was a misunderstanding but the man smiled sadly. "Yes, I know you asked for Captain Magari. I'm afraid he is dead. He was shot at the Airport three days ago, trying to stop some of the army boys from shooting down civilians. I understand from the guard that you are friends of his. . . ."

"Yes. . . ."

"I am sorry. I wondered if there was anything I could do. He was both a colleague and friend. If I could be of service to you in any way."

Ofeyi was only slowly taking in the message. "So Magari is dead?"

The officer remained silent. He took a swagger-stick that lay on the table in both hands and turned it over lightly between his fingers. "His own people shot him down" he said. "As a Cross-river man himself he was not expecting too much difficulty pacifying the swine. They told him to step aside. He didn't, so they gunned him down."

"And the civilians he tried to save?" Ofeyi asked.

"Oh you can guess. Wiped out to the last child."

Ofeyi stood up. "Thank you very much. We shan't take up any more of your time."

"Did you want anything. The guard said you had just driven all the way from Ilosa."

"Oh it was . . . we were looking for a girl. She was abducted by some soldiers who shot up a club where she was giving a performance. I'm sure you've heard of her—the Cocoa girl. . . ."

"Ah yes, a beautiful woman."

"Yes?"

Zaccheus eagerly continued, sensing the possibility of authoritative help at last. "I was in the club, it was my orchestra playing that night. In the middle of the performance they burst in, fired shots at everything in sight and took her away. I followed in a car to the house where she was taken—on Market Street. It's a big mansion, no one can mistake it. It's the only house of its kind."

The officer looked startled. "The big house on Market Street?"

"Yes. I watched the whole day but there was nothing I could do. The streets were not safe to walk in . . ."

"I know."

"Could you help?" Ofeyi pressed him. "Is there anything you can do? I want to find her. I'll give anything just to know what happened to her."

The young man shook his head sadly. "So it *was* the girl on the posters. She is the pin-up of the whole base."

Ofeyi checked. "You heard about the abduction then?"

"Yes, we hear all about our disgraces."

"Do you know where she is?"

The officer rose. "I did not know that that house was involved."

"Look Captain . . ."

"Lieutenant" the man smilingly corrected.

"Lieutenant then" Zaccheus rushed on, "You don't know what it means. If you could only put some of your men on it, just to help us find out. . . ."

The young officer looked from one to the other. Ofeyi's heart sank as he read the pity in his eyes.

"It will take months, if not years to sort out Cross-river, I mean really to sort it out. That includes . . ." He stopped short. "May I ask you this, is this your first stop since your arrival? I mean, have you made enquiries elsewhere?"

"We called at the central police station."

The officer sighed. "And I take it you gave them all the information you've just given me?"

"No, not everything. Zaccheus here did not suggest he was the eyewitness."

The officer looked visibly relieved. Then troubled again. "Even so . . ."

Ofeyi said quietly, "I have come here to find Iriyise, Lieutenant."

"I know. And the only service I can perform for you, believe me very sincerely, is to give you an escort to ensure your safety out of Cross-river."

"That is not the kind of help I am looking for."

"It isn't, but take my offer, quickly."

Ofeyi walked up to him and asked directly, "Who owns that house now Lieutenant Sayi? Who had the owners butchered?"

"Oh it won't tell you anything. And that is not really your province is it? Just take my advice, please."

"I can't do that."

"In that case . . ." He held out his hand.

"Thanks anyway" Ofeyi said, taking his hand. Zaccheus shook hands miserably. The look in his eyes could be taken to mean that he wished the lieutenant would place them forcibly under guard and escort them out of town. But the officer was busy guiding them out, transferring them to their escort and bowing back into his office. He gave them one last brief salute.

Once outside Zaccheus wailed. "She's dead Ofe. I feel it in my bones now. She's dead."

Ofeyi shook his head. "She's alive. I am sure of that."

"You don't seem to know Celestial. She would give those Jekú ruffians of the Cartel so much hell they would simply have to kill her to keep her quiet. And that baby was sick enough before it all happened. Ran high temperatures all that day before we went on stage. When I think I nearly forced her to stay back in the hotel!"

"They would have found her there. The thing to do is to find her. Where do we go next?"

"Home. Back south man, there is nothing to do here."

"Let's drive around. We will visit the night-haunts and listen to the gossip."

At the gate the guard stopped them at the sentry-box. "Which of you is Mr. Ofeyi?"

Ofeyi identified himself.

"The Lieutenant wishes to speak to you." He handed him a receiver through the square hole in the booth. The lieutenant's voice came through on the line.

"Is that you Mr. Ofeyi?"

"Yes."

"Do you know the suburbs of this town very well?"

"Fairly well."

"On the route to the airport, about four miles out of town there is a road which goes towards some agricultural settlements. You know those experimental farms that rather became the pattern? I believe the model came from down your way, some place called Aiyéró."

"Yes I think I know it."

"Well, if you take that road and go on a few more miles, you will find a few of those . . . er . . . native Christian churches. They are dotted all over the place, usually with no more than narrow footpaths leading to them. Now, two of those churches contain survivors in hiding. I suggest you try them."

"Thank you, I will."

"Be careful when you go there. They are understandably nervous and quite a few have weapons for their own protection. And of course be careful not to lead their hunters to them."

Ofeyi promised he would take all precaution.

"It is a waste of time of course, but I think it would help you if they told you how hopeless your quest is. They at least know what they are talking about. They should be able to convince you where I failed."

Ofeyi began to thank him but he cut him short. "No, I'm only offering it as the only alternative to making my men forcibly escort you out of town. I feel responsible for the safety of any friends of Magari."

"I pissed in my pants" Zaccheus said, "when that man stepped out and asked who was Ofeyi. And then I hoped it was to arrest you and bundle you out of town."

"He thought of it I'm sure, then thought better of it."

"So where are we heading now?"

"To find a church."

"A church!"

Ofeyi stopped the car in the middle of nowhere, stepped out and looked in every direction. "Of all the vague directions . . ." he muttered. He climbed to the top of the car while Zaccheus remained within, wishing himself five hundred miles from the spot. Ofeyi climbed down at last and opened the door on Zaccheus' side.

"I think we'll have to walk the rest of the way."

Zaccheus sighed. "Just tell me something. Do you know where we are?"

"Come on."

He sighed his resigned bulk out of the car. It seemed to him at that moment the most singly foolish act he had ever committed, leaving the safety of the vehicle in the middle of a clearly murder-filled environment. He hunched his shoulders to receive the first blow that would confirm their joint sanity.

"Ever heard of something the oyinbos call a suicide pact, maestro?"

"There are people around Zaccheus, but they are those who are used to other fugitives turning up."

Zaccheus gasped, staggered and nearly fell as Ofeyi pushed him aside suddenly. He pointed downwards to a spot from which a huge swarm of bluebottles had just risen.

"You nearly stepped into that mess."

The drone flies and a hundred other varieties settled back on the offal. Mostly it looked as if it had once been the intestines of some animal. The path fell silent again as they left the mess behind them, the bushes fell aside then closed about them.

"If only I'd remembered the cocoaine" Zaccheus continued to moan. "A suicide pact deserves a last drink before the end."

Abruptly the grass ended, gave way to a burnt swathe which stretched for some distance before them, a wide patch of black and grey ash and floating carbon wisps. The world stretched out on every side, brown, limp and arid. Against the landscape rose a single baobab, dry and stunted. Its trunk was broad and even up to a few feet, then it was overtaken by an abnormality or retardation that seemed, from the lumps, swellings and contortions, a blight of human infections—rickets, beri-beri, kwashiokor, and a variety of goitres. A distended belly in the middle of the trunk thrust its wrinkled navel at the black horizon. From malformed shoulders balanced on a flat chest writhed an abortion of limbs. Where the head might have been thinner branches hissed skywards, daring forked tongues in a venomous protection of whatever mystery hoard lay within the so-called tree of life. For there was nothing that called for protection from this wasted emanation.

At the edge of the arid stretch they paused. The baobab held both hypnotized. Zaccheus snapped his fingers round his head to ward off evil: "They can call the baobab their tree of life, I just call that one a bad omen."

"Let's go on" Ofeyi said.

"Look boss, let's sit down and plan this thing properly. Why don't we simply move back to civilization, have a square meal, dig up a friendly native and return to this place. I mean, we are not working scientifically."

"The church is around here" Ofeyi insisted.

"Who's been burning grass here? Them or us? And why?"

"Us, obviously. There is no sign of a building burnt down is there? So it can't be that the raiders found a hiding-place and set it on fire. The fire could only have been by the fugitives."

"I don't get the logic."

"So no one can sneak up on them. One of the churches must be beyond that next stretch of bushes. I'm sure they've posted guards and we'll be watched walking through the burnt patch."

"In which direction then?"

Ofeyi seized his arm and pulled him out of their camouflage. When they came to the baobab Zaccheus halted, leant against the tree and began to take off his shoes.

"Do they pinch?"

"Help me up this monster. If I can get a foot on that protuberance, I can make it to the top. Bad omens should be trampled on."

Ofeyi comprehended at once and hoisted him onto the look-out post, watched Zaccheus scan the horizon on all sides. After a long while he announced wearily, "Not a building in sight."

"You were looking too far out. Try and look into the bushes. See if you can detect movement or footpaths. Don't gaze into the bloody horizon man."

Zaccheus tried again. Suddenly his face lighted up. "Help me down. I think I've got it." He scrabbled down onto Ofeyi's shoulders, leapt down and retrieved his shoes. "Yes, I think it's over there, just where the bush is broken by that lemon shrub or something. Come on."

"Did you see movements?"

"Nothing. Just a break in the bush."

Sweaty and itchy from dust and ash and countless needles from the snapping twigs, they traversed the broken path for another half a mile, then came suddenly on a stockade of low stakes. The church, a mud structure painted yellow and white stood in the midst of the stockade. A graveyard, well-tended, stood a little to one corner of it. The entire surrounding was deserted.

Then the bushes broke behind them. Four men emerged from both sides, two armed with guns and the others with matchets.

"What do you want?" asked the foremost.

"We are friends" Ofeyi assured them.

But the men only continued to stare at the intruders and Zac-cheus shouted irritably, "Can't you see for heaven's sake we're not Cross-river people."

"Your names?"

They supplied them.

"Where were you born?"

They submitted to a prolonged interrogation.

The leader said at the end, "It isn't that we don't believe you are not natives of this damnable place. But we have had traitors among us who tried to buy off their own lives and property by betraying their own people. Many have done strange things. What do you want?"

"We are looking for some friends."

There was another silence while their spokesman gave them a further inspection. Then he signalled to his companions, adding in explanation to the two intruders, "You will have to be blind-folded. This church here is not our real hiding place."

They allowed themselves to be blindfolded. The leader contin-ued to speak. "We are waiting until we are fully prepared. Then we take the long journey home on foot. By river and through forests. We are placing no further faith in public transports and guarantees of safety. One of our camps believed in the radio claims of order and trooped out to the airport to fly to safety. They were butchered to a man."

"We heard about that" Zaccheus said.

"They should not have believed those lies. Their leader came here and we warned them. Better to trust in the forest and fight our way through any villages we encounter on the way. Sooner wild beasts than the human jackals we have just learnt to know. They should have listened to us."

The procession moved on. One man placed a hand underneath the upper arm of each of the blinded men and guided him forwards. They told them when to crouch and when to raise their feet. They forded a small, muddy pool and climbed over fallen logs. After thirty minutes of the fumbling walk they came to a halt. Hands touched their faces and they felt the blindfolds removed.

Zaccheus blinked. The sight that confronted them could only be called an armed camp. Hostile eyes surveyed them from all sides. Finally one of the captors asked, "Shall we take them to the old man's hut?"

There were imperceptible nods and the two captives were again nudged forward until they stood before an improvised shelter, a shack which appeared to have been constructed from odds and ends then roofed over with tarpaulin. "Wait here."

One of their escorts entered the hut. They heard low-voiced snatches of the conversation.

In the hut sat an old man, alone, his head bowed as if in thought. Before him was a bowl which contained some boiled maize, and a plate of groundnuts. There was no furniture in the room, their host was seated on a mat onto which he now waved them. Then he made a strange gesture over the bowl of food and muttered:

"Food is sacred."

Ofeyi gasped, looked up to encounter Ahime's eyes staring straight into his. The old man took up two corn-cobs and offered them to his guests.

"Try this" he invited.

They accepted the maize, began to eat, thoughtfully. The old man continued, "I sent word to a mutual acquaintance to trace you in Ilosa. He was to tell you that I was already on my way to Cross-river. I had the slight hope that it might make you return to Aiyéró—at least to look after things in my absence."

"I left as soon as Zaccheus returned with his news." Ofeyi stopped, struck now by the light mockery in the old man's voice. He asked, "A mutual acquaintance?"

"He traced you once before. Anyway it turned out that he also had already made for Cross-river."

Ofeyi waited but the old man said nothing further. Instead he asked, "What are your impressions of our camp?"

"Unreal" Ofeyi admitted. "Who organised it?"

"Our mutual friend." The flicker on Ahime's face widened to a grin. "Surely you can guess who it is by now?"

"Someone from Shage? I've recognized a few of the workers from there. And from the Mining Trust."

Ahime shook his head. "Only one man has the training to organize protection for such an open camp."

The elusive name flew to Ofeyi's tongue at once: "Not the Dentist!"

Ahime nodded. "I don't think of him by that name he has since acquired. Demakin is how we still refer to him in Aiyéró. And now I have to ask your forgiveness for the long deception. Your meeting abroad was no accident. Not what transpired between you two—that was your affair. But each time you sent me one of your postcards I wrote to our sons in that part of the world to look out for you. Demakin was only one of many."

Ofeyi digested the news with some measure of irritation as if he felt that he had been no more than an object of study to both men. Perhaps Ahime guessed what went on in his mind for he went on to add:

"He is very secretive by habit, perhaps it comes from his training. He wrote me that he had met you but he made me promise not to mention his links with me or with Aiyéró. That's the way he's always acted."

Then Ofeyi recalled some detail in the little of himself that the

Dentist ever revealed. "Was he lying" he asked, "when he said he was born in Irelu?"

"No. Like you he came to Aiyéró from the outside. But the effect of our community on him was to make him take off from the country. The last I heard of him was that he was off to join some liberation group. That is, until he found himself in flight to Europe when he wrote me a most bitter account and asked for news of home."

The noise of newcomers entering the camp interrupted them. "I think he's back" Ahime said.

A copper-haired head bent down to let himself into the tent and stopped at the sight of Ofeyi. They stared at each other for a wordless moment. Then the Dentist grinned, came fully into the tent. Zaccheus made room for him on the mat.

"Well. I wondered how long it would take you to find me."

"To find you out, you mean" Ofeyi countered.

The Dentist looked sharply at the old man who merely shrugged.

The Dentist spread out his arms. "Ah well, I should have told you a long time before."

"It's strange" Ofeyi conceded, "how it never occurred to me I would meet you in Cross-river."

"I came to try and stop four men—Amuri, Batoki, Biga and their uniformed stooge. It was the first chance we ever had to get all four together, at one blow; the situation was even appropriate, they were meeting to plot the fine details of this horror. Well, I needn't tell you we failed."

"What happened?"

"We were betrayed. We set the ambush on the road from their meeting. All the information was right—the hour, route, the place. Only, just before the motorcade came through, a helicopter began hovering above our heads. It wasn't even searching."

Ahime said, "What about tonight? What have you decided?"

"It can be done." He turned to Ofeyi. "We need a few more weapons for our own defence. I have just been scouting a police armoury and we raid it tonight. Would you like to help?"

Ahime said quickly, "Ofeyi has other things on his mind."

"Ah yes of course. The great search for a woman." There was an awkward silence. The Dentist himself broke it by asking, "Tell me, why is it important? I mean, you've taken the most suicidal pains over this, we know that."

Ofeyi returned his penetrating look, frankly. "Each person does what he is best at, remember?"

The Dentist, recollecting, said "Touché."

"But it is a little more than that" Ofeyi added. "I'm sure every man feels the need to seize for himself the enormity of what is happening, of the time in which it is happening. Perhaps deep down I realise that the search would immerse me in the meaning of the event, lead me to a new understanding of history."

The Dentist turned to Zaccheus. "And your friend here, what does he think? He has been with you most of the time hasn't he?"

Zaccheus shook his head vigorously. "No, don't ask me anything. I lost half my band in one of the very first attacks. I saw Celestial abducted. What am I to do? Sit down and die of self-pity?"

Zaccheus' outburst left them all evading one another's eyes, staring at the tent walls or at the floor. Ofeyi resumed eating, biting savagely into the maize.

Ahime tried to turn their minds away from that loss. "We plan that the camp should go into the furthest depths of the forest, join the river at the confluence and follow it home. For me this is a cleansing act. It will purify our present polluted humanity and cure our survivors of the dangers of self-pity."

The Dentist continued, "I insist on seeing it first as a good toughening exercise. The Aiyéró idea treks back to source, but it marks the route for a more determined return. Ofeyi, if you find the woman in time, would you join us on the trek?"

Ofeyi thought rapidly. "I don't know what her condition might be."

"Even if she were seriously ill . . . we know how to move fast through any terrain, even with our wounded."

The question seemed important to the Dentist. Ofeyi could not quite understand why and searched his face for a clue. Ahime waited on both.

"She may be dead" Zaccheus said, suddenly.

"Then we will take her body with us" the Dentist said.

If his intention was to shock, he was only too audibly success- ful. The Dentist ignored the gasps and went on calmly. "No, I haven't quite changed places with the cocoa-man here, who plucks symbols out of brothels. But we must acknowledge the fact— pimps, whores, thieves, and a thousand other felons are the famil- iar vanguard of the army of change. When the moment arrives a woman like Iriyise becomes for them a Chantal, a Deborah, torch and standard-bearer, super-mistress of universal insurgence. To abandon such a potential weapon in any struggle is to admit to a lack of foresight. Or imagination."

He stood up, thrust a handful of groundnuts in his pocket. "I must see to some urgent arrangements. If Pa Ahime hasn't told you already, we also have devoted some energy to searching for her. But we have to complement each other, I mean, even after she is found. I have already turned my mind to the strategy for the future."

"What's happened to the present one?"

"Was there really one? All I know is that the four men who should be dead by now got away from us."

He offered his hand to Ofeyi. "We may find her before you do. But with or without, I hope you will march with us."

Ofeyi shook hands but said nothing. After the Dentist was gone, Ahime continued to stare silently at the ground. Then he cleared his throat and placed his hand on Ofeyi's knee.

"I hope you will not think that I wish such a rapid end to your search that I hope for the worst result. But . . . it is best to begin with the worst. Have you . . . looked yet among the bodies in the mortuary?"

XII

"There is no more room in the mortuary."

Through the Casualty Ward, past rows of prefabricated laboratories trimmed round with bare lawns and connected by covered passages. They entered one of these, followed its twists and strove against gravity as it bore them down a gentle incline. The walls of the tunnel thickened as they went deeper, padded and roofed in grey asbestos. "No more room whatsoever" the doctor, their guide repeated. "It filled up in no time at all."

Before a massive lead-zinc door he produced a matching key and inserted it in the lock. The door opened sleekly, led to others. They passed through into yet another tunnel. It weighed on the searchers, still and airless. The doctor's words beat a refrain of variations in Ofeyi's head . . . no room in the morgue . . . no room in the morgue . . . no room at the inn . . .

Get out get out said the landlord
Shut his door in the face of the lord
Take up your rags Mr. Joseph and Mary
And pick up that brat with the face of a fairy
There's no more room in the morgue, in the
  morgue . . .

"Not bad not bad" he heard the doctor murmur. His voice had a soft but weighted inertia that seemed to hang in that dead air.

"What is not bad?" Ofeyi enquired. He had not said his jingle aloud, so the doctor could not have been referring to that.

"You don't look nervous or taut. Coming into a mortuary for the first time, most people do."

"No, in fact I suddenly made up a ballad." He stopped. "How curious. I haven't even hummed a tune in my head for nearly a week."

The medical turned. "Now that is most interesting."

"Not at all. In fact it was your 'no room in the morgue' that started me off. Reminded me of a tour I made through Europe not so long ago and the number of hotels which tried to pretend they had no more room."

"Ah" the doctor sighed. "You've been through that have you?"

"With a vengeance" Ofeyi said.

The doctor preceded them to the next door. "What was the ballad? I am most curious to hear it."

"It was not about that experience. My mind jumped to Herod's desperation for infanticide. And so on to the no-room-at-the-inn bit."

Zaccheus said, "Yep. I bet that's the way it was. You gotta know this guy doc. A word like that turns out a song like your dose of castor might shoot out a tape worm. If you'll pardon the analogy doc." His voice tapered out, seeing the doctor grimace.

"Well, how did the ballad go?"

Ofeyi forced a smile. "It is kind of you to try and take my mind off what we may find on the other side of that door. But I assure you it isn't necessary. I realize I have been doing that myself. Making up lyrics to take my mind off was part of it."

The man protested, "Not in the least, not in the least. It is a little indulgence I permit myself. Perhaps it helps me retain a healthy attitude in such morbid surroundings. Now your Nativity ballad—I say to myself—how curious! Then I wonder, does it reveal anything? Are you the kind whose mind instinctively joins up the entire cradle-grave cycle? Things like that. It stops me dwelling on what I really feel."

He pushed the last door wide open.

A band of cold encapsuled them at once. They entered on a carpet of cold, it crept up their feet and slowed up the flow of blood in their veins. Zaccheus shivered uncontrollably. The doctor remarked kindly, "Yes it is cold in here. That anterior passage helps a little to acclimatize the body."

"It didn't acclima nothing on this guy doc."

He and Ofeyi stood huddled by the door as if they did not dare come in any further into this icicle world. The doctor closed the door and moved towards a still life of five, mounted on a doubled trolley against the wall. Ofeyi moved forward as if in a trance, his eyes glued to a perfection of repose he had never yet encountered.

"These came last. We had hopes that we might save the child but it was a futile effort." He shrugged. "It would have made no difference in any case. The ones we did save, the killers came and finished them off—right on the operation table." He walked softly over to a corner of the concrete platform, pulled off a sheet. "Like him. I was rather proud of my work on this one. Heart and lungs badly perforated by bayonet thrusts but I worked under candlelight and managed to save him. Yes . . . I confess I felt very proud of that surgery."

They hardly took in the doctor's words. Eyes roamed round the oppressive stillness of every object. A ponderous stillness, a weight of eternity that seemed measurable clung to the smallest wad of cotton, pressed on the air and the grey fog of light in which the room was bathed. The temperature fell steadily, the living bodies felt clammy hands about them sucking their vitality into a universal deathness.

The chamber was split by raised concrete slabs, these also ranged around the walls, interrupted only by glass-and-zinc cupboards laden with test-tubes, slides, fluid-filled jars and human organs. On the slabs some of the bodies were already opened. Delicate instruments, scalpels and stainless forceps, glass tubes and hypodermic needles; then the heavy tools of the trade—choppers, hacksaws, meat-axes and huge weighing scales. They looked on grey frozen livers and congealed marrow. The brain was a fallen meteor: craters, ridges, a network of irrigation channels formed a microcosm of the world from which it had fallen. A heart sat in glazed aloneness on the top of a glass case, a funerary ornament above a body lying piecemeal, not in state.

Ofeyi felt the doctor's eyes on him. He returned his look and the man asked, "You don't feel faint or anything?"

"Why? Should I?"

"Some people do." He continued to finger something in his pocket.

Then there was a thud behind them. Zaccheus had collapsed, banging his head hard on the floor. The doctor rushed to his aid, smiling with undisguised satisfaction. He fished out the smelling-salts from his pocket and held it under the band-leader's wide nostrils. "Old-fashioned remedy" he commented, "but still the best. I was beginning to fear I would be disappointed."

Zaccheus woke to the gentle hum of the cooling plants. The doctor was still waving the phial to and fro under his nose while he blinked from one face to the other.

"You passed out" Ofeyi informed him.

"Never!" Zaccheus swore. "I must have slipped" he rubbed the back of his head, "there is a bump on the back of my head. That's what knocked me out."

The doctor shook his head, helped Zaccheus up and spoke in a disappointed voice. "Just the same I was wrong. The wrong man fainted."

"You mean it was I you . . ."

"I'm afraid so. I am losing my touch. This sudden inundation of death has dulled my judgement about the living . . . yes, I'll use that excuse I think." He turned brisk. "If your friend is fully recovered we had better begin our search hadn't we? I don't think you'll be able to survive this temperature for too long."

Zaccheus pulled at Ofeyi's sleeve. "If you ever tell anyone . . ."

"Are your legs all right?" the doctor asked, solicitous.

"Very well thank you. It was nothing."

"Good. Because we are about to start viewing them by the score."

Suddenly Ofeyi could contain himself no longer. As they passed a new body in which a cleaver still stood he burst out: "But Doctor, is this how you must treat a human body! Just like a butcher's shop? Two pounds of liver please a portion of spare ribs a prime cut from the haunch and a pound of breast. . . ."

"Ah yes, hm, it is rather like a butcher's shop I must admit."

"It is indecent!"

"Oh no I wouldn't say that. We don't find it indecent. We learn much about the human body here you know. Unfortunately . . . ah well, that will come in time too I suppose . . . but we don't seem to have learnt much about the human mind. What makes it act in this manner for instance . . . still, it is hopefully only a matter of time. . . ."

They resumed their progress through the trolleys and concrete slabs, stopped involuntarily at a family group. At least so they interpreted the pile—a father, a mother, three grown boys and a six-month pair of twins. The man and the eldest of the boys were badly charred, the others unmarked. Yellow ointment seeped through thick bandages on the eldest boy. A strangled cry came from Zaccheus: "Look at that!"

They followed the direction of his shaking finger. Hanging from a hook was a human rib-case. There was a repetition of the previous thud behind them and they turned at the sound.

"Oh dear, your friend has fainted again."

As the doctor bent over him Ofeyi said, "Maybe we should leave him there. I don't really need him for the search."

"In that case we must move him from the floor or he'll freeze to death."

They carried him onto a canvas stretcher, the doctor opened a cupboard, found a rug and covered him in it. "We shouldn't take long. I'll pull out the drawers, they come out head-first. Just nod No until Yes!"

As the doctor laid his hand on the first sliding compartment Ofeyi asked, "What was the history of that family group?"

"Oh that? They were locked in a room and the house set on fire. The others were simply asphyxiated, but the father and eldest son tried to make a break for it, tried to find an escape route for the rest."

Ofeyi nodded slowly. "All right. Let's see what we came here for."

The doctor pulled each drawer outwards on smooth rollers. A fresh gust of iciness revealed that it was still possible for the death chamber to deflate further the intruders' pretensions to warmth.

The trays slid forwards on smooth aluminium grooves and Ofeyi looked down directly on one death-mask after the other; the skins were drawn taut, grey and unreachable. Even those that bore labels had relinquished all pretensions to a human identity.

"Why don't I pull them out myself?" Ofeyi asked after the first twenty or more.

"All right. That ladder is for reaching the higher pallets. Just hook it against that rail."

He looked on one head after another, and he found himself thinking, how little one really knows of the top of a man's head. The face yes, a too familiar terrain. But the top of the head, one rarely sees that even through a life-time acquaintanceship. The doctor hovered anxiously below: "Are you sure wouldn't rather I pulled them out for you?"

"No, I think I can get through them quicker this way."

The doctor glanced up from time to time to catch the first sign of distress. Zaccheus recovered shortly afterwards and he made him sit down in a chair. They both watched Ofeyi and the movement of pallets in and out of the filing complex. Time and time again they caught a flicker of recognition but it was only Ofeyi's eternal alarm at human recognition—a frozen moment of thoughtfulness, of surprise, of hurt, anguish, of despair or of transcendental peace. Even a gruesome joy, but all forever frozen and greyed in a cold wind.

I'll lie here some moment in time, labelled perhaps or without the sham of identity. Perhaps only with a filing number—date, place where picked up, by whom picked up . . . too late for it to matter then, at least not to me whom it really concerns.

Third tier. Fourth, Fifth, Sixth. Two bodies to one compartment in some cases—these were the children . . . no, there was no more room in the morgue, the emptied hulk of Ofeyi would have to wait in the streets or rot in one of the makeshift graves.

As if it mattered. The feeling grew on him that Iriyise could not be here, that her living essence could not be summed up in one of these wax parodies of the human condition. Not one of these counterfeiting forms could desecrate her image by laying claim to a similarity in fate, so, why seek ye the living among the dead . . . still he continued . . . last row, last pallet. Out. In.

Relief? But I've known it all along. The ritual had to be undergone, no more.

When he came down he found the doctor holding up a piece of human tissue to the light. "Cancer" he explained. "Oh, not all the bodies here are from the recent carnage. This happened to be a case I was working on before my routine was forcibly suspended. That's a cancer tissue. We are isolating cancer tissues by the ton in every hospital all over the world but we still haven't worked out the causes." He replaced the tissue and smiled. "Well, at least you did not find her. There is hope."

"Yes . . . perhaps . . ."

He clapped him on the back. "There is hope. You mustn't let your spirits be cast down by the sobering experience of the search."

"Sobering . . . ? Yes. Yes I would call it that. In the face of every dead form there is something of all the humanity one has known, man or woman."

The doctor nodded. "Let's go back to my surgery. I have something there we usually requisition under the name Medical Comforts. I think you could do with a drop of it."

Ofeyi followed him out, nodding assent. Zaccheus shot out of the morgue yards before them.

A sensation—rather like a constriction in his breathing—held Ofeyi captive in the doctor's office the moment he let his body go lax in a chair. He fought down a sudden senseless heaving, an eruption in a little known part of him which struggled for release. Some long buried spring had welled into motion around his chest cavity; restricted, it threatened to burst through his mouth and nostrils, through ears, head and eyes, a violent memory awakened, an anger at loss only yet intuitively felt. It coursed through nerves long deadened by the incessant demands of the past months, and he strove powerlessly against a force that threatened humiliating release through tears. A cold claw clutched at his guts, savaging his breath. Then he felt gentle fingers pulling away his own which had formed a vise against his head and the commencement of a massage on his temples. The doctor spoke to him in a soft voice, almost as to a child:

"You should never try to stem back tears, not especially if you are unaccustomed to them. No, keep your eyes shut. Let your arms hang down. There, that's better."

Zaccheus stared at both in anxiety. "Is he sick doc?"

"No. Only a different version of what happened to you in there. I think he's fine now. How do you feel?"

"Better, thank you."

"Here's your drink. It is the local brand from your national distilleries I'm afraid. That is all the headquarters supply us these days. Quite right too but . . ."

Zaccheus laughed. "Couldn't agree with you more doc. Still—cheers!"

"I shall drink to a happy conclusion of your search."

"That is too much to hope" Ofeyi muttered.

"No, I believe you are wrong." He felt the two pairs of eyes on him—he had spoken with such considered emphasis—so he tried to explain. "I'm sorry, but it is really difficult to account for these things. When you came into this room earlier today and spoke about your search I . . . knew, yes, I knew that you were not talking about a dead person. She did not feel . . . did not emit—a dead aura." Feeling their eyes still dubiously on him he threw up his hands in frustration. "Oh words, words! A very long time ago I gave up this whole business of words. I started out to study history if you really want to know. Suddenly I switched over to medicine. Many things have happened since then but . . . take what took place here, in this very room only eight days ago. My senior nurse was killed in this room."

With a rapid movement he was across the room and had whipped off a pile of medical journals and books from the couch. A huge dark discoloration marked the beige cover. The doctor took out his pipe. He began to fill it from a tin.

"Yes, that stain was his. They followed him in here and killed him. Nobody would come near the hospital for days, I did all the cleaning myself, with the help of some patients, Cross-river natives of course. The others had fled or been killed. But I was about to tell you . . . when the murders began I was doing my ward rounds. From the wards I went straight to the surgery and there I remained for days on end. My nursing orderly never turned up. I moved from ward to surgery and back again, morning and night. I missed him dreadfully, but of course I hoped that he had made good his escape when the mob invaded us. His body never turned up you see, so I permitted myself to hope. It wasn't a very deep hope to tell the truth but you know how it is. The fellow had been so close to me throughout the years I've worked here, I couldn't quite accept the possibility of him not escaping. Then— yes, I remember—I was making my ward rounds again, I actually had my stethoscope against the chest of a geriatric, also taking his pulse. Then he asked me where my nurse was. And do you know, I just said straight out, without thinking, oh, my senior nurse? I think he is lying dead in my office."

He paused. The office grew oppressive with the presence of the murdered man. "Well you can imagine what happened. I was stunned, paralysed for some moments. Then I dashed upstairs. Sure enough the poor fellow was there lying across that couch.

Horribly gashed and mutilated poor man. Been dead for nearly a week."

Ofeyi took his glass and walked to the window, gazed at a vast tract of land, arid, stretched forever into emptiness. It was fissured all through as if it were a mudflat, only occasional tufts of grass broke the surface. A few crown birds sought grass seeds among these, stepping delicately through like stick-insects on swamp surface.

"Beautiful birds" the doctor murmured. "Such delicate head-feathers. Like coloured silk-cotton tassels."

"Yes, I suppose so." Ofeyi sank into more distant abstractions.

"Do you think the country will hold together?"

"After this? Who knows?"

"Well, let me ask instead—should it?"

Ofeyi turned to him. "Well, what do you think? What is your outsider's point of view?"

"A selfish one. Most of my medical work has been done here, so I know only the problems of the Cross-river people. They need the rest of the country, maybe down there you feel you don't need them. But they need you."

Ofeyi nodded in agreement. "Yes. And that is sufficient reason for us not to give up what we tried to do. But what do you think? Can these people ever understand the enormity of their crime?"

"They may not for another decade, but . . ." He stood beside him at the window. "Take that stretch of land, do you know it really is our unofficial hospital burial ground. Or was, until recently."

Zaccheus whistled and leapt up. "How come doc? I don't see no tombstones."

"There aren't any. The—er—well—the Cross-river Head of the Cartel—I am sure you know who I am talking about—yes, that character is really priceless." He pointed to the generous tract of land unbroken by tombstone or mound. "Whenever he went on his Islamic pilgrimages he brought back some minion to fill the high posts in the region. That included our own medical departments unfortunately. And the railways. You may recall the Kapagi disaster? Well, that train was driven by a senior railway engineer whom he had brought back from Pakistan as Senior Engineer. The man was only a station sweeper in his country."

"There was never an official report was there?"

"Naturally not. But the medical section paid dearest—well, the patients to be more accurate. A mere hospital orderly arrived here as a senior medical officer. He was in charge of this very hospital, so what was more natural than that he should begin to try his hand at surgery?"

Zaccheus swallowed his drink at a gulp and begged, "Doc, don't say it. Just don't tell me you had someone here slicing into patients and didn't know liver from kidney."

"Beyond the fact that he had been present in the operating room once or twice, wheeling patients in and out in Karachi, he had never been remotely near an operating table. It all came out at the enquiry. Oh yes, finally the fatalities grew too much. I mean, they were a matter of course." He waved his hand outside the window. "Scratch a few feet of those grounds and you'll find quicksands. In the rainy season you don't even need to dig. After an inch or two of rain has softened up the mud crust any deadweight on those flats simply gets sucked in. That's where that Pakistani surgeon buried his victims. Scores of them."

"How long did he last?"

"Some four years I think. Don't forget the Zaki's word is law here. Any talk which suggested something wrong and—the foolhardy mouth disappeared forever. Strange thing is, whenever Amuri himself took ill he did not use this place. He always sent for his private physicians from your university hospitals."

Zaccheus demanded, "But was he never put on trial, this butcher?"

The doctor shook his head. "There are no bodies to show. And no witnesses. The relations of the victims could be made to shut up." He raised the bottle. "Another drink? Matter of fact I too owe my job here to him. But I am qualified I assure you."

"You knew him?"

"Not him. Just a few of his ministers. They whispered in his ear. You see my father is quite a wealthy businessman. He and your politicians . . . well, let's just say they got on well."

Ofeyi looked the man fully in the face, studying him. The doctor met his gaze with some mild amusement. "What are you thinking, Mr. Ofeyi?"

Ofeyi admitted frankly, "Just wondering about you. Why have you remained—after all that happened? Many others simply packed and left."

"Oh I don't know. Guilt? A need to make some compensation. I can't help feeling that there is a chain-reaction in all this. My father is first and foremost a businessman. One of the richest men in Calcutta. He doesn't much care what sort of associates he makes. Profits Mr. Ofeyi. Profits. That is my old man's one philosophy. He had no scruples. He got on very well with your political leaders."

Zaccheus remained absorbed in the affair of the surgeon. "But look here doc, what happened to this butcher-man? Did they just send him packing off home and nothing more? I mean, what happened to the bastard?"

"I see you are not quite familiar with the realities of Crossriver. He was transferred to another hospital, retained his rank and—what do they call it now—emoluments. But he was forbidden all further surgery, that was all. In fact I ought to tell you, the only reason the affair got as near the public as it ever did was that one victim of his turned out to be a relation of one of Amuri's henchmen. It was all rather complicated. The henchman's cousin had been taken to this hospital on the recommendation of another Amuri follower. Naturally the bereaved man—well, it seemed there had been certain personal rivalries and so on—this henchman thought his rival had got his cousin killed deliberately. But for that internal cesspit of rivalries my colleague from Pakistan may have gone on doing his butchery forever and ever."

And now something, he could not remotely guess what, stirred in Ofeyi's memory. Abruptly he asked, "Where did you do your training?"

"Britain and Germany. But I do assure you . . ." he spread out his hands, "I'll show you my diplomas if you like."

"No no" Ofeyi reassured him. "I was not doubting you. It's just that . . . well you suddenly reminded me of someone I knew. An Asian . . . maybe someone I had met with in my student days."

"Never mind. We Asians all look alike."

They found relief in laughter. "Seriously, you don't look one bit alike. In fact, to quote yet another phrase you must be familiar with—you are not a typical Asian."

"So you know about that too. I practised in England for two years and I came in for quite a bit of those insular idioms. Did it used to annoy you as much as it did me?"

Ofeyi waved it aside impatiently. "Who remembers much of those reactions now? I realize they were luxuries—the emotional responses I mean. Who cares ultimately how those stupid master races reacted to you and me. The problem now is how to answer what is happening here."

There was a long silence. Their eyes and minds returned to the quicksand graves beyond the hospital walls. The crown birds had diminished but now flocks of egrets swept across the barren expanse, ghostly couriers in the twilight of a criminal silence buried in the mudflats. Their shadows danced over the graves.

"Well? What do you do now?"

"Continue searching." He laid down his glass and held out his hand. "You have been very generous with your time, thank you very much." The doctor opened a drawer and brought out a cyclostyled map. "This is where I live. If you feel like dropping in any time—in fact, why not tonight? Come over for dinner. I am certain you won't be looking all the time. What about to-night?"

Ofeyi hesitated.

"It is no trouble I assure you. My mother and sister are visiting, they came just before the troubles started. They'll do the cooking and we can talk." His voice sounded earnest. "Do come. They have never met anyone since they arrived so you would be doing me a favour. They arrived in the middle of a siege atmosphere, you can imagine it—locked and barred doors, screams in the neighbourhood and all that. You would be most welcome I promise you."

Zaccheus broke in. "Sure doc, why not. C'mon Ofe we ain't got much else to do."

Ofeyi nodded. "Thank you. I think we could do with a bit of sanity."

"Good. The map will get you there. Government reservation. If you get lost just ask anyone there for the medical quarters."

"We'll find it." He held out his hand again. "You really have been very helpful."

Outside, Zaccheus said, "What next maestro? It's getting dark."

Ofeyi pointed to the petrol gauge. "First we fill up, then we pay another call on that Police Inspector."

They were preparing to drive out of the station when Zaccheus pointed at a passing car and said, "That's the doc heading home. Man must be worked to death."

Ofeyi's headlights slewed round across the main road as the

doctor drove past. Beside him was seated a young woman, also with unmistakable Asian features. Involuntarily Ofeyi slammed on the brakes.

"What's the matter?"

"That girl Zaccheus. Did you see that girl?"

"Yah. Wasn't one bit like Celestial if that's what you mean."

Ofeyi sat behind the wheel, not moving. Then he shook his head and re-started the vehicle. "No, it's not possible. I am beginning to see things."

They found the house easily from the map. The doctor himself opened the door and they stepped into a carpeted lounge. A figure of Kali stood on a podium improvised from an elephant's foot. There was a smell of incense in the air. The skin of a wild cat, probably a leopard, hung from the wall and then in rapid succession Ofeyi's eyes followed one hunting trophy after another, followed the heavy trail of incense braiding fur and even clusters of ostrich feathers. He looked disbelievingly at the unlikely person of his host, and asked him if he hunted.

The doctor shook his head. "Our neighbour does. Or did. Some are gifts we had from him ages ago. The rest we are merely keeping for him while he's . . . away."

Ofeyi said, "I didn't think you looked like the hunting type."

The doctor gave an indulgent smile. "Are there really hunting types, or any definable human types?" Then he looked apologetic. "Excuse me, come into the sitting-room. Mother would never forgive me if she knew I had engaged you in argument the moment you walked in. But you are quite right. I hate all violent sports. Sports!"

Zaccheus grinned. "You're the opposite of maestro here. Give him a ghost of a chance and he'll blaze away at the cooingest pair of doves if they looked plump enough."

The doctor took the pipe from his mouth and looked surprised. "Now I have to confess I had not only typed but mis-typed you. I didn't think you looked the hunting type. Good gracious, how utterly wrong I was. Do you really enjoy hunting?"

Ofeyi hummed and hawed. "Well, a little you know. I don't often get the chance."

Zaccheus guffawed. "You should see him on those early tours of ours before things got so tough you didn't dare get caught with a bow and arrow. A little you know . . . ho ho! Some little!"

"You would have got on well with my neighbour. A real big game maniac. That elephant foot belonged to one of his victims. Mounting Kali on top of it is my sister's idea. She doesn't enjoy the blood sports either but she wallows in hunters' tales. You should see her sitting open-mouthed when Semi-dozen regales us with his adventures. Talk of Othello and Desdemona. You wait until she finds out you also hunt. . . ." He put his head round the passage door and called out, "Mother! Taiila! The guests are here what are you still doing back there?"

Ofeyi stood rock-still. The doctor turned to encounter his thunderstruck face.

Ofeyi turned in the direction of the passage down which the doctor had shouted, half-dreading an impossible confirmation. He did not know when his host came close up to him, looking anxiously into his eyes. "I say, are you all right?"

Ofeyi turned slowly to encounter his gaze. "I . . . did you say Taiila?"

"Yes, that's my sister. I told you she was staying with me."

"She was with you in the car this afternoon? I mean when you left the hospital?"

"Of course. In fact she had been waiting in the reception while we went in the mortuary. . . ."

Ofeyi shook his head violently. "No. It would be too much."

"Chalil."

All three turned at the voice. Ofeyi tried to shake himself awake. The same enormous goblets of eyes, lithe, gazelle limbs impossibly long . . . only the hair was different, drastically so. She had cut it close to the skull, black and glossy in a light hug down the nape of her Modigliani neck. He recalled too who had said that, the total stranger who had come across to them in the restaurant, unable to contain himself, and how offended she had been! So the copy is now the idiom for Nature, she complained, unmollified by the old-worldly homage of the smooth, Mephistophelian face. You must have a drink on me he had said. I wish to toast the most beautiful couple I have encountered in this wretched, grimy city. His accent sounded Italian. Couple? Ofeyi confessed himself charmed by the man's tact, and the offer of wine was more than gracious.

The brother occupied himself with glancing from one to the other, his pipe hanging slackly down his mouth. Finally his face proclaimed the light breaking through. He struck himself on the forehead and shouted:

"Don't tell me! Just don't tell me that this is your African!"

He leapt across to the passage and shouted, "Ma, ma! Come here. Come here and see what's happened. I think Taiila has found her African."

Taiila came forward, offering her hands. A frail sprightly woman followed, wiping her hands hurriedly on a dishcloth. Ramath hurried her from the doorway into the room. "Look! Ask her yourself. This must be the man!" He was hopping about like a tree-sprite, puffing in spasmodic excitement. "What do you think of that eh? What do you think of that? How come you never saw that in your dreams, just try and explain that."

Mrs. Ramath held out a very dignified hand to her guests. "You mustn't mind my son's foolishness. He thinks he can explain everything by cutting up people."

Ofeyi felt a warm hand thrust into his. She came barely up to his chest, a little swallow trying to peer above tall grasses. Neither the grey hair smoothed straight back into a neat bun at the base of her head nor the wrinkles above her uplifted gaze could diminish the child-inquisitive sensitivity of the face. A fragile neatness that did not belong to the world of kitchens, shouts, children wetting granny knees and irate hungry husbands. Her kindliness seemed far more generous and roomy. Instinctively Ofeyi felt that she could accommodate all the world on her knees and yet remain unruffled. Hands, brow and eyes of radiating calm and paradoxical alertness . . . Ofeyi caught himself, stopped trying to see the child Taiila in her.

"What about your aura now Ma?"

Taiila answered for her. "Ignore him. I had weird vibrations waiting for him in the reception room but I could not interpret them. I mean, it is such a vast country. How could I even dream . . ."

The doctor snorted. Taiila rounded on him. "Well didn't I tell you about them on the way back. Answer that, did I or didn't I?"

"The engine was misfiring at the time, I explained to you. The car always vibrates in protest."

It was all so remote. Time out. Time and place way way out. Could this family really be engaged in good-natured teasing over their psychic affectations and cynicisms. Again he felt the intruder, I, Ofeyi, the eternal intruder, what do I know of these family scenes, these insulated oases of peace, peace. These microcosms of Aiyéró. A wild improbable idea rose from within and suffused him—why don't I marry this being and forget the outer chaos. Now, this instant, accept the most tempting interpretation of improbabilities—her presence here, the manipulative sequence of the encounter, accept, accept . . . no, impose my own need for peace that passeth all misunderstanding. . . .

Ofeyi recollected the winter days, proclaimed foolishly, "You have retained your superstitions I see."

"How long ago Ofe?" she asked.

"Time has suddenly stood still. I am blank."

"I shall get the food" the mother said.

"And maybe I should look to the records." Chalil said. He turned to Zaccheus who merely stood and blinked from one to the other. "You want to come with me? Music is your field I gather."

"Sure doc, sure."

Alone in the lounge Taiila took his arm. "Let's go on the verandah."

They leant against the balustrade. Taiila chuckled suddenly. "Imagine that. So it was you he had with him in the mortuary all that time. I knew that was where he was, that's why I waited in the reception. To give him time to get rid of the stench of death. But I never felt for a moment it was you in there with him. In spite of the weird vibrations. Once, they came so thick I felt I might faint."

"Zaccheus did."

"Who? Oh, you mean your friend. In the mortuary?"

"Yes."

"Chalil is a ghoul. So you didn't faint?"

"No. But I had very strange sensations afterwards. I had seen enough of dead people in my time, motor accidents, and then, recently . . . But it was the first time I had seen them in filing cabinets. Or like meat on a butcher's slab."

"What did you feel Ofe? Tell me."

Ofeyi shook his head. "Now I see it's a family trait. Your brother kept asking me that question."

She waved him aside as if he was a different proposition entirely. "He is just a morbid joker Chalil; don't pay him any attention. Did he tell you it was his only hobby?"

Ofeyi, after some reflection conceded that the doctor had said something to that effect. Taiila nodded sagely. "It is too. I keep telling him it isn't healthy. And he is superstitious, though he always denies it. He really loves to take people through the morgue and watch their reactions. He claims it tells him much about humanity—does that make sense to you?"

The deductive possibilities struck him for the first time, but Taiila gave him no time for reply, plunging straight backwards in time to her initial, adolescent yet strangely wise encounter. "Are you surprised to find I am not in a nun's habit?"

Like the eyes, limbs, low-voiced timbre this other recollection took formal shape, the facility of her mind to accept, evince the minimal surprise and move into grooves of new actualities as though a time had never intervened. There had been that strange view of predestination she held . . . I on my radials, you on your laterals Ofeyi, we are bound to cross again and again because we are seeking the same goal of quietude, which is the centre of the web. And my only question Ofeyi is when you will tire of it all, when you will turn sharply from the circling laterals and take the slower, quieter path with me. Beyond that first momentary pause of disbelief, she had absorbed their reunion while he still groped for words and pondered what this would mean in terms of his initial quest, alarmed already at the disloyal comparisons his mind had begun between the infectious calm and the turbulent quest which would go beyond even the finding of Iriyise.

Taiila would make the point over and over again, in the midst of a battle in his mind for decision during the encounters of his brief banishment—you wish to fight every inch of the undergrowth when all you need do is step aside onto a direct path to the still centre of peace. And the wise knowing laughter to his scornful retort: who seeks peace? Who has the right to expect peace? You barely avoid the blasphemous equivalent, happiness, do you know that? I know better than to use it with you Ofeyi, she replied, but I don't really distinguish between the two.

Ofeyi spoke. "This afternoon, we were just turning out of a petrol station when your brother drove past. I saw you but I said, impossible!" There was silence between the two, then he asked, "Why did you come?"

She shrugged. "Why not? Chalil was here. Mother wanted to come and I had not yet taken my vows. There was every chance I might hear of you. You are not a very obscure person by nature."

"Ah yes, my aura of violent emanations, I haven't forgotten. . . ."

She laughed. "I didn't mean that. But I had a feeling. . . ."

"What has become of the nun?" he asked, trying to read into the depths of her mind. She tapped her breast and said, "She is still in here. Almost at the centre."

Ofeyi felt a sudden, unreasonable anger at her calmness, her floating untouched assurance. "Perhaps you think to reach it sooner out here. You have managed to float above it all haven't you? Or perhaps you have simply seen nothing."

She looked surprised. "Oh. Hasn't Chalil told you what happened here?"

"What do you mean, here? In the city centre?"

"Oh no, I mean right here. In these expatriate reservations . . . Oh I see, Chalil didn't tell you."

He felt his voice fall thin, crestfallen. "What happened here? All your brother did was take us round the mortuary."

She nodded slowly to herself, withdrawing deeper and deeper into herself. "You must get him to tell you about his houseboy. Our neighbour warned him but no one took him seriously." Her face was taut suddenly, tired. "What made you think that any spot in Cross-river was exempt from this madness Ofe?"

He stood looking over the sundowner golf-culture preserves

which the first colonial masters had created for themselves, far from native smell, protected by distance against the possibilities of sporadic rebellions. The distance warning system had continued for the new white-graded elites like himself, a few Asian expatriates like Chalil. In Cross-river white descendants of that first domination inhabited such isolated areas of gracious living, immune from the squalor and occasional pack wars among the congested rats in the urban tumescence. A shadow of defeat crossed his face. In a sense, Cross-river had been tackled too late. The slit-eyed packs had leant more and more heavily on such white expatriate neutrality and paternalism and, when that source of leavings became gradually depleted the resentful packs were shamed into self-hatred from the long beggar reliance on the alien condescending purses. Nothing to aid the possibility of self-rebuilding, the self that took its place. The new tenants of such preserves simply acquired the shell of distance; the rat-packs waited, ready for revenge and mischief.

Taiila's voice enquired, "You have many problems Ofe? You have been very unhappy?"

He laughed, self-deprecatingly. "Don't look for lines of the tragic romance of life on my face."

Crestfallen, she looked away. "I didn't mean . . ."

Gently, he took her hand. "Neither did I. All I meant was . . . I have been too busy or too wholesomely dissatisfied to be unhappy."

"Ah yes . . . your eternal discontent. . . ."

"Divine. What's happened since? It used to be divine discontent."

She shook her head. "I don't believe that any longer. It threatens to last a lifetime if life is what I observe . . . what I have observed since I came here. What I still see in you. Nothing that eats the human life away has the smallest touch of divinity. It is all so . . . insignificant, I mean, ultimately. Well isn't it?"

They looked down over successive gradients of low-turfed hills onto the distant city. Whatever life it held bore no relation to the privileged preserves. A few ribbons of lights marked the major roads. A will-o-wisp in and out of pools of darkness betrayed a lonely cyclist. The brighter, more powerful lamps moved swiftly, from point to point of safety. Motorists, they felt the most vulnerable even in their lethal capsules of steel.

Gazing at the sky Taiila said, "I used to think, up in the mountains at home, that we had the clearest night-sky in the world. But, just look at that. I swear the stars here actually twinkle. Twinkle! They radiate feelers, you know, like those silk-cotton seeds floating about. And each feeler is differently coloured, blue, green, orange. Look at that one. It really does twinkle, don't you think so?"

"I am thinking more of the smouldering pockets of terror below us."

"Let's go in then," she said abruptly. "Food is nearly ready anyway."

A pungent swirl of succulent odours assailed them—okro fingers, chicken, curry, dahl and garden eggs in a riot of permutations. They entered to the querulous voice of Zaccheus offering to fetch them. "I know they have a lot to talk about Mrs. Ramath but I am hungry."

"You are always hungry Zack. Full stop."

"There he goes again. Do we have to wait for you all night?"

"Peace" said Mrs. Ramath, and waved them all to their seats.

Zaccheus slipped a casual finger beneath the table. Chalil, pouring the drinks saw him and announced, "Ma, someone means business. The bandleader has just loosened his trouser zip."

"He's just a vulgar snoop" Taiila assured Zaccheus. "Take off your trousers if you like. Chalil will lend you the wrap he normally uses when he eats, the hypocrite."

"That's a loyal sister for you."

It is not real, Ofeyi murmured, and inwardly cursed his growing incapacity for immersing himself even in pauses of relief. The feeling persisted and grew that there could be no natural entitlement to this, that the moment's normality was doomed to be revealed a mere mockery, a sham of a dream. What business had they all with such a mundane activity of life? A foaming mug of beer . . . he took it from Chalil's hand, disbelieving in its materiality, sipping a recognizable tang of hops . . . and the little old lady filling his plate with chicken breast. . . .

"Remember those curries I made for you that winter?" Taiila asked.

He stammered. The mother asked, "Is she setting herself up to be as good a cook as I am?"

"Now let's see whether you are polite or loyal" Taiila challenged him.

Ofeyi pulled himself together suddenly, raised his beer-mug. "I tell you what. Let's drink to the greatest contribution to culinary civilization: Indian Curry."

"Coward!" Taiila sneered.

But Chalil had remained for the past few moments by the sideboard, staring into the darkness to the rear of the house. His voice took on a quiet tautness. Without taking his eyes off from the window he said: "Something is happening in the next house I think."

They were all huddled together at the window, straining into the darkness. The night shadows had taken on a sinister pulsation, alien to the moments before, an uninvited guest that lay about the sill peering in against gaiety and banter. Under his breath Zaccheus swore and murmured, "There is no peace for the sinner damn it." The dishes grew cold, forgotten by most.

The quiet, undemonstrative Chalil gasped aloud as a figure stepped out of the front door of the bungalow on which their attention was strained. A fat, paunchy man in a dirty singlet, slouched under a world-weariness and surrender. Nothing had ever so vividly expressed—in the knowledge of all—such a totality of collapse of the human will. His eyes were unseeing, the eyes of a man who had shut his eyes to hope or salvation.

"Look at his eyes" Chalil said. "The man is blank. He has lost his mind."

"Why is he here?" Mrs. Ramath demanded. "I thought you said he had left. I thought the house was empty."

"So did I" Chalil muttered drily.

"He's lost weight" Taiila said. "He is only half his weight," she insisted.

Ofeyi demanded, "Who is he?"

"The mining engineer I told you about, our neighbour. He assured me he was packing out. I don't understand how he comes to be here."

The eyes of the man who walked between the rows of croton hedges were those of a man dead to the world. He shuffled slowly forward, hesitated, turned and looked back towards the house and shuffled forward again. "It is as if he has leaked. Leaked through his trousers. He's only half his size Chalil."

It never occurred to any of his neighbours to call to him. In the outer encirclement of the light pool which the man had created by switching on his porch light—the abnormal event that had first attracted Chalil's attention—there hung a menace that communicated itself even to Ofeyi and Zaccheus who were strangers to the neighbourhood. They waited and watched.

"You say you can use a gun?" Chalil half-turned towards Ofeyi.

"Yes."

"Semi-dozen left a double-barrelled shotgun with us. It's hanging on . . ."

"Yes I saw it. You want me to get it?"

"Please. I am useless with those things. There are cartridges in the cardboard box on the chair."

Ofeyi moved swiftly in the direction of the gun.

"But how can a big man leak out like that? Just like that! Within a few days." Mrs. Ramath continued to wail.

"What was he doing in there all this time, that's all I want to know. I thought he had left."

Ofeyi returned with the gun, broken at the breech. The brass cups of two cartridges gleamed in the breech. "Listen" he began. "Just give me a vague idea what is happening."

Chalil's finger circled to indicate the cashew and bougainvillea trees surrounding the house. "I've only just understood it myself." There were flutterings of white among the green branches, sharp gleams of eyes. "But I still don't understand why the man is still here. Or why he has chosen to commit suicide." He turned to his sister. "Do you understand it? You were here when he brought his things to us for safe-keeping. Was there anything he said I might have missed?"

Taiila thought it all over . . . the big extrovert voice, downing one bottle of Guinness Stout one after the other, casual, relaxed. She had looked for a hint of fear in his face but there had been none. Drank his stout the way he always did, one bottle a gulp, rest, talk, laugh, the huge booming voice all over the house, his generous paunch overflowing the brevity of his evening singlet . . . what on earth could have gone on in his mind on that last visit! She saw him walking in through the front door, hearty, beefy and confident, not like this caricature of his former self now slouching to certain death between the crotons . . . "aha-a-ah! Thought I was gone didn't you? Fooled you, that's all I did. Planning to give you a surprise that was all your old Semi-dozen was up to. Neither more or less, like my faithful semi-dozen. I just stocked up, made everyone believe I was leaving and then lay low until the damned foolishness blew over. Only came out 'cause I was getting lonely with no one to talk to over my evening semi-dozen, what's wrong with that?"

A heaving belly of which he was so proud . . . when the insects swarmed in the wake of the rains he would shake with laughter . . . "no, they won't stay long around this body of mine. They know I make them sea-sick when I gulp down one of my nightly six. No, they won't sting me. It's you Doctor they're after. You're so thin they mistake you for a landing strip." The asbestos ceiling shook with his bellow. And the unfortunate sausage fly with curling sting really found itself hanging from the underlip of an enormous wave, dizzy and shaken, flying off to find a more secure base for the night's excursion. . . . Had there been an uncomfortable feeling about his gaiety that night? An excessive tone that bordered dangerously on a collapse?

"Oh Dr. Chalil I feel so light-hearted tonight, light in spirit, light in heart and impossibly light in the belly . . . yes, I saw them all off this afternoon, saw them off at the garage. By now they should be half-way home to safety. Tomorrow morning I follow them. Had to see to the final tidying up. You sure you don't mind looking after these heavyweight nuisances for me?"

"Good. And that's the last of the six for tonight. No, not another bottle for Semi-dozen. That's where the trouble begins. I never exceed my semi-dozen per night. After the regular, I stop. Then I start all over again ha, ha ha ha! No, but not tonight. Last-minute packing to be done. . . ."

And then he had looked up suddenly and seen Edwin.

She shivered, her eyes shut tight in recollection of the horror that had overtaken them because they ignored his warning.

"Edwin is still here?"

Chalil, complacently: "Oh yes of course. The safest place for him is here."

And Semi-dozen had shaken his head. "No no no no, send him away quickly. Quickly. There is another airlift tomorrow, get him on that. Don't even send him by road."

"We can protect Edwin" Chalil said. "But in any case they won't come this way at all. They haven't attacked any of the expatriate reservations."

"I've . . . I've sent my family . . . away," Semi-dozen repeated. And his voice sounded slurred, more slurred and drunken than they had ever known it. "I've sent them all home . . . safe."

"Sure" Chalil had replied. "Best not to take chances. But Edwin is quite safe here."

The big man lumbered up, put his hand to his eyes and wobbled about on his feet. Chalil sprang up, thinking he would collapse. He waved him aside. "I am all right . . . quite all right. I think I'll go to sleep now."

"I'll walk you across the lawn" Chalil offered.

The big man had brushed him savagely aside, wordlessly. Then staggered home.

"What is he doing now for god's bloody sake?" Zaccheus had ceased to make sense of it all.

The man with a flapping jacket over a dirty white singlet stood at the little wicket-gate that led into his garden. Shadows cast by the retreating porch-light created deeper shadows in his ample cheeks than seemed normal, even for those who had never met him. And then, to successive gasps from the dining-room, figures dropped from the hovering branches, the shrubbery sprouted heads, then shoulders; silent figures emerged from the shadows and converged on him.

Semi-dozen stared stupidly, then began his retreat towards the house, blinking. He retreated two or three steps to only one of his stalkers', they seemed concerned not to panic him, merely to close in on him, enjoy the sight of the big man breaking and pleading for his life.

Semi-dozen broke and ran. His pursuers responded by merely fanning round the house, surrounding it completely. The engineer ran into the supposed safety of the house. The watchers heard the rapid slam of bolts and locks. Then silence.

"Fool!" Chalil muttered aloud.

Zaccheus wrung his hands, slumped into a chair and wailed, "We can't just leave him there. I know the swine. They will break in any moment and butcher him."

What they had thought, the stalkers who had waited so long in the shadows was that the man had emerged to yield himself up for orderly slaughter. A change in their mood now took place, as if this was not how they had expected the game to be played. Suddenly the crash of stone against glass pane broke the momentary stillness, then another, and another. Ofeyi fingered the guard of the double trigger and admitted frankly, "I don't know what to do. What are we supposed to do in God's name?"

Zaccheus leapt up suddenly. "The telephone! Why haven't we telephoned the police?"

Chalil shook his head. "There is no telephone."

"But you are a doctor. This is medical quarters. What do you mean there is no telephone?"

It was Taiila who explained. "The house had one. They tore it off the day they came for Edwin—Chalil's houseboy. They killed him on our doorstep."

A long silence filled the room.

"We had no choice" Taiila went on. "Chalil had to give him up. There were over a hundred of them. We could do nothing." She broke down sobbing. The mother, straight-faced and riddled with the hurt of recollection told the rest of the story. "We had hidden him for the whole day. They simply waited. We couldn't leave the house. Chalil tried all he could, pleaded with them, and threatened. He defied them and . . . for that, they made us watch. Forced us to stand there, on the gravel path, while they cut his throat."

Ofeyi rose out of the silence. "It's dark. They don't know that anyone will come to his aid. But I don't know the neighbourhood very well. If you could just give me a layout of the place. There must be a backway to the house. . . ."

"I'll come with you," Chalil said.

"No!"

"We'll have to hurry" the doctor continued, unruffled. "I have just heard the fourth stone go into the house. The next missile might be a lighted torch. They will probably try to smoke him out."

"There is only this gun" Ofeyi pointed out. "And in any case you don't shoot."

Chalil had disappeared into the passage, vanished into one of the rooms that led off it. During the next few seconds of silence they listened to two more windows broken in the house. Then the doctor reappeared, and he had a bow in his hand. It looked a hardier version of the tourist brand sold in their hundreds at airports and outside expatriate clubs. He inspected an iron-tipped arrow from the quiver slung over his shoulders.

"Come on" he said. "I was once a student of contemplative archery, but I was a despair to my guru. There was a question of mine he never could satisfactorily answer: why is a non-target not a target? Since I could not be satisfied on that point I alternated constantly between both. I took pleasure in both. Let's go. Oh, does the band-leader drive?"

"Zaccheus? Of course."

"Good. Then perhaps whenever you are forced to let off the first shot he can take that as a signal to get in the car and dash off for help."

The mother screamed instantly, "Leaving us here alone?"

Ofeyi agreed with her. "No, he will have to take you with him. They will be too busy coping with the surprise of gunfire. I don't think they'd be expecting anything of the sort."

Chalil nodded in agreement. "If it's the same gang as killed Edwin—and I am certain it is—they would feel very confident we will not interfere."

"Don't stop for anything Zaccheus. If anyone jumps in the way, don't brake."

"I can drive with four flat tyres" Zaccheus promised.

"Ofeyi . . ." It was Taiila.

"Yes, we'll be careful."

They crept out through the back door.

A door was violently shaken in the besieged house. Chalil, crouched beside Ofeyi under a hedge asked, "Isn't it time to fire your scaring shot?"

"Not yet. And I don't think there should be warning shots."

"Can you see in this dark. Because I can't."

"Don't try and look for faces. Look for white smocks. They are mostly dressed in white—a dirty white anyway."

Chalil strained. "Ah yes, I get your point."

"Let's find that rear entrance you mentioned."

Chalil led. They dashed forward at a crouch. A few yards from the objective they stopped, beaten to it by a figure in white kaftan who now crouched beside it. In his hand were pieces of rags, and a tin which he threw aside. In that still night the acrid tang of petrol hit their nostrils.

Chalil whispered, "Hey mister, don't you think now . . . ?"

"Maybe we should try yours first. Are you sure you can hit with that thing?"

Chalil had already fitted an arrow to the bow. "Never tried a human target before."

"Except with a scalpel eh? Well, try and imagine it's the same thing. Shoot to heal."

The arrow pulled back into his right shoulder, Chalil said, "I admire your British-type jokes but I need instructions. I can't cope otherwise, so it's not a time to be ambiguous. Do you mean merely to wound him or what?"

"I meant that the engineer is your patient."

Chalil sighed. "A-ah" and let go the arrow. The sound that came from the action was a shotgun blast and a huge red flare in the darkness.

The crazy thought flashed through Ofeyi's mind before he could fathom the result—is this a magic potency of the oriental archer? Chalil himself, shattered by the result had ducked down into a crouch. The cry of the backdoor arsonist was drowned by the blast itself. It came, clearly, from some other part of the house. The next moment they saw a little window open, not far from the door which had been their goal. A face looked round anxiously, satisfied, it stuck a leg through and proceeded to squeeze his huge frame through the tiny opening.

Ofeyi saw him first and pointed. "Is that he?"

"Oh yes, it's Semi-dozen. Did the shot come from him?"

"Quickly. Go and help him through. I shall stay here and keep you covered."

"Good gracious! You really sound like . . ."

"Hurry!"

Ofeyi darted nervous eyes around, keeping an eye also on the incongruous sight at the window. Chalil seemed to have proceeded sensibly, identifying himself in a whisper before he seized the man round the waist and tried to man-handle him through the narrow aperture. There followed a brief silent argument, then he saw Chalil spring and catch hold of the window-sill and disappear into the room. Ofeyi was still absorbed in this insane development when he heard a sound on the dead leaves almost directly behind him. He froze. A man's breathing so close that it seemed his next step must stub his toes against his heels. He held his breath. Ofeyi was certain that the man was insensible to his own presence, that his eyes were riveted on the happenings at the window. The man took a step forward. Acting on his hearing alone Ofeyi spun on his knees and thrust the muzzle of the gun upwards in the direction where he judged the man's plexus would be. He heard a winded gasp and ducked sideways as the man, doubled in pain fell forwards on his face. Unhesitating, he reversed the gun and brought the stock crashing on the back of his skull. The man lay still.

Returning his attention to the window he saw Chalil handing another gun backwards to Semi-dozen, then leaping down beside him. They ran forward at a crouch. Chalil appeared to have to nudge the man forward. Panting slightly Chalil picked up his bow and quiver and pushed Semi-dozen towards his house muttering, "Come on friend. We've stayed out here much too long."

A heavy crash told them that a main door had been broken down at last. Beyond Ramath's own house they heard a car start up. Zaccheus, obviously mistaking the shot for Ofeyi's was carrying out his orders. Ramath shook his head in annoyance as he understood. They regained the house, locked the door. Ofeyi went to a window overlooking that rear section from which they had just come. Satisfied that they had not been observed he rejoined them in the lounge. Chalil was already at the sideboard. He returned a moment later with three glasses.

"I know you would rather have your Stout, but as your doctor I recommend this for now."

Wordlessly, the engineer obeyed. He drained the contents of the glass at one gulp, then sat with his head fallen of its own weight over his chest, staring stonily into the ground. He was like a shambling ape, doped half-insensible, still unaware of his surroundings.

"If you want a wash or anything . . ."

Surprisingly the man understood what was said to him. He shook his head. The action raised his eyes for the first time and they encountered a table laden with the untouched dinner. He stared at it for several moments as if he was trying to grapple with its meaning. Then he stood up with purpose, pulled out a chair, sat down and began to eat.

Chalil and Ofeyi looked at each other, shrugged and sat down with him.

They ate without speaking.

Outside they could hear the wreckage of the house in progress. The marauders had broken in and were searching for their quarry with increasing fury. The rescued man ate solidly, remorselessly. Chicken legs disappeared and a mound of curry-drenched rice vanished without a trace, accompanied by a dozen items from the side-dishes. Still no word. He finished eating at last, wiped his lips then reached over suddenly and took hold of Chalil's left wrist. But he only turned it aside to examine his watch. He gave a loud, prolonged belch, pushed his chair back and struck what was unmistakably a listening posture. Ofeyi looked questioningly at the doctor. He shrugged, then looked keenly at the man, nodded as if he finally understood and mouthed the word, "Shock." Ofeyi agreed with him.

About forty seconds later, an earthquake erupted against their ears. At least so it seemed. It began with a terrifying explosion, then a violent shaking of the ground beneath them. Earth flew against the windows and a huge sheet of flame leapt into the night-sky. Chalil and Ofeyi gyrated in every direction for the cause, the explosion seemed to come from all around them, leaving no choice of a direction in which to take shelter. Only the big man remained unmoved. In the quiet which followed a few moments later, broken only by the steady crackle of the burning house they heard Semi-dozen give a huge sigh. Then he began to speak, softly.

"Don't bother yourselves about the house. There is nothing in it to be saved. Nothing. It was kind of you to come doctor, but I really had no wish to be saved. All I wanted was to draw them into the house and take them with me."

Anticipating the event, but only half crediting the threat, Nnodi had decided on the favourite compromise, send the family southwards to safety but ride out the danger himself. The Mining Trust was a state within a state; it ran its own electric power, patrolled its territory with a private police force, maintained its own arbitrary wage structure, untouched by the industrial upheaval of the rest of the land. Naturally, it paid a negotiated tribute to the all-powerful Amuri of Cross-river. In return for this, the Cartel ensured that agitators vanished in the dead of night, even in open day, and no one dared enquire into their fate. Token black faces such as Nnodi were given the trappings of a senior grade and this answered the perennial break into the arrogant cocoon of the Mining Trust by firebreathing trade unionists south of the river. But the result was always predictable. Hounded by agents of the Cartel the trouble-maker was run out, rail-roaded on spurious charges or discovered lifeless on a deserted road. The native protectionists identified their interest with preservation of white Monopoly on their own soil, guaranteed its autonomy, a sovereign enterprise within their sovereign greed.

Inevitably the Mining Trust became a target for the men of Aiyéró.

All that Nnodi thought of however was the inviolability of the Mining Trust territory. If danger threatened he would move immediately into its premises and stop his field-work for a while. The field was his home—there he had no thought of danger, he had an equal chance of survival. Prospecting in the wilderness of Cross-river for ore, Nnodi had grown accustomed to camping out for weeks at a time in company with the denizens of the sparsely forested mountains, moving out of the path of nomad baboon families or tracking a mountain cat until the moment of the kill. A second generation citizen of Cross-river he knew no other home, became one of the first locals to be trained as prospector by the Mining Trust, travelled out for a degree at a mining college in Colorado and returned to be absorbed into the highly ranked post of a prospecting engineer. He could not accept this new definition of himself as alien in Cross-river, nor accept the early hints that this could bring on him the penalty of violent dispossession, expulsion or harassment, even repudiation by Cross-river neighbours. When rumours began of the possibility of far more lethal consequences it had to be explained to him slowly and methodically. Wrapped in the isolated protectionism of the Mining Trust, his circle of expatriate acquaintances and his own isolated passion of the hunt Nnodi remained blind to a degree that bordered on imbecility.

A few political villains had died. The white manager had once or twice summoned a meeting to discuss the menace of certain subversive doctrines spreading through long docile workers. The culprits, he recalled, were identified, chased from the Mining Trust. He recalled that much passion surrounded the name Aiyéró—a town he had never heard of—but that any of this should spell personal danger to him was inconceivable. Still, he sent the family away to friends outside the region. Beyond that, Nnodi refused to recognize the possibility of a change in his status as a gregarious, harmless consumer of the simple pleasures of an elevated social position.

Nnodi drove his family to the motor garage where he had booked the entire first-class compartment of a brand-new passenger lorry for his wife and four children. He gave the driver a professional inspection and was satisfied that he was a sober, responsible type, probably with a family to whom he was every bit as attached as Nnodi himself. He stood by while the lorry filled up with other passengers, then wondered why he had not thought of sending the cured skin of his latest kill as a present to his colleague whose hospitality they were going to enjoy in Ilosa. He asked the driver if there was time for him to dash home and back, twenty minutes at the most. The driver assured him that he could take his time.

On the way back the engineer began to sense the beginnings of panic. About half a mile from the garage he became convinced that a disaster had taken place or was about to overtake him, of a magnitude which turned his palms sweaty at the wheels and urged the car forward at a reckless pace. He rounded the last corner and found his way barred by police vehicles. From scattered points in the motor-park smoke belched thickly and three vehicles lay on their sides. A park which had teemed with a noisy haggling, touting, quarrelsome humanity was suddenly empty. It seemed impossible that such a transformation could have taken place in such a short time.

And then, between two Land Rovers parked across the park entrance, with figures of policemen flashing across the gap he saw the lorry which had contained his family. The policemen were pulling bodies from it and laying them on the ground.

There were a few moments of desperate hope. It was possible that his lorry had left and that that spot had been filled by another vehicle. It had to be a new transport lorry whose grisly load was now being unloaded. It had to be. How otherwise could it be, when their presence in the motor-park was solely to ensure their own safety. What other meaning could there be to the present activities except that the Nnodi family was already rolling happily towards safety in the brand-new lorry with a careful driver who took no chances on dangerous curves and did not overtake on the crest of a hill and knew at what moment not to stand on his rights and invite unnecessary delays when a simple bribe of a few shillings could open the toughest barriers of the traffic police. . . .

The First Class Compartment, the narrow strip built next to the driver's cabin, facing the direction of travel while the rest of the passengers sat with their back to it, that section he saw charred, blackened and smouldering from what must have been the most sudden and total conflagration ever yet to overtake a passenger vehicle. The police brought them out one by one, a woman, then a boy . . . Nnodi, with an animal cry sprang through the police cordon and raced for the spot. . . .

Petrol fumes penetrated every sense. The corner of his eyes remarked for the first time little skirmishes still in progress between the police and individual members of the gangs which had attacked the motor-park. Through puffs of smoke he recognized the shapes at last. Arrows stuck to the bodies and there were matchet cuts on the mother. The little girl's face was blown apart by what could only have been a shotgun blast at close range. As the last of the family group was brought out it struck him suddenly as an irrevocable moment, the abrupt cessation of laughter, mischief, domestic squabbles, school fees and school reports, midnight vigils by a fevered bedside, an end to vague bonds which, now that he thought of it all in one coherent whole, he felt he could define at last in terms of love . . . "my Semi-dozen Dr. Chalil, well, counting me the begetter and my assistant in the proceedings, I like to do everything in semi-dozens you see . . . well of course if another should chance along there will be a semi-dozen not counting me, and if another, well, it is still a semi-dozen not counting the mother. . . ."

His eyes took in the slashed tyres, the smashed windscreen. Then he saw the driver's body and recollected that he too was an alien in Cross-river.

Then a voice was at his ear, a hand on his shoulder. He turned and there stood a police officer asking him, "Did you have anyone in the lorry?"

The officer repeated his question a few times and Nnodi was surprised to hear himself answering "No. No one at all." And he turned and walked back to his car.

Hours later he walked from the loneliness of his home to where the Ramaths lived. When the doctor asked him if his family had left he said yes, they got away safely. The mother expressed relief, there had been trouble in the town from what Chalil reported. Yes, said Semi-dozen, yes I know. I am leaving early tomorrow myself, I just came to say good-bye and drink my last semi-dozen at your house. They all laughed.

He drove that night to the Mining Trust. He had his own key to the explosives store and he filled the car with gelignite. On his way out he informed the gate-keeper, a Cross-river native that he was going to his house on the reservation and would not step out of it until all the trouble was over. "I shall simply lock myself in" he grinned, "stock up on stout and drink the wahala dry. So if the management or anybody else wants to know why I haven't come to work, they know where to find me."

He drove home to wait. Nothing seemed more certain to him at that moment than that a visitation would be at his home before the week was out.

———

Zaccheus saw and heard the explosion, drove madly into the largest and most central hotel and made the women wait in the crowded lounge. His imagination painted the most lurid versions of the events which had taken place in and around the holocaust and he found himself lost and powerless but strangely clear-headed. Booking a double-room in the name of Mrs. Ramath he took the key, returned to where he had left them, pressed the key in their hands and instructed them to take immediate occupation, barricade themselves in until they heard his own or Chalil's or Ofeyi's voice. Before the women could voice a protest he had disappeared.

The debate, whether or not to summon the police took him a surprisingly long time. Before he could quite resolve it within the terms of the fantasies he had spun around the unexpected explosion he found himself already out of the city centre, speeding towards the expatriate reservation. Ah well, if the numerous patrols claimed not to see that virulent signal it meant that they did not want to see it. He was still uncertain which was the least menace, the murderous squads which roamed about at will, the army, equally murderous and uncontrollable, or the police who mostly meant well but were terrified of both.

Half a mile from the scene of the siege he abandoned the car and began to creep through the bushes. Without formally thinking out his next plan of action he had decided that it was best to reconnoitre. He picked his way carefully through the unfamiliar terrain, freezing in terror at every unfamiliar sound. He came on the spot unexpectedly.

The charnel house rose stark against the dark sky, gaunt, taller than its daylight intact reality. It blotted out the landscape, dwarfed and eliminated all other objects within sight—trees, bushes or neighbouring houses. His mind was already attuned to disaster but even so it was difficult for him to accept this actuality. Not for a moment did he doubt that by some freak combination of events both Ofeyi and the doctor had been engulfed within the holocaust. The gutted walls, the total, self-contained tottering horror was a conclusive shadow in the dark. An uninviting hole gaped through a side-wall leading into some unspeakable hell within. He skirted the house, keeping well within the bushes.

Then he saw his first sign of a casualty, a human limb charred and torn from the shoulder, blasted through a hole in the wall. It was caught and wedged in a cleft of a low cashew branch, a macabre joke fired from a circus spectacle. A few books lay scattered on the lawn. Glass splinters and bottle-necks everywhere, the relics of many semi-dozen nights of that strange character Mr. Semi-dozen.

There was no motion anywhere. Clearly there were no survivors. Zaccheus moved forward, gradually throwing all caution aside. He commenced his search through drunkenly swaying shelves, shattered porcelain, pushed his way through a table which was wedged tightly in a doorway. He began to wonder when a wall might collapse on him. It hardly mattered. A body lay beside a wardrobe, it seemed to have passed through a shredding machine, so neatly was the flesh severed by a thousand splinters of glass. A reek of cordite stung his nostrils. Suddenly he wondered if there were unexploded charges lying about. One false step . . . still no sign of the fat suicidal creature or of the two rescuers. It was the glass which was most in evidence, as if a powerful tornado had whirled through a glass-house forcing shrapnel at high pressure through every object and embedding them in walls, ceilings, and human bodies.

And then he saw a survivor. The man had half-crawled outwards through a hole in the bathroom door. Both his legs were shattered and a huge raw welt covered one side of his face. He could hardly see. But he had heard the sound of Zaccheus' movements and his hands were raised in a pleading gesture in his direction. Zaccheus stood a long time and watched the man, his feelings strangely numbed and untouched. He watched the man's strength dwindle slowly from his efforts until he collapsed again face downwards. Zaccheus wondered if he was dead. Then he heard him raise his head again and attempt to resume his outward crawl.

Suddenly Zaccheus was galvanized into further action. He raced through the house now, looking briefly at the bodies, lifting falling masonry and shattered furniture to find quick clues to recognition of the bodies that lay beneath. Satisfied, experiencing uncertain relief that neither Chalil nor Ofeyi lay within the centre of the holocaust nor in the immediate periphery he returned to the injured man as to the major problem of the night. Only then did it occur to him to wonder if his erstwhile companions were safely back at the house.

Zaccheus stood beside the wounded man, marvelling at this strange, prolonged blockage in his mind. It seemed unreal, that he had actually needlessly exposed himself to the hundred inherent dangers of burrowing through the charnel-house! His mind explored again the fears he had felt of other murderers still lurking in the vicinity of the blast and he shivered violently. It seemed beyond him, in fact he considered it the most marvellous part of his own participation in the night's events. Hauling the wounded man over his shoulder, he moved towards the house.

In the lounge Mr. Nnodi staggered up uncertainly and turned to the doctor. "Can I lie down on your couch? I want to sleep. I want to sleep for a whole week. I have not once shut my eyes in four days, waiting for those murderers to call on me."

"Come upstairs. There is a spare guest-room."

Zaccheus tried the back-door at that moment and all movement stopped. Ofeyi leapt for the shotgun and moved towards the window. Nnodi was instantly transformed, looked wildly around for a weapon, then grabbed the other gun for which he had made Chalil return at the moment of rescue. Ofeyi switched off the light. Zaccheus knocked again. But now he was terrified to announce his identity, the sudden dowsing of the light had raised new possibilities in his mind. It could quite easily be that survivors of the raiding party now occupied the house. He stood in utter confusion unable to think clearly any more.

Then Chalil switched on the rear porch light barking aloud at the same time: "Who is it?" Trembling both from the sudden exposure under the aggressive light as much as from relief Zaccheus announced himself. As the door was opened, his much weakened knees gave and he fell in with the wounded man, both covered in blood.

"Zaccheus! What has happened to you?" Apprehension in both men had flown to the fate of the women.

"I'm all right, I'm all right. The blood is from this wounded man."

Only then did they enquire about the women. The Asian bent down swiftly and began to examine the man's wounds. Zaccheus narrated his adventures.

It was Ofeyi who first noticed the change in the big man. There came the moment when it penetrated Nnodi's mind that the wounded man now being tended by Dr. Ramath was none other than one of his would-be murderers. He seized his gun again but Ofeyi beat him to it. In the struggle the gun went off, blasting off two of the dancing arms of Shiva and knocking off a pictureframe from the wall. There followed the struggle of the three men to overpower him as he next went for the throat of the wounded man. With maniacal strength he threw them off again and again, rolling-eyed and dribbling saliva from his mouth corners. His intended victim, blinded still by blood called continuously on heaven's protection, shivering in every limb. Finally Nnodi's strength appeared to slacken. He began, strangely enough to commence an attempt to struggle free towards the window. Ofeyi sensed the change and looked quickly to see if another weapon lay on the sill. There was none. Nnodi tried to speak, tried to indicate an urgent need but a huge obstruction lay in his throat. Suddenly he was violently sick.

Ofeyi led him towards the lavatory before the next convulsion began. The doctor moved towards his bag and laid out a syringe. Zaccheus gave up all further effort to comprehend it all, slumped from exhaustion into a chair.

XIII

A bold painted cross across a church steeple did not seem a likely prospect. Camouflage was far more likely for such areas of sanctuary. Yet where the steeple, obviously a recent addition, merged with the main body of the church, a wide arch blazed forth in loud red letters the legend TABERNACLE OF HOPE.

"Hope!" Ofeyi muttered. Taiila placed her hand on his lap and said, "Don't give up."

They left the car and walked towards the enclosure. Inside the gate someone had left a bundle of rags and a staff. Ofeyi looked around hoping for some sign of the owner. They moved on to the back of the church and Taiila, still looking over her shoulder clutched at Ofeyi's arm. Only to relax again.

"Oh, I'm sorry. I must be more scared than I thought."

"Not half as scared as I am don't you worry . . ."

"Look! It moved again. The heap of rags!"

Zaccheus whistled. "Yah. That thing we've just passed. I saw it too."

They watched it for some moments but it betrayed no further motion. Ofeyi shook his head. "I think you're both seeing things. I've been hearing things too."

"Hearing? You mean like a kind of low humming?"

Ofeyi nodded. "So you heard it too."

"Look boss, I don't believe in spooks but this place is spooky."

Taiila had never taken her eyes off the rags. "It could have been the wind" she said.

"Everything is too still. Everything is uncannily still."

They were quiet for a long while. Strain as they would, they could no longer hear even the former low monotone that seemed to seep from the bowels of earth.

Zaccheus fidgeted. "Let's get going. There is nothing here. We must have come to the wrong place."

Ofeyi moved forward. "No, there must be someone. I'll try a window round the back."

"Careful" Taiila cautioned. "If there is someone and he's scared he might attack you."

He moved round the back but came first to a door which looked as if it belonged to a vestry. He knocked softly. No reply. He next attacked the window, pulling back the bottom edge a little to provide a slit. All was dark within. Then as he straightened up he was certain that he had heard movements. He spun round to the distinct noise of a key turning in the lock of the door he had just passed. It opened a crack and a figure emerged fully to confront him. He wore a simple black cassock, frayed and discoloured. Ofeyi's quick glance took in his thin features that looked almost foreign, even to his near-light skin and downy hair. A nomad type from Cross-river.

"Do you need help?" the man asked. "My name is Elihu. I am the catechist here."

Taiila and Zaccheus coming up just then rescued Ofeyi from a momentary confusion. Zaccheus wished him a good morning and the catechist shook hands all round. Taiila explained their mission.

Ofeyi added, "Perhaps you know Lieutenant Sayi of the Air Force. He suggested we look in a few chapels like this. If she's not here perhaps you can direct us to others."

The name appeared to achieve the desired effect. The catechist nodded. "You had better come in and wait in the vestry. I shall make enquiries."

The bare room contained only one chair. "We have no furniture as you can see. Perhaps the lady can take the chair and you two gentlemen . . ."

"We are all right standing" Ofeyi assured him.

The man hesitated a while. His eyes were fixed on Taiila and he seemed to want to say something. Finally he smiled a little, the tenseness and work-burden that appeared to have knitted together the corners of his eyes dissolved. "You are a very beautiful lady" he said.

Surprised but pleased, Taiila thanked him but he continued, "Not just beautiful but full of light." He glanced round the dank room. "This room feels radiant, it must be your presence."

He turned to go, hesitated again at the door, and faced them again. "I wonder if . . . you would like to come yourselves. I could make the enquiry and let you know. But, perhaps I clutch at every straw . . . only I think that the sight of visitors might bring some cheer into the gloom."

Taiila sprang up at once. "Of course we'll come if you think it will help."

He shook his head. "Nothing of light or beauty has touched their lives here for some time. But come and see for yourself. Please mind your head. It is much better to crouch."

He opened a door and they were struck blind or else had moved into thick impenetrable darkness. But sounds came. And Ofeyi recognized the low murmuring he had heard before, the low resonance of hushed human activity and intimacy. There was a child's whisper. A heavy wooden object, probably a bench scraped the floor. A suction of bare feet.

Their eyes had not yet adjusted but they felt their guide stop at some obstacle and tap on it. They recognized then that they were in some kind of ante-room, a low rectangular box, a huge packing-case muffled and padded. Ofeyi felt along the sides, it was clearly wooden and seemed carved with unusual designs. He raised his head slightly and it came in contact with the roof at, he estimated, no higher than five feet. When a door opened in response to the priest's knock he realized that they were in fact entering the body of the church through the belly of the altar. The "door" was itself a solid barricade pulled aside by invisible hands. The sounds from within swelled to a rhythmic language of hives. As they emerged into a slight lessening of the dark the priest said to them,

"You will have to pick your feet one by one."

Their hands, feet, brushed against human textures, warm contours. Bodies they could not yet completely see yielded them passage. They waded carefully through a low dense thicket of limbs keeping an eye on the pale neck of the guide, watching the whites of eyes spring forth and fill the thicket like a swarm of glow-worms. A hundred eyes swept round towards them, flared brightly for a while then dimmed inwards into the dark. Ofeyi imagined an instinctive fear, hope, defiance in each eye-flare in the dark. Then there were those which seemed more like tiny moths; they fluttered blankly, expressionless. Ofeyi concluded that they were the children's.

Then they heard singing. Their passage ceased to usurp the feel of invisible graves lined with prone bodies for burial. From beyond the feel of upturned feet, from the further dark-massed corner of the temple voices fanned out towards them, deep, close and self-absorbed. Low though it was and cautious it formed a generous protective shawl denying fear or despair. One heard the watchfulness in it, the soft breathing of a dog that would cease abruptly at any alien sound, and sift it for menace.

Some light had been permitted in through narrow fanlights. Pale beams cut across the room parallel to the floor but remained high above it, so that walking upright their heads floated on the beams, disembodied. Ceiling and rafters began but vanished into the upper darkness, a brief portion of the walls floated in the sur-real haze, a few crude paintings of cherubs and angels and their extravagant haloes. The rest, peopled by the prone, squatting, dragging, whispering figures was a low long crypt roofed by pale mote-riddled beams of light.

Taiila whispered, awe-struck, "It feels like a subterranean camp!"

A leg dragged inwards just before them, a hand lifted languidly and fell back again. Again and again they saw their guide bend downwards, his hand deliver a pat or a caress. Once he rose with a child in his hands. They stopped while he stuck a finger under the child's nose and wobbled it in play. The child remained strangely silent, responding not even with the ghost of a smile much less a chuckle. He replaced it into waiting hands and they moved on, pursued then ignored by an eloquence of eyes.

At a concrete hexagon covered by a wooden board he stopped at last. The baptismal font was now a cauldron for food. It appeared to be feeding-time. A ladle dipped into the font, emerged with some form of stew, tipped itself into a bowl and vanished into waiting hands. They watched the bowl float from hand to hand all down the line and it occurred to Ofeyi for the first time that its contents were hot. Anticipating their amazement the priest explained.

"One of the men is an electrician. He rigged up the element in a cooker against the base of the font. We manage to have a hot meal at least once a day."

The sleeping forms were sitting up one after the other, the children betrayed animation. Cries followed, rebukes and soothing noises. With eyes that were now fully accustomed to the light the visitors began to make out a multitude of heads and arms. Patches of cloth grew light retentive. Objects stood out which had served till now for pillows. Portmanteaus, cloth bags, cardboard cartons, a radio, the cover of a sewing-machine but mostly bundles of the soft doughy testaments of the suddenness of catastrophe and flight, squashed for cushions and back-rests. In the slow-motion darkness these bundles appeared to pulse with the stubborn resilient yeast of life. Enamel, aluminium, clay or tin, the bowls that passed among limbs and heads dispensed the same warm essence of survival and Ofeyi found himself absorbing some of its stubborn hope.

The priest's eyes continued to search even as he spoke to the server at the font. She pointed with her ladle and they moved towards a further wing of darkness, in the direction in which the singing had begun. The dark here was a mere grey mist, pierced in a hundred places by fuzzed beams from slats high up in the tower. Breasts hung out from blouses and babies sucked noisily. A few figures swathed in heavily stained bandages lay unmoving. Heads lolled against pews which for the first time they could now see clearly. There were old people stretched out on these pews, some strained to read a few lines of the bible in the poor light. It was they also, the old ones, who broke into hymns from time to time, singing in hushed age-seasoned tones. A low murmur rose from a pair who sat side by side in the pew, prayer books in their hands but staring straight before them, intoning over and over . . . the Lord is my shepherd, I shall not want. He leadeth me in green pastures. Yea though I walk through the valley of the shadow of death . . .

"Father!"

They turned. A face risen from the grey sea approached them. Striated by beams it worked pain-strictured lips to bring out words. The priest placed his hand on his shoulder.

"What is it Michael? Is she worse?"

"I think she is dying Father."

The priest pushed past him and disappeared into the grey fog. A moment later the others had caught up with him. Taiila knelt beside a form lying on its side, knees drawn up against the chest. One side of her face was hidden under a huge wad of cotton, held in place by a string across her head. Her breaths came now with difficulty. Taiila lifted the head and placed it on her knees and the woman began to give up the struggle against death.

Ofeyi found himself face to face with a broken figure of anguish, a face contorted and giving slowly along the grain. The words struggled out from strangulation. "They are all dead. All of them. My sister, all our children. She is all that is left. If she goes I have nothing more, nothing . . . I should have died. They left us for dead, I should have died. . . ."

They heard Taiila move. She lay the woman's head gently on the floor and straightened out her body. She looked up at them and spoke quietly,

"She is dead."

The man crashed down beside the stilled body and began to sob. A few figures began to move towards them.

The priest's words seemed to come from a very long distance.

"It is our fourth death since they began to come in. We lost two children in succession. There was an old man before that. . . ."

A group had gathered about them. The priest appeared to bring himself back to his duties, bowed his head and murmured,

"The Lord giveth and the Lord taketh away; blessed be the name
of the Lord."

Knowledge of death filtered through the crypt, a chilly cur-
rent through air that had only begun to warm up. The shad-
owy inmates underwent changes of infinite subtleties, drawing
together even more, purging individual fears in the font of shared
loss. Prayers rose in hushed voices from one corner to the other, a
mother embraced her children in a sudden spasm of love, hugged
them until they hurt. Her tears fell in mourning for the unknown
one, death spread its cold tentacles through the festering gloom
but it bred no fear in the breasts of any. They had seen too much.

Perhaps the priest sensed their growing feeling of intrusive-
ness. He turned and said, "Let's return to the vestry. I shall ask the
man we need to see to meet us there."

Relieved, they followed his path-finding form through the
febrile chamber of grief. Ofeyi wondered how they looked to all
these fugitives, Taiila especially, foreign and beautiful in the midst
of such squalor and destitution. Yet her eyes as she rose from that
hard death-bed had held such oceans of sadness, reflecting a suffering that he had not thought possible in one so young. A nun's
cowl-framed compassion, held and eternalized in a pietà of luminous stone.

Ofeyi, oppressed by the feeling of superfluity found his discomfort turning to irritation when the priest stopped again to pick up
and quieten an agitated child, whisper a comfort to a new apparition from the gloom, and hold in both his hands the withered
fingers of an elderly invalid who had strained to raise his wasted
body and receive his greeting. The geriatric sank back in its bed,
a beatific look on its skull-face. There was no corresponding limb
sprouting from the other shoulder, only a wad of lint and a rubber
sheath. . . .

How long had they hidden in this grotto? How many more of

such catacombs awaited discovery before the search was over? . . .
Messala . . . Mesalla? The name rose in his mind . . . must, carbon-
dating, scrolls that disintegrated and writings that turned invisible at the first touch of sunlight . . . a brave self-immolation that
slept for a thousand years—was it Massada? Was this how it always
began, these treasures that brought scholarly salivation to the lips
of burrowing fanatics. Dead Sea Scrolls and dead men's bones that
are never permitted rest. He found himself casting an involuntary
glance at what had struck him as the weak, assailable parts of the
shelter, a sudden vision of the mob breaching the walls . . . fire,
sword and rapine. Walls in a slow-motion collapse beneath towers
of fire. A methodical extraction of the rubble, brick by brick. Dust
and ash, ghostly cinders in a harmattan wind. . . .

Why do they bother, these antiquarian hands forever disturbing the ghosts of history. With so much ever-present manifesta-
tion, why raise the old accusing stones and reveal powdery bones
of condemnation. Let it all be. Raise earth around and above it.
Let grass grow upon it all and let fresh, rich millet feed the children of survivors. And a hundred years from now when the land
makes a shift in iron development and metallic jaws chew up the
strange forgotten hillock don't let the grubbers in among pain-
sanctified potsherds, enamel chips. Or a concrete font with the
strange twisted wiring around its base. These futile reconstruc-
tions, of what use ultimately are they since they neither stop nor
caution against the reenactment . . . ah yes, poke poke poke . . .
a fascinating piece, most fascinating . . . poke poke poke . . . do
you observe this broken bolt? Take a good look. I would say the
marauders broke in through here wouldn't you? Poke poke poke.
This sector . . . I suggest we dig here, this sector . . . poke poke
poke . . . there, a rare piece of luck! A child skeleton entire. A bit
of the skull is gone, could have been done with an axe . . . now, we
had better scrape away carefully here . . . what did I tell you? A

most remarkable story. Unique graphic details. Mother obviously
trying to shield infant . . . most touching . . . with that glazed
coating it could almost be a Henry Moore . . . beautiful beautiful! Now this . . . yes, that posture, probably praying when struck
down. These twelve in the . . . must have been the vestry . . . can't
see any wound can you? Probably suffocated to death. Reminds
me of the Burghers of Calais. Such martyr composure even after
these years. This one at the altar, looks like he was wounded somewhere else but crawled all this way to die . . . we won't prize those
fingers off without breaking a bone or two I'm afraid. Much rather
preserve the altar, most quaint. Skeletons we have more than
enough of . . . I say, remember these antiquated sewing things?
Quite a find this. I suppose most of them were brought to Africa
by those Victorian missionaries. I happen to know about them you
see because one of my great forebearers . . .

Do you think it's the ash? Carbon? Carbon does act with
astounding preservative powers . . . we'll take it up with that
chap when he gets here. It's the layers of ash we have to thank
I believe. Truly remarkable. It must have been quite an inferno.
A very strange sect, not one I've ever encountered. Some sort of
fundamentalist Christians I think . . . given to quite primitiv-
ist representations of angels and things like that. Reminds me of
some of those Ethiopian Christian art . . . quite close to the Greek
Orthodox bunch that lot. Strange history . . . must look into what
evidence there is of a Nilotic link . . .

Caruthers! Come here quick! Take a look at this. Do you see?
Not in the least negroid. Female too. Look at that brooch! And
this necklace. Can't be a coincidence. Indian jewellery. And the
bones . . . here, take hold of the end of the tape will you . . . see
what I mean? Such fine bones, truly fantastic limbs. Beautiful?
She must have been phenomenal. Look at the jaw-lines. The man
is negroid all right. Badly broken from blows. Must have spent

some time dying, probably defending her to the last breath. Tough brute. We'll tag them Quasimodo and Esmeralda shall we? Here's another of them . . .

A child's hand reached out of the darkness and tugged him by the trousers. Ofeyi heard a churtle and looked down. On the floor he discerned patterns which the child had drawn. Some light fell there, covering about three square feet. On this the child had worked the figures of birds, houses, animals and abstract shapes. She wanted Ofeyi to admire it. Ofeyi stopped, placed his arms around the child's waist. Looking into her eyes he saw them turn to mere sockets, their gladness of achievement lost forever, even to the pick-wielding intruders who would not be shaken off from probing the ash-shrouded catacombs of the future.

Caruthers, yes, you *are* right. A child made these cave drawings but what does it matter now? And then Ofeyi's eyes switched to a far different grouping which began in the corner of the light patch and faded away up the darker wall. She had relegated her tragic memories of the catastrophe to this obscure surface—a baby's flight arrested in mid-air, plummeting towards a blazing fire . . . a tight-robed figure presiding over a scene of slaughter . . . a long line of waiting victims . . . as Ofeyi's eyes accustomed itself to the gloom he saw that the child had prolonged the line to the very edge of the floor, continuing the figures up the wall as far as her hands could reach. Then came her mound shapes. Sacramental loaves? Onion images? Or simply bundles? Every bit of space that was not taken by the sacrificial scenes had been covered with irregular loaves. Had someone come round distributing loaves of bread? Or was it the bundles which lay so liberally around, the symbol of dispersion, disintegration, the symbol of the final surrender of individuality?

He rose. He reached out a hand to pat the child on the head and stopped himself in time. The gesture seemed grossly patronizing.

He walked on briskly to rejoin the others. The wooden box was again moved aside and they passed through the altar and into the vestry. The catechist shut the door.

"A brother is making enquiries. They all know the lady from the posters. If they've heard or seen anything we shall know in a moment." He paused and turned to Taiila. "I hope you were not too distressed. Perhaps I should not have taken you in to see them but . . ."

"I am not as fragile as I look" Taiila assured him.

He nodded. "No. Still it was unfortunate that the woman should die just then. We are not always so gloomy."

"How do you feed them?" Ofeyi demanded.

He smiled. "The Lord provides. We have a very good little organizer. He warned us of your approach as a matter of fact. We owe him our very survival."

"A local?" Zaccheus asked.

"Oh yes. I see you did not discover him on your way in. But he had his eye on you all the time. Quite a fierce watchdog he is. Perhaps you ought to meet him. He knows his way around, he may be of use to you some time." He opened the door and called out, "Aliyu."

What they had taken to be a heap of rags stirred fully to life. It grew taller in a series of jerks, like a puppet being assembled, extending and retracting in horizontal directions—forwards, backwards and sideways, while somehow contriving to add a few inches to its height after each one of these motions. A central axis became gradually discernible, the staff which they had also observed tangled up in the bundle. Now they saw a wasted limb twine itself creeper-like around the staff; the other, hardly more fleshed or disorientated, but with more apparent pith stabbed the ground at an incongruous angle. Only the arms were strong, the entire locomotion of this strange human contraption appeared to depend on the propelling force of the arms. Above those arms and powerful shoulders a head was stuck with the barest suggestion of a neck. It was an elongated head with a distinctly horizontal axis, ravaged by smallpox marks and with one eye permanently closed. Its striking length was further accentuated by a conical cap at its rear end. At last he was stretched out complete and he moved towards them with strong practised hops. The shape became quite familiar to the visitors—the manifested resilience of the human body against sheer cussedness of the Cross-river environment, its frequent epidemics, blindness inflicting plagues, spinal infections and mind-drugging flies. Ofeyi wondered briefly, confronted by this half-human apparition, was the blood-lust that seized upon the populace just another legacy of climate? Another deformity like the effects of meningitis or the blood-poisoning of the tse-tse fly? A diminished responsibility created by a virus in the air, flooding the victims with a need to degrade more fortunate humanity in an image of their own pain and desecration? Or was there a truly metaphysic condition called evil, present in epidemic proportions that made them so open to the manipulation of coldly unscrupulous men? There had to be a cause beyond mere differences in culture, beyond material envy—for their victims were largely equals in the court of penury, there had to be a cause beyond resentment at the right of their victims to stay different in their midst. For this was not a mere question of slaughter. A relish had coloured their actions, a deep hunger of perversion both in inventiveness and magnitude, as if they sought to balance unnatural mutations, their human forms with a vengeful outrage on the face of humanity.

Ofeyi glanced at the residual being and was amazed at the happiness which suffused his pock-marked face, this object at which Nature had thrown everything in a singular concentration of spitefulness. Twisted, part-blinded, hunchbacked, visually unwholesome, a mockery of all that was human yet he greeted them with unfeigned friendliness and pleasure, threw a brave salute at the catechist and waited.

Elihu saluted in return and asked, "Everything okay Aliyu?"

He grinned back. "Ebrything Oooh-ke!"

"These are friends. . . . And this is Aliyu, sergeant-major, food organizer, watchman and general factotum for our little camp."

Impulsively Taiila held out her hand. Aliyu saluted again, suddenly stuck his staff under his arm-pit and balanced on it so that he could take her hand in both of his. Zaccheus, then Ofeyi both shook hands with him also, Zaccheus adding a salute to his greeting.

It seemed one way to reconcile oneself to humanity, to see in it nothing but the symbol of deformation, a cursed shell which grinned and survived all visitations. Elihu continued to speak in his praise: "You know what name our population here gave him? The Lion of the Tabernacle."

Aliyu's grin grew larger and larger. He gave a salute again and his massive teeth bared in a frothy curve through his debris-laden face. "Go in" Elihu said. "Find Mr. Ngosi and ask him if he's found out anything."

Aliyu's face looked instantly troubled and he cast a meaningful glance in the direction of his post. "It will be all right" the catechist reassured him. "We will remain here and keep a look-out."

The cripple looked dubious but he saluted and obeyed.

"They killed our minister" Elihu told them, "but no one else was touched. He went out to confront the mob and they struck him down. Aliyu had been with us for some time, he used to wait outside the temple on Sundays and beg for alms. One day the minister asked him if he would like to help with odd jobs, cleaning the premises and sweeping out the temple once in a while. That is how he became attached to us. Well, when he saw our leader struck down he rushed at the mob and attacked them with his staff—and a few curses too. They were all people from the next township, that's where Aliyu himself comes from, so he knew them quite well. He told them they would have to kill him to get at the temple. And that's the whole story. We were all waiting in there, barred and shuttered in fear and trembling. The leader had made us promise not to move until he had failed. He took only Aliyu with him."

Ofeyi was struck by a sudden certainty. "You are Cross-river yourself aren't you."

With a sad smile the man confirmed it. "Our minister wasn't. I should have gone to meet the mob. I spoke the language. But he wouldn't hear of it. Perhaps his fears were well-founded. Although we are all Cross-river we again have important differences. Where I come from our people tend to look down on others from Kuntua. The sight of me could have incensed them inordinately." Thoughtfully he added, "Who can tell if they won't even turn on us next. When all the so-called aliens have been hunted down or chased out, if the killing lust has not quite died down . . ." He shrugged.

"And they never came back?" Taiila asked.

"The killers? Oh yes they did. On the way back from some less fortunate settlement. We were barred in and silent, just as you found us today. Naturally they thought we had taken flight, abandoned the place. Even so they stopped, considered burning down the church. But Aliyu somehow drove them off. He said we had fled but had left him watchman over the place and were paying him well. God knows how he managed to make it sound convincing, but they just poked a bit of fun at him and took off. One of them threw him a severed head as parting gift. It is buried over there—by our minister."

The man he called Ngosi came through the vestry and stood at the door, staring in disbelieving horror. Elihu turned round and saw the expression on his face and laughed. "I think we had better go in. Mr. Ngosi thinks I am foolish to expose myself in this way. I keep telling them I am in no danger but they won't even let me go and forage for food with Aliyu except at night." Aliyu nodded vigorously, grinned and hopped towards his post.

Elihu led the way into the vestry and shut the door. "Mr. Ngosi, these are the people in question." He introduced them one after the other.

Ngosi, a big man who looked continuously over the heads of the visitors shook hands with them, distantly and solemnly. That ceremony over he coughed, and swallowed, continuing to stare into the wall.

"Well?" Elihu prompted.

"The news is not good Brother Elihu." He hesitated. "But neither is it certain."

"Go on" Elihu prompted. "These people have been searching for some time."

"We think she may be in Temoko, and that she is either dying or dead. A woman was brought into the compound with what looked like great efforts of secrecy. It took place at night and she came in in military ambulance. They kept even the normal guards away from the gates. Some of our people were hiding beside the walls of Temoko just before the ambulance brought this woman. They were trying to decide whether to knock for admittance or to run on. They saw the stretcher taken out of the lorry. There was a nurse they said, holding a bottle, and rubber tubes attached to her arm and to her nostrils. It was dark but they caught a glimpse of the face. She did not seem to breathe."

There was a long silence, then Ofeyi made a request. "I would like to talk to these witnesses."

"Call them" the catechist instructed.

Ofeyi felt Taiila's consoling fingers on his arm.

5

SPORES

XIV

"Now it's interesting you should be interested . . ."

Karaun Karaun Karaun . . .

"Most interesting you should be interested, in that particular laydeee . . ."

Karaun Karaun Karaun . . .

In vain he tried to keep his mind on the object of his search. So he turned it on the club-foot of the grinning governor of Temoko before him, most of whom was swallowed by the wide polished desk and terraces of files. Dwarf? He reminded him of a rounded egg on the back of an ant; that timber neck thrust over folded arms gave his back a strong suspicion of a hunch. Perhaps the recent encounter with Aliyu had begun to colour his sight. The music of the gongs rippled over the man's spine, bounced off his occiput and pinged across the table surface . . . *Karaun Karaun Karaun*—Pause

Karaun Karaun Karaun . . .

Clubfoot seemed indifferent to its influence yet his words seemed to follow that all-pervasive rhythm.

"Don't you agree?"

"I . . . why?"

"Why? You ask me why?"

Karaun Karaun Karaun . . .

This must stop. Concentrate. Have all your wits about you. A lost hint, a lost signal to the sixth sense. . . .

"It sounds an almost cheerful place." That came out in spite of himself.

The little man laughed. Red teeth. Black gaps. You could tell a colanut addict. "People outside think that this is a kind of morgue—abandon hope all who enter, something like that. But it isn't. A world of its own is what it is. A world of its own."

"Ye-e-es . . ."

Clubfoot's thoughts were as far from his words as Ofeyi's—a realization that was slow to come. His dome of a head was filled with questions about the intruder. His eyes, mere slits behind ludicrously tiny lenses concealed some kind of warning. A quest that seemed ordinary enough though risky slowly filled with foreboding. And that sing-song response to a straightforward Missing Persons Inquiry. . . .

Karaun Karaun Karaun

"Very interesting you should be interested."

Karaun Karaun Karaun

"In that particular laydee . . ."

Karaun Karaun Karaun

Ofeyi tried to reassure himself—Damn it all! I have a citizen's right to enquire! But even more concretely reassuring was the recollection that he had made Zaccheus remain outside the gates to await his return.

The outsize ant-egg had risen and was moving towards the

window, dragging a reluctant left foot behind him. He was now all too clearly dimunitive, though nothing remotely like the un-prepossessing figure of Aliyu. Short muscular arms pushed the window outwards and barked:

"Hey you there! Enough of that *karaun-karaun-karaun*. Take them away from here."

In spite of the leisurely volition of the left foot he seemed capable of moving swiftly. Back on his seat he grinned. "I could see that the noise disturbed you. You were not paying full attention to our conversation."

Conversation! Would that be the same word for tactical evasion? Ofe began to protest; no he wasn't in the least disturbed by the gongs. . . .

"It is quieter now" Clubfoot insisted. "We can hear ourselves think . . . Yes what is it?"

A man had come up to the door. He gave a smart salute.

"Yes, yes, what you want?"

"Sorry sir. I no hear the order wey you give me sir."

"Take your squad away from here. Their *karaun-karaun* is disturbing us."

"Yessir." He saluted and marched off.

"He's a liar" sighed Clubfoot. "He heard me." He waved his arms about in a gesture of boredom. "It's a joke they all enjoy at my expense. They think I don't know about it but all they want to hear me say is *karaun karaun.* I don't mind at all. I oblige them. Keeps them happy and consoles them when I discipline them— you know what karaun is?"

"Karaun . . . that's shell isn't it?"

He thumped the table. "Right! And that is just what they call me, the Boss! *Karaun Igbin*! A snail dragging its shell. I didn't know I was giving myself a nickname the first day I shouted to the work-gang to stop their *karaun-karaun.* But I don't mind it now."

"But you did at the time?" Ofe felt he had to say something.

"No one likes to be laughed at. Our people consider it sinful to laugh at natural disabilities so why should they do it to me? But of course they are not our own people. Mostly aliens. I don't mean to offend you but your people lack piety and respect, the way we understand the word. I thought at first they were merely laughing at the way I said the word. No, they just found it doubly funny that I should actually mouth their own insult to myself. We-ell, it doesn't matter. I taught myself to get used to it. Have you ever been an object of ridicule Mr. Ofe?"

"O-ah er . . . well . . . of course. It happens all the time."

"You are thinking of little jokes at one's expense, the occasional incident which makes one feel a fool. No, I mean to be an object *for* ridicule. Like me. As you can imagine, right from childhood. Throughout school—well, while I remained in school anyway. I am mostly a self-taught man. No money to complete my education so I had to do it all myself while working. Not like privileged people like you eh? Rich parents and relatives. I had to do it all by correspondence courses—very costly. And I just don't mean for exams only. All those pamphlets you see advertised—How to Make Friends and Win Confidence, Develop Your Sense of Humour, One Hundred and One Toasts and After-Dinner Speeches . . . not that I attend parties and things like that but, well, it all helped to get me where I am today." He stopped abruptly. "Ah yes, where are we today? I must stop giving you my life history. Yes, yes-yes-yes *yes*! Where were we Mr. Ofeyi?"

This time the telephone interrupted.

"Yes? Hallo . . . Hallo . . ." He covered the mouthpiece with a stubby hand, grinned abruptly and nodded to Ofe. "Those white men who were here before, this was something they admired— ingenuity. I was a very ingenious young man. I am not boasting, it is just a gift from heaven. You either have it or you don't. . . .

My fellow trainees could not understand why I was chosen to go for a specialist course in the U.K. There were only four places offered for our department throughout the country but I got one of them . . . yes yes, is that Headquarters? This is the Acting S.S. Office. I said Acting Senior Superintendent office. Yes? I asked for Headquarters, Headquarters! Waterworks?" He rattled the telephone rest in fury. "Who is on duty there? Hallo! hallo. You! Why have you got me the Waterworks? I asked for Headquarters nearly an hour ago. Don't Yessir me just get me the damned place."

Slapping down the receiver he took off his glasses and wiped them, squinting hard from near-blindness. "It is disgraceful. The Russians and Americans can speak to each other across the moon but we can't make a simple telephone call within the country." Then the abrupt grin, "I bet that officer is telling the others that Karaun has blown his top again."

Ofeyi grinned in sympathy, glanced at the wall as he saw a literal image of that cannonball head exploding and spattering grey matter in every direction. The head remained intact. Ofeyi could anticipate his next utterance when the glasses were back in position.

"And now what were we saying?"

"I am looking for . . ."

"Ah yes, that particular laydee . . ."

"If you could just check your records and tell me . . ."

"Records? Ah, but I had not got round to explaining. I have instructions about that very lady. Yes yes, that is why I found it very interesting that you should come so soon after my directives."

"Directives?"

"Anything about the lady, anything at all I must report to headquarters." He tapped one of the tiers of paper. "Several memoirs on the subject. Ha, ha, she must be a most important laydee."

"She is here then."

He wagged a playful finger and grinned. "Ha, I didn't say that no no no. You mustn't put words into my mouth."

"It is obvious. Why should you be sent instructions on someone who is not in your charge?"

"My friend, that is what is known as a mathematical fallacy. One thing does not necessarily follow the other. Really. I think I ought to lend you my course on Clear and Logical Thinking. Now I shall offer you the following alternative. One, that she has been here and then was transferred. Two, she has never been here but in another of our places. Since enquiries are expected it would be natural for headquarters to send circulars to all sections, generally. Three, she has never even been in any of our institutions but if she is missing or reported missing we would receive notifications just like other institutions—hospitals, railway stations, airports and what have you. Four . . ."

Ofe raised his hands in surrender. "All right sir. Is she here?"

"A-ah, now that is one question I cannot answer."

"Who can?"

"Headquarters."

Ofeyi made to rise but the telephone trilled suddenly.

"Yes? I don't want a progress report. Do you think I want to listen all day to your Graan-graan every two-two minutes just to tell me you have not yet succeeded? And—hallo, hallo—were you going to cut me off? How often must I tell you to wait until you're dismissed. Don't sorry-sir me. Send me Suberu. Right, Dismissed."

For such a thin slit, even with the aid of the powerful lens, what came next was a massive wink. The head made up for the rest. "I vary it for them you see. I say graan-graan for the telephone but karaun-karaun for when the gang-gong is going on in the yard . . ." He cocked his head at that, grinned. Suddenly he pulled out a drawer, withdrew a notebook and wrote laboriously . . . "gang-gong is going on . . . hm . . . I wish you could hear me when I slip that in at the next parade. I have to address them every morning on parade. Give them the day's instructions and all that. It's good for general morale when I give them something like that to throw around for the rest of the day. Firmness with humour, yes, firmness with humour, that's the secret of discipline."

Ofe stood up. "I think I shall pay a visit to your headquarters."

"Oh dear oh dear. You mean we cannot help you at all? That is a pity. It's these useless telephones . . ."

"It doesn't matter. You have your directives."

"I knew you would understand. There is nothing like an intelligent man I always say. You can talk to him. I have really enjoyed our conversation you know. Most stimulating to talk to someone like you. This can be a dull place. Sometimes I think my brain is getting fat, getting very fat. I still keep up with my correspondence courses but what's the use of that if you can't put them to use against people of your own calibre. . . ."

As Ofe extricated his hand a shadow fell in the doorway. He heard the stamp and muscle creak of a salute.

"Yes?"

"Telephone sir."

"Well put it through. Why do you have to march here to tell me?"

"It's on the direct line to S.S. office, sir. From Headquarters, sir."

"Headquarters? Perhaps you are lucky after all Mr. Ofeyi. Wait for me while I take the call."

"All right."

"Have something while you are waiting. Hey, bring the visitor a cup of cocoa. You like cocoa I hope. It is now the official beverage."

Ofe smiled. "I know."

"Good." He was already on his way out. "I shall not keep you long."

A brisk drag. It was the only way to describe his strange walk. Ofe glanced round the walls of the office, paused at the familiar poster for the Cocoa Campaign. A buxom hostess held out a "cup of patriotism" to a smiling foreigner. He thought again of the band who had gone on the last fatal tour. And Iriyise?

It was an old friend who brought the steaming cup. The same one who had acted more bodyguard than trusty when Ofeyi was first ushered into the governor's office. Hung at his back and watched him so steadfastly that Ofe grew uncomfortable and shifted in his chair to half face him. Karaun's miss-nothing eyes saw it and flung out the faithful dog. "Why do you have to stand there like the war memorial at Idumota. Go and supervise something!" Then the rambling apology after the giant's seemingly reluctant salute and exit. "He doesn't know what it is to think but he is first class. Very dependable man—as long as you give him precise orders. Not like my paid staff. They can't distinguish between initiative and contravention of orders. Especially this new breed they are recruiting fresh from school. They think they know everything. Too-know, that's the trouble with them. Suberu now, he has no education and he is supposed to be a prisoner, but he is my right-hand man. He can run the whole place single-handed if I am suddenly taken ill."

Ofeyi now watched Suberu, in his shapelessly ambiguous uniform fiddle with a jug and quickly stopped him. "No milk, thanks." Surprise all over Suberu's face. He waved his hands about in a language which plainly said, How is that possible? Ofe stared at the hands, fascinated. The fingers were gnarled blackened roots knobbed and knotted into place. He had no palms to speak of. Fingers and wrists seemed welded together into a weird flagellating contraption. As he straightened from setting down the tray Ofeyi thought that his head would hit the ceiling. He smiled and nodded thanks.

The man's facial muscles moved. Cicatrice or muscle, it was not possible to distinguish. Cicatrices or furrows between black muscle ridges, bunched skin and foot-glazed furrows, they all ran into one another in unending whorls. And the face matched his body. Large and long, thick cicatrices, glazed red eyes. Ofe stirred his cup, watched the man resume his favourite position by the door.

Ofeyi's eyes roamed across the yard to a distant barbed-wire topped wall. Was that the legendary wall? There was an unbroken roll of barbed wire held in position by evenly spaced bars, V-shaped on the top of that wall. The wires thus formed a V-tunnel. Perhaps it was the wall, it fitted the description he had heard that day when the pattern of unsanctioned traffic had been reversed and the world was trying to break into a citadel of ostracism. They beat on Temoko's gates as soon as other flood-gates were opened to terror and death. The animal noise of fear, the cowed whimper when the last exit is tried and that also is sealed . . . a sound so tangible he felt he could touch it.

A new sound appeared to come from the ceiling fan, a mixture of asthmatic wheeze and a panting dog . . . Ofe turned round. It was only Suberu's unique way of breathing. Ofeyi stirred his cocoa aimlessly and sipped the tepid mixture.

There were a few who escaped the first whirlpool of blood. They were sucked gratefully into the next, a quiet limbo of the mind where nothing happened and time stood still. The youth who walked as if eternally trapped in the tunnel of spikes . . . anything was welcome with that weight of fear behind. They impaled themselves on the broken-glass tops of the walls and battered the metal-studded gates. A mother took her child by the legs and swung it over the walls. It fell short, was hooked in the fanged tunnel. It lacked the sense to lay still. Last vision of the mother before the mob got her . . . the soft flesh of the child and the metal barbs sinking deeper . . .

Karaun ordered that the gates be flung open. It was the end of the peaceful kingdom over which he presided. They came in without forms, without inspection, registration, classification, filled the compound from wall to wall trampling the neat flower-beds and scattering the whitewashed stones. They pulled up the KEEP OFF THE GRASS signs in the last desperate effort to face the attackers. They hurled the whitewashed stones and stained them red. A squad of guards now fought to lock back the gates on their assailants, the bars were wrenched into place and the bolts forced home, and then the fugitives lay down and wept.

But some could not rise again.

Day after day, a trickle, a flood. The wicket door in the gate opened and shut, sucked in anxious little groups with ever backward glances. The clerks moved up and down, taking names. Food contractors came and went. Somehow, if only a crumb of bread, a handful of groundnuts or a fruit, they were fed. Karaun sent his clerks to the market. He ordered the nurse to buy dressings from non-existent budgets. They tore up sheets for bandages and created lint from wrapping paper. An emergency burial-ground was created next to the hanging yard. . . .

There was no precedent for the invasion. Nothing in the General Orders anticipated such an event. Nothing in the regulations allowed for a disruption in ordered traffic in and out of Temoko. Karaun found that he was ultimately on his own. He flourished under the imposition. And even when the pace had slowed, when a form of control had been established from without and Karaun was again a bureaucrat fulfilling quotas of exit and admittance

as requested by the scraps of paper and the voices on the telephone it still fell to him to decide who would go first and who
could be kept to the last, who shall be evacuated as a group and
who as individuals. And there were those reports to be filled out
and demands put forward by him on L.P.O.s and retrospective
approval of excess spending which he dared anyone even in that
overglorified headquarters to question. . . .

Then there was this new thing. Just when it seemed Temoko
must sink once more into the backwaters of obscurity, up came
this new affair.

The humdrum days were over. No, he did not yet fully understand the affair, but he had a nose for the "tide in the affairs of
men." He had had that same feeling just before his selection for
the break in his career—the restricted course . . . four places only
and he took one of them. It was the same feeling now. Of all
the possible hideouts at their disposal the Cartel had picked on
Temoko! If this wasn't the tide-in-the-affairs so constantly stressed
by his pamphlet on The Moment of Opportunity, then he had
wasted his entire spending on the correspondence tuition and he
should retire.

"I am counting on your discretion," the voice had said. "I am
informed that you are thoroughly trustworthy and can be relied
upon."

Whoever it was had spoken after Karaun's own boss had called
and promised him a "confidential directive" which he was to carry
out to the letter. Then the telephone was transferred to the anony-
mous one and he had received those directives direct. He was not
curious, so he filed the voice away as Very High Up. From then
on he only thought of the entire business in terms of—the V.H.U.
affair. All calls from V.H.U. came to him on the direct line to the
office of the S.S. Karaun was only acting S.S. But he knew that his
acting days were nearly over.

Karaun came back from the telephone call beaming. At the doorway a black pillar, a black marble capital on fluted khaki column
appeared to wobble yet retain its form as if it was only a trick of
light on shimmering skin, reared suddenly to a yet astonishing
height and saluted.

"At ease Suberu."

As he came past him by the doorway he was already speaking.
"I have news for you Suberu. I need not let you out on remission
just yet even though you've more than earned it. Things are not
settling back into routine as we hoped. We have a slight crisis on
our hands. I still need you while that crisis is on."

Suberu nodded obedience, otherwise there was no change of
expression. Karaun attempted an approving pat on the stiffened
shoulders but his hand reached only as high as Suberu's crude sash.
"Anyway you are happy here aren't you? You don't really want
your liberty do you? You've been so far out of the wicked world
outside you wouldn't know how to cope with it." He turned to
Ofeyi. "My good friend here barely escaped the rope. Since then
he has made himself the pillar of our little society. He's happy,
very happy. Each time his release papers come through he refuses
to sign them."

"Well then!" He sat on the edge of the table and beamed down
on Ofeyi. "The news" he said at last, "is positive."

"You have information?"

"Come with me Mr. Ofeyi."

They approached the narrow gate through lines of whitewashed
stones. Like an outing of lizards in the sun the fugitives gathered
on the sparse grass tufts on quadrangles, waiting in uncertainty.

The work-gangs had moved to the perimeter of the walls, their flexible cutlasses slashing through the weeds to the accompaniment of a metallic beat which bounced directly off the walls, filling the yard in the timbre of a pathetic defiance. Nothing could quite transcend the close-cropped hollowing of their skulls, nothing relieve the sychophantic humour which deferred to the guards' whiphand, even at the most caustic flights of their lyrics.

"Do you understand the words?" Karaun enquired of his companion, limping as if in deliberate counterpoint to the rhythm of the gong.

"No" Ofeyi lied. "What are they saying?"

The cripple laughed. "And you keeper, and me prisoner; both are one and the same." He looked slyly up at Ofeyi. "Do you think there is some truth in it?"

"It is a consoling point of view. What else do they sing?"

"Mostly unrepeatable stuff" Karaun answered. "But I never interfere in their composition. As long as it gets the work done."

"Yes. I suppose that is all that matters."

Turning a calculating eye on Ofeyi, he continued, "Another of their popular wisdoms goes like this: Me today, you tomorrow; Mister Mercedes, welcome home. Champagne bucket, latrine bucket; don't be shy sir, take your turn. . . ." Karaun's eye grew misty with laughter from some hidden joke. "I suppose" he giggled, "you wouldn't know what they mean by that?"

Ofeyi confessed he would not.

"Ah," putting back on his glasses. "I hope you never find out. They tend to administer their own justice among themselves and they have very strange ideas of punishment." He grimaced. "I watched them once at what they call their Assizes. Of course they didn't know I was watching. I do secret rounds in the night from time to time, keeps the guards on their toes naturally. It's the only way one can see what's going on."

"You don't trust your guards?"

"They are only human" Karaun sighed. "Don't forget the chant of the work-gang. Those felons are not complete fools you know."

One fenced-in yard led to another. A chamber of horrors revealed its nature slowly, without warning. The gongs and chanting of the work-gang had long faded when Ofeyi found himself face to face—a mere few yards between himself and the nearest of them— with a scattering of inmates who struck him instantly as being— this was his first definition—incomplete. A wide-sweeping glance described a canvas of missing parts; a moment later he realised that he was in a yard of lepers. Instinctively he shrunk closer to the boundary of the fence.

The guard who had opened the gate followed close behind. Ofeyi remarked that Karaun walked through these creatures without flinching, with a gait no different from that which he used in his office. So did Suberu who emerged from a hut beneath whose shadow the majority of the lepers were clustered, pushing checkers on a board with the stumps of their hands, even weaving baskets. Smoke issued forth through mere holes on one severely ravaged face. Perched on a trestle on which planks were still laid from a recent flogging a putty-faced object surveyed the scene through lidless eyes, shoved a parcel of obvious contraband under his rags as the visitors approached. From one came a mock obsequious bow, snuffing out even the attempt to shout his "Afternoon oga sah" through non-existent lips.

Ofeyi's eyes swept over the remnants of human bodies. Even in their varying degrees of physical curtailment they managed to run the familiar gamut of the sullen and gentle, viperous and chastened, predatory and hunted. They stared at the small procession with uniformly curious eyes, an initial expectancy doused early as the governor's pace indicated that he was not coming to break the monotony of their existence with any drastic announcement. From within the long hut a single altercatory noise died away in response to the knowledge—transmitted mysteriously—that Authority was within the premises. They traversed the yard in silence. Suberu rushed forward, knocked on the next gate and the guard on the other side pushed it open.

Karaun entered smoothly into his role of courier on guided tour. "We have just come through the Leper's yard." He smiled with a complacent sense of shrewd organisation. "This one contains the Death Cells. Our people have such a horror of lepers that most prisoners would think twice before trying to escape through their quarters. It is the best form of security."

"But the warders . . ." Ofeyi began.

"There isn't all that risk" Karaun assured him. "And anyway we submit them to frequent examination. Quite unnecessary. Not one of them has ever been infected. They are just as scared you see. You won't catch any of them moving too close to the occupants of this yard." He chuckled. "The ideas about leprosy are mostly old-fashioned. So the prison doctor tells me anyway and I believe him."

Defensively alert, Ofeyi turned to take a last look at the leper's ward before passing through the gate, saw two obscene gestures from fingerless hands freeze in the air. They had, he had no doubt, been directed at Suberu's retreating back. He bowed under the low gate as Karaun stood aside to let him pass. He also apparently caught the gestures.

"They hate my trusty of course. Because the warders will not get to grips with them if they make trouble they tend to be difficult. Fortunately Suberu can be called upon to deal with them in any situation. He has absolutely no fear of the disease."

"He was nearly hanged you said?" Ofeyi lowered his voice even though Suberu was already far ahead.

"Oh yes. Commuted to life. Not the kind of man any of those petty criminals would care to fool around with."

Ofeyi had the uncomfortable feeling, as Karaun looked at him to say this, that a warning had been directed at him. He shrugged off the presentiment; it was overtaken by the thought that Iriyise had been brought through this planned barrier of disease and physical revulsion. Again he experienced a disbelief in the existence of men who had planned this, minds which had brought it about. He forced down the bile in his throat to demand:

"Was it necessary to bring . . . was there no other place except through here?"

Karaun patted his back in an effort at kindliness that only galled him. "She saw nothing of this" he assured him. "It was night-time, and in any case she was not conscious."

The feeling of desecration remained. His mind seethed in a cauldron of futile vengefulness through which he sought to surface into a clearer purposeful air and the hundred decisions that awaited him outside the walls. What broke through from beyond his mind was an animal snarl, a guttural noise through twisted lips and words which approximated to: "Beast of no nation!"

The shout had come from the Leper's Ward where it was now feeding time. They turned to see a hoard of aluminium bowls, the food ready served in them, resting on a long work table. Three figures stood by the board, one the figure Ofeyi had observed, his nose eaten away, left only with tiny gobs of clay stuck on by a bored child in a kindergarten modelling class. The second figure was nearly blind. A third had rested his mud-padded crutch against the wall and was clutching at a bowl with both hands. Stumps, in strict accuracy.

They were smooth as the ends of the guards' riot batons, but they fastened to the sides of the bowl more tenaciously than any ten fingers. The noseless one was intent on pulling it away; it was clearly he who had snarled the fighting words, "Beast of no nation!"

With a sudden jerk that nearly cost him his balance, Stumps

snatched away the bowl, regained his crutch and, tucking the prize under an armpit hobbled away to a safe seat. The brief conflict seemed over. Gob-nose watched his disputant for a while, watched him as he burrowed under his rags and emerged with a spoon which he dug, using both stumps, into the mess and proceeded to eat. The others approached the trestle in comparative order and assumed their portions. Ofeyi observed what appeared to be some form of barter. A spoonful of food or a special lump within the bowl changed ownership. Something emerged from within caches and changed hands. Bargains were proposed, silently concluded.

Gob-nose continued to stare at Stumps. Soon only his bowl was left on the board.

Karaun looked nervously round, snapped his fingers. But Suberu had outpaced them and was already across the yard in which they now stood, waiting for them at the next gate.

Stumps looked up only once, saw that his challenger had not moved from his position. He tried to spoon some more of the food but grew nervous, got up and hobbled to a safer distance on legs of pestle. His watcher picked up his bowl, began to follow him at a slow deliberate pace. Neither was aware that the governor was still within sight, staring at them through the barbed-wire fence and showing concern. The yard was filled with sounds of slurping, scraping, grunts and hisses of discontent. A figure walked over to a fence and threw his food, bowl and contents over the fence, returned to his position and pulled out a wrapping from his anus. From within it he produced a cigarette stub and lit it. His face at first lit up with content, then he began to curse, slowly, deliberately, beginning with the prison cook and climbing up the ladder of an arbitrary hierarchy of his tormenters.

Ofeyi asked, "Is there going to be trouble?"

"It seems to be over," Karaun murmured rather dubiously. Again he clicked his fingers in the direction Suberu had gone as if by using his voice he would exacerbate the situation on the other side of the fence.

"But why are lepers kept in the same institution with normal prisoners?"

Karaun, still slightly absent, unable to take his eyes from the unresolved clash beyond the fence muttered impatiently that they committed crimes like normal beings. "They are human aren't they? And don't go wasting your sympathy on them. They take advantage of the fact that most people are afraid to touch them. That one over there, just by the fence. His speciality was frightening young hawkers into dropping their wares and running off. Then he took possession of what he called abandoned property. Believe it or not that was the term he used in court—abandoned property!" The tension had eased and Karaun had regained his good humour. He resumed his progress through the compound. "One was arrested with over three hundred pounds on him, hidden among his rags. It turned out to be part of the proceeds from a bank robbery. Seems he acted as look-out man for the more active bandits—there he is. Take a look at the sly rogue."

Moving towards the communal tap was the look-out man, walking with legs apart on stilts encased in canvas shoes. He walked jerkily, one ramrod planted in the ground before the next. An eye had vanished into a mess of flesh, pocked and chewed. But the shoulders appeared filled with immense power, his far too small tunic was bunched up at the shoulders, threatening to burst.

"He's in for ten years," Karaun continued. "But not for the bank jobs. They never convicted him on that. It was rape that brought him here. He was able to afford the best lawyer over the charge of being accessory to the robberies. Got off quite easily. In fact that came up in the first place only when he was charged with rape. That was when the money was found on him." Again Karaun gave one of his chuckles. "Oh the things we have to put up with here you can't imagine. That creature has actually sent a petition to the governor asking to be set free. Now Mr. Ofeyi, I give you three guesses. On what grounds do you think he demanded his freedom?"

Ofeyi thought for some moments. "Humanitarian grounds?"

"No. Try again."

Karaun stood in the middle of the Yard of the Condemned, both feet planted square, looking up at Ofeyi and enjoying his secret. Ofeyi looked back on the human refuse across the fence, observed that the original protagonists appeared to have vanished into or behind the hut. Turning back to his inquisitor he admitted defeat.

"No, I can't think of any reasons."

"No, I didn't think you could. I'll tell you. I have the duplicate in my office. Let me see if I can quote some of it . . . yes, listen to this . . . Sir, your Excellency, I wish to ask for full remission of my remaining sentence because I was charged on rape and now I hear that the Army have been taking young girls, raping them and sending others to leper colonies to be raped by lepers like me. So I respectfully ask you to send me back to one of these leper colonies because there is no justice in the world if I should be kept here any longer while everybody is enjoying himself and raping is no longer a crime . . . and so on in that tone for over two foolscap sheets. Well, what do you think of it my friend?"

"Did you forward it?" Ofeyi asked.

Karaun looked surprised at the question. "Of course. We are obliged to do so. I can censor or repress their letters to family and friends but we are duty bound to forward all petitions to the Authorities. He dictated it to one of my clerks who took it down and typed it out in triplicate." He winked in sly amusement. "The only problem came when he had to place his fingerprint over his name."

Ofeyi did a double take, then smiled in spite of himself. "Yes, and how did you get over that?"

"Oh, I signed for him. Even if he had his fingers I don't think headquarters would have appreciated receiving a letter touched by a leper no matter what their own appointed doctors say. We are still a most superstitious lot Mr. Ofeyi, never mind what it says in the prison handbook."

A scream halted them in their tracks once again. They heard a violent shout: "Leave my meat!" A figure emerged from behind the hut, followed by another supported by a crutch. It was the same pair who had struggled for the bowl at the very start of feeding-time. Held between the half-thumb and single-jointed fingers of his palm the contentious lump of meat was clearly discernible, snatched clean off the bowl of the other during the hidden duel that had taken place behind the hut.

Gob-nose spun round and stood his ground. "You took my cigarette yesterday and promised me your meat ration for today." And he turned round to the others to bear him out. Opinion seemed divided. Without further ado he shoved the meat in his mouth.

The robbed man leapt straight at him, casting aside his crutch, sank his teeth into his arm. The attack took Gob-nose by surprise and he yelled in pain. The part-chewed disputed meat appeared in the opening of his mouth and the next moment it was gone. Stumps had snatched it back and simply swallowed it whole. Gob-nose was now incoherent with rage, he seized his opponent by the throat and shook him, throwing him off balance. From nowhere a bowl of stew came hurtling through the air, contributed by one of the others whose sole aim was to expand the area of conflict and prolong the diversion. Some of its contents splashed over the rapist who stared in disbelief at his clothes. He looked round in a general appeal shouting,

"You see my jumper wey I wash only yesterday?"

Gob-nose now sank his teeth into his opponent's shoulder while he lay on the ground, worrying the flesh in his mouth as if determined to tear off weight for weight the amount of meat of which he had been robbed. The rapist assumed that the bowl had come from them and stumped towards the pair, lifted each head apart and banged them together. They slumped down and lay still. But by now the riot had spread. Bowls, crutches, spoons and checkers boards flew across the yard. Doors were rattled open, slammed, the dust-bins set up a din and improvised missiles flew across the fence in every direction. A chain of deliberate pandemonium had been forged. It was a sudden, violent contagion and in a few moments all discrimination was lost as the inmates sought to assuage their accidental injuries on the nearest and weaker prospect at hand. The smooth-ended stumps became vicious weapons, the heads were transformed into battering-rams.

Panic whistles blew from guards in the neighbouring yards and Suberu came sprinting towards the scene with no further prompting. A guard appeared from nowhere shouting, "Get the buckets! Buckets!" Other trusties had also appeared in what seemed a familiar exercise. They formed a chain and passed water-filled buckets to Suberu who had placed himself at the head, dousing the combatant in cold water and applying the bucket directly on the heads of individual heads which proved obdurate. When that failed he tore them apart with his own hands. More pails arrived, another line was formed, but Suberu alone was at the head of both, weaving fearlessly through the now promiscuous battleground, shouting down with a counter ferocity the demented noises which rose from the throats of the lepers. Single-handedly he began to herd them into their cells. A warder threw him a baton but it was hardly necessary. Once or twice Ofeyi heard its crack on a stubborn knuckle but that was rare. He mostly used his feet. More often it was the voice alone and the effect of his sudden appearance above a whirl of rags and flesh.

Ofeyi looked once at his guide. Karaun appeared shaken by the sight. "It's under control" he snapped suddenly. "Let's go."

"Are we close to where we're going?"

"There is only the Lunatic Yard after this." He hesitated. "I apologise for that disturbance."

"I don't see why you should. It must happen sometimes even in the calmest setting."

"It is most unfortunate that it should occur while you are here," the man insisted.

"I am not planning a report, if that's what bothers you. I am not a Government official or a journalist."

Karaun appeared about to speak, turned his face away and suddenly increased his pace. They were pursued by racking coughs from the subdued gladiators. There had indeed been moments when they appeared to be gladiators in a freak circus, with clubs that seemed integrated into their bodies, battle-scarred from the long struggle against cannibalistic foes, elbows used as terrible vises in whose grip the victim was mostly powerless . . . it was probably those choked victims whose retching sounds pursued them. Ofeyi cast a quick look backwards just before the yard vanished completely from sight. A few remained on the ground, still to writhing. A form hung over the fence, retching into the yard of the Condemned.

And now it seemed as if the commotion had gathered wings and was flying above their heads preceding them in the general direction in which they were bound. The infection of violence had spread. Beside him, Karaun checked, the frown of worry now deepening on his face. "It's a strange business" he murmured, "but this sort of thing has a way of spreading. If it gets to the Lunatic Yard we will have to take some very harsh measures."

"Why is that?" Ofeyi asked, and immediately felt it a foolish question. It was one thing for Suberu to wade in among the lepers, discarding even the long-range water deterrent, glaring murder through his compacted head and ripping apart the struggling mass with bare hands. Plucking them out individually like maggots from a festering lump of meat. As each layer was peeled off the next felt the exposure, rolled away or cringed from the poised blow, burrowed into deeper recesses of a fetid heap. What however would the lunatics understand of such tactics? Ofeyi recalled scenes of mindless mob viciousness in public places. In market places where a lunatic, besieged, stoned, tormented with every cruelty by a mob would charge again and again, insensible to the superior strength of his assailants. Would they be any different within walls?

He looked anxiously at the diminutive figure beside him, hurrying towards the new source of noise. "How many are in the lunatic ward?" he asked.

"Enough to create outright disaster" the man answered shortly, beginning to puff from the exercise. "We would have to beat them senseless."

"Where is Iriyise?"

There was no reply forthcoming from him.

"Is there a woman's ward beyond the Lunatics?"

"The rest of the prison is beyond these first three compounds we've come through Mr. Ofeyi. I thought I had already explained that to you."

"But the self-imprisoned fugitives are camped before these 'first three.' We came through them as we left your office. . . ."

"The lady is ill, very ill. . . ."

"The clinic was behind your office. Where the work-gang were cutting the grass before you drove them away. I saw it through the window, distinctly marked."

Keeping pace with his amazingly quick steps Ofeyi tried now to read into the man's face. It seemed suddenly important that he find out where and why Iriyise was hidden in the convoluted bowels of Temoko before another step brought him nearer the physical revelation. But there was only the twisted smile on the face of the man, one that he could not interpret beyond a bureaucrat's testiness at the presumption of an outsider. Again Ofeyi tried to force an answer, demanding, "Where exactly are you taking me? Inside or outside these walls?"

"You seem to know the geography of the place better than I" Karaun mocked. "You know where the clinic is, where the fugitives are housed, you seem to know the place better than I."

Ofeyi began to speak but he silenced him. "Listen to that!"

Differing from the slippery, squirming growls that were wrung from the embattled lepers, a cacophony of assorted sounds had welled up ahead and was rolling back towards them like cans and tins and fragmented rubble before the wind. Simultaneously a squad of guards in close formation swept past them, rushing towards the new source of the noise, armed with riot shields and preceded by batons at the ready.

A now chronic constriction commenced in his guts. Ofeyi experienced an urgent need to vomit as intuition overcame all hope and turned the world a sickening purple pottage that cloyed his throat. He hardly knew at what moment his hands took the small man by the shoulders and bore him round to face him, trembling.

"In the yard of lunatics, is that it?"

A stream of explanations, self-extenuation from the governor. Ofeyi could not grasp the coherence of all or part, if any, while the man fluctuated between terror and power. The warders were fully engaged in quelling the riot and Suberu was nowhere to be seen. His voice rose and fell from scream to whimper. "Believe me, that annexe is isolated. She has no contact with the lunatics, none at all!"

"Among the lunatics!" Ofeyi's demented shouts surmounted the din that raged about them. He shook the governor like a rag doll, saw tears come to his eyes.

"Those were my directives Mr. Ofeyi. Please stop being hysterical."

Ofeyi dropped him suddenly, began to race through the battle-ground, bawling. The crumpled form of a woman had come flying through the flail of batons. He plunged through and stooped to lift her up. Was she ever in his arms—the feel? Warmth? Breath? There came the sudden crumpling of his knees. A casual corner of his eye had remarked Suberu's approach but failed to convey a warning. Until the numbness in his skull, eyes closing on a twilight sky.

XV

Was this what they fought against, abdication of the will, resignation, withdrawal or enforced withdrawal—what did it matter?—the half-death state of inertia, neither-nor, sensing but unaffecting, the ultimate condition of the living death? Looking beyond her body for consolation he glanced through a barred window, through restricted openings at a handkerchief firmament. A few stars pocked the sky and he wondered whose constellation they might be, the detached movement of worlds which transgressed his present stagnation from one corner of the window to another, right over the edge of void.

He did not move from the spot where he had regained consciousness, he lay still on the hard floor, his eyes turned towards the camp-bed onto which Iriyise had been restored. No sign of the female nurse. Or was she simply a female warder? He could remember nothing of what uniform she wore, nothing beyond a blur of the frightened woman, cowering beside a tree.

Time? It had to be at least midnight for the stars to make so bold on the tiny patch of blue. In reality it might be earlier still. He gave up that problem too. There were things to remember quickly, as, for instance . . .

What?

The figure was very real on the camp-bed. What could those lunatics know of this object which the servants of the Cartel had brought and hidden in the annexe? In the contagious rampage they had broken through the nearest fence, broken into the hut and flung out the contents, chair, cupboard, medicaments, table, bed and the patient. That much he had seen. And the relief on seeing that Iriyise landed on soft soil, short-lived, because she did not move. . . .

Then picking up the limp form, or trying to. He recalled the approach of Suberu, the last-minute warning. Then flat on his back, a last moment of consciousness as his gaze picked out the stars in the twilight sky and his mind, true to form, repeating— like a long-legged fly upon the stream . . . her mind moves upon the silence. . . . Were those his last thoughts? On the cold cement floor where someone—surely Suberu—must have moved him, he wondered if he had meant the stars or the warm stillness of the woman in his arms.

He raised his eyes again to the barred window. A feeling grew on him now that it was nowhere close to midnight, that the evening had just begun. True the stars invaded the visible patch with a bold definition. Plough? Big Dipper? Even the sky was a circus of indifference, the thought provided some consolation.

Seared forever on his mind was the sight of that body flying through the air in the same whirlwind as propelled the net and the bed and what else?

Clubfoot? Where is that man of directives? Gone for more of the same? Ofeyi sat up suddenly as rationality seeped through and he realised that his situation was all too temporary. Unless, yes, unless in their ultimate plans, whatever these were, his presence in that annexe was unimportant, he would be moved, and soon. The self-made, self-promotions man was probably about it now. Ofeyi stopped abruptly. Why have I been shown in here at all except . . . ? Thinking was difficult. His head split with the effort and he realized that he was merely evading the issue. Comatose women tell no tales. Nor dead men.

He rose painfully, sat on the bed and prised open her eyelids with his fingers.

I am . . . trying to . . . break through . . .

Surely some such phrase, some such message must be uppermost in her mind. There would be a strain exerted against the present tyrannical hold. She must be conscious of my presence here! Leaden arms perhaps, a sensation of slow congealment, a memory left on the shore of consciousness among discarded clothing, a slowing pulse . . . even so there must be the invisible near-titanic strain against the gluttonous maul, a fight to free the mind from its fly-paper trap of silence. If a marriage of feelers could be effected by one magic moment, by a simultaneous evocation of the many thoughts they had shared . . . he tried to concentrate on his actions which were one with what she symbolized. He stressed his mind with the effort of concentration. But she lay still.

He continued to stare into the eyes held open by his fingers, tuning himself into a universal receptor, probing with a million antennae, sieving out distracting atmospherics, terrified to move lest he loose one sigh of pain, one silent anguish of the disordered world contracted into one camp-bed. Helpless, he looked up through the window and found that he had to struggle against the hynotic eye of the moon now drifting slowly past the window. Letting his head drop sharply back from weariness he winced from pain and located at last where the giant must have hit him. He hung the head forward in turn to relax the sore muscle, only to be rewarded again by a blur and a white blinding flash. The giant must have hit him more than once. Even so he could not remember struggling.

Or could it be that, while he lay flat dizzily counting the stars, some other warder had booted him in the head? It seemed to explain why he had failed to shake through the first dizzying blow which had knocked him down.

Rising to his feet a locomotive ran briefly round the rails which someone had placed in his skull, ran off the circular rails and plunged sizzling into some indeterminate pool somewhere in the base of the skull. He decided that there was something seriously wrong with his whole body. He let himself gently down, flat on his back, with his hands to cushion his head against the cold floor. The moon tugged him upwards, filled the sockets in his head and etched him cruciform on the floor. On its way towards him, it picked out the figure of Iriyise in cold relief. Ofeyi turned on his side to face her fully, shuddering at the thought of what ravages had induced this deep refuge in her volatile self.

Voices . . . voices . . . but through it all there was the clarity of events. Only the sequence was a little uncertain. Of course he had scooped up Iriyise in his hands . . . yes . . . and there was that volcano of loss against which the silly bureaucrat had tried to stand. What swept him under? Surely not he. There was of course his voice suddenly gone thin and insecure, uncertain how to relate the definitive consequence to the simple though devious manipulations that preceded it.

How strange the man was, choosing that moment to say to him, "I know you Mr. Ofeyi. And not just as the mastermind of the cocoa campaign. You brought the men of Aiyéró to Cross-river. . . ."

"She's dead!" Yes, he recalled saying that, softly, insistently. And the little man reiterating, "She's not dead. I tell you she has been in a coma."

Was it that possibility which made the governor hysterical? There was that sudden highpitched scream that came from him: "I had nothing to do with it. You saw how it happened. It spread. Just like an epidemic Mr. Ofeyi, just like an epidemic. . . ."

Just like the spread of the outer plague. He read that on his face.

"She is dead." He recalled that monotonous phrase, dripping from his lips.

Strange, the little functionaire had barred his way. If she was dead, if she was alive, but in a coma, she was his to take away, far from the madness and general contagion. Far from curtailed bodies and minds who slugged one another over half-chewed meat and buried their teeth in pestilent carrion. So what was he saying, this little man, what did he mean? But Karaun barred his way even as he whined and uttered gibberish, barred his path while the guards were engaged in quelling the madness in that compound, beating the lunatics senseless.

"You can see the gap yourself Mr. Ofeyi . . . they broke through that fence and tackled the guard from behind. Then they forced their way into the room where she was isolated. I swear to you she was well guarded, please believe me. No one could have predicted the sudden riot. And anyway no harm was done to her. She remained unconscious, just as you found her."

Barring his way just the same. This was what he could not understand. Oh yes, he had made one accusation, just that one: "You put her here. You kept her here. She is dead." Yes, he remembered that. And the functionaire's confident rebuttal.

"She is not! You can't blame me for what happened. She was kept quite safe. A female guard and nurse looked after her. The doctor visited her every day." And yak yak scream bang . . .

His recollection was clear enough. Iriyise in his arms, he at the gate to the yard of the Death Cells and the thick lenses of the man darting from him to the battle behind him and back again, speaking fast and saying much. Until it penetrated his mind that the man kept talking for a purpose, that he was merely waiting, waiting. But his mind was one huge cocoon of grief from which no chrysalis of reason could emerge. What had he said in that immense span of time, this cannonball head which effectively blocked his path? Strangely it was Suberu's face that came in between, whenever a glimmering commenced in his mind of the dwarf's long sermon. Suberu appearing from nowhere. Something had penetrated that cocoon of deadness at last and Ofeyi had turned; perhaps it was the glint in Clubfoot's eyes, a sudden expansion of his iris which bore no relation to the words that flowed from his mouth. Yes, it could have been no one else. Suberu had hit him in the back of the neck, and he had woken up on the hard floor of the annexe to the Lunatic Ward. Stretched on a camp-bed on the other side of the room was the inert form of Iriyise.

A barred window, high up on the wall on that side let in the moonlight, a full moon though it was still early evening. It had been midday when he first passed through the gates of Temoko.

What next? And why that belated accusation? He had after all been with the man in his office most of that day and there had been no mention, no hint of Aiyéró. He had come on a simple Missing Persons Inquiry. Why, in the midst of a freak riot and with the lifeless form of his quest dangling in his arms had he picked that moment to shout: "Well blame yourself! You brought the men of Aiyéró to Cross-river. Did we invite you?"

Ofeyi sat up with a jerk. A long peal of laughter had broken through his mind's meanderings. Slowly, carefully, he propped himself along the wall and came to the window. He listened. More voices. A hectoring voice, then a commanding thump as though by an auctioneer's gavel. And a smooth, methodical voice, marshalling arguments.

He climbed on the camp-bed and looked out.

The scene that lay below set him blinking hard and praying for sanity. Seated in a ring were the inmates of the lunatic yard. The ring was not quite complete. At its open end sat a portentous figure with a blanket round his shoulders and a headgear, clearly improvised to resemble a turban or a judicial wig—looking down it was impossible to be certain. A standing figure held his audience in rapt attention, full of urbane gestures and flourishes, bowing from time to time to that authoritative figure decked out in the regulation blanket. At the extreme end of the fence stood two guards, half-attentive to the scene. Prostrate before the bench— for the format had by now become even clearer—was another of the inmates, the victim or simply actor of whatever charade was afoot. A few moments' attentiveness left his interpretation in no further doubt; in that last hour before they were locked in for the night, the lunatics were holding court!

A bright moon. Each figure in the circle clearly delineated, every twitch of the face and conspiratorial glance. The abjectness of the accused and the proud oratorical mastery of the prosecutor lifting his face to the gallery somewhere on the lunar rim as he made a resonant summation. The circle cheered. The judge remained solemn, lifting his face in grave rebuke at any excess. Ofeyi found himself drawn into the sedate lunacy of the circle, losing himself so completely that it was a long while before he became conscious of the soft barrage of missiles that fell against the wall, penetrating the gaps between the bars to enter the cell. The sound had reached him for a while but it seemed part of the mad collisions of sausage flies and other winged insects, attracted by the lone bulb in the yard.

The persistence struck him at last and he looked closely at the seated ring, watching them for any surreptitious motion. But their eyes were fixed on the leading actors of the evening rites. Finally he looked along the fence until he reached the outside wall with its crown of bottle-tops and barbed-wire tunnels. A shea-butter tree rose over and dominated the wall from without. Unable at first to believe the apparition, he traced the moon face of Zaccheus, partly camouflaged by the leaves. Seeing himself perceived at last Zaccheus grinned from ear to ear, signalled to Ofeyi to wait at his post. His face disappeared only for a few moments; when it returned, he dangled a step-ladder a few inches over the wall, shook it gently and drew it back again. Ofeyi signalled that he understood, came down from his perch and sat down to think.

The principal motives were unravelled. One was resolved at his first glance through the window onto the scene below. Buried, if need be forever in the heart of lunacy there was no danger that Iriyise would uncover the assault on her nor identify the guilty ones. And there was the likely prospect that she would herself succumb to insanity, the first reality to which she would wake—if she ever did—rendering any future testimony of hers of no consequence if ever that day of reckoning did come.

Ofeyi stood up, knocked on the door and summoned the guard. The man came, leant against the door and demanded what he wanted.

"Water. I need some water."

"What for?"

"I need some water" he repeated.

The man scowled. "I am not here to fetch you water."

"I am ill" Ofeyi pleaded. "You can send the trusty for a cup of water, is that asking too much?"

The guard growled. He heard him going away, grumbling at criminals who imagined themselves in a hotel. But Suberu shambled in at last, unbarred the door and brought in the mercy cup.

Ofeyi took it and drained the contents while Suberu waited to take it back. He reached the cup towards him, then withdrew his hand, the cup still within it.

"Why do you never speak Suberu? Why is that? You understand everything but you never speak. I want to know why."

Suberu reached out his hand again for the cup, jingled the keys to indicate that he had to go round the cells shortly, locking up the inmates.

"Cigarette?" Ofeyi offered, patting his pockets only to realize that his pockets had been emptied while he lay unconscious. "I am sorry," giving him a rueful smile, "I thought I could offer you some but I have none."

The trusty dipped his hand in his pocket, brought out a packet from which he extracted two cigarettes. He offered both to Ofeyi, brought out matches and lit one for him. Even so, he shouted:

"What can I say to thank you? I am sorry I have nothing at all here with which I can repay you."

Suberu shook his head, reached out his hand again for the empty cup. Sighing in despair Ofeyi surrendered it, giving up forever all hope of reaching the dark hulk of silence. Even so he shouted:

"I would like to ask you why I am trapped in this place— because that is all it is my friend, trapped! And why this woman is here who should be in hospital, receiving specialized care. Does it not seem strange to you my friend? Or do you see it all as part of ordinary, normal existence I wonder? But you stay dumb. If you could pretend to be deaf I expect you would."

He shrugged with the hopelessness of it all and turned from him when he saw that the trusty had begun to rummage in some inner pocket of his uniform. He brought out a thick, neatly folded piece of paper, squatted on his haunches and began to unfold it on the floor. It was a poster, one of the very earliest of Iriyise. Shrouded in a filmy gauze which—he grimaced—claimed to represent a milky distillation of the creamy flesh of cocoa seeds, Iriyise was emerging from a neatly cracked golden egg-shape that represented the pod. Suberu pointed to the figure on the bed and, slowly, with laborious gestures, signalled that the figure on the bed was the same as the poster. Taken by surprise, Ofeyi watched the man mime his own enlightenment. The woman's condition was like that egg and Ofeyi must wait, patiently, for her emergence. Suberu solemnly folded back the poster, restored it to the recesses from where it had emerged, and turned towards the door.

Ofeyi cleared his throat, forced his voice to be as casual as possible. "Why don't you lock up those lunatics before me. I could use the few minutes to take some fresh air in the yard." He rubbed the back of his head pointedly and grimaced. "My head . . . why you had to hit me I don't know, but it has given me a headache. I am very ill. You owe me the fresh air."

Suberu considered. Ofeyi moved close against the giant, raised his eyes to his and held them with a desperate earnestness.

"Don't go yet Suberu, just listen to me for a moment. Damn, I wish I knew how to reach you. I know I can. You proved it just now, fishing out that poster to preach your hopeful message at me. I mean, who would have thought you a man of images?"

A stiffening from the giant alarmed Ofeyi and he sought frantically for a new idiom that would lessen the man's lifetime habit of suspicion.

"It's a compliment you understand? I mean, calling you a man of images. Essentially of course you remain a man of action. You grasp a situation of chaos and—bang bang—you impose your own order on it. Rather like those men of uniform who thereby claim to control other lives in perpetuity. Like a bull you quell the tantrums of a quarrelsome herd of females. I mean, I am impressed by your self-sacrificing dumbness, your gladiatorial valour among infectious lepers, who wouldn't be? The question is Suberu, why are you still here? You've served your time, you could have had your parole ages ago. Why are you still kept here?"

Suberu shuffled with impatience, his face retained the same mask of blankness that Ofeyi had encountered from the beginning. Desperately he hissed, "Do you know what it means to be exploited? To be kept in a death row all your life? Look, no wait, don't dangle your keys yet. You think you were reprieved but look what is happening. Look at the woman on this camp-bed. You are after all a dark horse of images so you should understand my meaning. Why can't you see you've been trapped like her in a capsule of death? The milk rots in the coconut if left too long. The child rots in the womb if it exceeds nine months, or else it emerges a monster—isn't that what your own people say? The life-yolk rots in the shell if it is not opened in time, it creates a poisonous world of fumes and is suffocated in the trap. Haven't you seen the butterfly struggle like mad out of the coccoon Suberu? What happens if your talisman is buried in rubble by your enemy? Tell me that. Don't you know that even the kernel in the palm nut turns rancid sooner or later, disease finds the weak eye in its hard shell and rots the inner flesh!"

His voice rose to a shout: "Can't I reach you at all Suberu? Can't I reach you in your coffin where you have been forced to lay these twenty years of your short life, responding not even to your own jangling of keys? Have we all wasted time trying to end the deadly exploitation which traps minds like yours in one lifelong indenture to emptiness?" He sighed, turned away "Good-night then. Your companions are waiting and you are the privileged slave who will place manacles on their held-out wrists. But for faithful dogs like you the Amuris of this world could not trample down humanity with such insolence. You snap at the heels of those who would confront them and afterwards you bury their bones in the back garden. But remember this Suberu . . ." he turned and faced him again, holding the trusty's eyes in his, "only you can sniff out the spot and root out the bones to accuse them. After the licks and the caresses, don't complain if the Amuris finally throw you a poisoned bone. Sleep well my friend."

Ofeyi sat on the edge of the bed, exhausted by the futile effort, his head held between his hands. Suberu remained motionless on the same spot, a film across his eyes, drifting back in time to a buried past. Hard though he tried to hold on to it, an earlier phase of knowledge continued to elude him when life had more volition, was not filtered exclusively through the heavy lenses of his master and the exhalations in dark corridors from adumbrated lives. He failed, but the distant stirrings remained to divorce him from the present.

From far away he heard the voice of the guard calling out his name. He came out of his semi-trance, stirred slowly, turned his head towards the door without really perceiving it. The call came again and he obeyed it at last, but in a slow reflex, a somnambulist following the source of a familiar sound struggling back from a strange, alien territory.

Ofeyi listened to his receding steps, turned his head in a mixture of certainty and misgiving. Suberu had passed through and left the door ajar. Ofeyi glanced briefly at the figure on the bed, touched her on the forehead and followed the trusty into the night.

He stopped in his tracks as two figures stepped out of the shadows. In the light of the outside bulbs the wiry copper hairs glinted unambiguously and the Dentist's face confronted his. The second figure he recognized as Chalil but the doctor muttered only a brief greeting as he stepped round him into the room, knelt beside the bed and began to examine the woman.

"Details later" the Dentist promised. "Right now we haven't much time. Is your head better?"

"What's going on?"

"Nothing much. We merely harnessed chaos to our own ends. Zaccheus brought news you had vanished into the bowels of Temoko. He's been playing look-out man on one of those trees . . ."

"Yes, I saw him just now . . ."

"Oh, he's back at his post is he? He is far more active than his shape suggests. Oh, I er have to confess I did a bit of eavesdropping just now, before the doctor joined me. Were you really trying to reach that ox?"

Exasperated now, Ofeyi hissed, "Will you just give me some idea . . ."

The Dentist gestured deprecation. "It was nothing elaborate. We broke in over the wall, under cover of the rioting. You had got yourself knocked out. I took a look at the woman and decided not to take the risk of hauling her out the way we came in. There was no choice but to take the governor under our protection and make him order us a doctor and er—a few other things. Zaccheus insisted on him." He gestured towards Chalil, then turned to meet Ofeyi's questioning gaze. He smiled. "Yes, I know it is her brother."

Ofeyi changed the subject. "Was your raid on the armoury successful?"

"We could not afford another failure. It went without a hitch."

The doctor completed his examination and rejoined them. His mind was not on the patient however, his eyes ceaselessly roved the interior of the hut. "It was clever" he muttered, "very clever. No one would have thought of looking in the waiting room."

Impatiently Ofeyi demanded, "What are you talking about?"

"This waiting room, that's what we call it. It's never used except on execution days. We all gather here—official witnesses, the magistrate, the governor's representatives, hangman and assistants, the doctor in attendance. When you work for the government you can be assigned to attend at any time. On those occasions, there is no quieter place in the universe."

A chill hung about them until Ofeyi pointed at the figure on the bed and demanded, "The patient, doctor, what about the patient."

"Oh yes your friend's guess was accurate. A very deep coma. As for this trek . . ."

Ofeyi felt increasing annoyance at the Dentist's habit of taking matters in his own hands. "Why have you been taking medical opinion on that?" he snapped. "We have not decided anything yet."

"Of course not. But it saves time to ask these questions ahead. What do you say doctor?"

Chalil looked uneasily from one to the other. "Well, it won't do her any harm. It could, on the other hand, result in bringing her out of the coma. Medical science is usually at a loss over this particular condition."

Ofeyi walked away from them, stopped and stared into the sky over the walls. The Dentist left him alone until he had assisted Chalil in dismantling the stretcher part of the bed and strapping Iriyise securely onto it. Then he went out and stood behind Ofeyi.

"I have to think of practical things. Our safety margin is wearing down fast. I also promised to overtake the rest of the camp before midnight. You have to decide."

Ofeyi turned round. "You are mistaken. I was not struggling over any decision, only with the past. I am ready when you are."

They rejoined the doctor. The Dentist and Ofeyi took up the stretcher, Ofeyi at the head. Suberu, who had been waiting for them at the inner gate fell in ahead of them and the procession passed through the sleeping yards. Nothing in Suberu's face indicated if he knew that the new orders which he now carried out for his master had been issued under duress. They passed by the office where the hapless keeper sat at his desk, mentally composing his report on the night's events.

At the gate, there was not even a guard. "You seem to have every detail well under control" the doctor remarked.

The Dentist shook his head. "It doesn't take much to organize a riot. We have enough of Chantal's army locked in here. They only await their opportunity to strike back at their tormentors."

They had expected Suberu to turn back at the gate but he stepped outside with them, bolted the gate behind and walked steadfastly ahead.

"Where is he going?" the doctor demanded.

"I think you'd better ask Ofeyi" the Dentist replied.

More men emerged from the shadows and fell in with them. The two men were relieved of the stretcher and, with the doctor they drew aside into a shadow of the walls. Zaccheus, slightly winded, soon joined them, self-conscious as he received Ofeyi's greeting.

The doctor spoke. "Remember you are not to worry about my part in this. You've made sure I am well covered."

"Just don't lose the governor's written instructions" the Dentist cautioned.

"After the trouble you took to get it out of him? Not likely."

"Good-bye then."

They shook hands and the Dentist strode swiftly away, gaining fast on the distinctive back of Suberu. The file had turned into a footpath and the figures vanished one by one into the bushes that bordered the path. They watched the Dentist as he gained the opening, his copper hair glinted for a moment and then he was gone.

"How to say thank you . . ." Ofeyi began.

"Don't."

"Is Taiila alright?"

"Of course. She wanted to come but I felt that the evening might turn dangerous."

"You were right. Tell her . . . well, tell her we'll meet again at the next intersection. She'll understand."

"I do" the brother replied.

Temoko was sealed against the world till dawn. The street emptied at last as the walls and borders shed their last hidden fruit. In the forests, life began to stir.

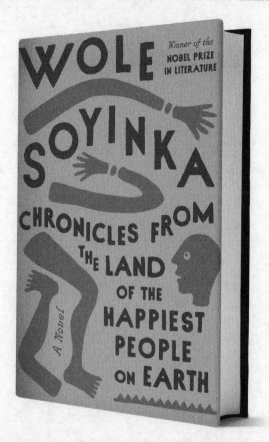

ALSO BY

WOLE SOYINKA

THE INTERPRETERS

They are the interpreters. Drawn together by their hopes, loves, dissatisfactions, and the daily lives and deaths around them, five young Nigerian intellectuals evoke a new lost and found generation. From their wild drinking bouts at the Club Cambana to their individual pursuits of personal and professional integrity, they simultaneously find themselves as seekers and prophets as they attempt to define their identity in a world where their cultural past and Western-influenced present are brought into conflict.

Fiction

AKÉ
The Years of Childhood

A dazzling memoir from Nobel Prize–winning Nigerian novelist, playwright, and poet Wole Soyinka, *Aké: The Years of Childhood* gives us the story of Soyinka's boyhood before and during World War II in a Yoruba village in western Nigeria called Aké. A relentlessly curious child who loved books and getting into trouble, Soyinka grew up on a parsonage compound, raised by Christian parents and by a grandfather who introduced him to Yoruba spiritual traditions. His vivid evocation of the colorful sights, sounds, and aromas of the world that shaped him is both lyrically beautiful and laced with humor and the sheer delight of a child's-eye view.

Memoir

VINTAGE INTERNATIONAL
Available wherever books are sold.
www.vintagebooks.com